THE VIEW OUT THE
WINDSHIELD WASN'T ENCOURAGING.

It looked as if he were skimming right on top of the forest canopy. Barely a second would go by without an outflung branch throwing ocher foliage across the nose of his craft.

Dom switched on the rear video. There wasn't any sign of pursuit. The attack didn't want him, or at least he wasn't a priority target. They were after the GA&A complex. That gave him room to breathe. *If* he could land this thing.

Woods shot by around Dom, getting closer. Godwin was still a good ten klicks away, and now that the grade below him had flattened out, he was losing altitude. The view out the nose was now totally obscured by dark foliage. Warning beeps sounded from every available speaker. The Hegira was shaking like someone having a seizure.

He needed to gain altitude—quick.

He lowered the back of the Hegira, hoping to use the main drive in the rear to boost him up.

The craft reached a forty-five degree angle and he stopped losing altitude. As the Hegira began rising on a ballistic arc, the violent shaking subsided, and the night sky drifted into view.

Just as Dom started smiling, the Hegira hit something. A final devastating thud shook the entire craft, and the remaining half of the warning lights came on in front of him. . . .

PROFITEER

Hostile Takeover #1

S. ANDREW SWANN

DAW BOOKS, INC.

DONALD A. WOLLHEIM, FOUNDER

375 Hudson Street, New York, NY 10014

ELIZABETH R. WOLLHEIM

SHEILA E. GILBERT

PUBLISHERS

First Printing, April 1995

1 2 3 4 5 6 7 8 9

DAW TRADEMARK REGISTERED
U.S. PAT. OFF. AND FOREIGN COUNTRIES
—MARCA REGISTRADA
HECHO EN U.S.A.

PRINTED IN THE U.S.A

For my sister Katy on her graduation,
something more than I ever did.

ACKNOWLEDGMENTS

Thanks to the following people who commented on this manuscript: Levin Armwood, Jerry Goodwin, Astrid Julian, Bonita Kale, Geoff Landis, Charlie Oberndorf, Jay Sullivan, and Mary Turzillo. All of you had some effect on this manuscript—if not necessarily the intended one.

GODWIN ARMS
-(SHOWING "BLOOD-TIDE")-

A. SECURITY
B. OFFICE COMPLEX (HGT. 60m)
C. CONTROL TOWER (HGT. 100m)
D. LANDING QUAD
E. WAREHOUSE ENTRANCE
F. RESIDENCE (HGT. 80m)
G. OBSERVATION DOME & DOM'S OFFICE (HGT. 90m)

DIDEROT MTS.

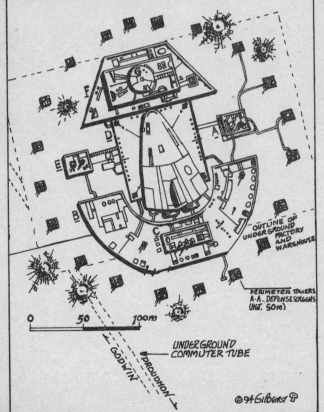

0   50   100m

OUTLINE OF UNDERGROUND FACTORY AND WAREHOUSE

PERIMETER TOWERS A·A· DEFENSE SCROGHS (HGT. 50m)

UNDERGROUND COMMUTER TUBE

GODWIN

PROUDHON

©94 GILBERT

DRAMATIS PERSONAE

CONFEDERACY

Pearce Adams—Confederacy representative for Archeron. Delegate to the TEC from the Alpha Centauri Alliance.

Ambrose—Dimitri Olmanov's bodyguard.

Kalin Green—Confederacy representative for Cynos. Delegate to the TEC from the Sirius-Eridani Economic Community.

Francesca Hernandez—Confederacy representative for Grimalkin. Delegate to the TEC from the Seven Worlds. Nonhuman descendant of genetically engineered animals.

Robert Kaunda—Confederacy representative for Mazimba. Delegate to the TEC from the Trianguli Austrailis Union of Independent Worlds.

Dimitri Olmanov—Head of the Terran Executive Command. The most powerful person in the Confederacy.

Sim Vashniya—Confederacy representative for Shiva. Delegate to the TEC from the People's Protectorate of Epsilon Indi.

OPERATION RASPUTIN

Klaus Dacham—Colonel, TEC. In command of the *Blood-Tide* and Operation Rasputin.

Mary Hougland—Corporal, Occisis marines. Attached to the *Blood-Tide*.

Eric Murphy—Second Lieutenant, Occisis marines. Attached to the *Blood-Tide*.

Kathy Shane—Captain, Occisis marines. Attached to the *Blood-Tide*.

Webster—Alias used by informant for Col. Dacham.

BAKUNIN

Flower—A birdlike alien. Expert on the Confederacy Military.

Cy Helmsman—VP in charge of operations for Godwin Arms and Armaments.

Ivor Jorgenson—Pilot and smuggler.

Johann Levy—Demolition expert and proprietor of Bolshevik Books.

Tjaele Mosasa—Electronics expert and proprietor of Mosasa Salvage.

Dominic Magnus—Ex-Colonel, TEC. Ex gunrunner. CEO of Godwin Arms and Armaments.

Kari Tetsami—Freelance hacker and data thief.

Random Walk—An artificial intelligence device. Mosasa's "partner."

Mariah Zanzibar—Chief of security for Godwin Arms and Armaments.

CONTENTS

PROLOGUE

Politics as Usual

"In politics, as in high finance, duplicity is regarded as a virtue."

—MIKHAIL A. BAKUNIN
(1814–1876)

CHAPTER ONE

Secret Agenda

"Foreign policy is dictated by powerful men's prejudices."

—*The Cynic's Book of Wisdom*

"Force and fraud are in war the two cardinal virtues."
—THOMAS HOBBES
(1588–1679)

For a hundred million years the two-kilometer-long Face had stared impassively up at the Martian sky. Dimitri Olmanov had only been visiting it regularly for the past century.

The first time he had seen it, Dimitri had needed a pressure suit and the sky had burned a hostile red. Today he survived wearing only a heavy parka. Today his breath fogged beneath an infinity of crystal blue that was only slightly tinted by clouds of engineered microorganisms.

His doctor would curse him for not using a respirator. *Dimitri,* he'd say, *your new heart has quite enough trouble with the stress of your job. Don't burden it with a too-thin atmosphere.*

His general staff would object to him being out in the open like this—even with the omnipresent Ambrose. Too much risk in his job without inviting assassins.

The Confed publicists wouldn't like to have it public knowledge that Dimitri—*the* Dimitri—had a sentimental streak. They made much of the mythical Iron Man at the head of the TEC.

He could ignore them with impunity.

The Face, Dimitri could not ignore.

He was the most powerful human being in the Confederacy. He needed to remind himself that there were things bigger than he was.

Dimitri turned to look at his bodyguard-companion. Ambrose appeared unmoved by the alien structure filling a third of their horizon. But, then, he never was. Ambrose stood at parade rest, wearing less covering than Dimitri did, breath hardly fogging the Martian air. Ambrose was two and a half meters tall, hairless and tan, and stared out at the world from behind black irises that nearly swallowed his pupils.

"Ever wonder why they died out?" Dimitri swung his cane in the general direction of the dome that supposedly protected the ancient artifact from the oxygenating atmosphere.

"No, sir." Ambrose shook his head.

Sometimes Dimitri wondered how much cognition really went on behind Ambrose's dark eyes. Most of Ambrose was construct. Only a quarter of his original brain was left. Ambrose's conversation had more to do with the computer programs that maintained the other three-quarters of his mind. Despite the brain damage, Ambrose was loyal, somewhat intelligent, efficient, and perfectly programmable—all without violating the Confederacy's taboos on AIs or genetic engineering.

But Ambrose would never be a great conversationalist.

Dimitri hobbled forward on his cane. "Was it a natural flaw? Some inherent weakness?"

"I wouldn't know, sir."

"They achieved so much . . ."

The Face was one of only a handful of remnants of a civilization that flourished and died before any of the known intelligent races achieved sentience. Humanity had originally called them Martians, believing the Face to be the product of a dead Martian race—

That was before humans had discovered a carved starmap that led them to Dolbri. Dolbri was an inhabitable planet that absolutely could not have evolved naturally. It was only the first example of extraterrestrial terraforming. Mars, it seemed, was an example of a similar effort. However, Mars—unlike Dolbri—had stalled halfway. The biosphere never took, the atmosphere thinned, and the water froze or evaporated.

It seemed that the ancient Dolbrians had died out at their zenith, and no one could figure out why.

"Is there a problem, sir?"

Dimitri realized he had trailed off in mid-sentence. "No, no." *I'm just thinking, Ambrose. Not having a stroke.* "It's just the Dolbrians reached such a point—may have been *gods* compared to us—and *still* destroyed themselves. What chance have we got?"

"Do you know that, sir?"

Dimitri smiled bitterly. "It's the nature of thinking animals to create Evil. And Evil is what destroys us."

Ambrose stared at him.

"You should realize that, Ambrose," Dimitri said. "We wade through it every day. Or I do. One hundred and sixty years of humanity's collective Evil. "That's what I am."

"If you say so, sir."

"Someday you may have to disagree with me, Ambrose." Dimitri bent down and pulled a strand of green-webbed demongrass from the dirt. It came reluctantly, trailing chunks of partially-dissolved rock and some of the engineered symbiotes that supported its simple ecosystem. He rolled the strand between his fingers, crushing tiny white insects. "What would you do if I tried to kill myself?"

A pained look crossed Ambrose's face. "Sir—"

"That would give you some problems. You'd have to leapfrog that programming of yours and use whatever judgment you have left."

"Don't." Ambrose seemed to have trouble talking.

Dimitri let the strand tumble from his fingers. "Don't worry. I'm cursed with the knowledge of what a succession battle would do to this Confederacy I'm supposed to protect. I will not allow myself to die." *Not until I know that my replacement isn't going to be worse than myself.*

The look of pain on Ambrose's face seemed to fade somewhat.

"The nature of the beast. The head executive is going to be a monster. But the monster has to have a scrap of a soul."

Ambrose had faded back into his natural mode, parade rest, nodding, saying, "Sir."

Dimitri barely noticed. He stood up from his too-long squat and felt the joints of his knees pop. "Remember to serve my successor as well as you serve me, Ambrose. You're going to outlive me."

"Perhaps, sir."

Dimitri sighed and started walking back to the aircar. He had seen enough of the Face. "Do you remember Helen, Ambrose?"

"No, sir."

"You wouldn't. It isn't relevant to you, is it? You don't retain anything that isn't relevant, do you?"

"No, sir."

"Helen was before your time, anyway. When I knew her personally, that is. I dealt with her fifteen years ago, and now I'm going to have to deal with her twins."

"Sir?"

They reached the aircar and Dimitri leaned on the hood. He decided that he probably should have brought a respirator. "The propagation of Evil, Ambrose. Sins of the fathers and so on—" Dimitri paused and caught his breath. In a few seconds he was racked with painful coughs that made him dizzy.

Ambrose was at his side before Dimitri could say, "Back!" He warded Ambrose off with his cane. "I'm fine! No doctors this week. They'll only replace another organ."

"Are you sure, sir?"

Dimitri nodded, even though his head was spinning. The aircar door was open and Dimitri slipped inside. Ambrose took the driver's seat and the door closed. Dimitri felt better when the car repressurized.

He looked out the window at the Face and realized that it was probably the last time he would see it. Whether he managed to create a successor or not, his doctors could keep him alive for only so much longer.

Dimitri didn't want to live any longer. He had lived too long already.

He had lived through the rise and fall of the Terran Council and the forced depopulation of the Earth. He had seen the wormhole network superseded by the first tachdrive starships and the subsequent explosion of mankind across the sky. Humans had founded colonies on fifty separate worlds since his birth, most of them in the last century. In his lifetime the Martian atmosphere had been made breathable and the majority of mankind had moved to the stars.

It was too much history for one man.

He was the head executive of the Terran Executive Command, the secret police, army, and enforcement arm of the eighty-three planet Confederacy. Dimitri and the TEC represented the only centralized authority over all of those eighty-three planets. Eighty-three independent governments that would gladly tear the Confederacy apart if it weren't for the thin diplomatic glue holding the whole thing together.

Sometimes it was nearly too much to bear.

And, speaking of diplomatic glue.

"Let's go, Ambrose. We have a meeting." As the vehicle lifted off, Dimitri added, "Someday you'll make me late for my own funeral."

Far away from Dimitri's aircar, in a Martian rock formation that could have been a Dolbrian artifact, or simply a weathered crest of rock, a lone figure lowered his binoculars. The man knew it was a risk to be this close to

Dimitri, especially with that creature, Ambrose, hanging around. In fact, he was just remembering how much of a risk it was. He had almost forgotten about Dimitri's pet golem.

Not forgot, just another thing I didn't want to remember. The man looked at the dull chrome cybernetic hand at the end of his right arm. The hand was scarred and pitted by years of use, and he walked on a leg that was similarly tarnished. *The old man has a habit of making people over in his own image.*

He backed down the rock, away from Dimitri's aircar. He was risking too much. Dimitri, the Confederacy's chief executive, was a white-hot nova of unwanted attention.

Once he was out of view of Dimitri's aircar, he put the optical binoculars back into their case.

He stayed immobile past the point where Dimitri's car should have disappeared beyond the Martian horizon. He maintained as low a profile as possible. It helped that they weren't looking for him.

No one was looking for him.

No one knew he existed.

He had spent nine years making sure that he had as little impact on the world around him as possible. It was very necessary that no one knew he was here. He was an anomaly, a temporal hiccup that could destabilize the events he was here to correct.

So much could be disrupted if he was discovered, if his crystalline caverns were discovered—and still, despite the need for caution, despite his fabricated—and all-too-real—nonexistence, he still made his pilgrimages to see the Face. He had braved this hive of academics many times over the past nine years, just to get a good look at the alien structure.

The Face reminded him of home.

He now knew the other reason he'd done it.

He had hoped to see Dimitri.

He had known about the old man's obsession with the Dolbrians and the Face. Deep down, despite his efforts

to remain unobserved, he had wanted to look upon the
man who was responsible for everything. He wanted to
see his former commander, a man he had respected at
one time.

Now, at the Face this last time, he'd finally seen
Dimitri as well. This close to exile's end, it had been an
unexpected shock.

And when he had finally seen Dimitri standing on the
Cydonia plain, all he could think of was how easy it
would be to kill the old man.

Even after nine years of self-imposed isolation, his hatred of the man who would give the orders was un-
dimmed. Worse. If his sacrifice was to mean *anything,*
he had to *let* that old man give the orders. To have a
chance of saving anything, he had to wait until the orders
had been given, wait until they had nearly been carried
out.

Wait until it was nearly over.

But he had waited nine years; he could wait four more
months.

At least, very soon, he could ship himself to Earth
without changing anything. He had always wanted to see
Earth.

After a long pause, when Dimitri and Ambrose were
long gone, he started the long walk back to his camp, a
crystal structure as impressive in its own way as the ancient polyceram of the Face. Unlike the Face, it was only
nine years old and hidden underground.

Dimitri's meeting was a dozen kilometers away from
the Face, in one of the abandoned academic stations clus-
tered around the alien structures known as the City. The
station was buried at the root of one of the ten-kilometer-
high atmosphere towers, one of the more spectacular artifacts of the human terraforming effort. The atmosphere
towers, built by intelligent self-replicating machines back
when mankind felt safe using such things, dotted Mars
like gigantic albino dandelions.

Dimitri liked thinking of the Terran Executive Command meeting under the roots of a weed. The metaphor gave one a sense of place in the universe.

The meeting room itself, chosen by Dimitri, was twenty meters underground. He had chosen it as much for security—all the TEC-commandeered structures on Mars were secure, by definition—as for his own convenience. Dimitri hadn't wanted to alter his trip to Mars, and it was easier to have the TEC meeting on Cydonia than it was to reschedule it.

Such was bureaucracy.

Dimitri was the last one to arrive. The five delegates were already seated at the table, waiting for him. Five delegates, two distinct sides. Dimitri went through the pro forma greetings, shaking hands and nodding.

On one side of the table were Pearce Adams for the Alpha Centauri Alliance and Kalin Green for the Sirius-Eridani Economic Community. The Centauri and Sirius arms almost always acted together in Confed policy matters. Their capital planets of Occisis and Cynos were nearly as rich and central as Terra herself.

On the other side of the table were Robert Kaunda, Sim Vashniya, and Francesca Hernandez. Kaunda represented the smallest arm of the Confederacy, the Union of Independent Worlds. Vashniya represented the largest, the Protectorate of Epsilon Indi. Hernandez represented the insular Seven Worlds and was the first delegate to appear from that arm of the Confederacy in at least two decades.

Hernandez also wasn't human.

Dimitri had to hold his breath when he held his hand out to her. She was a bipedal feline creature who stood taller than any human in the room. Her cat-face was totally unreadable.

The Confederacy would've liked to forget the past that the worlds beyond Tau Ceti represented. No one liked to think that humans once played around with genetics, creating intelligent creatures.

People could forget about the AIs. Those you could turn off.

You couldn't forget creatures like Hernandez. No matter how insular and xenophobic the Seven Worlds became, they were still *there*.

After the formal greeting—with the exception of Hernandez he knew all these people professionally—Dimitri slipped into the briefing on Operation Rasputin.

Like the handshakes and the greeting, his discussion of BD+50°1725 and the troublesome planet that circled it was perfunctory. Everyone here was aware of the planet Bakunin. Everyone here knew the economic drain it was for the Economic Community and, to a lesser extent, the Centauri Alliance. Everyone here knew Sirius' proposed solution.

The reason the five delegates were here had nothing to do with Dimitri's speech. It had to do with the vague permutations of physics. Confederacy law required a simultaneous vote on capital intelligence matters, and simultaneity was just not possible over interstellar distances, even if you used a planetary tach transmitter.

To satisfy both Confederacy *and* natural law all the voting parties had to be in the same reference frame. Which meant that Dimitri faced five individuals in this room, each bearing the proxy for one of the collective powers of the Confederacy.

Dimitri ended with, "It is important to remember that, since the planet Bakunin is not a member of the Confederacy, none of the legal constraints on Executive activity apply. None of what I've described to you is illegal under the Charter."

Dimitri overheard Kaunda mutter, "Meaning we throw the Charter out the window."

Dimitri ignored him. No one would like the precedent that this kind of invasion would set. No one but Sirius and Centauri, who were both in economic trouble even without the financial black hole of Bakunin sitting at their back door.

"If you'd please finalize your votes and pass me the chits."

Adams and Green slid their cards over simultaneously. Kaunda wrapped his dignity around him like a cloak and slowly slid his card to Dimitri. The gesture would have looked regal if it weren't for that fact that Dimitri knew that the Union only had one vote to cast in this matter; they only had one prime seat.

Hernandez clicked her claws on the card as she passed it over.

Vashniya hesitated. He looked at his card while everyone waited. He was a chocolate-brown man, bald with a heavy white beard, and very short. As he sat there, smiling enigmatically, he looked like a dwarf smiling over some golden horde.

Vashniya's expression was unaccountable. Dimitri certainly didn't understand the delegate's glee. Dimitri had already counted prime seats in his head. Even if Vashniya had his two allies solidly with him—even if Indi and company were unanimous against—they would still be one vote short, twenty-two to twenty-one.

Vashniya passed the card over.

Dimitri slid all five cards into a terminal set into the tabletop and read the results to himself before announcing them.

What? He almost said it out loud. He almost let surprise register in his face, something he never let himself do. It wasn't that Operation Rasputin failed. The measure passed, just as expected, and with a heavy margin.

It was *how* it passed.

In a dry voice, Dimitri read off the totals. "The final vote of the Executive Command stands: Twenty votes for, seven against, sixteen abstentions." When Dimitri read the number of abstentions, Kalin and Green looked shocked, and most of the people in the room turned to look at Vashniya, who was smiling impishly. "The motion carries," Dimitri concluded.

Why? Dimitri thought. *The entire block from Epsilon Indi abstained, all fifteen votes.* That wasn't all. There had been two defecting votes from Sirius. That meant that if Indi had voted against, Rasputin would have been blocked.

The Indi Protectorate constantly complains about Centauri and Sirius having de facto control over Confed policy. And Vashniya, after gathering the Union and the Seven Worlds into a coalition, just let Centauri and Sirius force through another proposal.

So why is he smiling?

Dimitri left the Executive meeting planning to assign a task force to study recent changes in internal Confederacy politics.

Ambrose met him at the door, as always. Dimitri's bodyguard was never more than fifty meters away from his charge, a distance Ambrose's enhanced body could clear in less than a second.

"Rasputin passed, Ambrose."

"Very good, sir."

They walked to the aircar. As they did, Dimitri decided he was going to miss Mars. If you left out the effects of the atmosphere, the lesser gravity made Dimitri feel half his age.

Unfortunately, half his age was eighty years standard.

"I suppose it is good, even if the circumstances were odd."

"Yes, sir." Anyone else would ask about the "odd circumstances." But Ambrose seemed to have no sense of curiosity. It was one of the things Dimitri liked about him.

"Good indeed. Sirius gets to pretend it's solving its economic problems, and I get to finally stage the climactic confrontation."

Ambrose opened the door for Dimitri, and Dimitri tapped the side of Ambrose's leg with the cane. "Do you get that? My swan song, finally."

"As you wish, sir."

Dimitri slipped into the back of the aircar, and Ambrose settled into the driver's position. "I've been waiting ten years to send Klaus to Bakunin." Dimitri closed his eyes. "With the need for my successor becoming more and more pressing, for a while there I thought I was go-

ing to have to exceed my authority—if that's possible—
and invent a mission for him."

"It is good you didn't have to, sir."

"Yes, Ambrose." Dimitri yawned. "Wake me when we
get to the spaceport."

CHAPTER TWO

Freedom Fighters

"War is simply honest diplomacy."
—*The Cynic's Book of Wisdom*

"We go to gain a little patch of ground
That hath in it no profit but the name."
—WILLIAM SHAKESPEARE
(1564–1616)

Captain Kathy Shane had a bad feeling about Operation Rasputin. It wasn't just the fact that this was the first time she'd been attached to a Confed Executive mission. If that had been it, she might have been able to discount the feeling. It wasn't even the fact that the two companies under her command were going to operate outside the Centauri Alliance, the first time she'd heard of the Occisis marines leaving that sphere.

No, that wasn't the problem. This was a cooperative effort with the TEC, which meant that her command could leave their nominal jurisdiction for anywhere in the Confederacy.

Anywhere in the Confederacy.

That was the problem.

The planet, Bakunin, was outside of the Confederacy's jurisdiction. It had never signed the Charter. It didn't even have a government with which to sign the Charter.

That lack of a government was the seed of the dilemma facing Captain Shane. One of the cornerstones of the Confederacy Charter was planetary sovereignty. Layers of sovereignty wrapped the Confederacy like an onion. Every planet was a force unto itself, the arms of the Confederacy keeping interplanetary order, and the TEC keeping interstellar order. Only two things were supposed to call for interstellar military action—

Defending a sovereign planet from external aggression, and defending a legitimate planetary government from internal rebellion.

Operation Rasputin was neither.

Shane lay in her bunk, thinking of her upcoming command. Her cabin was tiny, wedged to the rear of the troop compartment of the *Blood-Tide*. Even so, the accommodations on the troopship were palatial. She was command, and thus was the only Marine officer on board with private accommodations.

Normally a Barracuda-class ship could give most officers private quarters, but Shane's Occisis marines only formed two thirds of the ship's complement. The rest of the force was TEC civilians—and the colonel.

The troop-carrier *Blood-Tide* had left Occisis undermanned. Only two, of a possible three, marine companies rode the craft to Sol. In Sol orbit, the *Blood-Tide* picked up the Executive personnel, their command for this mission.

That was another thing that rubbed Shane wrong. Not so much working *with* the TEC, but the fact that their command was a TEC spook, Colonel Klaus Dacham.

Shane looked at a chrono set in the wall.

2400 hours Bakunin. They'd been on Bakunin's thirty-two-hour day ever since entering Sol space a week ago.

In a half-hour the *Blood-Tide* would engage its tach-drive.

Her ship communicator buzzed. "Captain Shane."

She picked the little device up from a dent in the wall that wanted to be an endtable. "Shane here."

"This is Colonel Dacham. I want the commanding officers to assemble in the briefing area for departure."

"Yes, sir," she said as the communicator went dead.

At 2415 the entire command staff aboard the *Blood-Tide* was assembled in the briefing room. Herself, six platoon commanders, and another half-dozen civilians. Even without the uniforms, anyone could have separated the civilians from the marines. The Occisis marines were all large-boned, squat, fair-skinned, and had a habit of sitting at attention. The civilians were much more racially diverse, and a few of them exceeded two meters in height— taller than any marine on board.

Colonel Dacham seemed to bridge the gap. He was olive-skinned rather than fair, and his near-black hair wasn't cut to military specs. However, he didn't tower over the marines—genetics, apparently, rather than gravity—and he walked like a military man. His body language was that of someone used to command, or at least someone used to giving orders.

He wore a generic uniform, black to match the marines, that was innocent of any insignia.

Colonel Dacham stood at the head of the briefing room, in front of a giant holo display. The display showed the cockpit view out the nose of the *Blood-Tide*. The scene was mostly black starry void, but Shane could see the tiny image of Saturn drifting over the colonel's right shoulder.

"In just an hour," said the colonel, "the *Blood-Tide* will enter Bakunin's airspace."

An hour for us, Shane thought. *The rest of the universe is going to lose track of us for nearly a month standard.*

The colonel addressed the marines. "Fifteen minutes after that, you will lead a surgical strike against Godwin Arms & Armaments. This surprise strike is pivotal to gaining our foothold on Bakunin. The assault and capture of this objective might seem a small target for two companies of marines. Don't let that appearance fool you into treating this mission lightly. This is only phase one of

Operation Rasputin, and it may be the most critical
phase."

Saturn drifted off the screen.

"Most important, after capture of the facility itself—I
cannot emphasize this enough—is the capture of the CEO
of Godwin Arms, Dominic Magnus."

Shane nodded absently as the colonel went on. He
wasn't covering any new ground. Everyone had under-
gone an intense week of preparation for the upcoming
mission, including a few mock assaults on the Martian
surface. Most of her people could do the mission blind-
folded by now.

In fact, even with the obscene corporate defenses bred
by the violent Bakunin environment, the fact was that the
Blood-Tide was an exercise in massive overkill. There
was no real question that the Godwin Arms facility would
fall to the TEC invaders.

Shane's thoughts kept returning to the fact that this
covert operation, if performed anywhere *within* the Confederacy, would represent an act of war that could tear the
Confederacy apart. The violent overthrow of GA&A—
even though it was a corporation and not a government—
was tearing the spirit, if not the letter, of the Charter to
shreds.

The worst part of this was the fact that Operation
Rasputin was cloaked in the same secrecy that shrouded
most of the TEC's activities. Shane knew absolutely nothing of what was to happen beyond phase one. That was
"need to know," and the grunts didn't.

During the colonel's talk, there was a brief whoop over
the PA system. Colonel Dacham stopped talking and
turned toward the holo.

With little sensation or fanfare, the display on the holo
shifted radically. The background stars remained more or
less fixed, but now in the foreground sat a small reddish
sun, and filling almost a quarter of the screen was the
planet Bakunin.

Bakunin was a white ball that was girdled by a wide
strip of ocean around its equator. Bakunin's one continent

was on the side opposite the *Blood-Tide*. The tach-in had gone flawlessly.

Colonel Dacham nodded and said, "Get into position for the assault."

PART ONE

Leveraged Buyout

"War was not invented by humanity, but we have perfected it."

—MARBURY SHANE
(2044–*2074)

CHAPTER THREE

The Military-Industrial Complex

"Capitalism is a dog-eat-dog system. However, with most other alternatives, the dog starves."
— *The Cynic's Book of Wisdom*

"Capitalism will kill competition."

—KARL MARX
(1818–1883)

"It isn't a hardware problem."

Dominic Magnus' voice came out in a whisper. His attention was focused on his left hand. Under the translucent flesh he saw no problem with the connections. The synthetic muscles still moved smoothly, and the abstract mirrors of the printed circuits hovered unbroken just under the surface of the flesh.

He had noted his fingers drumming unconsciously, and he had hoped to trace it to some concrete miswiring. Unfortunately, the finger tapping and the facial tic originated in his brain, not in the prosthetics. They'd always been with him, but lately—with some of the recent upsets in the munitions industry—the ties had been getting worse.

He kept hoping to find some sort of mechanical difficulty, something he could get a handle on. Something to fix. Something to control. He didn't like things he couldn't control.

He made the mistake of looking up from his hand and caught sight of his reflection in the black marble of his desk. He closed his eyes, but since the pigment was off, it didn't do any good.

Not that he didn't know what he looked like when he turned off the skin. He just didn't like the reminder.

Most of the time, Dom resembled any other man in his mid-thirties: olive-skinned, shorter than average, unremarkable. But with the pigment off, all the reconstruction was visible. Under the transparent skin, half his torso, as well as his entire left arm, snaked with wire filament and printed circuitry. All the musculature on that side of his body was synthetic and only slightly opaque. Underneath, the gunmetal gray bones glistened. A few of his remaining human organs were visible under his titanium ribs. On the right, a few natural muscles shone red, nourished by transparent capillaries carrying a watery fluid that passed for blood.

Worst of all was the face.

A titanium-alloy skull grinned from under the marble of his desk. Its teeth were too white to be real. A pair of brown, human-looking eyes stared up at him. He willed the pigment back and the skull was slowly obscured as his skin took on an olive cast, like slightly tarnished bronze.

The doctors had said he'd get used to the idea eventually. . . .

So far it had been ten years standard and he had yet to get used to it.

The klaxon sounded the half-hour warning, announcing the tach-in of a cargo ship. The ship was cruising in-system and should maneuver for planetfall any minute. The scheduled ship was the *Prometheus* out of Cynos.

Dom supposed the coming deal was why he'd felt a sudden wave of self-consciousness when he realized he'd been drumming his fingers on the desk. CEOs weren't supposed to get nervous.

Though, perhaps he had a right to be a little nervous. The *Prometheus* was a Hegira Aerospace C-545—a *damn* big cargo ship. It had contracted one of the biggest sales

Godwin Arms & Armaments had ever contemplated, on-planet or off.

The order was big enough for Dom to have forgone some of his normal caution. In the ten years he had spent building GA&A, Dom had played the corporate game more conservatively than most, more conservatively than *anyone* who did business on Bakunin. The lawless atmosphere of Bakunin bred corporations that seemed to thrive on risk.

Not Dom, not GA&A.

Not until now, anyway. Dom still had a few contacts in the Confederacy from his days after the TEC. He heard little from them nowadays. Not until one of his old intel sources close to the Terran Congress sent a tach-comm warning him that the *Prometheus* was a Confederacy front-job.

A few years ago that would have been enough for Dom to trash the whole megagram deal. However, during the past year Dom had winded an instability in the air, the sense of a storm on the horizon. Nothing concrete, but the paranoia was enough for him to sink a large chunk of capital into a mountainside bolt-hole. Even his chief of security, Mariah Zanzibar, thought that purchasing the virtually unknown commune wasn't the best financial move—even if it was an admirable precaution.

Ironically, after sinking the money into that commune, he wasn't in a position to refuse the *Prometheus*. Dom had to force himself to ignore his last disastrous involvement with the Confederacy, if not to forget it. Past was past, and Dom doubted that anyone in the Executive Command still knew his name—with one exception.

Dom slid a drawer out from his desk and contemplated what kind of sidearm he should carry into the deal.

The suit he wore was tailored for either a shoulder holster, or one on the hip. He chose both. On the hip he holstered a cartridge weapon, a slugthrower with nine-millimeter projectiles. It would do nothing against even halfway-decent body armor, but it was the custom on Bakunin to go into business dealings visibly armed.

The chromed antique would be both expected and non-threatening.

However, because he had a Bakuninite's distrust of the Confederacy, he wore a considerably more effective weapon in the concealed shoulder holster. A GA&A random-pulse variable-frequency antipersonnel laser was built to play hob with a personal field.

An Emerson field—force field was an unfortunate misnomer, since the Emerson effect dealt with energy, not fields of force—could suck up a considerable amount of energy at its target frequency. However, only the very high-end military models had processors able to compensate fast enough to defeat a laser that changed frequency at random microsecond intervals.

Once he was properly armed, he told his onboard computer to activate the observatory. He wanted to see the *Prometheus* land. The computer wired into his skull sent a coded pulse to the hemispherical white walls of his office, and they vanished from view.

His desk was on a raised dais in the center of the room, so he could sit behind it and get a panoramic view of the GA&A complex.

In the high-backed chair he could look down on the whole complex. The blinding glare reflecting off the landing quad splashed white light off of the mirrored U-shaped office complex. The smaller of Bakunin's two moons was rising behind the concrete tower of GA&A air traffic control, above the offices.

A slight heat shimmer above the perimeter towers obscured the Diderot Mountains beyond. The shimmer was a side effect of the defense screen generators in the towers, housed below the antiaircraft batteries.

Dom sat on top of the twenty-story residence tower. The deal he'd worked with the owner of the *Prometheus* would bring an influx of income that would not only compensate for his purchase in the mountains, but would be enough to give every one of the 1500 employees living below him a ten-percent bonus this year.

It was almost too good to be true.

The ten-minute klaxon sounded five minutes ahead of schedule.

Dom turned the chair away from the quad and faced west. It was a nice sunset. The ruddy orb of Kropotkin dominated the horizon, larger than either of Bakunin's moons. An awesome sight, a reminder that, in the cosmic scheme of things, life should not exist on this planet.

But then, Bakuninites had a habit of bucking the natural order of things.

Dom squinted. The ship was on its orbital approach. It would come over the city of Godwin to make its landfall. He'd see it in a few minutes.

A different klaxon sounded. The heat shimmer around the perimeter towers disappeared in a sheet of electric-blue light, the St. Elmo's fire from the defense screens' excess charge. The field had deactivated for the *Prometheus*' approach.

Something was wrong. He hadn't heard the all-clear first.

He told his onboard computer to call up the GA&A communications net. He needed to contact the control tower, *now*. Air traffic control was supposed to confirm the ID of any approaching craft and sound the all-clear before anyone even *thought* of lowering the defense screens.

He turned around and faced the holo projection above his desk.

Nobody was manning the control tower. He was looking at a totally empty room, lit only by the computer schematics showing the local airspace. There was no one to authorize downing the screens.

Dom called security.

The holo fuzzed and the empty control room was replaced by the dusky face of Mariah Zanzibar. "Yes, sir?"

"Red Alert. Prepare the defenses for immediate attack."

Alarms sounded, and the antiaircraft batteries began turning to track the incoming target. Dom had the feeling that it was already too late. He turned back to watch the approaching *Prometheus*.

The ship that was just becoming visible over the glowing sprawl of Godwin wasn't the *Prometheus,* or anything close to a Hegira cargo liner—

The lines were unmistakable, even at this distance. It was a Confed troopship.

"Damn it, Zanzibar, get those screens back up—"

Even as he spoke, he could see a streak of light emerge from the ship. It split into five arrows of fire, heading right for the perimeter towers. *EM-tracking missiles with independently targetable warheads. If the screens were up, the ECM would take out 70% of them.*

The screens did not go back up.

Five field generators and accompanying antiaircraft exploded into cherry-red balls of flame. Dom felt the building shake underneath him and knew that defending the complex now would be a futile gesture.

The realization was like a sheet of ice slicing through him. He was suddenly very calm.

He turned back to the holo. Zanzibar was facing away from him and shouting orders at her security team. She turned back. "We can't get the defense screens back up, Mr. Magnus. Someone scragged the independent power supply. We're trying to hook into the factory generators. That'll take another five minutes and the power supply will be vulnerable."

Dom nodded; he knew his own complex well enough. "Start evacuating personnel," he said, his voice a monotone. "It's a lost cause."

"Sir?"

"Get everyone you can to the Diderot Commune. That's an order."

"Yes, Mr. Magnus. Good luck."

Dom cut the connection.

Behind him the holographic walls flashed with more red light. *Five more warheads,* Dom thought, *another five perimeter towers.* Even if Zanzibar could get power to the remaining screen generators immediately, the screens would cover only three-quarters of the complex.

Dom looked toward the invader. The ship was slowing,

disgorging its landing craft. It wasn't going to blast the complex.

They were going to try to take it.

His thoughts were ice-fine and cold, like filaments of metallic hydrogen. Only briefly did he wonder *why* this was happening. But the fact that the invaders were shifting to a ground assault gave him a chance to salvage something—

Himself.

It also gave him a chance to deny them at least part of what they were after.

Dom called down to the computer core. The control center for GA&A, its heart and brains, was buried in a concrete bunker two klicks under the surface. Even a direct hit by a micronuke would leave GA&A's assets and records unharmed. If he'd had some warning of the attack, he could be down there and control most of the aspects of the complex, including defense.

By the time he had stopped talking to Zanzibar, the cold reptilian part of his mind had decided that there was a traitor, who he was, and where he had to be.

Cy Helmsman, his Vice President of Operations, was one of the more powerful cogs in the GA&A machine. Dom had built GA&A, but much of it had been on the foundation of Helmsman's expertise. In many senses, Helmsman was Dom's sword arm. Helmsman fought GA&A's secret battles, and had brought many of GA&A's competitors to their knees. Helmsman had come out of the same background that Dom had—war, espionage, the TEC.

Which all meant that Dom had never fully trusted him.

Helmsman was the man who answered the holo call down to the core. The core was the only place where it was possible to override the defense screens without Dom himself being present.

"I've been expecting you," Helmsman said.

Helmsman was middle-aged, white-haired, a slow, plodding, methodical man used to deception and double-think. Dom had felt he could keep Helmsman's ambition in check by using Helmsman's incredible cowardice. Dom had miscalculated.

Very slowly, Dom asked him, "How much did they offer?"

"Ownership of the company."

Helmsman had abandoned the TEC to save his own precious skin. Apparently he had returned to the fold because he thought he deserved a bigger slice of the pie.

Helmsman was a fool.

"Don't try to come down here," Helmsman went on. "I've planned this for quite a while. The blast-doors are all down and locked. I've reprogrammed all the access codes—"

Dom shook his head. Helmsman had thought everything through. He had made sure that he would pass through the battle unscathed, safe in the armored bunker at the core. Helmsman had made the assumption that he knew everything about GA&A's security setup.

"Good-bye, Cy."

"What?"

"Code Gehenna Hellfire."

The holo cut out and the power to GA&A died. There was an earthquake rumble as glass blew out from the office complex. The walls to Dom's office became temporarily opaque. It took the emergency generators three seconds to kick in.

Dom had activated a very small program buried in the communications software of GA&A. If Dom said those three words through any communications channel on the GA&A web during a full alert, the program switched a mechanical relay. Anyone who looked at the program wouldn't even know what it did unless he dug into the heart of the mainframe and traced the wires. Something Helmsman couldn't have done and maintain his little secret.

The relay activated a GA&A half-kiloton tactical warhead that was located about twenty meters away from Cy

Helmsman, deep in the core. Helmsman and the GA&A
mainframe, with its assets and sensitive information, had
just become an integral part of the bedrock two kilometers beneath the complex.

It was a desperation move, to prevent a good deal of
sensitive information from falling into unauthorized
hands. It would also make life hell for the people taking
over a complex operation that suddenly had no records,
no brain. It would save many people, clients and employees, a lot of grief.

It was also the equivalent of shooting a decade of his
blood in the head and leaving it to die.

Dom wanted to feel something.

The only thing there was a deep, aching chill in his
metallic bones that he really shouldn't be able to feel.

When the power came back, Dom looked behind him.
The walls went transparent on the scene of the troopship
hovering just outside the perimeter. Landing craft were
putting down inside the complex. The landing parties
looked like marines, though all he could make out from
this height in the dark were the battlesuits in striped urban camouflage.

Time to get the hell out of here.

The marines were at the base of the residence tower.
He stood up and walked to the curve of wall that faced
the ship. Dom saw the details on the ship now.

The hundred-meter long monster was a Paralian-
designed drop-ship, a Barracuda-class troop-carrier. Hovering, it blotted out most of the western sky—a
dead-black rectangle with a drooping nose and stub
wings. The drive section to the rear was half again the
size of the rest of the ship. Missiles clamped to hard-
points in the ranks across the skin of its midsection. Ten
landing craft had clung to parasitic blisters under the
wing like suckling young. Each could handle ten marines
in full battle dress, and all had dropped. A five-barrel
Gatling pulse cannon stuck out of the troopship's nose.
The cannon could waste the whole GA&A complex with
a single strafing run.

Dom didn't look at the ship long enough to determine if it had a full bombload.

Once he was close to the wall, he could make out where the door was. He found the switch and placed his hand against it. He could have had his onboard computer open it, but he wasn't going to risk a transmission.

The invisible door whooshed aside and let in the smell of smoke. Dom ran out onto the roof of the residence tower. Behind him, from the outside, his office was a matte-black hemisphere. As soon as he emerged, a high-freq laser lanced out from somewhere in the sky, to score on the dome. Don smelled kilos' worth of electronics crisping in the walls behind him.

Sounds drifted from below. Explosions and screams.

Without a wall between him and it, the Paralian ship seemed bigger than ever. It nearly blocked his view of Godwin. He ran, paralleling its profile, hoping another laser wouldn't target him.

Dom raced to the edge of the roof, where one corner was paved for a small landing area. In the center of the area was a canvas tarpaulin. Dom threw it aside to reveal a Hegira personal luxury transport. It wasn't armored and it wasn't armed. Dom had only used it to get around the GA&A complex—

There was a very ancient proverb about beggars and choices.

The canopy slid up slowly over the drive section and Dom jumped into the leather bucket seat. He started the power sequence wishing for wings, a hypersonic drive capability, life support capable of low orbit, a tach-drive—

A pulse laser strafed the roof in front of the car, leaving a blackened groove. Dom looked up and saw a marine landing craft heading for the roof.

The Hegira's vectored jets hadn't reached full pressure yet. Dom didn't wait for them. He hit the main drive units on full and rolled off the edge of the roof. The car was designed for vertical takeoff. It needed those vector jets to maneuver. It fell.

Dom had a great view of a platoon of marines below

him. They saw the descending craft and—probably a smart move—broke formation and ran. Behind him, the main drive blew out windows down the side of the residence complex.

He wasn't in free fall. The drive accelerated him faster than gravity wanted him to. Dom watched the pressure of the vector thrust build. Slow, too damn slow. The ground was too damn close.

He opened the vector jets prematurely and hoped it would be enough to maneuver the craft.

The Hegira shot away from the wall, and Dom desperately tried to get the nose up. The front end drifted upward, giving him a view of scattering marines, landing craft, and the blown perimeter defenses.

The G-force he pulled would have made him black out if he were still built with his original equipment.

According to the altimeter, he couldn't have dropped as far as it had felt like. He could have sworn he'd kissed the ground, but when the car's trajectory flattened out, he flew by just under the top of the fifty-meter-tall perimeter towers.

Once he cleared the edge of the GA&A property, the ground started dropping away. The foothills below him began to sprout thick purplish-orange forest as he shot west, away from the mountains.

Red lights began to flash across the control console. The Hegira had soaked up a few hits. Even as Dom started to assess the damage, the little craft began shaking.

The view out the windshield wasn't encouraging. It looked as if he were skimming right on the top of the forest canopy. Barely a second would go by without an outflung branch throwing ocher foliage across the nose.

He switched on the rear video. There wasn't any sign of pursuit. The attack didn't want him, or at least he wasn't a priority target. They were after the GA&A complex. That gave him room to breathe. *If* he could land this thing.

Woods shot by around him, getting closer. Godwin was still a good ten klicks away, and now that the grade below him had flattened out, he was losing altitude. The pressure in the vector jets wasn't enough to keep him airborne, and there was no way he could cut them and let the pressure build back up.

He should have budgeted for a contragrav.

The view out the nose was now totally obscured by dark foliage. Warning beeps sounded from every available speaker. The Hegira was shaking like someone having a seizure. It crashed through the canopy with a sound as though it was tearing the universe a new asshole.

He needed to gain altitude—quick.

He lowered the rear of the Hegira, hoping to use the main drive in the rear to boost him up.

The craft reached a forty-five-degree angle and he stopped losing altitude. As the Hegira began rising on a ballistic arc, the violent shaking subsided, and the night sky drifted into view.

Just as Dom started smiling, the Hegira hit something. A final devastating thud shook the entire craft, and the remaining half of the warning lights came on in front of him.

In the rear camera view, Dom could see a single tree pointing out of the canopy, about twenty meters more than it had a right to. It was broken and burning. He had clipped it with the main drive.

He assessed the damage. Rear vectors were out. All he had were the nose jets and the main drive, and the main drive acted erratically. He was in trouble. The damn thing now needed a runway—

The craft hit four hundred meters altitude and the main drive started stuttering. *Damn it!* He needed at least another fifty meters for the ejection seat—

Five klicks to Godwin and he was losing altitude and going three hundred klicks an hour. Time to start decelerating and hope for the best.

It was an opportune time to make that decision because the main drive quit altogether. He was going to ballistic into Godwin on only his maneuvering jets, a third of which were dead.

Dom pulled the crash harness around him just in time. The Hegira plowed into an abandoned warehouse on the east side of Godwin at one-fifty klicks an hour.

CHAPTER FOUR

Industrial Espionage

"Industry is amoral."
                    —*The Cynic's Book of Wisdom*

"Honor sinks where commerce long prevails."
                    —OLIVER GOLDSMITH
                    (1728–1774)

Tetsami had that sinking feeling she always got near the end of a job. This was the part she hated—the waiting.

She could cruise a proprietary operating system laced with lethal security without breaking a sweat. But now, sitting in the dark outside an old bunker waiting for the meet, she could feel her palms getting damp under her driving gloves. She straddled her jet-black Leggett Floater and idly eased the drive back and forth. The little contragrav bike obliged her by pacing back and forth in front of the loading bay.

She shouldn't have taken the Leggett. It was an expensive piece of hardware, and East Godwin was full of maggots.

Tetsami cussed herself. The time for second-guessing was before the operation. She had taken the Leggett for a very good reason. The few hours before the payoff were when things were most likely to go bad. It wasn't that she expected her employer to pull a double cross—if she had, she wouldn't be here—but it was a good idea to have an escape route, in case. . . .

Nice if I had a job where that wasn't a priority concern. Nice if I had a life *where that wasn't a priority concern.*

Tetsami put those thoughts out of her mind. Right now wasn't the time.

She concentrated on the meet.

The place the execs had chosen for the payoff seemed relatively clean. They'd found a place with one hell of an approach radius. The area around the bunker had been blasted clear for a few city blocks in any direction. Blasted by an artillery barrage or an orbital strike.

The bunker she waited by had once been a very secure building. It was the only survivor of whatever had reduced the surrounding blocks. The ruin still had shelter-quality armor, but the facade had been blown off. All that was left was blackened metal in the shape of a truncated pyramid.

The only entrance, the loading dock, had been blown inward by a direct hit from an energy weapon.

She wondered what this was the remains of. East Godwin had once been a corporate center before a few ugly company wars reduced a lot of the neighborhoods to rubble. The bunker could date from that blowup—around the time her parents had come to this ugly little planet.

Why Bakunin, Dad? she thought at her long-dead father. The question occurred to her even though she knew the answer. After Dakota, Bakunin was the only place that would accept their kind.

She wished the execs would show up.

Every minute she spent waiting for them to show, the data package under her seat got hotter. She wasn't made of time. The op had gone without a hitch. But that only meant that the spuds in Bleek Munitions weren't going to discover that their R&D database had been compromised until the next routine cataloging of the user list. In less than fifteen minutes now the spuds would see a red flag next to a user that logged out without any record of logging in.

The snag was unavoidable. Bleek's system was too tight for a dry run. She'd spent over a week planning the break-in, an hour weaving her magic into the system, and ten minutes on-line. After all that, she'd cut out with very little finesse or ceremony when she had what she wanted.

What the execs wanted.

If Bleek security ID'd her while she still had the data, things could get real hairy. She was a target until she passed the package to her employer. Once the exchange occurred, once she'd been passed the gold, she'd be free and clear.

Until then, she was hotter than a megawatt laser with a gigawatt power cell.

Think about the payoff, she told herself. Fifty kilos in the Insured Bank of the Adam Smith Collective. Not enough for her to retire on, but it might be enough to get her off-planet.

Off this slimy godforsaken rock. A graceful exit, as soon as possible. She wasn't like some software jockeys who went exponential until they crashed and burned. She knew she was pushing the envelope. If she didn't realize that, she had Ivor—her adopted father—to tell her she was eight years into a profession that chewed up and spit out most in less than three.

More than that, she wanted to abandon the planet that had killed her parents. Leave and forget that Bakunin ever existed.

She wished Ivor were in town right now. He was the only honorable, worthwhile human being on this planet, and she sensed that she'd need some handholding when this was all over.

There was a flash above her. She looked up.

A dead-black stub-winged drop-ship passed overhead, going east. It was a half-second until the bass rumble of the drives reached her. She could have sworn it had just fired something. It continued its stately progress across the night sky until she lost it behind the eastern skyline.

And there they were.

The execs were coming down a blasted stretch of road, toward the bunker. Three metallic-blue groundcars were weaving through the rubble, dust blowing out from under their skirts. They were armored for the neighborhood. Three cars. Godwin Arms might be slow, but when they show up, they put out the red carpet.

Tetsami didn't like red carpets. They tended to hide godawful piles of dust.

She stopped the Leggett and primed the grav unit for a five g vertical acceleration, just in case. Her palms were sweaty again.

Two of the cars pulled around to port and starboard, the third pulled in front of her. That left her with her back to the loading bay of the bunker. The door on the car in front glided open. Tetsami caught sight of a security goon—the goon was in civvies but Tetsami knew the type—before the corp walked out.

The corp wasn't her contact.

Shit.

The guy who stepped out was all teeth and smiles, with a generic face that came out of some production vat. Dark blue suit with a metallic shimmer on the edges. The guy dressed to match the cars.

The corp extended a hand, and left it there for a long time before he realized that Tetsami wasn't coming within five meters of him.

She moved her thumb toward the throttle. "Who the hell are you?"

"I'm assistant VP in charge of operations for GA&A. Mr. Helmsman is occupied back at the company—"

Helmsman was the GA&A veep in charge of operations. Tetsami knew him. Helmsman never delegated covert ops. Something was seriously wrong if the man didn't show.

"Bullshit," Tetsami said. "Whoever you are, I only deal with my employer." She kept her eyes on the junior veep, but she could hear a hiss as the doors on the other cars opened. More goons, probably armed. The only way she'd get out of this was if they didn't see her telegraph what she was going to do. She hoped they weren't armed with projectile weapons.

"My dear lady, your employer is GA&A, of whom I

am a representative. I can provide you with ample iden-
tification. If you would just provide us with the data, we
will transfer the gol—"

A dull subsonic thud reverberated through the clearing,
felt more than heard. It rippled in from the east, and she
could hear the piles of rubble shifting around. It felt like
a massive subsurface explosion, or an earthquake. The
veep toppled to the side as the ground shifted.

Tetsami couldn't ask for a better distraction. She hit
the throttle and keyed her personal field.

The Leggett slammed into her backside. It felt like the
bike was trying to split her up the middle as it shot
straight upward, straining the contragrav near the red line.
She felt a warm tingle as her field soaked up some sort of
energy weapon.

She looked down. The ground and the three cars were
rapidly receding below her. One of the goons had hit her
and was tracking her with his laser on full. Her field was
absorbing the beam's energy, but the heat was getting
bad. She could smell the ozone-transformer reek that announced that her field was close to failure.

Another laser hit and she'd be toast.

Time for some fancy maneuvering. She cut the
contragrav and leaned forward. The Leggett was compact,
top-heavy, and as aerodynamic as a brick. It dove nose-
first straight toward the ground.

The maneuver had the desired effect. She dropped out
from under the stare of that laser immediately.

However, while she'd pulled this stunt before, she'd
never done it this close to the ground. It took two seconds
for her contragrav to key in from a cold start—there was
a good chance she'd plow into something before she
gained power again.

She switched the contragrav back on and hoped she'd
done it soon enough.

She was pointed down, straight at the three cars. She
could see goons piling out of the cars and unlimbering
weapons, but they weren't pointing them at her—

"*Lord Mother Jesus Tap-Dancing Christ!*"

Her epithet was lost on the execs. The ground around

them had erupted with troops in powered armor. The execs were surrounded.

Tetsami felt extremely stupid. There must have been at least twenty men buried in the rubble around the bunker, and she'd called the place clean because the bunker was empty.

The contragrav kicked in when she was barely ten meters above the cars. The seat split her backside again, and her face slammed into the—thankfully padded—handlebars. It was just in time.

Through eyes watering with acceleration, she glimpsed something streak past the bunker and target the central groundcar. A smart missile. It maneuvered for the open door. The veep was in the way.

She had a subliminal flash of the corp folding over the missile and flying backward into the car. A split-second image of the junior veep doubled over, exhaust shooting out of his midsection.

Then the groundcar exploded.

The car's body was armored enough to hold its shape, but flame shot out the windows and the car landed back on its skirt.

For some reason, Tetsami thought of the last time she'd ever seen her father. He'd told her mother that the job was nothing to worry about, it was just a "routine penetration."

That word, "routine," flew through her brain like a runaway bullet.

She vectored the drive as she heard another groundcar taken out. The Leggett shot out at a tangent, past one of the armored soldiers—all white enamel and gold and looking nothing like Bleek infantry.

The Leggett was maxed at five gees, and Tetsami wished she could get more out of it.

She banked the bike toward the east side of the clearing. She streaked by only five meters above the ground. The velocity indicator shifted digits too fast to read.

Halfway to the surrounding buildings, and cover—

Something hit her. Something big.

It was an energy weapon, because the field soaked up

most of it. But the rear of the bike blew out as the power cells for the field overloaded explosively. The Leggett listed to port and banked away from the edge of the clearing. Tetsami tried to get the bike under control, but the explosion had damaged the grav unit.

She thanked God that personal transports only used catalytic injection grav units. They might power up slower than a quantum extraction unit, but they didn't turn into clouds of radioactive plasma when they malfunctioned.

The ground began sliding upward, and she wondered what would hit her first, the ground or another shot from that weapon.

It was the ground.

The left front of the Leggett clipped the corner of an old building foundation and flipped up and around in a slow spin that was only possible with a contragrav. Tetsami had a moment to see the ground spinning to meet her. She released herself from the bike and hoped her body armor would save her.

She hit the side of a sloping mound of dirt. Her helmet hit something hard and she could hear a crack. She was rolling too fast to see anything. It took her a second to realize that she was still alive.

Something above her exploded and showered dirt over her. She didn't know if it was her bike or a missile.

She came to a stop in a trickling river of slime at the base of the hill. She was nauseated, dizzy, and aching in every muscle of her body, but she seemed to have gotten off with little damage.

Tetsami raised her head—

She ripped off her helmet and threw up into it.

Elsewhere, the sounds of battle continued. If she was lucky, they counted her among the dead now. She raised herself upright, and this time the vertigo was easier to deal with.

She had rolled to the bottom of a large blast crater. The river in the bottom was the effluent from a broken sewer line. "Well, girl," she said to herself as she walked away from the battle. "You've been at this for eight years standard. You've finally hit the wall. What are you going to do now?" She didn't have an answer.

She still had to worry about getting out of this alive.

She climbed, haltingly, toward the lip of the crater. It was hard going, but her condition improved as she went. It got better when, halfway up, the sounds of fighting ceased.

She got to the edge believing she'd managed to survive the incident—

When she cleared the lip, she came face-to-face with a man in a battlesuit of chrome, gold, and polished white enamel. He wielded the nastiest energy weapon she had ever seen.

CHAPTER FIVE

The Underground Economy

"A criminal is a revolutionary without the pretense."
—*The Cynic's Book of Wisdom*

"After coming into contact with a religious man I always feel I must wash my hands."
—Friedrich Nietzsche
(1844–1900)

There might have been a worse place to ditch the Hegira than the east side of Godwin, but if so it wasn't on any of the eighty-three inhabited planets in the Confederacy.

Dom opened his eyes with the hope that what he was feeling was due to a screwed up balance circuit. It wasn't. He *was* hanging upside down from the crash harness.

There was a bright side. The drive hadn't blown.

The Hegira had plowed through the tenth floor of a fifteen-story warehouse and had flipped over. Perhaps it had rolled. Dom didn't remember anything after the small aircraft's impact with the building. It'd smashed through the other side, planting its nose in the roof of a neighboring building. The drive section balanced precariously on the bottom half of the window the Hegira had broken through.

Dom was suspended, headfirst, about thirty meters above a very hard-looking alley.

He waved a hand experimentally at the space where the windscreen had been. His hand brushed empty air.

As Dom scrambled to untangle parts of his body from the crash harness, he got subliminal glimpses of a group of spectators below him. The eidetic computer net wired into his brain dutifully recorded impressions of leather, metal, kevlar, and monocast with little rhyme or reason.

The most vivid detail that registered as Dom unwedged his artificial left leg from the Hegira footwell was the Proudhon Spaceport Security logo one of them wore.

That was before someone started to take potshots at him.

Suddenly, the group below him had Dom's full attention.

The shooter was shaved bald and wore an exec's monocast vest. Baldy was firing some hideous homemade weapon. The others were laughing as he paused to reload it. Even though Baldy was the one shooting, what scared Dom was the pulse carbine slung cross the back of the one with the spaceport shoulder patch.

Make short work of me and the Hegira—though it'd be difficult getting it recharged in this part of town.

Must be their idea of fun.

Dom pulled his body as far as he could into the shelter of the cockpit just as another shot hit the side of the Hegira.

He couldn't risk return fire. With his reflexes he might get two of them with his pulse laser, but that would inspire the survivor to use a real weapon.

He put his left hand, the fully cybernetic one, on the side of the canopy and clamped it there. Then he wrenched the crash harness off, swinging out the missing windscreen.

Dom dangled under the Hegira, his left hand clamped around a strut in the canopy.

The punks below applauded him.

Dom looked down. The gang was closely grouped under the Hegira.

Dom looked back along the drive section, at the window on the floor below. The window had been cracked by the Hegira's impact, but it was still there. It was a risk. . . .

He looked at his audience, who seemed to be enjoying the show.

If you liked that, he thought, *you'll* love *this*.

Dom reached up and pulled the emergency eject lever. His left hand was holding on to the canopy. When he pulled the emergency lever, two tons of gas pressure blew the canopy back on its track, shooting toward the drives. The ninth-story windows of the warehouse raced toward him. He let go, and slammed into the window.

For a split second he worried if the weakened window wouldn't give—

He smashed through.

As he crashed into the ninth story, rockets blew the driver's seat down, straight at the punks. The rocket had enough thrust to blow the chair up for fifty meters. It tried to level itself, but trapped by the alley it only managed to slam itself into the walls. The rocket would still be going when it hit the ground.

Dom rolled over broken glass to the receding thrum of the seat's thrusters. As he skidded to a stop, ruining his suit, he caught a brief glimpse of orange as the chute deployed all wrong, billowing itself up to the Hegira.

The few real parts of his body hurt.

He got on his hands and knees. The entire floor was one room. It was empty, stripped. Anything of value had long ago been ripped off—light fixtures, electronics, plumbing, carpeting, walls, furniture.

He had rolled to the far wall. Next to him was a deep shaft. Someone had made off with the elevator.

He turned away from the shaft. The floor was about five-hundred meters square. The only light came from anemic moonlight filtering through dust-hazed windows. No one could sneak up on him here. Just empty gray space. At first Dom was surprised at the lack of people or graffiti, but as he heightened the gain on his photoreceptors, he realized that there weren't any stairs.

The missing elevator had been the only access to the upper floors.

"Damnation and taxes." His voice echoed back at him, enforcing the sense of emptiness.

He shook with delayed reaction. He forced himself to stop.

A sickening screech shattered the silence, followed by a snapping sound. A grinding noise—accelerating in pitch—came from the window Dom had broken through.

He looked back as the majestic shadow of the Hegira slowly moved. The nose slid toward the ground. The grinding reached its apex and the entire craft jerked downward.

It slid by the window with comparative soundlessness.

A half-second later he heard the sound of tearing metal and shattering plastic. The concrete floor shuddered with the impact.

He paused a few seconds, rubbing his bruised right arm; then he walked to the broken window and risked a glance downward.

The Hegira was longer than the alley was wide. It hadn't fallen all the way to the street. It was wedged between the buildings again, four floors down. No sign of the punks.

Dom's nose itched with the acrid smell of burning synthetics.

He couldn't see it with the Hegira in the way, but he supposed that the ejection seat's rocket had ignited the chute during the descent. That wasn't supposed to happen, but Dom doubted the designers had anticipated their seat being deployed upside down in a narrow alley only thirty meters from the ground.

He cast a cursory glance at the building exterior, but there was no sign of a fire escape. He checked all four sides of the structure, kicking out the plastic windows. No luck. He hadn't expected any. This looked to be a secure building in its day. That meant one way in, one way out. When the neighborhood went bad, the owners took everything.

If it had been modular, they probably would have taken the building as well.

He walked back to the rectangular shaft that used to

hold the elevator. It had been a maglev, and bolts were anchored in the wall every few meters where the magnets had been attached.

He took hold of a projecting bolt and put his weight on it. It held.

He took a deep breath and began the descent.

It was slow going. He took the time to make sure the bolts were firmly attached and that his grip was solid. His scrupulousness paid off at least once, when one of the bolts bent under his foot and slid out of the wall in a shower of masonry dust.

As he climbed down, he tried to avoid thinking about what was happening.

He tried.

He failed.

The world had crumbled from underneath him. Again. The only real surprise was the fact that he hadn't expected it. He had naively thought that he had finally cemented his niche in the world and could forget his past.

He had thought that when the TEC had recruited him and his brother.

He had thought that when he had abandoned the TEC after Helen's death.

He had thought that when he had come to Bakunin after . . .

After he'd stopped being human.

A bolt bent in his left hand and he almost fell.

He calmed himself. It might be a nightmare. But it wasn't the worst possible nightmare. He'd already lived through that.

When he reached the fifth floor, he began to realize that something other than the chute was burning below him.

The signs of humanity had been growing as he descended. On the fifth floor were a few rat-gnawed mattresses and a few words written on the walls. Odds were that the first floor of this place was littered with combustible material.

As Dom paused to consider his options, a dull thud reverberated below him, followed by a wave of greasy black smoke that belched up the shaft.

He jumped out of the shaft and on to the fifth floor. He was in trouble.

He searched for an escape route. And there it was, the mangled drive section of the Hegira, sticking through a window.

Dom ran over to it and looked out a neighboring window. The nose of the craft had jammed itself into a window in the building across the alley.

It looked stable.

Dom climbed on top of the drive section. It was still warm from his escape. Although it felt as if the Hegira was solidly wedged between the buildings, Dom didn't want to trust that.

The floor behind him was already opaque with smoke. Breathing was difficult.

Down the length of the craft—a bare ten meters—was only a slight angle.

He held his breath and crawled out on to the Hegira's belly. The underside was smooth metal, and it was all Dom could do to maintain a slow pace that wouldn't have him sliding off into the alley below.

Below him was an inferno. Orange-red flame danced in the gaps between the roiling black smoke filling the alley. As he watched, a storage barrel shot up out of the smoke with a dull *foomp* sound, trailing fire.

What the hell was stored down there? He hoped another barrel didn't hit his craft.

The smoke got denser. Bangs and thuds continued as chemicals ignited behind and beneath him. He finally made it to the opposite window. He put his hand on a piece of twisted molding—

Behind him someone kicked open the gates of Hell.

The warehouse behind him and the ally below him exploded. No dull thud this time. This was a shuddering roar that belched a sheet of toxic fire up past him. If it weren't for the two tons of Hegira shielding him from the blast. . . .

The sound was overwhelming enough for his audio to

cut out for a second, leaving him in a violent whited-out silence.

The vehicle took the worst of it. Dom felt the craft rise up underneath him. The echoes of the blast were still fresh as the remains of the car dropped out from under him. Somehow he managed to grab the molding with his other hand.

The aircraft smashed drive-end first into the alley below, leaving Dom dangling from a broken window frame, five stories up. He swung a foot up and pulled himself into the window. He rolled, face first, into a rotting cardboard box filled with mildewed clothes. He came to a stop nose-to-nose with a dead rat that had crawled into the box to die. There were other things moving in the box.

He stayed until the explosion had dulled and his hearing returned. Then he pushed himself upright slowly, turning to face the warehouse.

The first two floors were invisible behind belching smoke, and he could see orange flickering as far up as the fourth floor. The explosion had blown out every window on the building.

He needed to get somewhere he could breathe.

He turned away from the window. He faced a hallway that was cloaked in graffiti and garbage. The place smelled of rot and mildew, but it was clear that people lived here. He passed open doorways that led into rooms with candles and soiled mattresses.

Eventually, he found stairs. He made it five floors down and to an exit without running into any of the natives.

Then he made the mistake of counting himself lucky.

As Dom opened the door to the outside, a bald punk in an exec's monocast vest grabbed his arm and threw him down the front stairs of the building. Dom hit the ground and heard his ceremonial slugthrower clatter out of his belt holster.

He landed, faceup, in the center of a ring of a half-dozen punks. They had the real weapons out.

Baldy, punk number one, picked up Dom's slugthrower, smiled in appreciation at the expensive antique, and aimed it at Dom.

Punk number two, the one with the Proudhon Spaceport shoulder patch, leveled a Griffith-Five High Frequency pulse carbine at him. The pulse carbine was a close-combat infantry weapon that, in a pinch, could be watted up to take on light armored vehicles.

Punk number three wore a black beret, leather jacket, and a three-fingered artificial hand. That hand was holding a fifteen-millimeter Dittrich High Mass Electromag. The HME rounds would be steel-cored uranium. If it hit the target, the target would drop. Even if the target wore powered armor. A testosterone weapon.

Punk four had vidlens eyes and a necklace of human teeth. The fact that he armed himself only with a machete in the midst of all that hardware made him a little scary. It also marked him as stupid, or crazy.

Punk five wore half a facial reconstruction in brushed chrome. He carried an antique frontier auto-shotgun. That thing was made for taking on large hostile fauna. He wore crossed bandoliers of shells.

Punk six had a smartgun. She had old unit tattoos on her face, from some off-planet marine force. Her custom job had wires jacked into her arm.

Dom would have preferred the Confed marines.

"A fucking corp," said Beret.

"Vent his ass," said the woman.

"Hell you say, Trace. Corp exec, ransom—" said the one with the shoulder patch.

"Sell 'im," the guy with half a face agreed.

"Vent him," said the woman as she began to power up her weapon.

"It's your call, Bull," said the man with video eyes.

The bald one looked down on him, shaking his head. "He *looks* like a corporate type. Could be worth something to someone—"

Patch and half-face gave satisfied nods to each other.

"—But I don't want to deal with the upkeep, and the bastard shot a chair at me." Baldy looked up at the woman. "Vent him, Trace."

"Just the head," said Beret, "We can harvest—"

Dom had been trying to think of a way he could either talk or fight his way out of this. He was about to say something, when Beret was interrupted by an impact that shook the ground. The punks all turned to face in the same direction.

"Shit, it's a fucking paladin!" That was the last thing Beret ever said. A beam of energy shot through his torso, cutting him neatly in half.

The one with the shoulder patch fired his pulse carbine, cutting a left flank swath while the woman with the smartgun cut in from the right. They should have caught the attacker in the cross fire.

A shadow passed over them. Whoever it was jumped. There was another impact, and the ground shook again.

Trace and Patch were cut down from behind.

Half-face returned fire with his auto-shotgun. It sounded like a jackhammer and was about as accurate. A beam of energy erased the remainder of his face.

In the interim, Baldy and the video-eyed machete wielder had run off for parts unknown.

Dom got to his feet, holding his arms wide, and faced the paladin. The paladin's body armor was spotless white, gold, and gleaming chrome. He had a narrow-aperture plasma weapon cabled into his backpack. The pack towered over the ovoid helmet, sign of a manpack contragrav unit. A gold cross was laminated on the paladin's right shoulder.

The voice that addressed Dom passed through a electronic filter and had the bass turned way up. "Lower your hands, citizen. I do the Lord's work."

Religious fanatic. "I appreciate your help—" Dom read a small chromed nameplate on the breast of the body armor. "Brother Rourke."

"Thanks are not required. It is our calling to combat the Devil's influence on this poor lawless world—"

Dom ignored Rourke's pitch. He spent the time looking over the four sinners that the nut had just erased. It wasn't that he objected to the killing. If there were ever four people that needed the express route off-planet, it was these punks. It was doing it in the name of God that grated. It was almost as bad as killing someone in the name of some government.

"—is customary to transfer a small tithe to the Church."

Dom looked up from Trace's corpse. "What?"

"Proper thanks to the Church of Christ, Avenger for your deliverance is made by tithing to—"

"That's what I thought you said." Great racket, save any poor bastard that looks like he has two grams to rub together and make a sure profit. It was just too bad for Brother Rourke this time. "All my assets have been taken over. I don't have any cash on me."

"That is unfortunate."

Rourke lifted another weapon before Dom could react. The paladin shot him, and the world blinked out of existence.

CHAPTER SIX

Coup d'État

"Might might not make right, but it makes a damn good argument for its position."
—*The Cynic's Book of Wisdom*

"Do not hold the delusion that your advancement is accomplished by crushing others."
—MARCUS TULLINUS CICERO
(106–43 BC)

At exactly 2542 hours, Godwin Local, Colonel Klaus Dacham strode into Dominic Magnus' office. Klaus was not in a pleasant mood. Ten years ago he'd convinced himself that it had been dealt with. Then came the discovery of Dominic Magnus' identity, and then this mission—

And at the critical moment the murdering bastard escaped.

The feeling strung Klaus' nerves tight, in an invisible tide, as if he were piloting his mental ship much too close to a point gravity source. It was a point he'd been orbiting for fifteen years.

Forget her, said a small heretic thought. *She's dead.*

The thought angered him even more. The fact that she *was* dead, beyond reach, beyond any reconciliation—that was the dark hole his soul orbited. Killed by her favorite.

The knowledge that the murderer had escaped justice this past decade tore all the wounds open.

The blood was still fresh.

And her murderer was still alive.

Sometimes Klaus wondered why he was obsessed with punishing the murderer of a woman he had hated. Hated and abandoned. Still hated. Every memory of her burned as badly as acid.

However, also burning in him was the sense that he was right. The necessity to punish the wrong was a scar on his soul deeper than even his duty to the TEC. A burning scar that, until recently, had been dormant.

Klaus should have been able to take Dominic, this time, without having to stretch the authority the TEC had given him.

And the murderer had still slipped through.

Klaus wondered if anyone at Executive Command—other than him—knew who Dominic *really* was. Did his superiors know why Klaus Dacham was so eager to command his first field mission since Paschal, at an age when most TEC agents were comfortably ensconced behind desks?

Klaus suspected that the old man Dimitri knew. If Dimitri Olmanov didn't know, he was certainly capable of knowing. It was rumored that the head of the TEC could know anything that he put effort into finding out.

Klaus was skeptical of omniscience. However, Klaus did believe that if Dimitri *knew* about Dominic and *still* ordered this mission, then Klaus had implicit permission to act as he saw fit.

"Dominic Magnus—" Klaus frowned at that. It was a pretentious alias.

Klaus had only recently learned that his quarry had fled to Bakunin. Apparently, "Dominic" had appeared here within a year of Klaus' last attempt to bring a belated end to the murderer's life.

Coming to Bakunin had been like falling into a black hole. Bakunin was not part of the Confederacy, and even the TEC couldn't penetrate beyond the scarred surface of its society. Klaus had been liaison between the TEC and

the SEEC intelligence community, a dusty desk job, when
he had learned of his quarry's continued existence.

The file on "Dominic Magnus" had been buried in with
a mass of reportage dealing with the arms industry on
Bakunin. Klaus would never have seen it if the information packet hadn't been mislabeled. The report had been
requested by Klaus' opposite number in the SEEC, and
Klaus was only supposed to be a courier. Instead, someone had keyed the file "ATT'N: Klaus Dacham."

That file had been a minor part of Sirius' and
Centauri's massive preparatory effort for Operation
Rasputin. Seeing "Dominic Magnus" buried in those files
had resurrected old phantoms Klaus had long thought ex-
orcised.

Even when he maneuvered to be part of Operation
Rasputin, Klaus had never thought he'd receive authorization to go to the planet himself.

Then, suddenly, Dimitri placed Klaus in command of
the mission.

Not only a command, a real force, but a chance to—

Klaus slammed his fist into the wall of the hemispherical observatory.

It had been prefect! Stage one of Operation Rasputin
was to take a munitions company. *A munitions company.*
The objective was almost tailored for him to target
"Dominic."

He looked out the holo-transparent walls and watched
the mop-up operation. Klaus' ship was settled in the landing quad, a Barracuda-class troop-carrier with oversized
engines. It was modified and fitted with enough weaponry to conduct an air assault on a small city. The
Paralian-designed ship was named *Kalcthwee'rat*. The
translation was *Blood-Tide*.

The ship and 130 Occisis-trained marines, and the murderer got away.

"Colonel?"

Klaus turned toward the voice.

The woman addressing him was still in field combat armor, though she'd removed her helmet. Her hair was
shaved into the transverse stripes that were the trademark

of the Occisis marines. Her red hair and stocky build marked her as a native. She was the captain, the ranking officer among Klaus' marines.

Klaus didn't like her. He had been given a week to prepare himself for the mission and another week with the marines in Earth orbit. The briefings he gave on Bakunin and their mission—the part the marines knew about anyway—had been successful, for the most part. He felt he could count on the large majority of his troops.

But Captain Kathy Shane had remained aloof. She had paid attention to Klaus' strategic holos, and the mission specs, but she'd remained uninvolved in Klaus' discussion of Bakunin itself. She acted like a sympathizer.

Klaus turned to face a blackened spot where a laser had penetrated the wall. It obscured the world beyond. "Captain Shane."

"You wanted to see me, sir?"

That wasn't quite true. What he wanted to do was get some priorities straight. "I understand that you didn't fire upon Dominic Magnus as he escaped toward Godwin. Is this correct?"

"Yes, sir."

Klaus ran his hand over the marble desk. A corner was charred by the same shot that had pierced the wall. So close.

"Was there confusion about the identity of the target?"

"No, sir."

Klaus turned back to the marine captain. Same nonexpression on her face. That annoyed him. "Perhaps you can clarify exactly why you didn't fire on him?"

"Sir, we have standing orders from the Terran Executive Command not to widen the scope of any conflict on Bakunin—"

Klaus nodded. "Until our primary mission has reached the stage—etcetera, etcetera. I know that. You have not answered my question. *Why* did you not fire on him?"

Was that a trickle of sweat on her upper lip? Good. "Sir. By the time we had the craft targeted, he had left the perimeter of the complex. Our orders were not to expand—"

"I see." Klaus paced around the desk. "Now, listen closely, *Captain*. Who is in charge of this operation?"

"You are, sir."

"I am glad we have that straight." Klaus sat in the chair behind the desk. "From now on I want you to act like it."

"Sir?"

"TEC isn't commanding this mission. I am. *And when I give you a priority target, you take the target out!*"

"But sir, our orders from command—"

"Only concern me."

"Yes, sir." Yes, he had her sweating all right. Now the hard edge in her voice was becoming a little more strained, a little more forced.

"I'm glad we have an understanding. Now here's an *order*, and it takes precedence over everything—understand?"

"Yes, sir."

"Even Executive Command."

"Yes, sir."

"Good. Your orders are— If anyone, I mean anyone, sees 'Dominic Magnus,' they are to kill him on sight. I do not care if this means dropping a warhead in the center of Godwin. He is to be eliminated. No qualifications. No exceptions. No excuses. This isn't going to happen again."

She looked a little pale now. "Yes, sir."

Klaus nodded, smiled to himself, and turned the chair around. He didn't hear her leave. "Is there something you want to say, Shane?"

"Sir, there's a question about what to do with the prisoners—"

Klaus closed his eyes and sighed. "What's to question? Shoot them."

Her voice finally cracked. "Sir?"

"Was I unclear?"

"No, sir."

"I'm glad we had this chance to talk. Dismissed."

Klaus listened to her leave. He hoped he wouldn't have any more problems from that quarter, but he doubted it. Shane was on the top of a list of people Klaus saw as spots of potential disloyalty. Spots that would need to be cleaned before he went on to the second phase of this operation.

But not yet. First he had to get GA&A up and running.

The holo lit up above Dominic's desk and Klaus turned to face it. It was the ground team's chief engineer, Atef Bin Said. The TEC had recruited the tech on Khamsin, right out of Hegira Aerospace's R&D department.

"Damage report."

"Go ahead." Klaus closed his eyes because the holo projection had been damaged. The unsteady image wildly shifted perspective and it hurt his eyes.

"As expected, the perimeter air defenses of the complex are a total loss. The attack wiped them out. The field generators and weaponry aboard the *Blood-Tide* can cover the same area until we can rebuild the ground units. Damage to the aboveground structures is superficial. I estimate repairs to be in the neighborhood of a hundred-thousand credits—"

"Gold, Said, we're on Bakunin now. Gold or the equivalent—"

"Ah, yes, sir— I'll get the estimates converted."

"What else?"

"Well, I said *most* of the aboveground damage is superficial. One building—GA&A security from our intel schematics—is a near total loss. This is, again, something we can handle from the *Blood-Tide*. In fact it would be recommended that we do that, in any event, until we have thoroughly examined GA&A's security setup. There could be some nasty surprises, given the environment."

"I understand. Anything else?"

"Yes, and I am afraid it is something we didn't anticipate. Ninety percent of GA&A's processing capability, its records and mainframes, was bunkered two klicks below the surface. TEC didn't anticipate any battle damage—"

Klaus nodded. "Booby-trapped. That was the subsurface detonation we detected, wasn't it?"

"Yes. It's too hot to make a direct assessment of the damage, but we can assume a total loss. The *Blood-Tide* doesn't have the processing capacity we need for an operation like this. It's a military vessel and the computers are too specialized."

Klaus rubbed his forehead. The TEC's little traitor, Helmsman, was to have been waiting in the bunker. Well, this saved Klaus the trouble of dealing with Helmsman himself. The agent down here had made a messy little deal to get Helmsman to even consider turning, but now there wasn't any question of who was in charge.

Klaus ran GA&A, period.

"How long before we can replace the computers?"

"Do you want to import the units?"

"Hell, yes! We can*not* have any native Bakuninites enter the complex—for *any* reason."

Said paused in thought. "Fortunately, our finances aren't limited. The closest Confed planet is Dolbri, but they wouldn't have what we need. Next closest is Earth—"

"God, no. We can't go anywhere near the capitals. Too many people are watching."

Said scratched his chin. "Cynos is out?"

Klaus nodded.

"Styx doesn't have an export industry . . . hmm— Banlieue is a little farther away, and expensive, but they'll have what we need and it's in the other direction from the Confed capitals. Will that do?"

Klaus nodded.

"Then I'll prepare a tach-comm to order what we need. If we use a military transport, it'll take about twenty-three days standard. About eighteen days Bakunin."

"Installation?"

"Two days at most."

The delay grated. But there was little Klaus could do about it. "Make the order. Any good news?"

"Yes, there is. The *Shaftsbury* has tached in ahead of schedule. We'll be able to start downloading personnel from orbit as soon as we have the living quarters cleaned out."

"Good. Keep me posted, and call me as soon as you know *exactly* when we can expect those computers."

"Yes, sir."

The holo faded.

Klaus' thoughts returned to "Dominic Magnus." He didn't expect his marines to get anywhere near him again. His sudden reappearance showed that if there was one thing the half-human bastard knew how to do, it was preserve his own hide.

Fortunately, Klaus had contingencies. Contingencies that had nothing to do with TEC covert operations. He had not relied on the TEC-supplied commandos to fulfill his own personal agenda, especially back when it seemed unlikely that he would be part of the Bakunin operation. He had made other arrangements.

Klaus walked to the door where he had left his case. He picked it up and carried it to the desk and set it down. He stuck his thumb in a hole in the side and waited for the mechanism to identify his genetic material.

The secure holo was a costly personal extravagance when the TEC would provide its officers with communications just as secure. Of course, the communications provided by the TEC weren't secure from the TEC.

The lid opened and the holo's lasers carved a blue spherical test pattern in the air over the base. Klaus tapped a twenty-three digit number seed into the keypad to start the scrambler on its work. Then he called a number in Godwin.

The holo display proved superfluous, since the recipient only transmitted audio back. "Greetings, Colonel."

"It is time we discuss our arrangement, Mr. Webster." Webster was an alias for a man—or woman, the voice could easily be a construct—that Klaus had never met. Klaus had worked a long time getting a few contacts on Bakunin. Now that he had actually come to Bakunin, he had made one of these contacts lead him to someone who seemed to have fingers in every rotten pie in Godwin.

To Klaus, Webster was nothing more than a high-priced informant, a messenger boy—

But informants had their uses.

"I've been expecting your call," Webster said. "I have

been quite thorough in assuring that the proper people are aware of the value you've placed on GA&A's personnel."

Klaus smiled. The TEC might accept half-measures, but Klaus was not going to take a chance that there were *any* of Dominic's loyalists at large. It was an easy thing to get GA&A's personnel list from Helmsman. No one had even questioned why he had needed it.

"There's a special one on the list. One that *has* to be eliminated."

"Dominic Magnus."

"Good guess."

"How much is this one?"

"My finances are unlimited. He must die. Even if you have to do the job personally. My security teams tracked him into East Godwin."

There was a dry chuckle on the other end. "I don't do anything personally. Besides, East Godwin would do the job for free. But—"

"But what?"

"I believe your target, and someone else on your list, are in the hands of the Church."

"What do you mean?"

"The Bakunin Church of Christ, Avenger. I gave them your list. BCCA is always open to new means for receiving donations."

"Is he dead?" It would be appropriate for a church to dispense justice, after what he had done—

"BCCA is—hmm—unusual. They do things their own way. He'll be alive until airtime. The show starts in a few minutes. Your holo can probably pick up their transmission."

"I don't like delays."

"If there's a problem, feel free to call back. Think of it this way, you get to watch."

Webster cut the connection.

The show?

Klaus adjusted the holo receiver and tried to find BCCA's broadcast. It took a while. The airwaves on this planet were hopelessly cluttered and followed no logical progression.

When he locked on to the BCCA broadcast, it was a scene featuring a priest on stage in front of a massive tote board labeled "Gold for God."

The priest yelled at an unseen crowd. "Welcome to our program of retribution."

There were cheers.

Klaus settled back to watch the broadcast.

Ten years he'd waited to get this close to Jonah.

Fifteen since their mother, Helen Dacham, had died.

"Death is the best you can hope for, brother," Klaus said.

CHAPTER SEVEN

Criminal Justice

"An efficient legal system operates on the assumption that everyone is guilty of something."
—*The Cynic's Book of Wisdom*

"Justice in government is as rare as a rich [man] in prison."

—DATIA RAJASTAHN
(?–2042)

Dominic dreamed ugly dreams.

Dominic dreamed of a forested ball of racism called Waldgrave, his home planet. He dreamed of his mother's drunken rages. He dreamed of her paranoia. He dreamed of the salvation the TEC recruiter offered.

Dominic dreamed of an ugly little planet in the Sigma Draconis system, a planet named Styx. He dreamed of thirty-five thousand people vaporizing as two tons of polyceram monomolecular filament struck from orbit. He dreamed of a city that no longer existed.

Dominic dreamed of the day that city had caught up with him. He dreamed of the slug slamming into his shoulder. He dreamed of falling over the railing, the endless fall. He dreamed of his body's reconstruction.

Dominic dreamed of the destruction of GA&A.

He dreamed his life was a massive glass sculpture,

shattering again and again. Every time it broke, a few
more pieces were missing. Now it seemed all he had left
was a few twisted shards.

As the stunner gradually wore off, the outside world
leaked back in. Dom heard people talking.

Someone with an insincere voice yelled at a crowd.
"Welcome to your program of retribution." Cheers. "First
off, I want to welcome back part of our viewing audience.
The Zeno Commune has finally repaired the battle damage to their vidsat substation—"

The emcee was drowned out by more cheers. Dom was
still fogged, but he could tell he was overhearing a holo
broadcast.

"And now, our first criminal. He was caught by one of
our roving patrols raping a teenage girl—

"So what are we going to do to him?"

"Fry him!"

"I can't hear you."

"FRY HIM!"

"And why are we going to fry him?"

"BECAUSE HE'S SCUM!"

The audience broke into applause.

"Well, we certainly hope so. But you know the rules.
Our lines are open for pledges, and our target with this
boy is a full kilogram."

Whistles from the audience.

"If we don't meet or exceed our target—we let him
go!"

Boos from the audience.

"So, while the home audience is making up their
minds, let's roll the video of the attack—"

"You, CEO-man, you awake yet?"

Dom opened his eyes. The last voice was a lot closer.

He was on the floor of a small concrete cell, and a
young woman was bending over him. Her age was somewhere between seventeen and twenty-two years standard.
She was only one-fifty centimeters tall. She had straight
black hair cut on an asymmetrical diagonal, almond-

shaped green eyes, and a concavity in the flesh of her neck that was the sign of an electronic biolink.

"I'm awake. Where is this?" he asked as he got to his feet.

He looked around for the holo he heard in the background. The cell itself was empty, but one wall opened into a carpeted lobby. The room beyond was where the holo was playing.

"Prime time, that's where this is. We're going to be making money for the mother Church—"

The lobby was done up like an exec office, static holo landscapes on the walls, soft-white indirect lighting. A uniformed guard sat in a plush red-velvet office chair, watching a holo mounted on a receptionist's desk. The desk must have faced the entrance to the room, but any exit was far to the right, out of his field of view.

The entrance to the cell was open, with the exception of a sphere mounted on a column, standing in the middle of the doorway. It didn't take a genius to figure that it was an Emerson field generator, the same idea as the paladin's stunner, a field programmed to raise havoc with human neural impulses. Walking through it would be painful, and you'd come out the other end unconscious.

Dom had a glimmer of an idea.

"The name's Tetsami," his cellmate went on. "Let me guess, you tried to shaft them on payment for their samaritan deal."

"How'd you know?" He kept his eye on the guard. The guard seemed intent on the holo broadcast and wasn't even looking in their direction.

"The only way they'd end up with a corp type. They take tithing very seriously. They're doing background checks on you now, to get something to put you on trial for. They need to recoup their costs."

After an overlong pause she asked, "So what do they call you?"

"I'm called Dominic Magnus." He debated with himself over what he was about to do.

Unless you pumped a hell of a lot of power into it, or it was tuned to a visible EM frequency, a static Emerson field was invisible. There'd be no way to see how the thing was tuned unless something passed through it.

He could make a few assumptions, though.

The Emerson effect's peak absorption band was based on the power you pumped into it. Widening the band increased the power consumption logarithmically—if someone pumped an infinite power supply into an Emerson field, you'd have a black hole—but at normal power ranges the fields were narrow-band things. There was a good chance that the field on this door was keyed only to interfere with a biological nervous system.

Of course, like most defensive screens, it could have a processor ready to adjust the frequency of the peak absorption band based on the field's own feedback.

In that case he would be in trouble.

Tetsami snorted. "*Sounds* like a corp name. You know, they're going to put one hell of a price on you. An exec would pull hellacious pledges from the communes."

"What'd you do?" There was also the small chance that the field was powered up to interfere with more things on the EM spectrum.

That would also be trouble.

"Same deal, bad luck to be saved before I got paid. Unfortunately, my normal employment is on their sins list."

"So what do you do for a living?"

Dom ran his photoreceptors through the whole range of possible configurations. There was no visible sign of the field's presence. Which only meant that, at the moment, it wasn't interfering with any of the EM spectrum he could pick up.

"Software, industrial espionage, that sort of thing. Apparently that makes me a thief. But I'll be better off than you will."

Dom inched up to the edge of the field. It could've come off of GA&A's assembly line. GA&A had a specialty in small-scale field jobs.

"Why do you say that?"

Tetsami seemed to realize something abnormal was going on. She kept her voice calm, but Dom felt her slide up next to him to watch his hands. "They told me the script. I'm the multiple-choice criminal today. Three pledge totals, the viewers are going to vote on whether I die, am maimed, or set free. I'll be set free."

"Why are you so sure?" Odds were it was just the neural field. Dom doubted there were any more fancy, or expensive, security measures. At least, that's what he was hoping.

After all, if there were anything beyond the field, they'd dispense with the guard.

Dom gritted his teeth and stuck his left hand through the field. If he was wrong and the field was broader-spectrum than he expected, there was a good chance he'd fry the cybernetics in his arm.

Nothing happened.

He saw Tetsami wince; obviously she had tried this before. However, Tetsami probably had natural limbs, while Dom's left arm was totally artificial.

There was a tingle, but no paralysis, no pain, and no alarms. He had to elbow Tetsami to continue the conversation; they couldn't have the guard looking around now.

"You see," she continued, "they're giving me five minutes for my own defense."

Dom felt along the other side of the central sphere. It was the obvious place for the control. There had to be a cutoff. Dom hoped it was within reach. "You're going to convince the audience you're innocent?"

Tetsami laughed. It sounded a little forced, but the guard didn't notice. "Hell, no. I'm going to promise to fuck anyone who donates a kilogram to let me go."

Dom found the switch.

He pressed the button, and again no alarms.

To test it, he put his right hand through the area where the field was. Nothing. The screen had dropped.

He waved Tetsami forward. "That's a dangerous offer."

Tetsami hesitantly stepped over the threshold. "My philosophy is to take things as they come. Get free, worry about the consequences later."

Dom stepped through himself, releasing the switch. According to the readout, the field sprang back up.

Now he had to deal with the guard. "Are you sure that

you want to promise something you might not want to go through with?"

The guard was still oblivious.

Tetsami hung back, letting him take the lead. "If someone gets me out of this mess ..."

The guard didn't show any sign that he knew his prisoners had escaped until Dom had slipped directly behind him. The guard began to turn in his seat and saw Tetsami. As the guard's hand went for his gun, Dom wrapped his left arm around the guard's neck.

"... I owe him that much," Tetsami finished.

Dom got the guard in a sleeper hold. He hoped the guard didn't have any enhancements in the neck area. "Tetsami, get his weapon."

Tetsami ran up and emptied the guard's holster. The guard thrashed a lot, kicking over the holo before losing consciousness. Dom let him go. The guard slid off the chair and landed facedown on the ground.

Tetsami covered the guard with her new weapon. It was a GA&A pulse laser.

The exit was a fairly normal chromed metal door, but above it was a red blinking light that said "on the air." This was a staging area, a holding cell for guests about to go in front of the audience.

"What now?" Tetsami asked.

"We dispose of the guard. Go over and hit the switch for the cell's field."

Tetsami did so, and Dom dragged the guard into the cell.

"Do you know the layout of the building?" he asked as he patted the guard down for IDs or card keys. No such luck.

She shook her head. "I was as zoned as you were when they brought me in. All I know is that this room is right off the stage, and they can only open it from the other side."

The room was small enough that Dom could see at a glance that there was only the one door. He searched around a bit, but nothing offered itself as a control to open it. Tetsami was probably right.

"We'll have to ambush them when they come for us." He went to the desk and pulled the holo projector upright. One of the lasers inside it had been knocked out of alignment, wildly distorting the blue part of the image, but they could still see the show. "This should give us some warning."

They stood in silence for a while on either side of the chrome door.

The show went on.

They had fried the rapist. The emcee, a slick hawker in a cassock and black pompadour, was going on about the next criminal. A mass murderer, he said.

After a few minutes, Tetsami asked, "How'd you put your arm through that thing?"

Dom kept watching the show. They were showing a video of the current subject emptying a Dittrich Hyper-Velocity Railgun into an East Godwin apartment complex.

"A biofield has to intersect a human nervous system to disable someone. My arm's a construct."

Tetsami gave him an appraising look, and they went back to waiting in silence.

They topped ten kilograms on the murderer. They burnt him alive, to the applause of the studio audience. Once the corpse sputtered out, the emcee came back. "Once again we've achieved divine retribution directed by your pledges. When we come back from our sponsor's message, we have a very special person to put on the block. The target is going to be a hundred kilograms. You won't want to miss this one."

The holo started to play a recruitment commercial for the Girolamo Commune. It took a dozen kilograms to buy a share.

Tetsami leveled the laser at the door. "A hundred K! You've got to be on next. Get ready—"

As if Tetsami had cued it, the door whooshed open.

Two guards were coming in. They weren't expecting trouble. Dom reached through and grabbed a wad of faithful. He held the leader by the gun arm and kneed him in the crotch.

Tetsami fired through the open door and a pulsing polychromatic beam burned the air. It got the second guard in the shoulder.

Dom brought his left fist down on the back of the leader, who was doubled over in front of him. The guard dropped to the floor.

The one with the burned shoulder committed a tactical blunder. He should have ducked for cover and called for help. Instead, he tried to close the door. The chrome door closed. The first guard was draped across the threshold and the door slammed into his side, prompting a groan.

Dom pumped through the gap. The mobile guard pulled his weapon and tried to track him. Tetsami shot him in the other shoulder. The guard's arm jerked, sending his shot wide as Dom got behind him.

Dom linked his hands and slammed both fists across the guard's back. The guard bounced off the far wall with a thud. The guard's laser dropped. Dom didn't wait for Tetsami to shoot again; he rushed the guard's back, grabbed him by the hair, and slammed his face into the wall.

The guard collapsed at Dom's feet. Dom glanced back at the door and saw that both guards were now unconscious. Tetsami stepped through the door as he bent and retrieved the guard's weapon. She was holding two guns herself, having disarmed the guard blocking the door.

They were in a short hallway with only one open exit. First came a half-dozen closed chromed doors. Then there was a curtain at the end of the hall. Beyond the curtain, Dom could hear a roaring crowd and the emcee's patter. No one seemed to have heard the commotion.

Tetsami stared at the curtain. "Think the alarm's raised yet?"

"Not yet. Not until the end of the commercial break."

"What now? Got to be a thousand people out there screaming for blood."

Dom started adjusting his audio pickup. He ran it through the onboard computer, and there was something repetitive about the waveform. "I don't think so."

"What did you say?"

"Have you ever seen that studio?"

"No—"

"Come on."

Dom headed straight for the curtain. He emerged right behind the emcee, put his arm around his neck, and put the guard's laser up to the man's ear. Dom faced the cameras. "This is called a powerful negotiating position."

Tetsami followed. She covered the broadcast studio.

The audience stopped applauding as the tech manning the speakers cut the feed. There wasn't a live audience, or even space for an audience. There was just the bare stage, lights, tote board, the holo cameras, and, behind a glass partition, a tech manning the broadcast and the electronics. There were two guards, but they were busy removing a charred corpse from the stage.

The guy in the cassock lost his cool. "Guards!"

Tetsami pointed one of her lasers at the two men on the corpse. She kept the other pointed at the tech. "Nope."

There was a door to the control room, and Dom headed for it, dragging his hostage. The emcee was still bleating. "Help. Someone call the tac units. Get a paladin up here—*gack*."

Dom had been increasing the pressure on the guy's windpipe to make him shut up. He shouldered through the soundproofed door to the control room while Tetsami covered the tech and the guards. Dom threw the emcee to the ground in front of the console and addressed the tech. "Put on a prerecorded show, more commercials, something—"

The emcee found his voice. "Don't do it Hanson, sound the alarm—"

Dom shot the emcee in the gut. The emcee screamed, and the tech lost all the color from his face. "Your host will probably survive that wound. Do what I say or he's going to look like your criminal of the week." Dom cocked his head toward the charred corpse.

Dom emphasized the statement by upping the power control on the laser. The iris on the firing aperture obligingly dilated a few fractions of a millimeter. The power cell could only supply five shots at the maximum setting. But they were shots best not contemplated.

The tech did as he was told.

The viewing public was about to be treated to a full hour of prerecorded commercials. It would be a little time before anyone in the Church organization realized that something had gone desperately wrong with their programming. By then he hoped to be out of the building.

Once the commercials got under way, Tetsami covered the guards and the tech back to the cell room. Dom had to drag the wounded emcee, who was crying. All six—including the two unconscious guards—ended up in the cell. Dom didn't bother deactivating the field, he pushed them through, one at a time, to fall unconscious on the other side.

"Now—" he began.

"Now," Tetsami finished, "we get the hell out of here."

CHAPTER EIGHT

Mergers

"Alliances are based on the premise that the parties involved benefit more from screwing the rest of the world than from screwing each other."
> —*The Cynic's Book of Wisdom*

"Money degrades all the gods of man and converts them into commodities."
> —KARL MARX
> (1818–1883)

Just outside the door of the high-tech holo studio was an anachronistic maze of stone corridors. The hall was dimly lit by recessed fixtures that tried to imitate torchlight. In recessed niches sat religious statues. The statues were either martial in nature, or they were horrific.

Either the Crusades or the Inquisition.

As they ran through the halls searching for an exit from the catacombs, Dom passed one that was particularly disturbing. He only caught a glimpse of it out of the corner of his eye, but it was enough for the whole picture to register. The sculpture showed a pair of hooded figures lowering a pathetic-looking individual into a vat. What was in the vat wasn't clear, but the victim's expression left little doubt that it was extremely unpleasant.

Dom did not like the memories that conjured up.

Too many nightmares to wake up from.

"You didn't handle yourself—" Tetsami paused for breath "—like an exec back there." From the tone of Tetsami's voice, it was a compliment. "And what do people. Really call you? I'm not going to be. Yelling 'Dominic Magnus.' In the middle. Of the next. firefight."

They were fugitives running for their lives and he almost told her to call him Mr. Magnus. He had to remind himself he wasn't at GA&A anymore. He was just another piece of human flotsam washed up on the shores of Godwin now.

But only for the moment.

"Call me Dom."

Tetsami nodded.

The catacombs were endless. They ran past dozens of heavy iron doors. The doors were windowless, but Dom figured that behind them sat material for future programming. Every few seconds he stopped at one and tried to open it.

He stopped when one finally opened, releasing the fetid stench of mold and rot. Beyond the door was a windowless cube, the stone walls covered with black-green slime. In the center, a humanoid skeleton that still bore a few scraps of flesh completed the effect.

Flabby white vermin scurried away from the light.

Behind him a breathless Tetsami said, "Ugh."

They went another five minutes without finding stairs or a window. The farther they went while still in the Church's domain, the greater the chance God's servants were going to land on them.

Dom stopped Tetsami at an intersection. "We've got to get some bearings before they start after us."

"We're getting nowhere," Tetsami agreed, panting.

They must be underground. From the stone and the low-tech construction, the place they were in could date from the first colonization of Bakunin. Back before the cities decided to jell. These corridors were built, probably, when the Church was sovereign over a large section of what was now part of Godwin. These halls could snake under the city forever.

However, he had the feeling that there was a cathedral above them somewhere.

Now that they had stopped, the only sound was the echo of dripping water.

"So where—"

Dom put his fingers to his lips and began to increase the gain on his audio input. He thought he could hear something else.

Tetsami's breathing became a thunderous bellows in his ears as he upped the gain. He tried to have his onboard computer filter out the noise and was only partially successful. He muted her breathing, but suffered a periodic deafness every time Tetsami exhaled—

But there *was* something else.

He might not know a word of Latin, but he knew where it was coming from.

"This way." Dom followed the sound.

It was long going, with a lot of false turns and back-tracking. But eventually they came to a wooden door behind which was a spiral staircase. From up the staircase came the sounds of a midnight service. Dom took the lead and started upward. Tetsami followed.

They circled upward, past more wooden doors that opened onto more underground corridors. When the stairs ran out, they found themselves in a niche recessed behind a Gothic stone arch. Dom looked out of the darkened space and into the floodlit cavern of a stone cathedral.

He grabbed Tetsami and started for the doors. They ran in the shadowed space beneath the choir loft, along the narthex.

The Church of Christ, Avenger, had tried to recapture the architectural glory of the Terran Middle Ages. The ceiling arched way above the assembly, dwarfing the human worshipers. A Hegira C-545 could be comfortably parked in the nave. The silhouette of Schwitzguebel, Bakunin's largest moon, was visible behind a stained-glass rose window high above the altar.

As they ran, Dom desperately hoped that no one noticed them.

Their shadowed hallway followed the main chamber. To their left, the only thing separating Dom and Tetsami from the ranks of seated worshipers was a fluted stone pillar every three meters. To their right they passed niches containing the odd—some very odd—saint.

Dom kept an eye on the throngs of faithful gathered in the pews of the nave. The crowd had a few nonhumans—though no true aliens—and seemed to be quite involved in their devotion. What worried Dom was the fact that every ten meters or so, they passed the back of a paladin's body armor. The Church's muscle was invariably facing the crowd. He couldn't count on that to last.

They stopped short of the main entrance, opposing the altar. There were two paladins guarding the doors, facing into the nave.

"Shit."

Tetsami shook her head. "They go to a lot of trouble to keep their faithful in line—"

"Let's get off the floor before someone spots us."

They faded into another niche recessed into the right wall of the narthex. It was another spiral staircase, this one going upward. They ended up on a balcony overlooking the service and all the paladins.

Dom was running out of ideas. "Know how this place operates?"

"Caught their holo show a few times." She shrugged and continued to catch her breath.

"Does it look like the battlesuits are guarding the worshipers?"

Tetsami nodded. "Must take tithing *very* seriously."

If the guards were for an external threat, they wouldn't be watching the faithful quite as closely. Dom retreated from the balcony. "If we're lucky, the guards will disappear when the crowd leaves. We just have to wait."

So they waited.

They sat on a stone bench carved into the wall. Tetsami faced down one end of the hall, Dom the other. The paladins didn't move.

There was a long pause before Tetsami asked, "You native to Bakunin?"

"I thought it was bad form to ask that."

Dom heard her chuckle. "No, the question you *don't* ask is why a nonnative *came* to the planet in the first place."

"No, I'm not native."

There was another long pause. Then Dom asked, "Why do you ask?"

"Sometimes seems Bakunin's got the monopoly on god-junkies." Dom had never really thought of it that way. "Do things get this weird off-planet?"

"It's not easily escaped. Wasn't this planet founded on socialist atheism?"

Tetsami chuckled again and waved at the cathedral. "The Founding Commune would toss their collective lunch if they saw this display."

"At least there isn't a state religion."

"There will be—five minutes after someone founds a state on Bakunin."

"We should both live that long."

The priest went on interminably. It was beginning to become clear why there was heavy security. It had slowly dawned on Dom that two-thirds of the worshipers wore restraint buckles on wrists and ankles. He was looking at a captive audience. Most of them were prisoners of the Church.

After a while Tetsami asked, "Would it be bad form to ask what nuked you?"

"Meaning?"

"Your suit's worth a kilo. They put a hundred-K bill on your head. You look like an exec. You fight like a brunet refugee from the New Aryan Front. And you smell like an East Godwin maggot-brain—"

"You forgot the cybernetic limb."

"Yeah, so where do you come from?"

Dom clenched his teeth. They were artificial, smooth, and fit together perfectly. He got no pleasure from grinding them. "You just told me you weren't supposed to ask that."

"Well, fuck me, Dom. I have an unhealthy curiosity. Won't force it."

There was an uncomfortable silence.

Dom relented. "My company, Godwin Arms, was attacked—shot out from under me. My escape crashed me into East Godwin."

"Oh, shit." Tetsami only managed a hoarse whisper.

"What?" Dom turned to face her and her normally pale skin had faded to white.

"Shit shit shit." Tetsami shook her head violently.

"What?" He repeated, more forcefully this time.

She sucked in a breath. "The biggest contract I ever got blew up in my face during the final meet. My contacts were scragged by a paladin hit team . . ." She shook her head again, as if she didn't believe what she was saying. "Guy, I was working for GA&A."

"Wait a minute—"

"No, I don't believe in coincidence. Those paladins came out of nowhere. You got tagged by them, too—"

Tetsami's nervousness was rubbing off on him. "Slow down. Let me think."

"Think? Someone's got a contract out on us."

"I don't like this."

"What's not to like?" Tetsami put her head in her hands.

Dom went on. "Having GA&A fail like that is one thing—but going after field employees is another."

Tetsami seemed not to hear him. "It was the job, right? Had to be. Espionage is a dangerous biz . . ."

Dom thought of the invasion, and the hardware that the Confederacy had brought to bear against GA&A. "I don't think the hit squad had anything to do with your line of work. It was who you were working for."

Dom heard the service breaking up below. He stood up and watched the crowd of involuntary worshipers filing out, escorted by the paladins. The two-thirds with the restraint buckles were vanishing into the sides of the church, presumably to be locked into the catacombs that he and Tetsami had vacated. The free third left through the main doors at the front of the cathedral.

Tetsami was looking up at him. "Don't say that."

"I think that explains why they treated us differently."

"What do you mean?"

"There has to be quite a lead time before they put a victim on their show. They seem to have at least five hundred selected criminals in their charge, but they scheduled us the same day they locked on to us. They didn't even spend the time to program one of those restraint buckles. They wanted us on the air *tonight*."

The silence between them was tangible.

Tetsami looked him in the face. He could feel his facial tic start up and he turned away.

"It *is* a contract," she said.

"There's probably a standing bounty for the heads of GA&A's personnel."

"No. This shit ain't got nothing to do with me. I'm a freelancer—"

"The kill list is going to be based on the payroll records. If you had contracted work for GA&A, you'd be on the list."

There was a long pause, and for the first time Tetsami sounded as young as she looked. "Damn it, you're scaring me."

Dom had scared himself. He had prepped that commune in the mountains for an emergency such as this. But he had never thought that GA&A's personnel would become targets. The top execs, maybe. A few corporations weren't above the occasional assassination. But going after employees, that made no sense. Even if they were loyal to the previous management—

Dom resolved not to lead anyone to the commune until he knew exactly what was going on.

That meant staying in the cold a little longer.

Damn.

Dom kept looking down into the nave. The last paladin was vanishing into the back, leaving the cathedral empty of evidence of the Church's enforcement arm. The small collection of people below were unrestrained, here of their own free will.

Sick bastards.

"Why?" she asked in a very small voice.

"If I knew that, I'd feel better."

There was a footstep behind them.

Dom turned and saw a paladin in a full suit, ten meters down the length of the balcony. The paladin froze in shock for a moment. Then he started yelling on his radio and unlimbered his weapon.

Five more minutes and they'd have been out of there with no trouble.

Tetsami shot. Her aim was exemplary. She focused on the faceplate. But the hand laser wasn't very effective against a military-quality field. Her shot did give them a few seconds to spare. The paladin's faceplate darkened instantly, blinding him in the dim lighting.

Dom grabbed Tetsami. "Brace yourself."

"What the fuck?"

Dom lifted her, stepped up on the railing, and jumped off.

Brief memory of flipping backward over the metal railing, tumbling endlessly into the hungry slime below—

He didn't like doing it, even though it was only ten meters. There was a chance he could land on his real leg. The remaining few worshipers were turning to watch with growing expressions of shock on their faces. The few underneath him were scrambling out of the way.

His left foot, the artificial one, landed on the seat of a pew, sending a vibrating impact up his body. A circuit somewhere was overloaded, and for a split second his entire left side was frozen and numb.

He didn't stop moving. The pew splintered and gave under his weight, and then his right leg hit the ground. A shuddering wave of pain crashed over his right side as his leg buckled under him. Fortunately, Tetsami was prepared when Dom let her go. He had managed to soak up most of the impact, and she only had to roll into the aisle and get to her feet.

The overloaded circuit started working again, and Dom could stand up. Tetsami was firing again. The paladin on the balcony was still blinded, but Dom's enhanced ears picked up the sound of more armor approaching.

"Reinforcements are coming."

Tetsami turned to him and noticed his limp. "Can you walk?"

"The question is, can I run?"

Dom started for the main doors. Tetsami came up behind him and pulled his right arm around her shoulders. She ran, pulling him along. It was a good thing she did. Dom thought his right ankle might be sprained, if not broken.

It seemed to take much too long to get to the doors, but they made it before more paladins showed.

They made it down the front steps of the cathedral and Dom was gratified not to see the war zone of East Godwin—

But he had no idea what part of the city he *was* in. He had spent way too much time sequestered in his suite at the GA&A complex.

He let Tetsami lead. She seemed to know where they were.

They'd gone barely thirty meters down the road when she turned him down a brick street that'd be too narrow for half the traffic in Godwin. They passed two skinny doorways and she pushed him into a third. This doorway was a kiosk that someone had constructed a building around. No door, only stairs down. In the darkness, Dom automatically adjusted his photoreceptors until he saw a monochrome light-enhanced image of a frozen escalator descending five stories below street level.

"Where are we going?"

"The Bakunin underground—" Tetsami snorted. When they hit a landing, she continued. "Five years ago someone tried to run a passenger commuter train from Godwin to Proudhon. For some reason it went bankrupt about three months before they finished construction. Some bank owns it now."

They left a short corridor and ended up on an abandoned train platform. Tetsami appeared unable to see in the darkness, but she moved as if she knew the place. She felt along a wall and found a control box.

About half the panels set in the wall started glowing. Dom killed the gain on his eyes and found himself fac-

ing the tracks for a high-speed maglev tube. A chromed
sign was set in the wall. It read, "Wilson Station." He
still had no idea what part of town they were in.

"The Church's goons can search for us, but if we go
about a hundred meters down the tube, they haven't stolen all the magnets yet—"

Dom knew what she meant. He knew the sensors the
paladins would be carrying, and sitting under one of those
magnets, and under a dozen meters of concrete and earth,
would be effective defense against anything but an eyeball search.

"Okay. Kill that light. I can see without it, and it won't
help down the tube anyway."

She killed it and reached out for him. He grabbed her
hand and started limping down the tube. "How'd you
know about this place?"

"There are stations all over Godwin."

True to her prediction, after a short walk, the huge
magnets still lined the rails in both floor and ceiling, sunk
into the concrete. Even though no power ran through
them, they still had enough residual magnetism to slightly
blur his vision.

They sat down, next to each other.

"So," she asked, "after we get out of this, what are we
going to do?"

What were they going to do?

What *could* they do?

Dom called up his personal database and started taking
a mental inventory of all the assets he had off the GA&A
complex.

CHAPTER NINE

Insurance Fraud

"People prefer deals where only they benefit to one of
mutual benefit between themselves and others."
                                    —*The Cynic's Book of Wisdom*

"Nobody has money who ought to have it."
                                    —Benjamin Disraeli
                                    (1804–1881)

Tetsami sat across from Dom. They were in a waiting
room inside the Reynolds Insurance Building, and she
wasn't quite sure why she was here. They should've been
holed up under a rock somewhere. She didn't expect to
see her 50 K, in the IBASC or anywhere else, no matter
what Dom said. It was too easy to move money around
when you didn't have any.

Despite that, instinct told her to stick with this guy—
and her instincts had taken her five years past the point
anyone in her line of work had a right to go.

Dom was a survivor. Not only that, there was something buried under the impassive facade. There was
power there, nearly hidden. She had the feeling that if
they split up, *she'd* be the one someone canceled.

Still, she wished he had the sense to hole up somewhere. It was barely eight hours since they'd skipped out
on the Church. Here they were, though, sitting in a corp

lobby, and he flipped channels on the complimentary holo as though nothing had happened.

He barely showed any emotion at all. The only real change she'd seen on his face was a twitch at the corner of his mouth. Not the most reassuring of facial expressions.

The door to the inner offices slid aside, and Tetsami had to restrain a frantic impulse to draw her laser and shoot the secretary. She was too wired. She needed sleep. A luxury that Dom seemed to be able to go without.

The secretary was a chiseled blond whose body looked as though it had cost a small fortune in cosmetic augmentation. He talked to Dom, ignoring Tetsami completely. "Mr. Brodie will see you now."

Dom turned off the holo. Tetsami had a brief glimpse of stock reports before the picture faded. Dom stood up and ran his hands down the front of his suit. It didn't help. With what his clothes had been through, he looked more like a refugee from a commune war than a corp type.

Dom walked up to the door and turned around when she didn't follow. "Come on. This concerns you as well."

She shrugged and got up. The secretary showed no sign of caring one way or the other. He led them down a plush corridor done up in imported woods, crystal, and off-planet artwork—mostly aquatic sculpture by the Paralians. Incredibly expensive stuff to transport, all webworks of threadlike coral that had to be kept in pressurized cylinders.

What in hell was she doing here? Tetsami got nervous this close to money, at least when it wasn't hers.

And, how much would a policy against the failure of a corp enterprise be worth? Her paranoia was kicking in again. Her palms were sweaty. It was too close to a payoff.

She felt things could go ballistic very easily.

The blond secretary stopped in front of a large door and motioned them through. The door was manual, a slightly irritating conceit. Dom led the way, and Tetsami

had to put a hand out to stop the door from swinging back
and hitting her. The secretary stayed in the hall.

Brodie's office did its best to scream money. None of
the wood was native to Bakunin. It was mostly the purple
close-grained hardwood from the Kanaka rain forests.
The wood gave the room a slight tang of bay leaves and
rancid mint.

Brodie was planted behind a U-shaped desk topped
with red-and-green-veined marble. The light in the room
was provided by the most ostentatious display that
Tetsami had ever seen. In the wall behind the desk was a
window about ten by four meters. Behind it was a huge
Paralian coral sculpture, and darting back and forth in its
midst were tiny aquatic life-forms that had to be from
Paralia themselves. What the upkeep on that must
cost. . . .

In contrast to the luxurious surroundings, Brodie
looked like a cheap hood. Tetsami saw Brodie's lean,
hungry face and had no trouble picturing him doing the
soft-core hustle on the fringes of East Godwin. Brodie
looked like a dealer in flesh, drugs, or money who'd
made good.

But then, what was insurance but a high-class protection racket?

Brodie waved them to a pair of plush chairs that were
placed an uncomfortable distance from the desk. They sat
and Brodie leaned forward and addressed Dom.

"Account number?"

Dom rattled off a twenty-digit number in response.

"Voiceprint checks," Brodie said as his gaze lit on
some display out of Tetsami's field of vision. Tetsami realized that Brodie only knew Dom as a twenty-digit account number.

Brodie *sounded* like a hood. He had an East Godwin
accent that he didn't try to hide. "I have reviewed your
file and your claim."

A small holo display lit up above the desk. The image
looked to be from a spy sat aimed at the Diderot foothills.
The buildings in the image must have been the GA&A
complex. Brodie leaned back and put his hands behind his

head. "We've confirmed that Godwin Arms and Armaments was attacked and seized by hostile forces, as you've claimed. Our attempts to contact the new management of GA&A have proved unsuccessful."

As Brodie spoke, Tetsami saw a craft float into the holo's point of view. Explosions peppered the perimeter of the buildings. Brodie did something that froze the image.

"We have confirmation that GA&A was attacked by a Paralian-built Confederacy troopship. The *Blood-Tide*." Brodie indicated the ship floating just outside the ring of explosions on the holo. Tetsami looked over at Dom. *You said nothing about the Confederacy.*

Why the hell would the Confederacy take over GA&A?

A smile crossed Brodie's lips. "This, of course, means we cannot pay out your claim."

"WHAT?"

Tetsami tensed and her hand drifted toward her laser. Dom was half out of the chair. Brodie was leaning back and Tetsami could sense an edge of violence in the air. She started cataloging escape routes in her mind.

Brodie either didn't sense the impending violence, or he didn't care. "Sit down." Brodie hit a hidden keypad and one of the Kanakan-wood walls began to display glowing blue text. "I've worked in claims for nearly a decade. I have rarely come across a clearer case. You just aren't covered for a military takeover. Rival corporations, yes. Other Bakunin organizations, yes. Confed military, no."

Dom sat down slowly. "It's semantics. What difference is there between a corporate takeover and the Confederacy . . . ?"

"The one's covered. The other isn't." Brodie looked like he enjoyed what he was doing. "You're a businessman. You know semantics is the name of the game. This is a *contract*, and we're not in this for our health."

"I could call LCI for an enforcement."

Brodie laughed. "You knew, when you had Lucifer Contracts witness the agreement, that they only pay attention to the letter of the contract. As I said, I've rarely had a clearer case of an unsupported claim."

Tetsami saw the corner of Dom's mouth jerk upward. He brought a hand up to his face, as if to hide it. "I see."

"I'm sorry that I couldn't be more helpful." Brodie couldn't have been less sorry.

Dom nodded. "If that is the case, I would like to cash in the equity of the policy."

Brodie's smile froze. "You must be kidding."

Dom was speaking in a cold voice that would have suited a machine. It chilled Tetsami. "Read your own contract. I can cash in the policy, as long as my premiums are up to date, at any time while the policy is in force—"

The idea that he might actually have to pay something out seemed to shrink Brodie in his chair. "This is highly irregular."

"The whole situation is irregular. But you did say Lucifer enforces the *letter* of the contract. Shall we consult LCI?"

Brodie raised his hands and shook his head. "No need to involve them. You do understand that premature withdrawal incurs a stiff penalty—"

Dom kept the cold edge in his voice. "I understand perfectly."

Brodie started typing on his hidden keypad, and the glowing blue text on the wall started changing. Brodie nodded to himself a few times.

"Cashing the policy now would realize 587.92 kilograms, after the penalty."

Tetsami's jaw dropped. Half a meg, and Dom looked disappointed. How much would it have been if the policy paid out?

Brodie looked at Dom. "How do you want that?"

"Whatever form that will facilitate an immediate transfer."

Brodie humphed and started typing. It took him nearly ten minutes.

"Okay, we have one hundred seventy-five K in currency from the Insured Bank of the Adam Smith Collective. Fifty K in bonds issued by the Proudhon Spaceport

Development Corporation. Sixty K in off-world credit in the Confederacy Central Bank. Two hundred eleven K in script from the Girolamo Commune. Fifteen K in bonds from Griffith Energy. Twenty-seven K in our own currency. And Fifty K in miscellaneous local currencies that shouldn't vary more than three percent from the base exchange."

Dom nodded. "That's acceptable, excepting the off-world credit."

"It's a numbered account."

"It doesn't matter. I don't want anything from off-planet except hard currency."

Brodie shook his head and went back to his typing. Tetsami was still reeling from the numbers Brodie was tossing around. One hundred seventy-five K in the IBASC? Two hundred eleven K from Girolamo? Not only were the numbers huge, but scrip from those places was overvalued by thirty percent on the street because of its stability, and scarcity. It was hard to believe that over two hundred kilos of Girolamo currency was in circulation.

Brodie sighed. "We're scraping the outside of the liquid assets. We have a speculation portfolio of off-world hard currency that's currently valued at forty-five K. We can only guarantee that value within five percent over the next three days—"

"I can deal with that."

"Finally, we have fifteen K worth of stock in Bleek Munitions. Will that be acceptable?" Dom nodded. "Good, then let's start transferring accounts."

They left Brodie's office with a hand comm that recorded assets that totaled nearly six hundred K. They were in the maglev elevator off the waiting room before Tetsami spoke.

"Can I have my money?"

She noticed Dom twitch the corner of his mouth. "When I said that, I thought I was going to receive the full value of the policy—"

Tetsami grunted. She hadn't expected much more.

Dom shook his head. "It's not that. You'll be paid. I

have an obligation to all my employees. I'm going to do right by them."

Tetsami looked at the exec. No sign of sarcasm. He was serious. "How many people are you talking about?"

"I just have to—"

"Fifteen hundred?"

"Something like that."

"How in the hell do you think you're going to— Hell, what is it that you *think* you're going to do?"

Dom sighed. "I'm not sure right now. I was hoping for an adequate flow of capital to start operations somewhere else. But cashing the policy only resulted in enough to— maybe—invest in a small inventory of personal hardware."

The maglev whooshed to a stop and the doors opened. Tetsami scanned the lobby of the office building. She didn't see anything she thought dangerous. But they were deep into Central Godwin, not her territory. The exec with the chrome suit could be the spotter for a hit and she wouldn't know.

Calm down, she told herself.

"You were planning to start over from scratch?"

Dom led her toward the doors. There was little emotion in his voice. "I did it once. I'll do it again."

The doors slid open, and they walked out on to West Vanzetti. Now that day had hit, crossing the street was out of the question. Groundcars were zooming by, apparently at random. Dom seemed at a bit of a loss. He didn't seem to know how to get around in the city.

Tetsami tapped his shoulder. "Let me borrow your hand comm."

A trace of suspicion crossed Dom's face even though she didn't know the codes. He handed it over.

Tetsami walked as close as she dared to the speeding traffic and raised her right hand, holding the comm up toward the air traffic.

It took three seconds for a Leggett Luxury contragrav to swing a dangerous arc and pull to a low hover in front of Tetsami, barely above the speeding groundcar traffic.

Three aircraft had to swerve to avoid it, one pulling a full vertical.

The Leggett cab slid over the pedestrian walkway, pivoting its passenger doors toward Dom and Tetsami.

She handed the comm back to Dom. "Where do we want to go?"

"Let's just get airborne."

CHAPTER TEN

High-Risk Investments

"Money can be neither created or destroyed. It can only be taken from other people."
—*The Cynic's Book of Wisdom*

"Money often costs too much."
—RALPH WALDO EMERSON
(1803–1882)

The aircar was laid out more like a limo than a cab. The back of the Leggett was a study in leather and earth tones. It was obvious that the driver was an independent doing business with the corp HQs in Central Godwin. They both got in the back before the driver could get a good look at the condition of Dom's suit and have second thoughts.

The driver didn't look enthusiastic. "Let's see some money, folks."

Sheesh, another perfectly chiseled blond. Tetsami wondered if it was contagious. Dom wordlessly typed a command on the comm and the driver looked at the balance change on his meter. The driver nodded. He didn't seem too surprised. "Where?"

Dom looked at Tetsami and said to the driver, "Circle the city for a while. And close the partition."

Tetsami saw a knowing expression cross the driver's

face as the partition closing the driver's section opaqued. Things had been going so fast lately that it took her a few seconds to realize the conclusion the driver must have jumped to.

Yeah, she thought, *I wish.*

Dom looked all right. *Okay, admit it, he looks* damn *good. Especially after all the maggots you been hanging with, girl.* But there were computers that showed more emotion than he did. Tetsami tried to picture Dom having an orgasm, or even getting slightly aroused. She couldn't.

Tetsami wondered exactly what was going on behind those brown eyes of his. She knew that there was a lot more under there than he let up to the surface. She'd caught glimpses of it—

Like the fact he hadn't let on that the Confederacy had been the folks who took down GA&A. That was the biggest operation she'd ever heard of the Confederacy pulling on this rock. The risk—GA&A was now guaranteed to have a dozen paramilitary groups attack it, just on the grounds that the Confederacy was involved—and the cost of the operation made it pretty obvious that Dom was pretty high on someone's shit list.

Maybe it was his deadpan personality, in the face of all that, that made her believe him when he said she was going to eventually get her fifty kilos.

But when?

"How much you need to start operations again?"

Dom took a few minutes to answer her. He stared out the window, watching Godwin rush by below them.

"GA&A was covered for a thousand megs, give or take. But that's a bit more than I need. That would assume rebuilding from the ground up. A friendly takeover of an existing operation, I could leverage that with two hundred—maybe less."

"Two hundred megagrams?"

Dom nodded.

What did he have? A third of a percent of that?

She was *never* going to get her money. She was never going to get off this rock. *What'd he expect to do,* she thought, *rob a bank?* Yeah, and what's to prevent the bank from devaluing the currency afterward?

"Who the hell has that much money?" She was barely aware she spoke aloud.

Dom heard her. "There are more millionaires per capita on Bakunin than anywhere else in the Confederacy."

Tetsami snorted. "Also more rackets, screwballs, hustlers, political dissidents, and religious fanatics."

"—and two hundred megagrams is not really that much."

Tetsami gaped. *"Not that much?"*

"Not in corporate terms. GA&A had at least three, maybe five, hundred megs in hard currency on the premises just for clandestine expenses. For things we didn't want records— Problem?"

"No." *You couldn't rob a bank . . .* "Tell the cab to put down somewhere."

Dom looked out the window. "Where?"

"Anywhere."

Dom tapped on the partition. It went transparent again. "Put us down at the nearest hotel."

There was another knowing look from the driver as they started down.

"What's on your mind?" Dom asked her.

"Wait."

The Leggett set down on the roof of a high-rise on the west side. Tetsami figured it was expensive as hell, but Dom could afford it. They stepped out on to a small landing field next to a restaurant that took up half the roof. The cab lifted off, leaving them alone in the center of a number of parked contragravs.

The restaurant was enclosed by a transparent dome and seemed to be doing a healthy business with the breakfast crowd. Tetsami walked away from it until she reached the railing marking the edge of the roof.

She noticed a slight hesitation before Dom joined her by the railing.

Fear of heights? she wondered.

When Dom asked her again, he had to raise his voice over the sound of the wind. "Now, what is it?"

"Where *is* all this money?"

Dom turned toward her, and cast a glance back at the restaurant. No one was paying attention to them. "A safe bunkered in the third sublevel of the office complex at Godwin Arms." Realization seemed to strike him. "You can't be thinking—"

Tetsami laughed. "What the hell else would I be thinking?"

The hotel was set on a rise. They were maybe half a klick above the city. Hell of a view of East Godwin, craters and all. Dom was staring east, toward the mountains.

"Do you have any idea—" he started, shaking his head. "A Confederacy troop-carrier. A Paralian-built Barracuda-class drop-ship. That means at least a hundred marines, ten secondary transports, weaponry that I don't even want to think about."

"Look, if you can tell me that two hundred megs isn't much money. I can tell you that the quickest way to get it is to break into your own safe."

"You don't understand the security on that complex—"

"Do you understand the security?"

"I designed most of it."

Tetsami turned around and grinned at Dom. She brushed windblown hair out of her eyes. "So, with your knowledge and six hundred K on our side, tell me it can't be done."

"It can't be done."

She snorted and turned her face out of the wind, leaning on the railing. "Yeah. And you think it's more likely that you are going to build that six hundred K into another Godwin Arms?"

"I built GA&A."

Suddenly he shows some emotion, she thought. "How much money did you start with?"

There was a pause.

"Hell of a lot more than you have now, right?"

A longer pause, then Dom's voice was back to normal. "This is your area of expertise, not mine. What did you have in mind?" He looked off at the eastern mountains again.

She looked toward the range herself. She could see some purple-orange, where East Godwin disintegrated into forest. There used to be suburbs back that way, but they'd been abandoned when East Godwin went to its own little hell. Most of the real development was behind her, where Godwin built westward, as if the urban center were slowly crawling away from its thousand square kilometers of infected slum.

That's what East Godwin is, a trail of slime left by the city as it crawls away from the mountains.

Tetsami decided that her lack of sleep was allowing her mind to wander.

What the hell *did* she have in mind? Whatever Dom said, this wasn't exactly her area of expertise. She was a systems expert, a data thief. She'd never planned a job to physically go into a target. Before yesterday, she'd never even fired a laser in anger.

Cool it, she told herself, *that's the number one screwup—don't ever start doubting yourself. Never on the job.* That's what gave the young software jockeys the edge. They were too inexperienced to worry about the risks.

She told herself to concentrate on her assets. The primary asset was the fact that she had access to the designer of a previous generation security setup. She'd be willing to crack almost anything with that edge.

"We obviously need a team to go in—"

"Obviously."

Wow, she thought, *what sage advice. Sheesh.* "We'll need someone to handle the comm in the complex. That's my specialty, running around the systems in there—"

"The mainframes were destroyed."

"Well, whatever's left." *What else?* "We need an expert on Paralian ship design, and another software jockey to handle the ship's system. Chances are it's isolated."

Dom nodded.

"We need some muscle, weapons people to protect the specialists that go in. Not too many. The more people, the harder this will be to pull off." *How many?* "Two people.

It looks like two teams going in. One for the ship and one for the safe."

Dom nodded again. What the hell was he thinking? Did this *sound* like she was making it up as she went along? "We need a demolition expert, to make sure we crack the place with the money, and we'll need an electronics expert to help prep us. Those and a driver."

"That's six more people."

Six? Tetsami made a head count. "I count seven."

"We only need one spear carrier."

Spear carrier? Oh, the muscle. "Believe me, we need at least one per team."

"We'll have one per team." Dom looked straight at her and she suddenly realized what he must be thinking.

"You?"

"I'll go with the team to the safe."

"I don't think you—"

Dom shook his head. "I'll probably be the only one who knows the complex firsthand."

"We're going to need someone with combat experience and weapons expertise—"

Dom nodded. "I know."

Tetsami looked at the exec and waited for an explanation.

Eventually, one came. "Ten years in the TEC. Special forces, retired."

She looked around by reflex, to see if anyone had overheard him. The landing pad was still empty of people. She broke out into a chill anyway. She suddenly had second thoughts that had nothing to do with her own competence.

It was a Bakunin tradition to dislike the Confederacy. It was another Bakunin tradition to *hate* the TEC. Some of the more radical communes had regular executions of "TEC spies." Bakunin was, in one sense, a planet of dissidents, and the TEC's major function in the Confederacy was crushing dissidence.

Tetsami began to realize that the attack on GA&A must have been a TEC operation, and she mentally revised the number of assaults the new management was going to

have to repel. GA&A was probably going to be hit at
least once by every military-capable fringe group within
fifty klicks of Godwin.

She could see someone lobbing a nuke just because the
TEC was involved.

Dom turned away from the edge of the roof and started
walking back toward the restaurant and the entrance to
the hotel. "Okay, Tetsami, I'll back your idea. I've risked
money on less promising enterprises."

Tetsami stayed by the railing. She was still dealing
with his admission. After a few seconds, she cursed herself and followed Dom.

Dom booked rooms for both of them. There was
enough money, and most of it wouldn't be traceable.
They should be safe for a while at least.

The hotel was the Waldgrave and it sat slightly west of
Central Godwin. It tried to emulate its namesake planet in
a number of ways, all with varying success. Wood was
everywhere, though none of the rich Waldgrave stock that
was the planet's primary export—if you didn't count fas-
cism.

The hotel tried for a Germanic flavor, which ended up
in silly affected accents and sillier uniforms. The staff's
only successes in its homage were in the expense of a
stay, which approached what a stay on Waldgrave might
really cost, and the absolutely feudal organization of the
staff.

In the end, Tetsami decided she couldn't have cared
less. By the time they got their rooms she was thoroughly
bored with the place. What she wanted was sleep. After
some rest, maybe her pitch to Dom might not seem as insane as it did right now.

Glibly throwing requirements around was one thing.
Just talk. However, coming through with a workable plan
was something else entirely. Even coming up with people
with the required skills—

Just thinking about it gave Tetsami a headache.

Top all of that off with the fact that people were out to
kill her and Dom. That showed how insane this all was.

The guy in lederhosen who led them to their rooms didn't stick around for a tip.

Dom opened his door and turned to her. "After we both get some rest, we're going to have to talk about your plans."

Tetsami nodded and watched him go in. She stood in the hall and held the card key for the neighboring room. She looked at it and thought about how much it cost. Dom had booked them for two days. It might come to just under a kilo.

It wasn't much, but she knew scams well enough that she could go to reception and cash the key in. It would be enough running expenses to get her as far as Proudhon. She couldn't buy passage, but there were ways around that. She could manipulate a ship's manifest as easily as a corp's database.

But she was no surer now than she had ever been of making such a software jimmy last all the way to the destination. There were just too many people to fool for too long a period of time. Ships were too careful when they made landfall on Bakunin. And stowaways often found themselves spaced, or tagged as inventory for planets with rather repressive ideas about personal freedom. Even the best case would get her to another planet, yes, but stranded, with no cash. In a situation where her only marketable skills were probably frowned upon.

She rolled the card between her fingers.

She had also made a deal. It had been her idea, and she had convinced Dom to go along.

Tetsami had never thought of herself as a particularly honorable person. She'd always pictured herself as riding the midline of corruption on Bakunin. Looking out for number one was the overriding priority.

Despite that, she realized she wouldn't skip.

But she was going to ask for a hell of a lot more than 50 kilos if they pulled this off.

Tetsami ran the card through the reader and walked into her room.

CHAPTER ELEVEN

Depreciation

"History is written by those in power to justify the present. Memory is the same thing on a smaller scale."
—*The Cynic's Book of Wisdom*

"The slaves to the past are all volunteers for its tyranny."

—Jean Honoré Cheviot
(2065–2128)

Dom did not sleep.

Ten years of chronic insomnia, and it never bothered him as much as it did now. He was sprawled, naked, on a bed in a luxury suite in the Waldgrave, and he couldn't stop thinking. His first chance to sleep, and he couldn't wrest his mind away from what had happened. He picked over the events of the past thirty-two hours like some ghoulish spectator who couldn't tear himself away from the bloody remains of an aircar pileup.

Could he have done better?

Could he *feel* something?

Dom sat up, feeling the side of his face vibrate. The room was dark, and he didn't bother heightening the gain on his photoreceptors to compensate.

The nightmares were bad.

The memories were worse.

"Damn it," Davis had said, back during his last day on Banlieue, "you're not a machine."

It had been ten years and the memory was still a fresh scar. "Yes, I am, Dave," he had responded. He had been a machine even before the "accident." He had been an automaton ever since Styx. The cybernetics were simply an external manifestation of his inner landscape.

He was a machine, but an imperfect one. A perfect machine wouldn't agonize over its own continued existence.

Davis MacIntyre was his second in command, the man who now controlled the small arms empire Dom had built after his "retirement" from the TEC. Davis was from Earth and had nearly as many unsavory contacts in the Confederacy as Dom did himself. He was, arguably, the man who had saved Dom's life.

"You would prefer it if we had left you in that tank?"

They were standing on a small porch adorning one of Banlieue's millionaire's villas. The view looked over a small vineyard, which the company also owned. Dom tapped his fingers on the railing. "Maybe it would have been better."

"Do you actually buy into Klaus' bullshit?"

Dom didn't answer.

Was it Helen's death? Or was it simply what her death represented for him? If he had known, ahead of time, that she was one of those thirty-five thousand people, would he have acted differently?

He had joined the TEC to *escape* her.

Her death had made escape impossible.

He kept staring out at the vineyard, tapping his finger.

David grabbed him by the shoulder and spun him around. "*Say something, you ungrateful bastard!* Rage, scream, cry, something! It's still *you* in there. The brain was one of the few things the bacteria didn't get to."

Dom found himself wishing he could do something to comfort his old friend. After a while he said, "I do appreciate what you did for me."

Davis dropped his shoulder as if that wasn't the right

thing to say at all. "You're burying this. It won't go away."

Dom nodded. It never went away. People died, but their accusations lived long after them.

He'd almost fooled himself into believing he was over it. Then Klaus had appeared, nearly killing him. Now, it was as if the wounds had become gangrenous, killing the nerves, leaving him numb.

Davis was still talking. "Someday all that pent-up anger is going to explode on you."

"I know."

"You're a different person than you were."

"I know."

Davis shook his head and headed for the door. "We have the transport and the account transfer ready for you— Are you sure you want to do this?"

Dom nodded.

"Just because I can handle the company without you doesn't mean we don't need you."

"You know you can't afford to hide one of your officers from the TEC indefinitely. You've done it too long already."

"But Bakunin?"

"A new name, a new planet—I can disappear there."

Davis gave him a backward look over his shoulder that told Dom that he doubted he could disappear anywhere. After a pause, he said. "We had to, you know. With all the damage to you and the TEC on our necks, there was no time to clone a real body."

Dom raised his hand to the side of his face to hide the tic he was developing. "I know that. It's nobody's fault." Besides, if Dom were to be really honest with himself, the cybernetics weren't the real problem."

"It's Klaus' fault, damn you!" Davis left, leaving Dom with no opportunity to think of a response.

Dom had been left, standing on the porch of the villa, trying to scrape together a hatred for his brother. Like every effort to pull together the pieces of his broken mind, it left him with no tangible results.

That was the last time he had seen Davis MacIntyre.

The last time he had someone he could call a friend.

Dom got off of the bed. *After all this, if all I can feel for the loss of ten years of work is this vague unease, what's the point?*

He walked into the plush bathroom and up to the wash-basin. At a touch, the chrome-metal basin began to fill from an invisible faucet. He placed his right hand, the mostly real one, in the basin, covering the drain. The metal was cool against his hand, and the sink beeped at him as the basin began to overflow.

With the left hand he turned on the lights. The panels around the mirror in front of him lit.

Water washed over the counter and splashed his thighs.

He put his left hand on one of the lit panels that surrounded the mirror. He began to slowly apply pressure to the plastic covering the light.

Water washed across his thighs, his calves, and his feet.

He had thought of this a few times since his reconstruction. A clean way to do it. The veins that pumped the clear fluid that passed for blood were self-sealing. His digestive system was artificial and would filter out most of the poisons he could think of. Most falls and projectiles wouldn't touch his brain within its chromed prison.

A long time ago he had decided that there were two ways he could do this cleanly.

One way was to step out of an air lock without an environmental suit.

The other was an adequately grounded electrocution.

The plastic on the panel cracked and his left hand came in contact with the cool surface of the glowing light beneath. A little more pressure and the frosted chemical illumination would crumble and his hand would be touching the live contacts, ending it all.

He wondered what his mother had thought before Perdition had been reduced to gravel.

Dom chanced to look at the mirror in front of him. The expression he saw on his own face made him jerk back. His foot slipped on the wet tile beneath him and he fell backward. He caught himself on the toilet before his head slammed into anything. As if it would damage him.

He sat, unmoving, wondering what had happened.

Above him, he heard the drain slurp itself empty.

He slowly got to his feet and looked in the mirror. He touched the surface, to reassure himself that it was, indeed, a mirror. The face beneath it was familiar, impassive, his own. There was no sign of the agonized mask he had seen a few moments ago.

Could he really wear an expression that held so much pain when he felt nothing himself?

Dom grabbed a towel and silently returned to his bed.

PART TWO

Fellow Travelers

"Rebellion to tyrants is obedience to God."
—JOHN BRADSHAW
(1602–1659)

CHAPTER TWELVE

Book Value

"Anyone who believes in free speech has never tried to make a living as a writer."
—*The Cynic's Book of Wisdom*

"All revolutionaries are criminals meeting in secret."
—YOWERI ADYEBO
(b. 2303)

It had been a busy three days for Dom.

The first and most massive undertaking had been laundering the money he had received from Reynolds Insurance. No names had ever been attached to the account, but the nature of the policy—insuring GA&A—meant that someone might eventually trace the money to him. Dom had spent a whole thirty-two-hour Bakunin day on the hotel's comm, wrangling financial deals ranging from commodities trading to currency speculation.

He came out of that day with a profit and an untraceable portfolio.

The second day he'd spent checking on names Tetsami had given him—the potential team members. There were a number of freelance security corporations in Godwin offering services to the two thousand corporations that formed the knotted heart of the city. Most of them would profile *anyone* for a price. It was simple for Dom to order up dossiers on the first two people Tetsami suggested contacting.

Ivor Jorgenson and Johann Levy.

He also called up a report on Tetsami herself.

Within a day of his order, Argus Datasearch supplied him with three thick packets of information. All of them he'd downloaded into his onboard computer to peruse at his leisure.

According to Argus' data, Tetsami's parents had come to Bakunin over two standard decades ago, from Dakota. That was interesting. Dakota was one of the Seven Worlds, and that entire arm of the Confederacy was populated by the descendants of Terran genetic engineering. Most of the people of the Seven Worlds were as radically nonhuman as one of the squid-delphine natives of Paralia. The natives of Dakota, however, were descended from gene-engineered humans. Unfortunately, all the data indicated was origin—not what made the Tetsamis different.

Tetsami's parents had gone to work for Holographic DataComm, a broadcast network that no longer existed. The reason HDC no longer existed was a dirty little corporate war over broadcast airspace. A war that fried every one of HDC's on-line hardwire console jockeys when the competition lobbed an electromagnetic pulse at the corporate HQ. HDC's computers were EMP hardened—unfortunately, the console jocks weren't.

Scratch Tetsami's parents.

Seven years later, Tetsami went into their line of work. Strictly freelance, though. She could've made a lot more by latching on to some corporation. She'd been hacking the comm net for eight years standard.

There was another interesting thing in her file.

No wonder she trusts Jorgenson.

Ivor Jorgenson had come to Bakunin from Styx within three years of Tetsami's parents. He had worked transport for HDC until the shit hit the fan. The file had little personal data, but Dom was adept at reading between the lines. The parallel addresses listed for both Tetsami and Jorgenson over a seven-year stretch was enough.

Jorgenson must've been a friend of the Tetsamis' and had taken care of the kid after the balloon went up.

Another thing Dom noted was the fact that Jorgenson and Tetsami diverged when Tetsami took up her parents' profession. From the record, she was only thirteen at the time.

The other data on Jorgenson showed that, indeed, he'd make a good driver for the job. Spotless record in nearly twenty years standard. Freelancer since HDC. Most importantly, no connection to the Confederacy in any way, shape, or form.

However, for some reason that man made him uneasy. Dom supposed it was the reminder about Styx.

The third file was Johann Levy.

The data here was sparse, but Levy seemed to be what Tetsami claimed he'd be, a wired-in part of Godwin's seamy underside. The data said that Levy had been involved in the uprising against the theocracy on his home planet of Paschal. That seemed to give him a good reputation in this part of Godwin.

The uprising on Paschal had happened after Dom left the TEC, but he had heard about it. A collection of teachers, lawyers, and students demonstrating against the more extreme excesses of the Paschal government.

When the Paschal Elders called in the TEC, the revolution found out exactly what extreme was. As far as Dom knew, the mass grave didn't even have a marker.

Dom had heard rumors that Paschal was where his brother got his commission, and a promotion to a desk job.

More important, though, the ex-lawyer Levy had made a reputation for himself as a safecracker.

As they waited outside Levy's bookstore, Dom wondered if he had enough data on Levy to trust him.

Answer: he didn't have enough data on anyone.

The bookstore they waited outside felt ironic to Dom. Just the fact that Bolshevik Books sold *books,* expensive, paperbound tomes of a generally political nature, gave Dom a feeling the place marched about half a cycle out of phase with the rest of the universe. Truly ironic was the fact that the place had a distinctly anticapitalist slant, and they were going to ask the owner to help resurrect a corporate enterprise.

Dom sat next to Tetsami in the front seat of a used Royt groundcar. They were both similarly clad in leather-covered monocast armor, and they both now wore personal field generators. His old exec suit had found its way into a disposal shaft in the Waldgrave the second day of their stay.

Today, Dom had moved them into cheaper accommodations. Dom had rented a small warehouse from Bleek Munitions. He rented the warehouse because it sat on top of the main spur of the same Godwin-Proudhon commuter tube that he and Tetsami had hidden in after escaping the Church.

Dom noticed that he was drumming his fingers on the control console and forced himself to stop. They had been waiting for two hours.

They were parked across the intersection of Sacco and West Lenin from the store, waiting for it to close. Tetsami had said she didn't want anyone walking in while they talked to the owner.

"What do *you* know about this Johann Levy? Other than the fact he's a demolition expert."

Tetsami yawned and turned to face him. If she noticed the emphasis on his statement, she didn't show it. "Known him years. Never been on a job together, but he has a reputation in the community—hooked into everything. Never heard of him going out in the field, but he's got more than his share of hatred for the Confederacy."

Dom looked at the bookstore and the rampant anticapitalism plastered all over the facade. "So he might be willing to join our enterprise despite his politics—"

"Doesn't have any politics. He just stocks the bookstore so it'll fit the neighborhood. Makes his real money with special-order ordinance, hooking contacts together, and helping locals deal with the Confed legal system."

Ex-lawyer, Dom thought. *That's how nuts Bakunin is. An anarchy and lawyers can still find work.*

"Supposed to have been involved in a revolution

against the Paschal theocracy," she continued. "Gives him lots of points with the politicos around here."

Paschal again, nothing that Argus' data package hadn't told him—

Dom felt a brief twinge of something—guilt?—over the data he'd ordered from Argus. Of course, he hadn't told Tetsami about it. Playing things close to himself was an ancient habit, from even before the TEC had slammed security procedures into his skull.

He hadn't told her.

Should he have?

Tetsami tapped him on the shoulder and pointed. "There he is. Let's go."

A short, balding gentleman was locking up the front door of the bookstore. As Dom followed Tetsami across the street, he had trouble picturing the man as either a revolutionary or a demolition expert. Dom also couldn't picture him as part of the spearhead going into the occupied GA&A complex.

They got up behind the guy just as he was turning away from locking up the door. Levy seemed distracted. He didn't notice Tetsami until he almost bumped into her.

Levy drew up short. "What?"

Tetsami smiled. "Hi, Johann."

Levy let his back fall against the door and he wiped his hand across his forehead. "My dear ... I thought you'd be safely off-planet by now."

Tetsami shrugged. "Something came up. We need to talk."

Levy broke into a sweat. *What a great recruit,* Dom thought. "Do you know there's a price on your head?"

She nodded. "Can we go in?"

Levy nodded as he gave a furtive glances up and down the street. He fumbled open the lock and hustled them into the bookstore.

Levy directed them through a display area dominated by tall shelves whose size made the man seem even smaller. The place smelled of old paper and had a sense of permanence about of it that was out of place in

Godwin. The free space on the walls was taken up by portraits of socialist deities—Marx, Lenin, Mao, Cheviot.

The three of them ended up in a small windowless office in the back of the bookstore. Levy was careful to close the door behind him. He sat behind a green metal desk that was half-buried in books and papers. Tetsami opened her mouth, but Levy shushed her as he rummaged in one of the drawers.

He came out with a small electronic box. Dom recognized it. It was a basic countersurveillance field generator. It wouldn't be perfect—it only caused a pulsing distortion of RF signals—but it was the first sign that this guy had something on the ball.

"Who's your friend?"

Tetsami smiled. "We can talk now?"

"Believe me, I would have known long before now if my place wasn't clean." Levy wiped his forehead again. "Please, what's going on?"

Dom and Tetsami had agreed that she would pitch their job. So Dom was in the unusual position of being the observer.

"As for my friend, Johann, he's my current employer. More you don't want to know."

"You're starting a job *now*?"

Tetsami nodded.

"They're hunting for you! You and five, six hundred other people. There are hits every day. People are laying low just because of the crossfire. I could be set for life if I just shot you—"

"You won't."

Dom felt an icy chill fill his gut. Did anyone get away from this? Would there be anyone at the commune when he finally got there? If they were looking for only six hundred people, that meant that nearly a thousand were still—

Don't think about it, you can't do anything right now.

"Why are you so sure I won't?" The way Levy said that made Dom tense.

"You're too damn curious. You *know* I'm sitting on

something pretty damn interesting if I'm out in the open at a time like this."

Levy nodded with a weak grin. "I'm interested. I'll admit that. What are we talking about?"

"We are talking about a share in at least a hundred megs or partnership in a corp enterprise."

Levy's skin took on a grayish cast. "That's an order of magnitude way beyond anything—" He took a deep breath. "What do you need me for?"

"We need someone to crack a box."

"What kind of safe are we talking about?"

Tetsami turned toward Dom. GA&A's security was his area of expertise. "The safe is a custom job from Kaivaku Security. It was shipped from Kanaka five years ago and incorporated in the foundation of the building. Solid bedrock on four sides. The foundation of the building sits on top of it."

"You have to go through the front."

Dom nodded. "Two doors that are interlocked. Not supposed to open at the same time."

"Doors the same construction?"

"No, the outer door is simply a delaying measure. The real problem is the inner door. It's a meter thick. The exterior is covered with twenty centimeters of microalloyed steel. Inside the door, behind a casing of woven diamondwire monofilament, is an Emerson field generator with its own power supply. The door's locked in place electromagnetically and is held up by a hydraulic system—"

Levy held up his hand. "I am getting a picture here, and I don't think I can help you."

Tetsami shook her head. "I saw you nodding, Johann. You know you can crack that safe."

"Perhaps I can— but I'd need to be there. This isn't a recipe job. You need an expert in the field when you try to pull this off."

"We know," said Tetsami.

There was an extended silence. Levy looked at Tetsami, then at Dom. The gray cast to his skin had gotten worse.

After a while Levy started shaking his head. "No."

Tetsami tried to interrupt, but Levy kept talking. "You know I don't get involved in the jobs. I can make plans for you. I can build an explosive to nearly any specification. Given enough time I can train you to get into any hardened— No. I don't go into the field. I'm too old to get my hands dirty."

Dom felt the corner of his mouth twitch. He tried to suppress it. "Do you know where this safe is, Mr. Levy?"

"That doesn't matter—"

"Yes, it does," Dom said. "The safe belongs to Godwin Arms."

Levy was staring at him now. Dom allowed himself a smile. His cheek stopped wanting to twitch. "GA&A, the company the Confederacy took over."

Realization seemed to dawn slowly on Levy. "The TEC ... I'm going to need serial numbers and exact specifications on that safe—"

Dom felt the dimple of the bio-interface on his neck. Out of the corner of his eye he saw Tetsami notice his hand move. Her eyebrow arched. She still didn't know how much of him was hardware. Didn't matter. "I can give you all the specs you need, all I need is a terminal interface."

Levy wiped his forehead. "I am still not going to commit to anything until I know how you plan to move in and out without two companies of Confederacy marines erasing the team."

Tetsami looked at Dom. Dom motioned to her to go ahead. It was still her show. "We know, Johann. Everyone is going to share the risk and the profit. No one goes in who isn't sure about the plan."

"Who else?"

"You're the first we've contacted. We had to be sure we can crack the safe when we get there."

"How many?"

"Two software jocks, two muscle, an electronics whiz, a driver, someone who knows Paralian ship design, and you."

Levy looked at Dom and asked, "Is he electronics or software?"

Dom answered, "Muscle."

"As well as our expert on the pre-Confederacy security setup at GA&A," Tetsami said.

Levy seemed to be calming down. He had stopped sweating and the color was back in his face. "I gathered that from his description of the safe. You'd better have an expert on the inside setup. I'd feel a lot better if he were still inside."

Dom shrugged. "If I were still inside, this job wouldn't even be under consideration."

"I suppose not." Levy had an expression as though he knew something Dom didn't. "Have you picked out the other team members?"

Tetsami shook her head. "Not all. I wanted to know if you have any ideas. You're wired into the community. You'd know who's available and who'd be interested."

Levy sighed. "I should charge you for the info."

Dom pulled out a kilogram note from the IBASC and placed it on top of one of the stacks of paper. "Consider that a retainer."

"You don't believe in half-measures, do you?" The kilogram note disappeared. "Off the top of my head, for your electronics and software, talk to Tjaele Mosasa. He's two of the best free agents on this rock."

"Two?" Dom asked.

"Talk to him."

"Where?" Tetsami asked.

"Mosasa works out of Proudhon. He has a surplus place off the spaceport. He'll be interested. It'll appeal to his general misanthropy."

Dom stood up and held out his hand. Levy didn't take it. "Let's wait until we have a deal."

Dom shrugged. "You'll hear from us."

Levy nodded. "I'll find that ship expert for you."

CHAPTER THIRTEEN

War Crimes

"Ethics only become a problem when taken seriously."
—*The Cynic's Book of Wisdom*

"We are at a great disadvantage when we make war on people who have nothing to lose."
—FRANCESCO GUICCIARDINI
(1483–1540)

It was the fifth Bakunin night since the operation had taken GA&A. During the previous two nights, perimeter defense had kept its hands full by repulsing nuisance attacks from a coalition of northern communes. There were people on this planet who really did *not* like the Confederacy. Even so, no real Bakunin resistance had reared its head yet.

As long as the Confed forces confined themselves to the single property, anything more was unlikely.

Tonight was quiet.

Quiet enough to allow Captain Kathy Shane to contemplate the end of her career.

Eight hundred and thirty-seven prisoners huddled below her, crammed behind the impromptu electrified barrier.

Eight hundred and thirty-seven.

That number was etched in her mind. Yesterday it was

eight hundred and forty-three. Two lost to exposure, two to injuries sustained in the attack, one attempted escape, one suicide.

The suicide had been pregnant.

Eight hundred and thirty-seven.

Four hundred and ten men. Three hundred and eighty-nine women.

Thirty-eight children.

Shane stood alone on the platform the engineers had built on top of the remains of GA&A antiaircraft battery number seventeen. Kropotkin had long since set and the tiny lump of Guillaume was passing in front of the waning form of Schwitzguebel. The two moons didn't quite give the scene a double shadow, but the presence of Guillaume managed to fuzz the edges.

Even in the dim lighting, she could make out the forms of individual prisoners. Few of them were military. They were office workers, secretaries, engineers, scientists, laborers.

As well as their families.

The armed defense of GA&A either died in the assault, or defended the evacuation of approximately six hundred personnel—nearly half of them children. The colonel was sending squads of marines on search and destroy missions to target the evacuees.

It was the fifth Bakunin night since the operation had taken GA&A.

The fifth Bakunin night since Colonel Klaus Dacham had ordered the death of all the GA&A workers.

Shane had stalled and delayed things as much as her rank and position would allow. The prisoners were to be cleared out in the morning.

What really scared Shane—and until now she had never thought herself capable of fearing anything—was the acceptance by her people of the coming atrocity. Men and women she'd been to hell with and back suddenly were strangers who talked of the impending murder of eight hundred civilians as if these people were simply another enemy asset to be disposed of.

During dinner, Second Lieutenant Murphy, a man she

had known since his training on Occisis, a man she considered a good friend, had started a dispassionate discussion on the best way to dispose of the bodies. Shane had to excuse herself, go to the head, and throw up.

She shivered.

She crossed the platform of the makeshift guard tower. Engineering had been busy during dinner. Someone had actually taken Murphy seriously. Engineering had mounted a wide-aperture plasma cannon on the platform. Unlike the other perimeter defenses, this one covered the small space given the prisoners. If it was used on the civilians, they would only leave a slight shadow etched in the bedrock. Something easily bulldozed over—no disposal problem.

Shane closed her eyes and pictured the half-second the cannon would need to reach full power. A half second when eight hundred and thirty-seven people would feel the flesh melt off their bones. A half-second before they would be flashed into eternity.

Half a second could be a very long time.

It was going to be her hand on the switch.

Captain Kathy Shane cried for the first time since she'd joined the marines.

She had to be the one to carry out the order. She couldn't let any of her people bear the responsibility of such an act. She could not pass on such a command.

But she just wasn't capable.

She would falter, and Murphy, pragmatic as he was, would push her aside and fire the weapon. She could see him doing that, and he wouldn't feel a damn thing.

She used to like Murphy.

Damn Colonel Dacham. Damn him straight to Hell. He was the scariest part of all of this. Shane seemed to be the only one who realized that they were under the command of a psychopath.

She was an officer, but she had risen up through the ranks. In her heart she was a grunt, and she had a grunt's appreciation of the fact that more often than not, command was truly fucked.

She looked down at the prisoners and realized that this was beyond fucked.

The colonel should never have gotten a commission, much less a command. Even the intelligence arm of the Confederacy should have known better— Her people had been delivered into the hands of a crazy man.

Shane walked to the rail on the edge of the platform and saw Corporal Conner on watch in a nest fifty meters from the west edge of the electrified containment area. Conner was in full battlesuit and was bearing his weapon as though he hoped that someone would try to escape.

She used to like Conner, too.

She was wrong. Her people hadn't been delivered to the colonel. They were no longer her people, and she doubted that they ever could be again.

Shane turned, passing her gaze over the huddled shadows of the civilians, and saw Corporal Hougland in the nest to the east. Hougland was also in a full suit. She seemed less tense than Conner.

Shane found herself wishing something would happen. They might be civilians down there, but there were eight hundred of them. There were only the three marines guarding them, including herself. Everything else was concentrated on defending the outside perimeter. The fence around them was far from maximum security.

Come on, she urged them mentally, *you know what's going to happen. You're scientists down there, managers, you aren't stupid. Don't you realize that if you all decided to break for it at once, we couldn't stop you? You haven't got anything to lose—*

Shane stopped still. A chill wind iced across sweat on her brow. She smiled.

"Neither do I."

Her radio spoke in her ear. "What was that, Captain?" It was Conner. He was way too hyped.

Shane put her helmet on and switched on the night enhancement. After all, she really *didn't* have anything to lose. Even if she managed to follow orders, any officers involved in the massacre would be fed to a Confederacy court-martial while the colonel vanished back into the TEC.

Shane would rather be court-martialed for mutiny.

"Corporal Conner, I thought I saw some motion beyond the perimeter. West flank, your area."

Conner acted predictably, whipping around to cover his rear. He turned his back to Shane. "I don't see anything, Captain."

"Cover your flank, Conner. You, too, Hougland."

Hougland gave her a thumbs up and turned away from Shane.

The only problem now was the range on her stunner. Shane killed her transponder and started down from the platform. She'd have to get Conner first. He was the one most likely to do some damage.

She got to the ground, which was still cracked and blackened from the missile hit on the tower. Hougland radioed her. "Captain, I don't see anything."

"Keep your area covered. I've seen movement west of Conner's position. I've called the ship for backup."

Conner was hearing this. He was green; this operation was his first fire mission. Shane knew he was going to see the shadows grabbing for him. She had to reach him before he started shooting, or the other marines would land on her real quick.

What are you doing, Shane? she asked herself. This was her whole life she was about to fuck with.

She could feel her pulse in her ears, and she had a copper taste in her mouth. She became aware of things she'd been safely ignoring a few minutes ago: the soft crunch of her boots on the burnt ground, the sound of her breathing echoing in her helmet, the rhythmic—almost subliminal—movement of the prisoners behind the fence to her left, the way the suit's harness pulled into her crotch and her shoulders with each step.

She called up the tactical database. It projected the status of Hougland and Conner on the inside of her visor. Hougland's suit was on full power, but Conner was only running on three-quarters because he had his suit on full environmental containment. If she wasn't about to attack him, Shane would have reprimanded him for wasting the power. As it was, with the recycler going in his suit, a Paralia Leviathan could sneak up on the corporal.

Shane reached the corner of the prisoner compound and stopped. She wasn't committed yet.

She told the computer to interpret Conner and Hougland as targets. The computer took in the information without comment and immediately the threat alarm beeped in her ear. 28.5 meters and 105.3 meters. Conner's form was outlined in red on her visor and the computer started going through the spectrum to get a full image of him, even through the sloped dirt lip of the nest.

"Captain, where the fuck are you?" Shit, Hougland had something on the ball. She'd probably noticed Shane wasn't on the tac database any more. Now what?

"I'm scouting the perimeter. We're in a threat situation, I want radio silence. Kill your transponders. Hold your flank. I don't want to hear anything unless you're in trouble."

Shane smiled. That bought some time. Hougland wouldn't question orders in the middle of combat, no matter what she thought of them. Conner and Hougland dropped from the database as they killed their transponders. The computer was smart enough to retain the last information and integrate it into the threat analysis computer.

Shane advanced on Conner. According to the last information on the tac database, he had—predictably—his personal field on full. That would have caused Shane some problems if she wanted to clean him with an energy weapon. Fortunately, this mission had equipped everyone for covert ops. So Shane had a high-energy personal stunner. It was a special military issue that sucked energy like a plasma rifle, but it was designed to interact with standard-issue military defenses. It would turn a defense screen into a momentary stun field.

Its only problem was the fact that it only had a five-meter range.

Shane was within ten meters of Conner's position, and she activated her suit's ECM capability. It was another power drain, but she didn't want Conner to be able to reach anyone on his radio, or track her on his own threat computer. Hougland might notice a distortion by Conner, but the risk of that was less than the risk of Conner IDing her to the whole compound.

Seven meters to Conner and the corporal started panicking. Shane knew he had just noticed the ECM. His radio was jammed, his radar was probably blowing all over his scope, and his display was probably fuzzed and rolling. *Remember your training, Conner,* she urged him. *Don't shoot until you have a target. If you don't panic, we'll both get out of this alive.*

Six meters. This was her last chance to turn back.

Five meters and Conner turned around. Shane could see his eyes widen. He was sweating and hyperventilating in his suit. His weapon bore down on her, and for a moment Shane thought Conner was hyped so much that he would shoot first.

Instead, Conner's face showed recognition, and he was visibly relieved to see her.

Shane shot him with the stunner.

An electric-blue ripple of static electricity shot across Conner's suit, and the corporal dropped. Shane killed the ECM. Hougland's transponder was still off-line, and there were no transmissions back to the ship. Hougland didn't know Conner had dropped.

Conner was draped face-first over the lip of the hole that formed the nest. Shane put her foot on his shoulder and pushed him back in. She turned around and saw, ten meters back, a line of prisoners hovering beyond the fence, watching her. Not knowing what to do, she held up one finger to her visor and hoped that they had enough sense not to fuck up their own rescue.

That was it. Shane was committed now. Things would be over for her the second Conner woke up. That could be anywhere between one and three hours.

Shane headed east, toward Hougland. To Shane's right, in the prisoners' compound, more of the civilians were waking and turning toward her. Shane prayed that it wouldn't draw Hougland's attention. If Hougland turned before she got within ten meters, Shane might have to use deadly force.

If at all possible, Shane would like to avoid that.

So far, Hougland was covering her flank like the professional she was. Hougland was counting on Shane and Conner to cover her back.

Shane was fifty meters along the containment database, and there was a blip on the tac database.

Shit. Shane almost said it out loud. It was Murphy. He had just turned on the transponder in his suit. One hundred twenty seven meters south-southeast and closing. Damn it, Murphy was supposed to be off-duty at this time of night.

She was thirty meters from Hougland and running out of options.

She couldn't have Hougland picking up any radio, so Shane activated the ECM. It was much too soon. If Hougland was in range, it was just barely. Shane started running full tilt toward her.

Fifteen meters and Shane cleared the edge of the prisoners' compound. Hougland was trying to ID the source jamming her electronics. It was only going to be a second before she looked back and saw Shane running toward her like a maniac.

Shane looked to her right, and she saw Murphy. He wasn't moving with any urgency—

Maybe she could still pull it off.

Hougland turned around and leveled a standard-issue MacMillan-Schmitt wide-aperture plasma rifle at Shane. Without even thinking about it, Shane made the universal gesture to hit the dirt. She hoped that her expression showed all the fear of God to Hougland. The corporal had a split-second decision to make.

Hougland took cover in the nest.

Shane reached the lip of the nest and dived in, firing the stunner. Even when she woke up, Hougland might not be sure what hit her.

Shane landed on top of Hougland's body armor and killed the ECM. The tac database showed Murphy closing on her position. However, she wasn't picking up any radio traffic. She was in luck, Murphy hadn't seen her dive in on Hougland. Or, if he did, he wasn't sure what he saw.

Now what?

Murphy was a pro. He might only be out for a walk, but once he closed on the prisoners, he'd turn on his database and notice the absence of all three transponders. He'd radio that kind of regulation breach back to base immediately.

He was now within seventy meters.

Thank God the prisoners were being quiet.

She was going to have to meet him out there and try to bull her way through.

Shane turned her transponder back on and climbed out of the nest. She took a few deep breaths to calm herself, and started walking toward Murphy. She could feel eyes looking at her out of the darkness. Suddenly the whole GA&A complex was enemy territory. She was heading toward the *Blood-Tide,* and the heavily-armed drop-ship was no longer reassuring. It was sinister.

Shane and Murphy approached each other, and Shane prayed she reached him before he turned on his database.

"Captain, what are you doing out here?"

Murphy was radioing her. She was still over fifty meters away from him. "I couldn't sleep. I relieved Clarke." That was true, as far as it went.

She could hear Murphy snort over the radio. Murphy had no tolerance for things that didn't go according to program. He rarely, if ever, voiced his displeasure when a superior decided to improvise, but it seemed that this was one of those rare occasions.

"With all respect, Captain, you should be back at the compound at Clarke's position. I believe you've heard my opinion that your guard detail on the prisoners is under-staffed as it is."

Shane knew that well. She kept advancing. Twenty meters. "There weren't any personnel allowances made for guarding that number of people. If it weren't for the missions into Godwin—"

"Again, with all respect, we wouldn't have this problem if you had been more timely in carrying out the colonel's orders." Murphy actually interrupted her. He must be *really* stressed.

Fifteen meters. "I don't believe there is a problem."

"Captain," Shane could make out Murphy's face now. It was lined and he was practically grimacing. She was beginning to detect the anger in Murphy's voice. He didn't know, but he suspected. "I think you've had a problem with this mission ever since planetfall."

Since before that.

They were within ten meters of each other now. To their right was the burnt-out foundation of the old GA&A security building. A slight smell of smoke still filled the air and managed to be cycled into Shane's suit.

Murphy stopped his approach.

"I've voiced my reservations to the colonel. I don't see how they're your concern, *Lieutenant*."

Seven meters. Murphy unlimbered his weapon and pointed it at Shane. "The mission is my concern, and it is my concern when my superior officer is behaving erratically."

Oh, God, Shane thought, *this is it.* She slowed her approach. Was he monitoring the radio traffic at the compound? Was that why he was here? "Are you going to shoot me with that, Murphy?"

Murphy backed up a step. "I think you intend some sort of mutiny."

"You're going to kill your superior officer because of your own paranoia?"

This obviously wasn't going as Murphy had planned. "I heard your radio transmission to Conner and Hougland— There's no enemy out there. What the hell do you think you have them doing?"

Shane began closing. She hoped her renewed confidence was showing in her voice. "You dimwit, Murphy, you know how green Conner is. The only way his performance is going to improve is if I throw him some curves—"

Six meters.

"You should have cleared it with—"

She had him now. "I was not under the impression that regulations required me to clear training exercises with *inferior* officers. I'm going to ask you again, Lieutenant Murphy, are you going to shoot me with that thing?"

Murphy was no longer angry. He was scared. He should have been. If Shane had been telling the truth, he was the one looking at a court-martial. He lowered the gun.

Shane smiled and shook her head. "You're lucky you didn't get shot, Murphy. Go back to your quarters, consider yourself under house arrest."

Murphy wordlessly nodded behind his helmet and began to walk back to the ship. Shane followed him, five meters behind. "One question, Lieutenant. Do you have any accomplices in this fiasco, or did you engineer this on your own initiative?"

Murphy sighed. "I did this on my own. No one even knows I'm out here."

Shane turned on the ECM and shot him with the stunner. Murphy dropped like a stone before he knew what hit him.

Shane stood beside Murphy, waiting for the alarms to sound. None did. Nobody had seen Murphy drop. He'd told the truth. No one knew he was out here.

Shane rolled him into the ruin of the old GA&A security building and pulled some wreckage over him.

Then, with one last look at the *Blood-Tide,* she turned toward the prisoners' compound. She would have an hour, an hour and a half at best.

She sincerely hoped that someone in the mass of prisoners would know where the hell they could go.

CHAPTER FOURTEEN

Executive Session

"Governments are always more at risk from their subjects than they are from external threats."
—*The Cynic's Book of Wisdom*

"A Great Power doesn't ask if it *should* dominate lesser nations. If it's a Great Power, it can, and it does."
—BORIS KALECSKY
(2103–2200)

It had been a month and a half since the intel briefing on Mars. The diplomatic invasion of Earth had begun.

Dimitri Olmanov had participated in every Terran Congress since the drafting of the Charter. The coming Congress was number eleven, the first one of the Confederacy's second century.

The Congress would convene in a little over two standard months. The politicking had started in earnest.

The Congress had three functions: rewriting the political boundaries of the Confederacy, admitting and promoting member planets and, most importantly, modifying the Confederacy Charter, the document that made the whole shebang run.

The most important dynamic was the number of prime seats in the Congress. Dimitri was reminded of that every time he thought of Bakunin. Primes consisted of forty-three seats out of seventy-five—or eighty-three if you counted the probationary members admitted in the last Congress.

Sirius and Centauri, between them, had twenty-two of those prime seats. They'd controlled a majority of primes since the founding of the Confederacy. That meant that, for a century, the two wealthiest and—as the other three arms were fond of pointing out—most European arms of the Confederacy had dominated the Congress.

Nothing lasts forever.

The 11th Congress might see the power shift. Promoting planetary seats was a basic function of the Congress. A planet usually rose through the ranks—probationary, nonvoting, voting, full, and, finally, prime.

Conventional wisdom had it that six planets would jump from full to prime. Two from the Alpha Centauri Alliance, one from the Sirius Community, three from the remaining arms of the Confederacy. If conventional wisdom held, that meant that Cynos and Occisis would retain their one prime majority, the slimmest majority they'd ever had, but still a majority.

The problem with conventional wisdom was that it was usually wrong.

Dimitri walked through the diplomatic compound with Ambrose. It was the first time he'd been out of Confederacy tower since his return from Mars. The building rose behind the two of them, nearly a kilometer into the Australian sky. The spire was a monument to hubris, a large proportion, Dimitri knew, his own.

"Another sin," Dimitri said, swatting the landscaping with his cane.

"Sir?" Ambrose said.

Dimitri shook his head. "Pride. I wonder if the Dolbrians were as proud of their Face as we are of our government."

"I wouldn't know, sir."

"Of course you don't. No one does. That's the beauty of it. A hundred million years and this will all be so much dust. All this so-important bean counting."

Dimitri saw the plaintive nonexpression that usually meant that the remains of his companion's brain had lost the thread of the conversation. The literal-minded Ambrose was probably picturing the counting of beans.

Dimitri sighed.

The secure diplomatic compound huddled around the foot of the tower, as if in worship. The area was landscaped within an inch of its life. Every single speck of gravel had been hand-placed and was monitored by security. Bushes, fountains, and flowers were everywhere.

The scene was about as natural as Ambrose.

The knowledge that every second bush held monitoring equipment deadened the garden for Dimitri even more. It was a much more concentrated form of the same maniacal human control that was strangling Mars.

Eventually he walked into a utilitarian building inside the Centauri compound. The unpretentious building was unmarked. It could have been a storehouse or gardener's shack.

In fact, it housed the offices of the second most powerful man in the Confederacy.

Dimitri was here to see Pearce Adams, Archeron representative to the Terran Congress, Centauri Alliance delegate to the Terran Executive Command, vice-president in charge of security for the Centauri Trading Company, and the head man of the Centauri intelligence community.

Ambrose followed Dimitri down stairs that led underground and into an office complex three times the size of the building above. Dimitri pressed no buttons, used no keys, and talked to no guards, but the secure doors opened for him anyway.

In the security-blanketed area around the tower, Dimitri doubted that there was a single door that wouldn't.

When Dimitri walked into Adams' Terran office, the first thing he noted was that Adams had the temperature down to its lowest setting. Adams sat at his desk, in shirtsleeves, and still looked uncomfortably hot. Dimitri didn't shed his jacket. The cold brought back joint aches he remembered from Mars.

Dimitri wondered whether Adams was homesick or simply trying to irritate him.

The only decoration in the office was a holo on the wall, an image of low-gravity mountains gripped in an endless sunlit blizzard. Occasionally the virtual ice caught the double sun and cast multiple rain—actually ice—bows.

Dimitri decided that Adams was homesick.

"I'd prefer to talk alone," Adams said by way of introduction.

Ambrose showed no reaction.

Dimitri looked at his companion and decided it would gain him nothing to argue the point, even though the last thing Ambrose was was a security risk. "Wait outside, Ambrose," Dimitri said.

"Very good, sir."

Ambrose would walk out until he'd reached fifty meters and stop. The door closed behind him, leaving Dimitri and Adams alone with the Archeron blizzard on the wall.

"What did you want to see me about?" Adams asked.

Dimitri didn't sit. He folded both hands on top of his cane and leaned forward. "I wanted to know why two of the SEEC seats dissented on the Rasputin vote."

Adams looked at Dimitri a little oddly. "Perhaps you should talk to the Sirius Community about—"

"I don't wish to talk to Kalin Green—yet."

Adams sat with an impassive expression, unmoved.

"Shall I expound a theory of mine?" Dimitri asked.

"Go ahead. I still fail to see your point."

"You will." Dimitri turned toward the holo as he talked. "Setting Rasputin up for a proposal required a few years of preparation. Preparation that fell mostly to you and the Community, because it was a Sirius-Centauri proposal."

"So?"

"Those two dissenting Community votes, theoretically, could have cost those years of investment."

"If it wasn't for Indi abstaining."

Dimitri smiled at the frozen holographic landscape. "Now why did they do that?"

Adams didn't respond.

"The coalition Indi is crafting shouldn't like Rasputin, should they? They see the whole operation, legalities aside, as a bad precedent for TEC interference in planetary affairs. And because of the Centauri-Sirius monopoly on prime seats, they see the TEC as a tool of the Europeans."

Dimitri turned around and faced Adams. "Obviously, Indi decided to ignore the obvious. They wanted Rasputin to pass."

Adams smiled. "Why would they want to do that?"

"The same reason you wanted it to fail."

"Can you get to the point without the obscure Machiavellianism?"

Adams was one of the few members of the Terran Congress who wasn't enamored of diplomatic forms and procedures. If Dimitri admired Adams for anything, it was his bluntness. That and the fact that Adams was secure enough to talk that way to Dimitri. Few others dared.

"The point," Dimitri said, "is the fact that this coming Congress has the potential of disrupting the power structure of the Confederacy. Indi is on the ascendancy. Their expansion during the last century is paying them with seats on the Congress; their coalition will have a majority on a straight vote shortly into the promotion process."

"So far this is all common knowledge."

"Is it common knowledge that Indi plans to bump some nonvoting seats in the Congress straight to prime?"

Adams' expression cracked a bit. It was fractional, the man had terrific control, but it was obvious that Dimitri had just hit a point that disturbed him greatly. Slowly Adams said, "That is a severe breach of form."

"Form, yes," Dimitri said. "Law, no. Promotion through the ranks is traditional but not compulsory. All a planet has to achieve is continuous human occupation for eighty years and a population over half a billion."

"And its name on the Charter."

Dimitri nodded. "And its name on the Charter. There's even a precedent—"

"The first five primes were promoted immediately upon signing the Charter. Yes I'm aware of that. I fail to see what any of this has to do with Rasputin."

"Everything," Dimitri said.

Robert Kaunda sat in one of the Hotel Victoria's private dining rooms. The hemispherical holo that surrounded him and the Protectorate delegate created the illusion that they were alone on the roof of the hotel. The open sky and the Pacific's surf were both fake, as was the sprawl of the Confederacy's capital city behind them. In reality, they were a few layers behind guards and other diners.

What counted was the fact that they were isolated behind that holo just as well as if they were really dining alone on top of Sydney's premier hotel.

Kaunda drank his tea and repeated himself. "Even if it is, as you say, a win-win situation, I do not like giving the Confederacy—especially the Executive—this kind of power."

Sim Vashniya, the delegate to the Executive Command from the People's Protectorate of Epsilon Indi, representative to the Terran Congress from Shiva, and the Gods knew what else, reclined on a chair considerably higher than Kaunda's, his expression betraying nothing but slight amusement. "You were satisfied with my reasoning before—"

"That was when we were counting seats. As you kept pointing out, the Centauri Alliance and the Sirius Community had a majority. But with those two Sirius dissenters we *could* have blocked the whole thing."

Vashniya sat impassively. Kaunda thought that the dwarfish Shivan looked like some graven icon, carved from nutwood. Like something the gift shops on Mazimba might sell to rich tourists from Waldgrave or Banlieue. The kind of thing that old women in Mulawayo knocked off by the hundreds to sell to the off-worlders at 100 credits each. After the tourist shops took their cut, it amounted to a credit an hour—if the women were lucky. It let them eat.

"Well?" Kaunda asked.

"Yes, we could have blocked it. That, in fact, was *why* two of the Sirius votes dissented."

Kaunda set down his tea. "Pardon?" He didn't like these intelligence games, political games. He'd gotten to represent the intelligence community of the Union of Independent Worlds—such as it was—by being a strong leader and taking no shit from his seconds. The trail might be a little bloody, but it was less bloody than those of most of his contemporaries on Mazimba. However, being chief of police in Mulawayo, and then chief of intelligence for the whole planet of Mazimba, had never trained him for subtlety. It forced him to trust his betters in those matters, like Vashniya, and he didn't like trusting people.

"Nothing in an Executive delegation happens by accident. Those two Sirius votes were well planned."

"They wanted the proposal to fail." Kaunda kept his voice flat, betraying none of his surprise.

After a moment of thought, Kaunda realized that they might not *want* TEC involvement. "They expected us to be solidly against and defeat them twenty-two to twenty. But if they wanted it to fail, why bring up the proposal?"

Vashniya patted his beard. "Rasputin is no spur of the moment enterprise. The latter phases of the plan have required nearly five years of delicate groundwork by the Centauri and SEEC intelligence services. They needed the TEC to allow them that."

"I see."

The TEC jealously guarded its place in the Confederacy intel community. If any planet, or group of planets, decided to do this kind of covert action unilaterally . . .

Well, it would be bad.

"So," Kaunda said, "the proposal to the TEC was a smoke screen—"

"To cover the realignment of the Centauri and Sirius intelligence apparatus. They wanted the idea to be shot down."

"But they were—still are—primed to slip in on their own before the TEC could intervene." Politics was a twisted arena. Things were much simpler when he was just a policeman.

"Just so. The plan was to set up the groundwork for Rasputin, have the TEC proposal fail, then slip in SEEC or Alliance military with no TEC involvement, and take over. Then they'd present the Congress with a *fait accompli.*"

"But because of the Protectorate's abstention, the TEC *is* in charge of this."

"And *we* have a hand in." Vashniya smiled a little wider.

"I think I liked it better when we were simply divorcing ourselves from the operation."

"Oh, we've done that. And more." Vashniya looked out over Sydney. "When the dust settles, when the Congress meets for the first time in this new century, we are finally going to see the Europeans lose their primacy. Take the long view, Kaunda."

Kaunda looked out over Sydney as well but said nothing.

"If the operation fails, it fails. But if it succeeds . . ."

"*If,*" Kaunda said.

It took him over a month to leave Mars.

It was harder to do than he had ever imagined. In his nine years he had grown attached to the severe landscape, the lethal weather, and, most of all, the isolation.

Even the knowledge that, fifteen light-years away, all hell was about to break loose on Bakunin, couldn't hurry him. The events on Bakunin were, in a real sense, over already. What mattered was the coming Terran Congress and what would happen there.

After all this time, what disturbed him was the fact that he would be among large numbers of people for the first time in nine years.

Eventually he left the empty crystalline fairyland he'd lived in for so long, paid his respects at a lonely grave, and started the long walk to the nearest settlement.

CHAPTER FIFTEEN

Silent Partners

"Artificial Intelligences are feared more for the latter than the former."

—*The Cynic's Book of Wisdom*

"These thinking machines are an offense against God!"

—AUGUST BENITO GALIANI
(2019–*2105)

Dom kept his eyes on the road while Tetsami kept her gaze locked on him. The new contragrav truck slid down the tunnel as if the tube were designed for it, not for maglev commuter traffic.

"I don't see why you had to buy it," she said when the silence got too long.

"We need the tunnel to make this work."

"I know," Tetsami said. She turned away from his deadpan expression.

The Godwin-Proudhon commuter tunnel shot by them, the magnets sliding past like a silent heartbeat in a giant concrete vein. They were well under the forest east of Godwin now. If they were lucky, ahead lay an unbroken subterranean highway that traveled nearly all the way to Proudhon.

They were combining an inspection tour with their visit

to their potential electronics whiz, and—Tetsami had to admit—this was certainly a low-profile way to travel.

"But did you have to *buy* it? It's not like anyone's guarding the entrance."

"You're concerned about the money?"

"Hell, yes, I'm concerned about the money. I never thought I'd see the day when half a meg seemed like limited resources—"

"The tunnel was a relatively cheap investment."

"Cheap?" Tetsami nearly gagged. "Put aside the fact I doubt those leeches at the Mahajan bank have ever given *anyone* a deal. You shelled out nearly one hundred K for this white elephant."

"Like I said, an *investment*." Dom's finger began tapping on the control stick. "Tetsami, don't think of the money we're spending. At this point I am *totally* committed to this operation."

"What if something goes wrong with it?"

Dom put a hand to the side of his face. "For me, that is not an option."

The flat way Dom said that chilled Tetsami. It was not the first time she was a little scared of her partner. She looked away from the expressionless stare he was casting out down the tunnel. The computer was guiding the contragrav, but he had yet to look at her during their conversation. She wondered if there were something down the tunnel only he could see.

Tetsami wished she'd gotten hold of Ivor. She'd feel better with him in the driver's seat, even though the computer was driving. Unfortunately, Ivor's old message drop said he was out on a run somewhere and wouldn't be back for three days or so.

She looked at Dom and moved the conversation to a different subject.

"How's the cover story holding up?"

"The bankers bought the innuendo, and the rumors are spreading nicely. One place where I was pricing mining lasers, the proprietor informed me that he could direct me to an off-planet buyer who would be *very* interested in Dolbrian artifacts."

Was that actually a ghost of a smile she saw?

Their cover was a very simple deception, explaining the purchase of the defunct Godwin-Proudhon commuter tube as well as masses of digging equipment, lasers, and things more esoteric. The Dolbrians—named for the first planet where concrete evidence was found of successful nonhuman terraforming—were a race that flourished perhaps a million centuries ago. The Dolbrians had scattered traces of themselves all over Confederacy space, not the least of which were the massive structures on the plains of Cydonia on Mars.

However, the most common artifacts to survive the hundred million years since their disappearance weren't ruins, buildings, or any form of technology. The most common evidence of the Dolbrians was the planets they'd terraformed.

Depending on the expert, there were anywhere from five to two dozen Dolbrian planets in the Confederacy. Planets that shouldn't—couldn't—have life, an atmosphere, or be remotely habitable without some form of intelligent intervention. Planets in triple sun systems, planets orbiting too close to—or far from—their primary, planets orbiting suns too young, too old, too weak. . . .

As far as Dolbrian planets went, Bakunin—orbiting a weak orange-red sun that never even rated a real name before humans arrived—was on the shortlist of possibilities. Very short, considering that Dolbri was Bakunin's closest inhabited neighbor. Every once in a while a herd of academics would brave the violent politics and go up in the hills, or out in the ocean, and try to unearth some physical evidence of the Dolbrian presence.

The fact that not so much as one kilo of worked stone had surfaced did not discourage them. After all, a hundred million years is a long time.

And treasure hunting for alien artifacts was just the kind of harebrained scheme that some wealthy home-grown Bakunin nutballs might come up with. It certainly covered for their plans for much more practical treasure-hunting, as well as explaining the digging equipment.

"Do you think there might actually be some Dolbrian artifacts under the Diderot range?" she asked.

She saw a smile, perhaps, or maybe only a trick of the light reflecting back through the windshield. "The Dolbrians," Dom said, "are a myth propagated to explain a handful of Martian rock formations and the fact that we have no coherent theory explaining the evolution of habitable planets."

As usual, she couldn't read his expression. "You believe that?"

He shook his head. "Not any more . . ."

After a few seconds, Tetsami said, "You trailed off, what were you about to say?"

"Sorry, caught myself in a memory. A long time ago."

Tetsami decided to let it lie. She knew practically nothing about Dominic's background, and she had decided, after he admitted to once being a TEC officer, that it was a good thing. Since their discussion on top of the Waldgrave Hotel, she had avoided questioning him on any part of his life prior to his involvement in Godwin Arms & Armaments. She tried hard not to acknowledge the curiosity she felt.

Dom might have sensed her unvoiced inquiry, or he might have just been in an unusually loquacious mood. In any case, he volunteered, "I've been to Cydonia."

"You have?" Against her better judgment she felt her curiosity piqued.

Dom nodded. "Long time ago. When I was still in the Executive Command. Since the atmosphere became breathable, a lot of old bunkers, terraforming bases, academic retreats were mothballed. The TEC uses them occasionally for secure meetings, safe houses, private retreats. The largest concentration of them is around Cydonia."

Tetsami couldn't help but smile. It was rather amusing picturing the archaeological find of the millennium swarming with spies and secret police. Certainly, it was out of the way.

"Anyway," Dom continued, "when I expressed my belief to a superior on Mars, he took me out on the plains to show me the Face. Said he wanted to teach me a little about humility."

The van drove on in silence for a while before Tetsami said, "Did it?"

"Hmm?"

"Did it teach you humility?"

For the first time since she'd met him, she heard Dominic Magnus laugh.

The ill-fated commuter tube never quite made it to the Proudhon Spaceport, its intended destination. The tunnel ended a few klicks away from the city limits in a tangle of scaffolding and abandoned equipment. Financial disaster had killed the project in mid-stroke.

Dom parked the contragrav behind a massive digging machine that no one seemed to have thought worthy of salvage. He departed to find some access to the surface, and Tetsami was left by the scaffolding. It looked like the two of them might be the first people down this way since the project collapsed. Certainly no one had come down here from the Godwin end. Down by Godwin, the tunnels were a warren of garbage, graffiti, and the occasional squatter.

Here, under the frosted glare of the truck's headlights, the tunnel was almost pristine. Up to the start of the scaffolding, the rock tunnel was sheathed in white tile, and the magnets were still firmly fixed behind their white plastic housing. Chrome trim was only slightly dimmed by an old layer of dust. The digging machine filled the dead end of the tunnel, behind ten meters of scaffolding. It resembled a giant insect frozen in the midst of a kill, arms stopped halfway to the rough rock wall. A burrowing monster that a mountain range couldn't stop.

Tetsami opened the door in the head of the beast and looked over the thing, pulling herself inside. It was obvious why it had been abandoned. The magnets in the walls reduced the effective diameter of the tunnel by a meter. The machine would've had to be disassembled to get it out.

Tetsami smiled as she settled into the control seat and

ran her hands over the inactive control panels. Nice little beast, this. A cylindrical body resting on all-terrain treads, a dozen arms in the front bearing drills, lasers, digging gear, built like a tank. Definitely an unsubtle vehicle. Tetsami liked it.

Too bad there was no way to get it out of its hole.

After a while, Dom returned. He'd found an access port that made it all the way to the surface. Tetsami left the digging machine, noting that it had a port for a bio-interface.

The maintenance shaft opened on a gentle slope that was relatively free of trees. The vantage gave a panoramic view of the city of Proudhon, and especially of the sprawl of the spaceport.

It was the first time Tetsami had seen a city other than Godwin. At least it was the first time she'd seen one when she wasn't on the business end of a wire.

As they walked down the gravel slope, more and more of the port became visible. Barely ten seconds would pass without something lifting off or landing. It was impossible, for a while, to separate the port from the city. It might have been because, for the most part, the port *was* the city. Proudhon Spaceport was like a mutant chrome-neon plant that sent branches sprawling across the land, sprouting landing facilities like giant concrete leaves. Parts of it weaved into the city, surrounded it, to the point where old landing strips became avenues for ground traffic, grounded luxury liners became hotels, and high-rises became control towers.

The sprawl was lorded over by a knot of white marble towers in the center of the city, the only sign of order in the midst of the chaos. Those white towers were the home of the Proudhon Spaceport Development Corporation, probably the wealthiest enterprise on the planet.

Thinking how hard it must be to direct traffic in that chaos gave Tetsami a headache. Then, again, the Proudhon Spaceport Development Corporation was pretty firm in its enforcement of their traffic patterns. They had a *lot* of antiaircraft batteries.

"Do you know where we're going?" Tetsami asked as she realized just how big the spaceport was.

Dom nodded. "Mosasa's Surplus place is over there."

He pointed at the fringe of the city/spaceport. In a vast, flat, stretch of land that spread away from both the foothills and the city, were ranks upon ranks of parked spacecraft. As Tetsami stared, she realized that all those craft, parked in formation below her, were derelicts. Some were missing control surfaces, others lacked drive sections, cabins, landing gear. In many cases, the original markings were obscured by age, but what she could see came from all quarters of the Confederacy.

A few of those ships could have been military, and a lot of them looked as though they'd been shot down.

No one stopped them as they descended from the foothills and began to walk between the endless ranks of dead spacecraft. It was eerily quiet; even the hectic activity of Proudhon Spaceport didn't seem to leak in here.

"Damn," Tetsami said, "Tjaele Mosasa must have the concession on every abandoned or shot-up spacecraft that passes through this place."

"It's quite a profitable salvage arrangement with Proudhon Spaceport Security." The voice wasn't Dom's.

They both turned around to see a squashed sphere, about a meter along its wide diameter. It was floating about eye-level with Tetsami. It aimed at least three different sensor devices at them. The voice came from somewhere within the brushed metal shell. "The lady and the cyborg, here to see Mosasa?"

Cyborg? What's that thing looking at?

The device began a slow orbit around them, just wide enough to avoid bumping into the spacecraft that marched away on either side of them.

"Afraid he's busy," it said. "Can I help you?"

Tetsami watched the floating lump of salvage, fascinated. There had to be a contragrav unit in there.

"We need to see Mr. Mosasa."

The machine made a derisive noise, as if it had been insulted. Tetsami began to wonder who, exactly, was operating the thing. It didn't sound like they were conversing with a security program.

"May I ask who's calling?"

Dom said, "No."

The machine tilted itself at what could only be called a sarcastic angle. "Oh, *really* now. Do you expect for me to disturb him for a couple of street flotsam who won't even—"

"Johann sent us," Dom said.

The robot righted itself and said, somewhat petulantly, "You could have said that right off. Follow me."

With that, the flattened sphere spun on its axis and sped down the aisle between the spacecraft at a brisk walking space. It floated off for about ten meters, spun back, and asked, "What are you waiting for?"

They followed.

As they walked behind the device, weaving between the ranks of spacecraft, Tetsami asked, "Who do you suppose is flying that thing?"

Ahead, without changing course or slowing down, the robot turned around against and regarded her with its triple video array. "The name is Random Walk, Miss. An advanced holographic crystal matrix late of the Race— who are rather late themselves—currently full partner in Mosasa Salvage Incorporated."

The robot turned a corner as Tetsami felt a chill run through her. *An AI? But that was . . .*

She stopped herself before she thought the word, "illegal," or, just as bad, "immoral." There really wasn't any reason why Mosasa couldn't be working with an artificial intelligence on Bakunin. It would be the only place in the Confederacy he could.

Well, only because Bakunin wasn't part of the Confederacy.

Considering where her ancestors came from, feeling uncomfortable around an AI was hypocritical. After all, a lot of people would feel the same way about her. If they knew where her parents came from.

They rounded the gutted remains of a Hegira luxury

transport, and found Tjaele Mosasa standing at the edge of a circular clearing.

Mosasa was an extremely tall black man with a dour expression. He was hairless, without eyebrows or lashes. He wore khaki shorts, a tool belt, a half-dozen earrings, and nothing else. He was adjusting a device on a tripod that pointed across the clearing at a gigantic ring that seemed to have come from the drive section of a military transport.

He looked up at them, and Tetsami saw that most of the left side of his body was dominated by a gigantic dragon tattoo. The tattoo was luminescent and changed color in the ruddy light of Kropotkin. It looked as though it was some photoreactive dye. The dragon's neck curled around Mosasa's and its head curled around his left ear. When Mosasa looked at them, it was with three eyes, one of them from the dragon's profile.

"I'll talk to you in a moment," he said, and bent back over the tripod. The device looked like some sort of particle beam. The upright torus it was aimed at was about ten meters in diameter.

The robot—*Random Walk,* Tetsami corrected herself—floated up next to her and Dom and said in a self-satisfied tone, "I told you he was busy."

Great, Tetsami thought, a snide computer. Worse, it and Mosasa were a package. The thought of working with a self-aware computer gave her a crawling sensation under her scalp.

Mosasa continued to work on his little particle beam.

"What's he doing?" Dom asked the floating robot.

"If you tell me who you are."

Dom looked at her. She shrugged. It was his show. She was scrambling to keep him from realizing just how out of her depth she was. Somehow she'd kept from locking up when they went over the beginnings of her plan—but the scope of the thing still scared the shit out of her.

An AI, too, why the fuck not?

"Come on," said Random, "we *are* a team. And if Johann sent you, you want both of us."

"Dominic and Tetsami," Dom said. "That's enough until we find out if you're working for us."

Tetsami nearly jumped when the robot circled around and stopped about three centimeters from her face. "Tetsami?"

She complimented herself for not yelping in surprise. "Y–yes?" she managed. Dom looked at her oddly, as if noticing her discomfort for the first time. *Dom,* she thought, *can you really be that oblivious?*

"I know that name—but then, of course I would—that is the same family I'm thinking of, isn't it?"

Damn it. Tetsami was a common name on Dakota, but that wasn't even common knowledge in the rest of the Seven Worlds. If someone bothered to dig into the history of the late twenty-first century, specifically the Genocide War against the Race, they might unearth a few important Tetsamis. Otherwise, for most people, it would be just a name. That was one of the reasons Tetsami had never changed it.

However, considering that the Tetsami genetics had been engineered for human-machine interface, and considering the peculiar rapport they achieved with captured Race AIs—

Of course this thing knew her. It had to be at least as old as the war.

Tetsami tried to say something, found her mouth too dry, and simply nodded.

"What luck. Someday we'll have to talk shop, comrade—"

That thing was much too close to her. She could feel herself shaking. Dom finally saved her by saying, "You were going to tell us what he's doing—"

"Oh, yes—" The robot sped over to Dom's side and Tetsami could breathe again. *It knows me,* she thought, *the damn thing knows me.*

She backed up and sat down on a pile of dismantled armor. She ran her fingers over the scars left by dozens of micrometeors and listened to Random Walk with half an ear.

"—in other words, he's trying to program an Emerson field to stop a bullet."

"Engineers have been trying that ever since they could reproduce the Emerson Effect in the lab."

"I've been telling him that," said the robot, "but he's convinced he can get the field to damp the kinetic energy of a particle."

"I don't see how. The effect is energy based, but if the field is on a massy particle's frequency—"

"He's finding it damn difficult—oh, boy. You better turn around, if this test is like any of the others . . ."

Tetsami wasn't facing the clearing, but she could feel the heat of the giant white flash that must have originated by the massive torus. Even though she was looking away, the reflection off the sandy ground dazzled her.

She turned around, rubbing her eyes, expecting to see the entire apparatus melted into slag. However the ring was still there, and Mosasa was next to it, looking at readout screens and nodding.

The floating robot tilted itself and rotated slightly, amazingly like a human shaking his head sadly. "He's convinced it's only a software problem."

Tetsami stood up and walked over to Dom.

"What was that flash?"

Dom waved at the ring, "A force field converting a few micrograms of carbon into energy."

"A field can do that?" She felt her hand going toward the personal screen on her belt. Suddenly she didn't feel too safe with it on.

Dom smiled when he saw her hand move. "Don't worry, a personal field—even a military-grade one—isn't calibrated to handle the wavelength of a massy object heavier than an electron."

"Besides," said Random Walk, "a field with that small an energy sink would collapse from the overload. I better check with Mosasa before he becomes too engrossed with the data to talk to you two."

The robot sped off toward Mosasa and the giant ring.

She kept looking at the torus. "That's a field generator?

When I first saw it, I thought it was the drive section from a spacecraft."

"It is."

Tetsami looked at him.

"Same technology that lets that box on your hip damp a laser beam lets that ring drive a sublight ship in-system. Plasma or hydrogen gas in one end, a coherent stream of high-energy photons out the other."

"Uh-uh," Tetsami said.

"You have some odd gaps in your knowledge."

She shrugged.

"Your name seemed to mean something to the computer there."

"I haven't asked you about your past," she snapped. She was sorry she said it. She should have glossed over the fact; instead she had drawn attention to it. However, Dom didn't follow it up. He simply looked at her, nodded, and dropped the subject.

After a while, Random Walk led Mosasa up to them, and Dom got to make his pitch.

Twenty minutes and a kilogram note later, the two were in.

CHAPTER SIXTEEN

Golden Parachute

"True enemies are as rare as true friends."
　　　　　　　　　—*The Cynic's Book of Wisdom*

"It is easier to forgive an Enemy than to forgive a Friend."

　　　　　　　　　—WILLIAM BLAKE
　　　　　　　　　(1757–1827)

Objectively speaking, the escape couldn't have gone better.

Shane had opened a thirty-six-degree hole in the marines' northern defense perimeter simply by taking herself, Hougland, and Conner out of the loop. Somehow she managed to funnel the prisoners through security's cone of blindness. Members of GA&A's original security managed to maintain order within the ranks of the prisoners as she guarded the rear and waited for one of the colonel's search and destroy missions to overtake them.

Within an hour they were under the cover of the forest, safe from most spy sats but not from overflights. Shane let two of the security people lead the way; they seemed to know where to go—and they were going away from Godwin. Shane didn't want to go toward the city. She knew that the colonel would concentrate any search for the prisoners in the space between GA&A and Godwin.

Even so, the mass of prisoners would be impossible to hide once a concentrated search started. Even though their path seemed to take them directly away from Bakunin's excuse for civilization.

Shane knew the whole project was doomed. They were still close enough to the GA&A complex to know when the alarm was raised.

She guarded the fatalistic march into the Diderot Mountains, waiting for a miracle.

In two hours, a miracle occurred.

The escape couldn't have gone better. Shane still thought that, five overlong Bakunin days later.

Kathy Shane lay sprawled on her cot, thinking about the briefing holos they'd shown on the *Blood-Tide* before the jump to Bakunin space. The planetary briefings they gave the marines before a drop were always heavy propaganda jobs. All good soldiers knew that, deep down. Just a little bit of spiritual bullshit to help everyone believe that they were on the side of the Angels; they were helping the helpless; God was on their side saying, "Rah! Rah! Rah!"

Of course you believed every word, or at least fooled yourself into believing every word.

"It was too good. Wasn't it, Murphy?"

Good enough for almost all her people to forget what they'd learned about illegal orders. Good enough not to question the colonel. Good enough to make her people believe that the people of Bakunin deserved what they got.

She should have had her own briefings after those holos. She'd known they were over the top when she saw them. . . .

Bakunin, home of a million perversions.

Bakunin, where every citizen is a thief and a murderer.

Bakunin, economic black hole trying to pull the Confederacy into its anarchic chaos.

Bakunin, where your typical inhabitant would shoot

you, rape you, and steal your boots simply because there was no law that said he couldn't.

Shane knew that by the time Dacham had given the order to vaporize the prisoners, her people had begun to think of Bakunin less as a planet and more like the first circle of Hell. If Dacham ordered carpet bombing the continent with micronukes, Shane thought most of his command would go along without any question. Those who'd question were probably too scared to do anything.

His command.

Shane shivered.

The room they'd put her in wasn't originally designed as a cell. The mattress she lay on was an electrostatic fluid of variable viscosity, much more comfortable than her bunk aboard the *Blood-Tide*. There was a separate bathroom that seemed to have an unlimited supply of hot water. There was a half kitchen that allowed her to call up her own menu at any time. There was even a full holo entertainment system on the far wall from the door.

The only thing to show that she was a prisoner was the fact that the door was locked.

For perhaps the dozenth time in the last four days Shane wondered if she should have simply split off from the prisoners once she got them safely outside the perimeter. And again, the same answer: She'd done the right thing.

She had chucked her career—hell, she had chucked her whole life—to free those people, and she'd make damn sure they made it to safety. She'd been the only armed member of the escape, and if she'd split off from them, they'd have been defenseless.

Fortunately for the prisoners, there was an emergency rendezvous set up by the former CEO, Dominic Magnus. They'd been barely three hours out of GA&A when the patrol at the commune here saw them and took them in, through one of the hidden caves that dotted the Diderot Range.

Unfortunately for Shane, the command here took a dim

view of her. The guards would have wasted her if the prisoners hadn't spoken up on her behalf.

So, instead of summary execution it was, "Thank you, Captain Shane; drop your weapon, Captain Shane; do not move, Captain Shane; follow us, Captain Shane; remove the armor, Captain Shane; we'll talk to you later, Captain Shane . . ."

At which point the door slid shut on her, leaving her alone in this room wearing only her sweaty underwear. She had not seen or heard from her captors since. Since the room had its own food and water, they could keep her isolated here indefinitely.

Preferable to the brig on the *Blood-Tide* anyway.

Shane ran her hand over her head. The even nap of hair felt odd to her. She had been here long enough for her hair to grow back somewhat, and instead of shaving the Occisis stripes back, she decided to do her hair in an even crewcut. The transverse stripes were a symbol of the marines, and it seemed a bit disrespectful for her to maintain them in her situation.

Waiting for something to happen was getting on her nerves.

Hell, maybe they've forgotten about me.

Shane chuckled. More likely, since she had discovered the location of their hideout, they'd chucked her in here while they moved the body of GA&A's personnel elsewhere. In which case she could be abandoned in an empty building being run by a computer, and eventually the food and water would give out. Perhaps a few years from now—

Oh, come on. If they'd do that, it would be much simpler to shoot me in the head to keep themselves safe.

The worst thing about this all was that she could see their point of view. She wouldn't trust her in this situation. Defectors in any situation were terribly unreliable. In fact, she could see Colonel Dacham setting up this whole charade to find out where the GA&A personnel could be hiding. It was a TEC kind of trick. If she didn't know better, she could easily picture herself as one of his agents.

As if that thought had triggered some sort of security alarm, the door decided just then to open for the first time in five days. Shane leaped off of the cot in surprise, taking a defensive stance across from the door as if it would do any good against a laser carbine. She stood there, naked except for a pair of Occisis-issue briefs, as the door whooshed fully open.

Standing there was the dark lithe form of Sergeant Mariah Zanzibar, the person who—as far as Shane could tell—was in charge of security for this place. Flanking her were a pair of guards in black monocast armor; each had a snub-nosed antipersonnel laser. Looked like Griffith Three-As from where she was. She didn't get a closer look at them, because Zanzibar stepped through the door and it slid shut behind her.

Shane relaxed a little bit, but not much.

Zanzibar stood in front of the door, looking down at Shane. Probably couldn't have found two more different-looking women in the Confederacy if you tried. Zanzibar was lean, tall, and built like a panther. The comparison made Shane look like a heavy–boned attack dog. Zanzibar was so dark and Shane so pale that the labels black and white were as accurate as they could be with any pair of humans. Where Shane was rounded, Zanzibar was flat. Where Shane was heavily muscled, Zanzibar was svelte. Where Shane looked like she could walk through an obstacle, Zanzibar looked like she'd flow around it.

Zanzibar, at the moment, was wearing the gray jumpsuit that seemed to be the uniform around this place, and she carried a small briefcase. She tossed the case on the bed and said, "Get dressed. Someone wants to meet you."

"Who?" Shane asked.

Zanzibar said nothing.

For a moment, Shane considered refusing, but she thought better of it. After all, what was the point? They could come in and drag her wherever, clothes or no clothes. Shane picked up the case, looked at Zanzibar, and sighed when Zanzibar made no sign of leaving to give her some privacy. Shane opened the case and put on the clothes she found inside, another gray jumpsuit.

Once she was dressed, Zanzibar nodded. As if in response, the door slid open.

Zanzibar led, and the two guards followed. They walked her through an endless warren of corridors, many of them with open panels in the walls revealing pipes and sheaves of unconnected optical cable. Many of the lights weren't working. It all felt as though it had just been taken out of the packing material after a long time in storage.

From what little she'd seen, the complex looked like just another of the self-sufficient communes that dotted the almost barren surface of Bakunin. Inside, under the complex—the route she and the prisoners had been ushered through—a shaft dug down to the water table, and another dug down to a shielded power plant. As far as she knew, none of the commune even broke the surface.

All in all, a nice little bolt-hole which Colonel Dacham, obviously, had no idea existed. If he did, it would've been a crater by now.

It gave Shane a perverse pleasure to think that most of GA&A's personnel, as far as Colonel Dacham was concerned, had fallen off the face of the planet.

After a while, the tone of the corridors changed. Instead of apartments, they now passed offices, and eventually they boarded an elevator. Zanzibar said something to the control panel in a language Shane didn't recognize, and the elevator began going up.

And up.

And up.

When the elevator had passed two-dozen floors, it announced that it'd reached ground level. The counter changed color as they passed, and kept going. Twenty floors above ground level, the elevator stopped.

Penthouse suite, Shane thought.

What the elevator opened on wasn't a suite, but it was familiar. The doors opened on one side of a transparent—probably armored—partition, on the other side of which was a command center, probably for the whole commune.

Zanzibar led her off, but in her brief view of the room filled with a dozen people or so she could see holos showing air-traffic patterns, perimeter security, stats on the power plant, and—of all things—at least a half-dozen examples of local Bakunin entertainment programming.

Then they were past the partition, and Shane noticed that she and Zanzibar had lost their escort.

Zanzibar led her down the corridor, through three security checks and two armored doors.

Eventually, after they had passed more security than she'd have needed to go through to board the *Blood-Tide,* Zanzibar stopped in front of an unmarked door.

The door whooshed open on a plushly appointed office decorated in mirrors and off-world woods. For a brain-numbing moment she thought that the person sitting behind the desk was Colonel Klaus Dacham.

The brain-lock lasted only a few seconds. The man behind the desk was slightly taller, less stocky, his face and hands less lined.

But he could be the colonel's son, he looked so similar.

The man waved to a chair opposite the desk and said, "Please sit."

Shane took a step forward, and the door whooshed shut behind her. She felt every muscle in her body twitch at the noise. That was the point at which she realized exactly how nervous she was. Shane was suddenly aware of the way her heart was pounding and that her face was flushed and sweating—

You'd think I was just about to enter combat.

She looked back at the man behind the desk. He regarded her with eyes as polished brown as the wood lining his office.

Maybe I am.

Shane took the offered seat and began to realize whom she was facing. "You're Dominic Magnus, aren't you? CEO of Godwin Arms."

He tilted his head in an almost imperceptible nod. "And you're Captain Katherine Shane, one of the officers who divested me of that title." The flat way he said that was more frightening than the colonel's trembling rages.

"I think I may have divested myself of my own title," Shane said.

The small nod again. "So it would seem." Damn it, did he think that she was a plant? Did they think all those prisoners were a cover to get her in here?

Well, Shane thought, *it's what I would think.*

He continued. "You committed no small act by freeing my employees. You could be charged with treason, mutiny, and desertion. Not to mention a score of other charges."

Shane sat up straight. "It was an illegal order, sir."

Huh? Why was she justifying herself to him?

"You were obligated only to refuse the order. Not to give aid and comfort to the enemy."

Maybe it was the colonel in some sort of disguise, here to torment her.

"Simply refusing the order would have landed me in the brig, sir."

"But then you could have defended your actions. No court-martial would have convicted you."

"But there would have been eight hundred corpses, sir."

"Treason carries the death penalty, Shane."

"You're assuming I could live with the alternative on my conscience, sir."

There was a long pause. Then he said, "Do me a favor and stop calling me 'sir.' "

"What should I call you?"

"Dom, Mr. Magnus, 'hey you.' At this point, 'sir' is not very appropriate." He stood up and faced a long mirror behind his desk. He clasped his hands behind him; one finger was twitching rhythmically. "Forgive the questions, but I need to have a good idea of your state of mind."

"Why?"

"I'll get to that. First, though, I want you to know how grateful I am that you did save my people.

"Look, it was—"

"I know something of what you went through, making that decision. I had a similar trial, fifteen years ago. I know what kind of wounds that can leave." His hands dropped.

Shane stayed quiet. Colonel Dacham had personally briefed the team on this man. She knew that Magnus had been an officer high in the Executive Command up until fifteen years ago. Colonel Dacham insisted that Magnus had turned traitor, began fighting everything the Confederacy stood for, etcetera.

Shane felt an involuntary wave of sympathy for the man in front of her.

He turned around, putting his hands on the desk. "Something like this doesn't happen suddenly."

"What do you mean?" Was he accusing her of something? It didn't sound like it. But it didn't seem his emotions ever touched his voice.

"You must have been dissatisfied with your command, the marines, long before you'd be *able* to make a decision like that."

"But—" Shane began to object, but she had the sinking feeling that Dominic Magnus was right. For a long time, especially after she became an officer, she'd been hiding a growing disillusionment with the marines—even from herself. When had she thought of herself, in the few moments she'd been brutally honest, as anything other than a government-sanctioned mercenary? How long had it been since she'd honestly believed what the briefings said, that they were on the side of the angels?

How long?

Years.

He was nodding at her, as if he could read her chain of thought. "What commanded your loyalty, Shane?"

Good question. She thought about it for a long time. It wasn't the Confederacy, which she'd always seen as a self-perpetuating bureaucracy only interested in preserving the status quo. It wasn't the planetary governments, a lot of whom were pretty nasty and deserved the rebellions that it was her job to put down. Certainly not the TEC. Not even the Occisis marines themselves. That realization hit home, because there was a time when the marines were everything, the marines were her honor. It had been a long time since she'd felt that, she realized. The dozen petty little conflicts she'd been witness to had sapped that out of her.

There really was only one thing that had commanded her loyalty in the end.

"My people," she said.

Her people, her team, her command, her *friends*. All of whom had become strangers ever since Colonel Dacham had taken charge. She felt warmth by her eyes and hoped Magnus wouldn't notice her tears.

"My people," she repeated coldly.

"That's good," Magnus said. "That's the only loyalty worth anything." He sank back into his seat, nodding. "So what do you want to do, Shane?"

Put my hands around Klaus Dacham's neck and slam his head into a bulkhead until his brains ooze out of his mouth.

"I don't know," she said.

He made a steeple of his fingers and looked at her over his tapping forefingers. "Perhaps I can offer a suggestion or two."

CHAPTER SEVENTEEN

Loyal Opposition

"The future is the past's revenge."
                    —*The Cynic's Book of Wisdom*

"We are dead men on furlough."
                    —VLADIMIR ILYICH LENIN
                    (1870–1924)

Dominic Magnus was barely aware he was going to recruit Shane until he had done it. It made little sense on the surface, especially as careful as he was being with every other potential member of the team.

It might have been a wave of empathy he felt for Shane. Her forced renunciation of the Confederacy was painfully akin to his own.

Of course, she was lucky enough to come to her decision before people died.

Once he had extended his hand, the corporate leader took over, and he found that he couldn't withdraw it. Even as Shane stared and tried to refuse his offer, Dom found himself playing Lucifer and turning the offer into something she couldn't deny.

It wouldn't be a betrayal, he told her. If she were involved in their heist, her information might actually save the lives of the marines. Perhaps it could even be an act of contrition.

Dom hated himself for the words even as he said them. She was vulnerable, and he was twisting her ...

But the corporation needed her. His people needed her. He wove his argument seamlessly, even after Shane told him who was in command of the GA&A takeover.

Dom left the interview amazed at how calm he was acting. He walked around to the observation room, hands clenching unconsciously. For once, his nervous tics were the farthest thing from his mind.

The door slid aside on Tetsami and Zanzibar, who sat on the other side of the massive one-way mirror behind the desk in the interview room. He could see Shane, still sitting in the room beyond the mirror. Shane had a bemused expression. Dom thought he might have left a little abruptly.

Zanzibar was seated at the monitor's station, but right now she was ignoring the displays recording Shane's blood pressure, skin galvanity, pupil dilation, etcetera. Instead, she was looking at Dom with an expression of concern.

"Sir," Zanzibar's voice was softer now than it normally was. "She could be lying about—"

"Escort her back to her room. I'll finish the interview later." Dom said it slowly and deliberately. He wasn't sure his mouth would work.

Zanzibar looked at him for a long moment, slowly nodded, and left.

Tetsami looked back through the mirror at Shane. "Are you sure it's a good idea involving her?"

"The information she has is invaluable."

"What if she's a plant?"

"She's not a plant," Dom said coldly.

Tetsami turned around slowly and looked at him, really looked at him, for the first time since he'd come into the room. Her expression now showed some of the concern that had crossed Zanzibar's. Dom realized his cheek was twitching.

"Are you all right?" she asked.

"A plant would not have mentioned my—" Dom raised

a shaking hand to his face. "Would not have mentioned
Klaus Dacham to me."

"Can I do some—"

"I need to be alone," Dom whispered.

"But—"

"Now!"

Tetsami circled around him, looking as though she
was trying to decide whether or not to be scared. She was
through the door before Dom could see which won.

Dom was alone in the observation room.

"Klaus," he whispered. The harsh name scraped his
throat.

He watched as Zanzibar entered the interview room
and escorted Shane out. Zanzibar had known him for the
better part of a decade, and she could only suspect what
this meant. She'd seen only the fringes of the wound that
Klaus Dacham was clawing open. Tetsami had no idea.
And Shane—

She thought that GA&A had just been stage one in
some larger TEC operation.

Did that matter? Would it matter to Klaus?

Helen Dacham's death had affected both of her sons.
Perhaps Klaus even more than him. Amazing how trag-
edy could sharpen parts of life once thought faded.

Helen was their only parent. She had not been a good
mother. She'd been prone to extreme emotion. She drank.
She beat her sons. She had her sons beg from Waldgrave's tourists.

The Executive Command had been a way for both of
them, him and Klaus, to escape.

Escape.

Escape was all Dom had ever tried to do.

His hands were on top of the observation chair Zanzibar had been sitting in. His left hand clenched through the
upholstery on the headrest, all the way to the chair's metallic skeleton.

It had been after Dom's greatest success as a TEC officer. He had single-handedly "suppressed" a military
coup on Styx without losing a single TEC operative. He

had received commendations on the deftness of the surgical strike.

It was in the glow of that victory that he had received word that Helen Dacham had been on Styx, in Perdition.

Perdition, a city that no longer existed.

He deserted the TEC and had lived within the cracks of the Confederacy until—

For the first time in a decade, he had to face something totally unexpected. And, again, it was his brother.

He looked up at the empty observation room and realized that his whole body was shaking.

"My God, Klaus. *Wasn't it* enough *for you?*"

He pulled on the chair, and his left hand yanked it free of the shaft in the floor. There was a screech as the metal under his left hand bent. He barely felt the pseudoflesh on his fingers crush and give way.

"You killed me already!"

Dom swung the chair at the observation window. The one-way mirror was armored, and the chair bounced off it, starring the view of the interview room and setting off a dozen red lights on the observation console. Dom swung the chair again. . . .

"*What the hell are you doing here, Klaus?*"
"*Don't you know?*"
"*The Command?*"
Klaus laughs.

The chair hit the window again. It bounced, leaving a concave depression where it hit.

"*Gunrunning is low on the Executive priority list at the moment. This is personal.*" *Klaus is no longer laughing.*

"*What are you talking about?*" *Jonah backs to the railing, wondering where his security is. He's been out of the game since Styx. Five years. Longer since he'd seen his brother.*

"*You could have saved her, Dominic.*"

God, no.

* * *

Dom swung the chair harder. The sound was even louder this time, and white dust blew from the cracks in the window. The view into the interview room became fractured and rainbow-colored. Somewhere a siren blared.

"What could I, anyone, have done?"
"Shut up! It was that damn Styx operation!"
"Talk sense! That was a black op. There was no way the TEC—"

Dom swung the chair and the observation window exploded.

Klaus' gun fires and Jonah tumbles over the railing, a hole in his shoulder.

The chair sailed through in a cloud of polymer glass fragments.

Jonah tumbles through the air. Above him is a blue cloudless sky. Below him is the green foam of the waste reclamation tank. Blue. Green. Blue. Green.

The pieces of the window twinkled as they fell, a mutant snowfall, alternately seeming transparent and mirrored. Glass. Mirror. Glass. Mirror.

Blue. Green.

Glass. Mirror.

He splashes into the waste tank. The tailored bacteria begin to feed. The pain begins.

There was a crash as the remains of the window hit the ground. The chair bounced off the desk in the interview room, spun, and tumbled to the ground. In the distance, the sirens continued.

Dom raised his left hand and saw lacerations on the

pseudoflesh leaking clear liquid. The pigment was off, and it looked as though he was beholding a flayed chromium skeleton.

Dom wanted to cry but found himself unable to.

CHAPTER EIGHTEEN

Glass Ceilings

"We hate that which is too much like ourselves."
—*The Cynic's Book of Wisdom*

"There is as much difference between us and ourselves
as between us and others."
—MICHEL DE MONTAIGNE
(1533–1592)

Tetsami followed Zanzibar and Shane out of the control
center and almost jumped out of her skin when the alarm
sounded.

Ahead of her, Zanzibar inclined her head slightly, as if
listening to something, and turned around. "That's nothing to be concerned about."

From your face, it don't look it, lady.

However, Tetsami didn't challenge her. It was probably
the truth—as far as it went. The only one in any immediate danger was probably Dom. Whatever mainspring had
been tightening in the CEO-man's skull had been close to
snapping ever since she'd met the guy.

Tetsami rode in the elevator with Zanzibar and the
prisoner, and decided that she was pretty damn sick of
surprises.

This whole damn complex was one of Dom's surprises—just like the insurance money. It seemed that ev-

ery time she almost believed he thought of her as a
partner in this heist, every time she believed that they
might actually have an equal share of this crap, something was sprung to remind her that she was way out of
her depth.

Damn it, it was *her* job. Dom might be backing the enterprise, but without her he'd be lost. He wouldn't even
know what he needed. If this were any other group of
Godwin freelancers, she'd be in command of this heist.

But Dom wasn't another Godwin freelancer. He was a
CEO-man who breathed his own superiority as if it was
air.

She wanted to strangle him.

"Since we made it unobserved to Proudhon, I think it's
probably safe to link up with some of my people on the
way back," he'd said.

Some of his people, sheesh.

"Some people" turned out to be just about fourteen
hundred employees who had managed to escape the invasion of GA&A, and the linkup place happened to be a
massive commune that Dom had apparently invested in
sometime during the past year.

A bolt-hole known *only* to him and his security people,
just in case, as though he was expecting all this crap.

In other words, he owned the place outright. The
Diderot Commune was an asset that was worth that
cashed-in insurance policy several times over.

The elevator reached one of the residential sublevels
and Zanzibar deposited the prisoner—or was Shane an
ally now? Once the door closed, the two of them were left
alone in the corridor. Tetsami noted the absence of the
two guards that had accompanied Shane up to the control
center and decided that Shane was, indeed, an ally.

Dom's security chief was looking at her with an expression of vague disapproval. "We'll need to find you
quarters for the night, and get you on the security computers."

Tetsami shrugged. Zanzibar was another surprise, one
that Tetsami didn't like, though she couldn't say why.

No, that was a little self-deception. Tetsami knew exactly why she didn't like Zanzibar. It was because Zanzibar seemed to know Dom so much better than she did. A stupid thing to be irritated by. After all, Zanzibar had apparently been working for Dom ever since GA&A got off the ground.

"Follow me." Zanzibar waved her along. As Tetsami followed her, she decided that Zanzibar's height didn't help.

Tetsami startled herself by asking Zanzibar, "You don't like me, do you?"

The question seemed to take Zanzibar aback. She stopped walking and looked down at Tetsami. They had stopped in one of the ubiquitous half-finished corridors that peppered the massive commune building like cholesterol deposits in an old circulatory system. "Why do you say that?"

"Come on. Ever since I got here, you've been treating me like an active germ culture—or maybe a census taker. You look like you really want to throw me in with our marine friend."

Zanzibar shook her head and resumed walking. "You exaggerate."

"Yeah, if your voice got any colder, you'd lose your tongue to frostbite."

Zanzibar didn't stop, but cast a withering glance over her shoulder at Tetsami.

Great, Tetsami thought, *alienate Dom's employees. He's already suggested that Zanzibar might make part of the team—*

That was just it. Tetsami was the one planning the damn break-in, and she didn't like Zanzibar. Not at all. From the looks of things, the feeling was very mutual.

Tetsami ended the day in a little modular apartment near the core of the commune. A place she supposed was pretty much like the place where they'd filed Captain Shane. Zanzibar had programmed Tetsami's security clearance into the base computer looking as though she were undergoing an amputation without an anesthetic.

When Tetsami was left alone in her room, the first thing she did was make sure the door was unlocked.

"I'm not having second thoughts—more like tenth or twentieth."

She sighed and sat in a recliner facing the built-in holo. There were controls on the armrest, and she switched the holo through the local airspace without really paying much attention to it. She stopped on a scene where two overlapping channels were warring on the air, playing the game "Who's got more wattage?"

She stared through the rainbow-blurred imagery and thought of the job she was supposed to do.

Objectively, she was doing well. The people they needed were falling into place. Even if she didn't *like* Zanzibar, Zanzibar had been chief of security at GA&A before the Confederacy happened to the place. Was there anyone she'd prefer to have in on the break-in?

Shane, a defecting member of the team that took GA&A over had to be high on the list.

And even if she didn't like AIs—no, that was too kind. They were creepy, perverted, and scared the bejesus out of her. But, even if she didn't like Mosasa's little machine, Random Walk, a Race-built AI machine could run rings around any human-built computer. That's why they were one of the few things that were illegal throughout the Confederacy. Capital crime to run one.

That, and genetically engineering a sentient being, Tetsami thought.

"Admit it, you don't like Mosasa's toy because it reminds you—"

Reminds me that I'm not really human.

Random Walk's circuitry was a relic of a few centuries past, just as Tetsami's genes were a relic. The birth of the Tetsami clan occurred back when every nation was still jammed onto one planet, when the scientists were still klutzing around with the stuff of life.

When the Wars of Unification came, the UN command decided that engineering human-level intelligences wasn't a good idea. Every citizen whose genes had been fiddled with got shot down a convenient wormhole like the rest of the undesirables.

In the end the genetic undesirables got Tau Ceti, a system lucky enough to have two inhabitable planets. The Tetsamis got the frozen ball of Dakota, along with all the other engineered humans. All the other genetic products got Haven and, eventually, five planets beyond.

The Seven Worlds was now one of the five arms of the Confederacy.

Tetsami's parents had escaped Dakota—a rather unpleasant place with one of the more despotic regimes in the Confederacy—and came here, Bakunin. The pair of them managed to parley their genetic and technical heritage into high-paying high-class jobs as executive combat hackers.

It was a prestige job that, in the end, got them killed.

Tetsami was barely old enough to understand what was going on when Ivor Jorgenson smuggled her out of the wreckage. Eventually, despite Ivor's objections, Tetsami followed in her parents' footsteps—up to a point.

Tetsami distrusted all corporations and had long ago promised herself that she would be a permanent freelancer. She'd never sell her soul to a corporation, even though she might make ten times what she lived on in the streets.

And, eventually, she would abandon this shithole of a planet.

What burned her was the fact that to do that, she would have to disguise her heritage. If someone discovered her roots, they were likely to look at her the way she looked at Random Walk. This despite the fact that by the time the Tetsamis' bloodline had reached her generation, her genes were as human as the next woman's. A thorough gene scan on her probably wouldn't even show anything unusual.

The only gift from her parents was her exceptional facility with a bio-interface.

Even though she could prove her humanity with a gene scan, she'd *still* be treated like a freak.

Maybe *that* was Zanzibar's problem.

Her train of thought was derailed by an annoying buzz. The buzz repeated a few times before she realized that it was the door. She opened her eyes, realizing that she'd nodded off long enough for the gladiatorial contest to win the wattage war over the demolition derby.

She went to the door and opened it. Standing outside, in the hall, was Dominic Magnus. He looked—*odd*.

"Can I come in?"

Tetsami shrugged and stood aside, not quite certain whether or not she was irritated at her "partner."

Dom walked in and spared a glance at the holo, where two hypertrophic steroid junkies were dueling with a pair of chain saws. He shook his head slightly and settled on the edge of her bed.

"I wouldn't blame you for being angry at me," he said.

Tetsami settled into the chair and killed the holo during a particularly gruesome parry. "Dom, I don't know if I'm pissed or not yet."

Dom sighed. Tetsami decided why he looked so strange. He looked tired. The look of fatigue was radically out of place on his face. It was as if a marble statue had suddenly sneezed. "I'm sorry for snapping at you back there. The news caught me a lit—"

Tetsami suddenly realized that they were on two very different wavelengths. "Whoa there, hold it a minute."

"What?"

"You think that you being upset is why I should be pissed?"

Dom looked confused.

"Okay, I didn't say that quite right." She took a breath and started again. "Dom, if I'm angry at you, it's not because you flipped a gear back there."

Something she said actually made him wince.

"But I wanna know, CEO-man, if I'm your partner in this, or if I'm just another frigging employee."

"Partner," Dom said quietly, as if he didn't quite understand the word.

She was beginning to realize that Dom hadn't been thinking along these lines at all. "Damn straight. You might be financing this op, but I'm *planning* this thing.

We pulled each other out of the shit. We'd be dead without each other—and this heist would never've been born."

"I know."

"I thought we were in this together."

"We are."

"Oh, we are?" Tetsami stood up and kicked the holo display. "Then why the fuck didn't you let on about this place?"

Dom inhaled. "I was keeping it secret. They're after GA&A employees and I didn't want to lead—"

"That kept you from telling *me*? You've pulled Zanzibar and Shane on to the team without even talking to me!"

"They fill the requirements, and Shane knows—"

"I don't give a shit what Shane knows! For *all* you know she could be the ever-loving colonel's mistress. And that ain't the point."

Dom sat there, quietly, for a long time. After a while he said, "I suppose it isn't."

"So, am I your partner? Or am I just another employee you get to order around?"

"And if I say you're an employee?"

Oh, you fucking bastard. "I'll get that box cracked if you give me a kangaroo to work with. But I'm gone once I get paid. Way gone."

"What if you're my partner?"

What's the difference, really? She was planning to blow this rock whatever happened. "I don't know."

"I came here for another reason, too."

"What?" She didn't like him just changing the subject like that.

"The window is closing. According to Shane, GA&A is part of a larger Confed operation. Once they get GA&A fully operational, they go on to Phase Two."

"Which is?"

Dom shrugged. "Need to know, Shane didn't. Anyway, getting GA&A operational requires a new mainframe. They're importing one from off-planet. It'll be here in little over a week. Ten days, installed."

"And a new mainframe means a new security system."
Great, just what we needed.

"So we have to go before it goes on-line or me, Zanzibar, and a dozen Paralian ship experts won't make a difference."

"You just made my day. A week?"

"Ten days, *partner.*"

Tetsami looked at Dom and smiled. "You bastard."

"I've been called worse."

"I'm sure."

"We need to fill the holes left in the team, and you need to polish up our plan for getting in."

"And out."

"And out," Dom agreed.

"All we need is a ship expert and a driver. Levy said he knew a ship expert, and the pilot I contacted is back in Godwin by now."

"Good, take Zanzibar and Shane back to Godwin and get things moving."

"What about you?" Tetsami tentatively stuck out her hand toward him.

"I'll meet you at the warehouse in a couple of days. I have to do things here." He reached in the pocket of his jumpsuit and pulled out a small computer and placed it in Tetsami's outstretched hand. "Here's a line on our liquid assets, in case you need anything."

Tetsami stared at her hand, taken by surprise *again.*

She could swear that she could feel the weight of the three hundred-some K they had left in the account. Dom left her there, staring at the computer that held all that money in virtual limbo.

She felt vaguely pissed again, but for no real reason.
I'm his partner all right.
Bastard.
Only a week. . . .

CHAPTER NINETEEN

Leaks

"We are the property of those we hate."
—*The Cynic's Book of Wisdom*

"It is a strange desire to seek power and to lose
liberty."

—FRANCIS BACON
(1561–1626)

"I don't like insubordination, *Captain* Murphy."

Murphy was rigid and as unmoving as a statue. "No,
sir."

Klaus was receiving Murphy is his current command
center, Dominic's old office. By all rights, Klaus should
have been happy with the way the operation was going.
Phase one of Rasputin was proceeding apace. In eight
Bakunin days the new mainframe would arrive. The residence tower was now filled with Confederacy people, his
people.

However, Klaus wasn't happy.

First there'd been his brother.

Then there was Shane.

Now this.

"I don't like disobedience."

"No, sir."

Klaus sighed. Was he getting through to this man? Did

Murphy understand what this meant? First there was Shane, then these five marines, then ... It was like a virus, it had to be excised before the entire company was infected.

"What am I going to do with these people?"

"I have them under house arrest, sir."

"Is that a suitable punishment for mutiny, Murphy?"

Murphy's gaze looked shallow and far away.

"The teams I'm sending into Godwin are necessary to this mission. I cannot accept *any* disobedience. Especially because, thanks to one traitor, there are nearly fourteen hundred enemy agents still unaccounted for."

"Yes, sir."

"An extreme circumstance calls for extreme measures, don't you think?"

Murphy was silent.

"Don't you think, *Captain* Murphy?"

After a long pause, Murphy said, "Yes, sir."

"Good. I want the first of them, the squad leader, prepped for the interrogation room in the *Blood-Tide*. The rest, I want them to observe."

Murphy stood there.

"Dismissed."

Murphy turned on his heel and left.

Klaus knew he was having this trouble because of Shane. If it weren't for her sending the containment operation balls-up, none of these solders would even think of disobeying his orders.

Shane and command at TEC. His subordinates were quoting TEC orders back at him. "No widening of the operation beyond the complex until phase one is completed."

Damn it. *He* was the one on the ground here. He was the one who gave the orders. He was the one who answered to the TEC. He was in control of an operation once it hit dirt—

Why did they sabotage his authority?

Why did Dimitri sabotage his authority? Klaus knew he was doing what the old man wanted. Klaus had thought long and hard, and he'd decided that neutralizing

"Dominic Magnus" had to be part of his unwritten mission.

Otherwise, why send him?

Klaus turned the chair and faced Godwin out the side of the transparent dome. The city looked like a glowing fungus in the sunset. Some malignant growth that you'd find under a rock. All of Bakunin was like that, a throbbing cancer in the side of the Confederacy.

He was the surgeon.

He would have advocated blasting this place to the bedrock. Flash this entire criminal nation into infinity from orbit. That would have solved both problems, his and the Confederacy's.

No, Klaus thought, *that would be too easy. And they need a planet with a population of a half-billion or so. Half a billion people and eighty years standard.*

Bakunin had over a billion people, and it'd been occupied for a hundred and four years.

"You did pick the perfect place to nest, didn't you—brother?"

A cesspit of disease and perversion. A boiling swamp just like the one Klaus had thought his brother had died in.

No mistakes this time. Klaus wouldn't finish until he had Dom's corpse in his arms.

The holo built into his desk beeped for his attention. Someone had finally gotten around to fixing the thing so it didn't give Klaus headaches every time he looked at it. He answered the call.

Looking out of the holo was Jonathan Whissen-Hall, one of the civilians who'd come on the *Blood-Tide*. He was the TEC communications officer, the one with the security clearance to handle the coded messages.

"What is it, Mr. Hall?" Klaus was aware that truncating his hyphenated name was irritating to Whissen-Hall, but the damn thing was too long, and Whissen-Hall kept any irritation below the level of insubordination.

"Our first synchronization call came in on the tach-comm."

"Oh?" Things were speeding along. "How's our schedule?"

"Well within the margin. The first sync signal was pulsed from Earth day three-oh after we left."

"Good. How long do we have to the Congress?"

"Counting the lag, sixty-five days standard."

That was a tight deadline, until Klaus factored in the duration of the Congress—which would stay in session for nearly six months. "Anything important sent with the sync message?" Klaus asked.

"Late intel on Bakunin, some other things. I'll upload a secure package to your office."

Klaus nodded and broke the connection.

Well, he and the Executive were on the same clocks now. And now that he thought of clocks—

He looked over his shoulder at Godwin. The overlarge red-yellow orb of Kropotkin was setting. It was time to talk to Webster.

He checked to make sure that the outer door was locked and took out his secure holo. He put it on the desk, let it check his DNA, and typed in the seed.

Soon, Webster's voice came from the blue spherical test pattern. "Hello, Colonel."

"Any news?"

"The score stands at Bakuninite gunrunners, one thousand three hundred eighty-seven. Confederacy, zero."

"No one's unearthed *any* more GA&A personnel?"

"Funny thing about people, Colonel. You start shooting at them, they hide." Klaus didn't like Webster's sarcastic tone. However, Webster was the only operative he had who was free of Executive interference.

"You *can't* hide that many people."

"Colonel, this is a *planet* you're talking about. Godwin itself has a population of ten million, and your targets could have disappeared anywhere between Troy and Proudhon by now. If they made Proudhon, they could be off-planet."

Klaus pounded the side of the chair with his fist. He didn't like needing people like Webster. "They have to be together, somewhere. Somewhere close."

Eight hundred people couldn't just vanish into the woods in less than three hours.

"The only people who would know would be Dominic's people." Webster sounded strange, as though he wasn't telling Klaus everything. Klaus hated that.

"Any news about Dominic?"

"Yes."

"He's holed up with his people?"

"No. He's been spreading stories about searching for Dolbrian artifacts in the mountains." Webster sounded as though he found that amusing.

"Huh?"

"That's the information I have. A cover for something."

I can see that, Klaus thought. "No current location?"

"It might be a good idea to prep for something against GA&A."

Dominic would be a fool to try to retake GA&A. "I'll take that under advisement."

"Cheer up, I do have some good news."

"What?"

"Remember that 'traitorous bitch,' as I believe you called her? Kathy Shane?"

Klaus leaned toward the holo, suddenly interested. "Yes?"

"I have some information on where she's going to be. . . ."

CHAPTER TWENTY

Executive Action

"Bravery comes when there are no other options."
—*The Cynic's Book of Wisdom*

"It is the policy of this government to fire when fired upon."

—DAMION CASTLE
(1996–2065)

Tetsami was concentrating on maneuvering through the chaotic Godwin traffic, so she missed it the first time Shane asked.

"What?" Tetsami asked as she turned the van on to one of the elevated roads into Central Godwin.

"Does that tunnel really go right under the GA&A complex?"

"Yep."

The traffic on the overpass was a little better mannered. Commuting execs mostly, even though it was pretty close to midnight. One thing Godwin didn't do was keep regular hours.

"A glaring hole in security," Zanzibar said, with enough annoyance that one might think she was still in charge of security for the complex.

Tetsami shrugged. Security's loss was their gain. "It wasn't there when the complex was built. The project went bankrupt, I hear, because of angry people who didn't like their foundations undermined. They laid siege to the backers until they agreed to pay them off."

Shane looked at Tetsami as though she'd said something unusual. "You don't mean they sued, do you?"

Tetsami burst out laughing, and even Zanzibar seemed to crack a smile.

Shane shook her head and looked out at the high-rises that were sliding by the van. "Do you know anything about this 'Paralian ship expert' your friend is introducing us to?"

"No," Tetsami said. "We kept our communication as short as possible." With barely concealed irritation she added, "Dom said this 'Flower' guy checks."

Of course Dom had waited until they were leaving to volunteer that information. He'd said it in an aside, as if it wasn't really that important that he was double-checking everything himself, in secret.

So, Dom? Do I check? The bastard probably had a file on her. The bastard probably had a file on everybody.

They were coming up on a major intersection, and Tetsami began slowing the contragrav van. In front of them, beyond the cross-street, another Godwin monolith was going up. Right now it was just a metal skeleton bracketed by four gigantic robot cranes, their arms reaching over the street and the neighboring—shorter—buildings.

As Tetsami slowed the van, Shane said, "Flower—" From the sound, Shane had a low opinion of any expert on Paralian ship design that could be found on Bakunin.

"Just because—" Tetsami began.

"Down!" Shane yelled suddenly, folding into her own footwell. She barely got out the word, "Sniper!" when a line of razor-straight polychromatic brilliance sliced through the body of the van.

Tetsami clicked on her personal field even as she realized that it was going to do little against the carbine the sniper was wielding. It had sliced through the van in a well-aimed shot that had taken out all the maneuvering controls. All she had left was the power to the contragrav.

Without thinking about what she was doing—only that she had to get away—Tetsami goosed the contragrav.

As the van slid forward, accelerating and rising, something large and explosive clipped the rear. A dull boom shook the van and suddenly the air inside was hot and rancid. One of the loading doors in the rear fell away—Tetsami heard it. Zanzibar cursed in a language Tetsami didn't understand.

Something slammed into the side of the van—vehicle or weapon she couldn't tell—and suddenly *all* the van's controls were unresponsive. The van drifted off the road, still going top speed. They lost altitude and shot toward the construction.

With the controls dead and the construction zooming at her, Tetsami closed her eyes and covered her face with her arms.

More shots. The van hit something and vibrated like a bass drum. A dull explosion and an ozone smell told Tetsami that the batteries had exploded. The van tilted and, after an excruciating half-second, rolled. Then, abruptly, it slammed to a bone-jarring halt.

"Fuck. Fuck. Fuck." Tetsami began to untangle herself from the harness. The van was on its side, the floor wrapped around the base of one of the crane towers. "Who's hurt?"

Zanzibar was crawling out from a pile of boxes that littered the back of the van. The boxes had been carrying Shane's powered armor, and Zanzibar—still cursing—finished ripping open one crate and pulled out an assault weapon. Beyond the security chief, the rear half of the van was gone.

"Shane!" Zanzibar yelled, ignoring Tetsami. "Shane! Who are they? How many? Where?"

Damn it, Zanzibar, she might be dead. Tetsami uncurled from the seat and found footing to stand upright. They only had minutes, maybe seconds—and Shane was the only one to see their attackers. Tetsami looked at Shane, who was still wedged in the passenger footwell where she'd taken cover. Shane was now in a fetal position, glued to the ground by the chair and the warped front of the van.

"Shane?" Tetsami said.

There was a groan and Zanzibar almost pushed Tetsami aside to get at Shane. That was enough. "Damn it, Zanzibar! Cover our ass. You've got the fucking weapon!"

Zanzibar looked startled.

"NOW!"

The mental logjam broke, and Zanzibar took cover and watched out the broken rear of the van.

That was a waste of three seconds. "Shane?"

Another moan. Then, "I think I'm trapped in here."

"Where are they?"

"Only saw the one. Octagonal high-rise. Roof. North." Shane began to breathe heavy. "Marines. Colonel's cleanup crew."

"How many?"

Shane took a long time to answer. After another moan she said, "At least three. Snipers cover the intersection, ambush. Ground team, maybe."

Shane had to pause to breathe. Her voice sounded wet. "Circle to get us . . ." Shane's voice faded and she didn't respond when Tetsami tried to rouse her. At least her breathing was steady.

After too long assessing Shane's condition, Tetsami asked, "You hear that, Zanzibar?"

"Yes, damn it. This weapon gives us shit for cover from those snipers. It's a short-range plasma rifle. It'd hold off a ground team, for a while. But the snipers can hold us down here indefinitely. All they have to do is frag the van."

"You see any snipers?"

"One. The guy who took off the rear of the van is halfway up the trapezoidal building to the east of the intersection."

"Any cover out there?"

"The construction above us blocks the guy to the north. But the guy to our east—" She waved out the missing rear of the van with her gun. "I could look right at him if I took a step outside. Right on the other side of the highway from us."

"Does the road offer any cover?"

"Thirty meters of open dirt with no cover between here and there. We'd never make it."

"No idea where number three is?"

"Not even if there *is* a number three."

Now what? Tetsami looked out the shattered windscreen in the front of the van. The van had come to rest at the southeast corner of the construction. She was looking down the length of the south side of the building, looking at robot workers, stacks of construction equipment, the foreman's command trailer, and the base of one of the massive, now-frozen construction cranes.

Tetsami got an idea.

She scrambled over next to Zanzibar at the other end of the van to see out the back.

"Watch it! A few more centimeters and you'll be in the line of fire."

Across the dirt no-man's-land was the highway, on the other side of the highway was the base of the tower that supported the second sniper, and over the intersection was the ass end of the northeast crane—shorter than the business end, it stuck out well over the intersection.

Tetsami stumbled over to the front and the windshield, but she couldn't see the business end of the crane. She tried to remember if it was one that carried a girder. As she tried to see it up through the skeleton of the new building, she decided it had been.

"Zanzibar, I'm going to try something."

"What?"

"I'm making for the foreman's trailer."

"What?" Zanzibar looked over her shoulder at Tetsami, then toward the windshield and the trailer. "That's fifty meters, in the open, with no idea where the third sniper is."

"I'm covered from the first two, and I have a force field."

"One and a half seconds max against a military laser carbine."

"Cover me if someone starts firing."

"Damn it, this thing has no range."

"It's a bright light that'll screw up their aim."

"Oh, shit," Zanzibar ducked and made over to the windshield so she could cover Tetsami's run.

"Do you have any better ideas?"

"No, and that's the problem."

Tetsami spared one glance at the green light on her field generator. It was lit. Her otherwise-invisible field was operating.

She nodded at Zanzibar, stepped out the broken windshield, and began running. A flash dazzled her and she felt a fiery dagger lance into her right shoulder. Her force field had soaked up some of a carbine blast, but a lot had gotten through. She could smell synthetic fibers smoldering.

Tetsami was under the sights of the third sniper.

She kept running.

She weaved out from under the laser for a moment, and suddenly her shadow was dancing ahead of her, pointing toward the trailer. The massive ruddy light had to be Zanzibar's return fire. The plasma rifle was like a signal flare behind her.

Tetsami spared a breathless glance at her field generator, the indicator light faded from red to amber. Another beam lanced ahead of her and Tetsami ducked and rolled in the dirt.

Halfway there.

The third sniper was above her and to the right. That would put him somewhere up in the building's metal skeleton. Figured.

Tetsami leaped to her feet and kept running toward the trailer, and cover.

Another shot of energy hit her. The beam struck her leg, and she felt burning heat in her calf and smelled her jumpsuit starting to smolder. She looked down. A line of strobing color was diffracting into rainbow circles that flashed along the perimeter of her field over her leg, as if the laser had hit an invisible elliptical shell surrounding

her. The fact she saw anything at all meant that her field
generator was about a second from overload.

The box at her belt that generated that ellipsoid field
was flashing a red warning light and beeping at her furi-
ously. Her leg was beginning to cook.

Five meters from the trailer, she removed the generator
from her belt, tossing it as she jumped for the side of the
trailer.

She hit cover against the side of the foreman's trailer at
the same time her field generator exploded. Tetsami
crumpled to the ground, breathing heavily, waiting for
that laser carbine to slice her unprotected body in half.
After a few seconds it seemed that wasn't going to happen.

She looked up and back. Zanzibar was poking the
plasma rifle out the windshield and up toward the murky
scaffolding. As Tetsami watched, she pumped off a cone
of red-orange energy that hurt to look at and lit the entire
construction site. Zanzibar must've cranked the beam all
the way up. She glanced in Tetsami's direction and gave
her a thumbs-up.

Tetsami had been fortunate. The trailer was parked at
an angle to the construction. Its shadow blocked the third
sniper's view of her.

She stood up, right leg a little wobbly, and slid along
the trailer, back glued to its side. Near the rear she came
to an entrance. She tried the handle.

Locked—

"Damn it."

Such a simple thing, and it really fucked her plans. She
didn't have time to jimmy a lock.

*Okay, but what're the odds that there's someone in
there? Pretty good, right?* Tetsami nodded to herself.
Most folks would have at least one human supervisor on
a project like this. That was the guy who had shut things
down when the shit hit the fan.

Guy probably got a big bribe to let sniper number three
take his position up there.

External sensors had to see her, so how to do this?

"All right, I'm addressing the a-hole inside this can."

Tetsami put a hand in her coat and put on her best crazy expression. "I'm carrying a few AM grenades—you know how twitchy they are—if I buy it out here, you probably won't have to wait for my partner back there to frag the trailer." Zanzibar punctuated that with another spectacular shot into the superstructure. Tetsami silently thanked her.

Hell, if she had been carrying some antimatter grenades and the bottles went, they could probably say good-bye to the whole building. AM was a sneak weapon, no one was fool enough to carry it into open combat where a stray shot or EM pulse could turn you into a two-hundred-meter crater. Terrorists liked them because they were small and you couldn't really detect one—except when they malfunctioned.

Whether it was the AM threat, or Zanzibar behind her taking potshots with a plasma rifle, the door slid open for her. She piled inside, pushing aside a pale straw-haired guy who couldn't be any older than she was. He stammered, "L–look I don't know what's going on. I don't want any trouble here. The company is going to—"

"The company's going to hang you, boy, for letting that marine geek up there."

"I had nothing to do—"

"Shut up."

Tetsami made her way down the length of the trailer. One end was dominated by a control center. The walls were alive with screens showing the POV of various robot workers. There was a massive computer board, displays showing elevations of the structure being built, blinking lights—a lot of fire warnings, Tetsami noted—a comm tap into the wider computer net, and—just what Tetsami was looking for—a bio-interface jack.

She pulled a small optical cable out of her pocket and checked the connections. They matched.

"Hey, you can't—"

"Don't fuck with me, Blondie, or I'll slice your balls off and jam them up your nose."

Blondie shut up.

She made the connection into the jack and made sure

the terminal was slaved to it. Then she took a few breaths to calm herself, and held the rounded end of the cable to the concavity in the skin at the base of her neck.

The magnetic end of the cable went home with a click audible through the bones of her skull. It took a fraction of a second for software and hardware to engage each other. It always seemed an eternity to her. She knew that it was her time sense telescoping, even before the hardwired interface programming got up to running speed. In a sense, her brain had been hardwired for the job even before she'd been born.

Time stretched into infinity. Her senses shut down. She fell into the bio-interface's shell programming. First there was a solid blue infinity, white noise, the smell of oranges, the feeling of pins and needles washing over her body. Then there was a jerk as the bio-interface's reality fell into place and gave her back the senses it didn't want.

It kept her vision and filled her point of view with a fairly pedestrian field full of control options: cubes labeled with icons, sliding over the same blue background. Her hearing dropped back to the real world, and she could hear Blondie's breathing. It sounded much too slow to her, as her time sense of the virtual world sped up way ahead of realtime. Kinesthetic and tactile senses dropped out too, except for her right hand, which apparently was the control surface.

The setup was primitive as hell, and buggy, too—she still smelled oranges.

Since the terminal software had given up her skin, she could feel a smile stab her cheeks.

Tetsami began walking through the software. Three levels into the surveillance option, she found out that the oranges weren't a bug. She tripped something, and the orange smell turned rotten and became a putrid stab through her forebrain. A security measure that would have knocked her out of the shell program if she weren't a pro.

She had barely noticed the smell change when she'd already started an internal dialogue with the hardware in her skull. She had cut out the olfactory I/O before the odor became crippling.

Should have done that earlier. Should have known the oranges weren't an artifact.

Didn't matter. Most folks couldn't cut out a slaved sense on the fly without losing the contact, but she had, so no harm done.

Since she was on a priority terminal for the construction computers, she didn't run afoul of any more stringent security. Most of the access-denied stuff was straddling external inputs. In less than three seconds she had cubes up showing windows on the construction scene.

She scanned the views as fast as she could, looking at the world through the eyes of dozens of robots. At one point, she heard Blondie's breathing change tempo and come closer. She yelled, "Don'teventhinkit."

She didn't know if he understood what she said at the speed she was operating, but it sounded as though he stopped moving.

Lock.

She found what she was looking for. She had the view from the northeast crane. The other views scrolled until she found cameras with views she wanted. A view looking at the armored marine on the roof of the building to the north, one looking at the sniper halfway up and in the corner of the eastern building, and another of the guy firing on the van from the tenth floor of the construction.

Now to hack the operations software.

Tetsami had to drop to the code to bypass some safety programs, all of which were frighteningly easy to override. It only took a little prodding to get the arm on the northeast crane to allow itself to go a complete 360.

She slipped into the control system of the crane while spinning off a few improv hyperprograms linking her multiple views of two of the snipers to the on-line engineering programs.

The crane was lifting a two-ton girder and rotating north as she fed the vectors and speeds to the engineering program.

The engineering program did as she asked and ran up a velocity profile and overlaid a schematic on her view out the crane's camera. Tetsami smiled again. The crane itself didn't reach, but since she'd killed the safety protocols, the engineering program had used its new freedom to get the girder where she wanted. It was easy now that she didn't require the girder's velocity to be zero at the end of its track.

She gave the program the okay to take over the placement of the girder.

The crane arm backed up a few degrees and began a rotation north, accelerating near the failure point of the mechanism. The end of the cable shot to the end of the crane arm, and the girder swung out over the road like a stick on a string. At a very specific point, the winches holding the cables let go and the girder was in free fall.

The sniper on the roof of the octagonal sky-rise must not have been watching above him. At almost the last minute he looked up, and the left half of the girder took him off at the knees.

The sniper was mulched by the two-ton bar of steel. The girder kept rolling, tearing up the roof, smashing antennas, landing lights, a few aircars, and the entrance to an elevator.

By then Tetsami had the northwest crane on-line, and that girder was already slicing through the corner of the twentieth story of the trapezoidal high-rise. This girder didn't have to go into free fall to do its job, and it stabbed through the corner of the building like a pin through a folded flap of skin.

Tetsami was lucky. She saw the sniper as he was thrown through the side of the building and tumbled toward the ground. She wouldn't have to swing the crane again.

Blondie began to scream.

It was a hideous slow-motion bellow that Tetsami first thought belonged to the carnage she was wreaking. Her nose, now stranded in realtime, told her otherwise. There was the smell of burning synthetics, overloaded circuitry, and burning flesh.

Sniper three wasn't a dope. He'd seen his friends get wasted and was trying to frag the control trailer. She was smelling a near miss. In a moment or two the geek was going to waste her.

So much for tactical genius. You should have wasted him first.

Tetsami got a fix on a camera with a view of the goof. He was in full armor, sort of half leaning and half clamped on the edge of floor ten. He was pointing his carbine down—toward her no doubt. As she watched, there was the stroboscopic flare from below—Zanzibar and the plasma rifle.

She expected to be blinded, but the cameras on the robot she was looking through adjusted to the light level without so much as a twitch. She looked for the ID of the robot. It was a plasma welder.

She took control of the thing and realized that she couldn't move it any nearer to the sniper without alerting him. The specs on this beast had it going no more than a klick an hour, max, and it was as big as he was with sinister looking manipulators and jets everywhere. With the plasma tanks on it, it looked like a bomb. . . .

Hell, it is *a bomb.*

Her connection fuzzed, and the trailer filled with the smell of another near miss. She didn't allow it to screw up her programming. The safety locks on the welder were a little tougher than the safety locks on the cranes, but she broke it in three seconds.

Even as her control died, she shot the improv program to the core of the welding robot.

Three simple commands: Close the welding aperture to zero, power up the plasma generators to max, and—after waiting a second—lose the magnetic containment.

The trailer rocked again, in the wake of a giant explosion. Tetsami jacked out the cable and fell into the real world. Blondie quivered in the corner. No laser sliced the trailer.

Her shot had been right on target.

CHAPTER TWENTY-ONE

Foreign Relations

"The difference between us and the alien is the belief
that we know ourselves that much better. The simi-
larity lies in the fact that we are ignorant of both."
—*The Cynic's Book of Wisdom*

"The ink of the scholar is more sacred than the blood
of the martyr."

—MUHAMMAD
(570–632)

Sergeant Mariah Zanzibar, for the first time in seven
years, found herself questioning Mr. Magnus' judgment.
Those doubts were perhaps the most painful thoughts to
cross her mind in those seven years. She had given her
loyalty to Dominic Magnus, and personal disloyalty was
one of the worst crimes she could think of—up there with
incest and fratricide.

She had tried to convince him, preach caution, warn
him about the people he was using. However, she'd
known she was preaching to deaf ears even before his interview with Shane.

She should have resigned then.

Instead, she had accepted his decision to go on with the
bizarre plan. He was right about her knowledge of GA&A
security. They needed her.

She should still have resigned in protest. It might have made him reconsider, though Zanzibar knew him well enough to know that would have been unlikely.

So, after having her protests brushed aside, she had gone along . . .

To end up shot full of holes in the middle of Godwin with the two people in Magnus' new organization that she trusted the least.

Even as she approached the intersection of Sacco and West Lenin, she still found it incredible that they had escaped from the ambush with their lives. Worse, she kept feeling unprofessional irritation at the fact that it was Tetsami who had saved them. Mr. Magnus had placed Tetsami in command of the trio, and she'd performed well—

That made Zanzibar mad.

Neither Tetsami nor Shane deserved his trust. Tetsami was a freelance software jock with no loyalty except to herself. Shane was a *traitor;* she had sold out every trust she had ever earned.

Zanzibar spat into the middle of the intersection. She checked the chronometer on her wrist—fifteen minutes late for the meeting. Not bad, considering she was on foot. Tetsami had stolen a truck from the construction site to evac Shane and get her to a medic, leaving Zanzibar to meet with their bookish contact, Levy, and the Paralian ship expert named "Flower."

What a name.

Zanzibar scanned the surrounding buildings for an ambush, and saw nothing. She tracked with the nearly discharged plasma rifle anyway. There might only be a half-second burst left on the thing, but its deterrence value helped keep the casual Bakunin night crawlers at a distance.

After one last survey of the night-emptied landscape, she slung her weapon and walked up to the entrance of Bolshevik Books. The windows were opaqued, and the store was obviously closed. She paused before she pressed the call button.

Could she have been followed?

It was a paranoid thought but one worth reviewing. There was the possibility of a ground team of marines out there. She had avoided further ambush by going underground at the construction site. The Godwin sewer system was hideously complex. No one knew it all, but Zanzibar was aware of the best subterranean highways. She'd surfaced nearly ten klicks away from the construction site.

Was that good enough?

She never got a chance to answer her own question. The intercom came alive, a laser began scanning her, and a small holo of a nervous-looking gentleman asked, "Who's there?"

The man was balding, middle-aged, and had an accent that Zanzibar thought belonged to either Paschal or Thubohu. It was probably Levy. She gave the password, "I'm a patriot."

"There are no patriots on Bakunin."

"Then perhaps I'm a partisan."

"Enter, comrade." The "comrade" part was laced with audible sarcasm. Zanzibar shrugged. The exchange had gone as she expected. Now all she had to do was meet this Flower, and see if the "expert" was what the plan needed.

What the plan needs is a miracle.

The door opened, and Johann Levy ushered her into his bookstore. She followed him through the stacks of paperbound books. Levy led her into a windowless office awash in clutter. The only concession to order was a clear spot on the metallic green desk upon which sat a countersurveillance generator, a wide-band signal detector, and a secure holo communicator unit. Everything was off except for the countersurveillance box, since you couldn't transmit in or out of an RF-damping field.

Flower was sitting behind the desk.

Zanzibar suppressed a gasp when she crossed the threshold, and she had to summon a reserve of composure to continue striding over to Levy's offered seat without showing her surprise.

She hadn't expected Flower to be nonhuman.

Not only nonhuman, *alien.*

Nonhumans were fairly common in the Confederacy, on Bakunin at least. Most people had met at least one descendant of pre-Unification genetic projects. The Seven Worlds, the Tau Ceti arm of the Confederacy, were all populated by those Terran nonhumans. There were over a hundred species of them.

But whatever mistrust—even horror—existed between humans and their creations, they weren't *aliens*.

In three centuries, the humans of the Confederacy had found evidence of only five intelligent extraterrestrial species.

There were the Dolbrians, who had died out over a hundred million years ago, leaving very few traces.

There was the Race, who had fought humanity and had been nearly exterminated in the Genocide War. The Race now never ventured off their world orbiting Procyon, where old United Nations battle stations still blasted anything that achieved orbit.

There were the Paralians, an aquatic civilization with little technological base, but who were so advanced in mathematics and theoretical physics that they had known the structure of tach-space centuries before humans launched a wormhole at Vega.

There were the worms of Helminth, with whom Confederacy scientists were still, as far as Zanzibar knew, trying to communicate.

Then there were Flower's people, the Volerans.

Volera was discovered during the Indi Protectorate's massive colonial expansion. Sixty-two years ago, one of the hundreds of Indi scouts had come across a highly attractive planet circling Tau Puppis, a star not only on the fringes of the Indi Protectorate, but on the fringes of the Confederacy.

It was found to be inhabited by a small population of highly technological avian creatures while it was still called Tau Puppis IV. Sometime after the planet was named Volera, it was realized that this planet was actually a remote outpost of another interstellar civilization.

Ever since, diplomats from the five arms of the Confederacy and the Voleran "Empire" had been engaged in a delicate dance on the fringes of both civilizations, trying to prevent any potentially disastrous contacts. That diplomatic dance was going on on the other side of the Indi Protectorate from Bakunin, almost ninety light-years away.

And, here, sitting behind a green metal desk was a Voleran named Flower who was purporting to be an expert on *Paralian* ship design.

Zanzibar slowly sat down, trying not to stare.

Levy closed the door. It looked like a simple swinging wood door, but Zanzibar heard a telltale static hiss when it closed—either more antisurveillance or some physical protection. Zanzibar assumed both. She could see almost instantly that all the clutter in Levy's office was carefully staged and ordered. The rumpled little man was probably never out of arm's reach of a weapon while he was in the store.

The little ones were always the most dangerous.

"Your name is Mariah Zanzibar, is it not?" he asked.

"And you're Mr. Johann Levy."

He nodded. "I've found you an expert on Paralian ship design who might be willing to work on this escapade."

Zanzibar nodded and took the opportunity to look at the Voleran. It looked like a cross between a snake, a bird, and some sort of bush. Wings rose from a set of broad shoulders and were at the moment, draped about it like a cape. Its torso was long, broad, and tapered down to become—Zanzibar could only suppose as the desk was in the way—a tail.

The feathers—if that's what you called them—were red, brown, and yellow, lighter on the underside and darker on top. They were flat and veined like leaves.

The neck was extremely long. Fully extended it would be a third of its height. The neck was bare of feathers—or was it foliage?—revealing leathery-looking brown skin.

Equally bare were its limbs. Each seemed double-jointed and had an extra knee/elbow. They all ended with three opposable digits. Two arms rested on the table in front of it, fingers locked in a disturbingly human gesture.

In a very *un*human gesture, it had one leg—built

exactly like one of its arms, only longer and more muscular—bent up, *backward,* to support its head in a cupped three-toe foot.

Its head looked to be off some sort of dinosaur. A long bony beak emerged from a domed skull dominated by huge jaw muscles. It all sloped seamlessly back into a neck arched like a question mark. Zanzibar looked for a face in among the mottled yellow and black markings on the head, but couldn't find one. Except for the mouth, its head was as featureless as a bullet.

"Hello," Zanzibar said. "As Mr. Levy mentioned, I'm Sergeant Zanzibar." She hoped she was looking at the right place when she talked. She considered offering her hand, and decided not to. "You are?"

"My name has translated himself as Flower." It conducted an elaborate gesture with its hands that Zanzibar supposed was a greeting. "I am pleased to discover your need."

Its voice was extremely odd: high-pitched, nasal, and very deliberately phrased. It was like listening to someone perpetually on the verge of a sneeze. "It has been long since I have heard someone who requires my expertise."

"That's what I'm here to find out. Whether or not you're what we're looking for." *Listen to yourself. You don't even approve of the project.* Zanzibar put those thoughts aside. Her job right now was finding someone who knew the ins and outs of that ship in the GA&A landing quad. She wasn't here to second-guess. Not herself, not her duty. "We need someone with extensive knowledge of systems, mechanics, weaponry, etcetera, of Paralian-designed ships. We need someone who knows everything about a particular ship design, including the classified particulars and Confederacy in-house modifications."

It made an imitation of a human nod, which amounted to a bobbing of the head on the end of its long neck. "It is right for you to be skeptical."

"Forgive me if I have my doubts."

"Shall I explain myself?" Zanzibar wondered how it

talked. The serrated beak was rigid, and barely opened when it spoke. The few glimpses Zanzibar got inside its mouth showed an intricate palate made of ridged holes and muscular flaps. Flower seemed to have at least three tongues.

Zanzibar thought it looked like someone playing a flute from the inside.

"Go ahead," she said.

"I have resided within the Terran Confederacy for thirty standard years. Many Diplomatic Envoys owned me as an Imperial Military Observer for twenty-three of those years."

Zanzibar felt a half-smile reach the corner of her mouth. "You were a spy?"

"I was an Observer. One of the Emperor's hands picks the academies for scholars to be its ears. I was one of those ears, and my observations were of the Confederacy military."

"So you're no longer an Observer?"

"My term of service to the Emperor ended himself. I still study human warfare, but only for my own ears."

"Quite a hobby."

Flower made a circular gesture with its free foot. Zanzibar interpreted it as a shrug. "I was studying the topic even when I was male. If I return to the Empire, I return to my academy. I do not because an alien culture provides more interest than my own. Bakunin allows me to have a free hand in my studies. Freer than when I was an extension of the Emperor's hand."

"I see. So you do know the kind of information we need?"

"You require information the *Kalcthwee'rat* provides me." it was the first time Zanzibar had heard a native Paralian term pronounced with anything approaching authenticity "The *Kalcthwee'rat* translates himself as *Blood-Tide*. He is a Paralian-designed, Confederacy-built drop-ship. He modifies on the Barracuda class-five troop-carrier. He sizes between the Manta fighter and the Hammerhead light bomber. He moves in tach-space, in-system, and can maneuver atmospheric with and without contragrav assistance. The Barracuda design was originally—"

"Okay," Zanzibar said, holding up her hand. "Has Mr. Levy informed you of what we need you for?"

"Not in any detail. I do know that you are offering me a chance to observe firsthand a human military operation. I would find such an experience invaluable even if no payment was offered."

I'll be damned, Zanzibar thought, *a thrill-seeking alien.*

CHAPTER TWENTY-TWO

Family Values

"There is no aspect of politics that was not first invented within the confines of a human family."
—*The Cynic's Book of Wisdom*

"If Absolute Sovereignty be not necessary in a State, how come it to be so in a family?"
—MARY ASTELL
(1666–1731)

Tetsami thought that the name, the Stemmer Facility, sounded more like a factory than a hospital. From the outside, it *looked* like a factory. The whole building was a one-piece blank-gray truncated pyramid that was typical of the bunkerlike architecture infecting most of Godwin. It had no windows, a shortage of surface access, and no external indication that it *was* a hospital, and one far removed from the biological chop-shops she'd known back in the old days.

Tetsami snorted. All of her previous life was now the "old days." She disliked the fact that she was waxing nostalgic about her years as one of the best freelance hackers in the Godwin corporate shithole.

There *was* a reason. In those eight years she'd never been involved in this kind of shitstorm. Because of the way her parents died, she'd shunned any sort of corporate identity—no matter what it cost her in potential kilograms—to avoid being targeted in the dirty little wars that constantly rippled through the sea of Bakunin economics. Now she was stuck in the middle of a whole flood of the same shit that'd killed them.

No wonder she was pining for the "good old days."

Days when the only laser she'd deal with would be piped through an optical datalink.

The only thing on the plus side at the moment was the fact that, now that she'd entered the rarefied atmosphere of corporate economics, the medical treatment was that much better. Shane was getting the full exec layout right in the middle of Central Godwin. It would have been cheaper to boot to the East Side. Tetsami *did* know some hacks there who were safe.

However, it was a given that the East Side of Godwin was crawling with informants and blabbing maggots.

Here in Stemmer, she had a chance of getting Shane fixed up without the honcho in charge of GA&A finding out about it. The docs here cost—but they wouldn't sell you out. Couldn't, since everything was cash up front, and all it would take for Stemmer to lose most of its lucrative executive clientele would be one info leak.

Tetsami stood in one of the private waiting rooms, hoping for word on Shane.

"Don't let this be a fuckup," she whispered to herself occasionally. Hell, it looked as though someone had set them up. Tetsami kind of hoped that it wasn't Shane who'd done it. However, Shane was the only person that Dom hadn't checked five light-years from everywhere. Which meant that if it wasn't Shane, it could be anybody—

"Hey, 'lil girl, heard you were looking for me."

Tetsami turned around to face the man who had just walked into the room. "Ivor!"

Ivor Jorgenson filled the door behind her. He stood over two meters, a head and a half over Tetsami. His hair was snow white, and his eyes were an icy blue.

She ran up and hugged him.

He patted her on the back and said, "Glad to see you, too, but what the hell's going on?"

"Sit down." She disengaged and perched herself on one of the overstuffed lounge chairs. "I'll tell you about it."

Ivor nodded and thrust his bulk down on another chair. "You better, punkin—you gave me one hell of a fright. First a coded message on my comm telling me you got a job for me. Then a message to meet you at Stemmer—you *could've* mentioned that it wasn't you who got busted up."

Tetsami saw the concern on Ivor's face and didn't know whether to laugh or cry. "Sorry—I was in such a rush here, I barely got the message out. If you ain't an exec, it takes a lot of grease to get them pulling here."

"Well, I'm glad it wasn't you. But what the hell are you doing out in the open? I've heard—"

"It's true."

Ivor's face became very cold. "Who backed the contract?"

"Ivor—"

"Tell me the bastard who put money on your head—"

"Ivor—"

"I'll kill the son of a—"

"IVOR!" Tetsami held up her hands until Ivor quieted. "Look, it's a bit bigger than that. You couldn't take them by yourself, anyway. Even if I wanted you to."

He sighed and shook his head. "What have you gotten mixed up in this time, punkin?"

"Maybe the biggest payoff for one job either of us could ever see."

As she talked to Ivor, she had to admit that seeing her not-quite-father again gave her an inordinate amount of reassurance. It was both calming and an annoyance for someone who had spent half her life in pursuit of fanatical self-sufficiency.

And as she went over the high points and the horrors of her last dozen days, she began to question involving her white-haired "uncle."

It wasn't because her initial impulse to pull him in was either sentimental or unprofessional. As far as pilots went, Ivor was the best one she knew or knew of. He had once been the ranking member of the Stygian Presidential

Guard, Airborne. Ivor Jorgenson once had—twenty years
or so ago—control of the entire planetary defense of the
planet Styx. Tetsami might be the only one on the planet
who knew that little fact, and even she didn't know the
name under which he'd served. Ivor's connection with
Styx had long ago withered and been abandoned. His reputation as a pilot on Bakunin had been built over the
twenty years of his residence here.

Yes, he was the best pilot she knew, and there was no
question about her being able to trust him.

Her second thoughts had a deeper origin.

This shit was dangerous, and she didn't want to lose
what was left of her family. All through the discussion,
she kept remembering the corporate war that had destroyed Holographic DataComm. The EMP that toasted
her parents spared her only because she had no hardware
in her skull at the time. Ivor, who was HDC's data
smuggler—slipping copies of product into the closed me-
dia environments of certain communes—had realized that
Tetsami's genetic heritage made her a potential corporate
asset. If Ivor hadn't evacked her, she'd probably've had a
short brilliant career as a pet corporate hacker for the
Troy Broadcasting Corporation. A career that would most
likely end where her parents' had ended.

When she'd gotten her biolink implanted, it was the
only time she'd known Ivor—with his explosive
temper—to have come close to striking her.

As she pulled Ivor farther into her proposal, she became more and more ambivalent about involving him in
her dangerous game. She began to understand what his
fears had been when she'd finally entered her parents'
line of work.

After Tetsami had spent an hour explaining things, Ivor
said, "To think, when you were six, I thought you were
cute."

"And I thought you were dashing, Uncle Ivor—you're
evading the question." Tetsami wasn't sure what answer
she wanted to hear.

"You know I've got commitments—"

"Hauling produce up to Jefferson? Come on?"

"Don't denigrate an honest living."

"You never worked an honest day in your life."

Ivor stood up and paced, running large hands through white hair. "You know I hate this, don't you? The only family I've had since I landed on this rock—do you go out of your way to put yourself in these scrapes? You've driven my hair white, you want me to go bald as well?"

"You had white hair ten years before I was born."

"That's not the point."

"Neither is your hair."

Ivor sighed and stopped pacing. "You *know* you've sold me, don't you?"

Tetsami nodded slowly, feeling relieved and disturbed at the same time.

"But only to keep an eye on you," Ivor finished.

"Of course."

After that, the conversation drifted into safer channels. It had been close to a year standard since they'd seen each other, and there was a lot of catching up to do. It took Tetsami a little while to get Ivor to admit that the produce run was a scam; he was really smuggling propaganda out of Jefferson City to the outlying communes that supplied it with food.

"What's the point?"

Ivor shrugged. "The Jefferson Congress decided that if some of the communes went democro-capitalist, they'd get a better deal on the food. I think it's revenge. Those fanatic Americans really *don't* like it when they're called the Thomas Jefferson Commune."

"But they are one, aren't they?"

Ivor laughed. "Just don't tell them that."

"I mean, if they ain't a commune, and they ain't a corporation, then they're a State, and someone would have to do something about that—"

The door to the waiting room slid aside, revealing a man wearing a blue one-piece cleansuit. His face was hidden behind a plastic mask that turned his eyes into tiny optical cameras and his mouth into a speaker grille. He asked, "You are waiting for patient D5/789/3467?"

Tetsami nodded.

"You can see the patient. The injuries were not as extensive as first expected. The remaining balance of your security deposit was refunded to your account."

Tetsami stood up, tugged Ivor's elbow, and followed the doctor.

The two of them walked through wood-paneled corridors, across plush carpets from the Protectorate. Ivor faded back behind her and whispered, "Patient D5-slash-78-whatever? Doesn't your marine have a name?"

"As far as these exec docs are concerned, no."

The room Shane was in did its best to look like a hotel room.

Shane looked undiminished by her experience. She was sitting up on the edge of the bed; the gown they'd given her resembled a kimono more than the paper hospital thingie Tetsami expected. The only sign of injury was a purple bruise surrounding a sealed gash that ran down the right side of her face. Shane looked up at Tetsami and gave a little half-smile. "This has got a shipboard infirmary beat all to hell."

"How're you feeling?" Tetsami asked.

"Well—physically."

"Up to getting out of here?"

Shane nodded. "They said I'm fine. They didn't even need to cut me open. Though—" She looked in Ivor's direction. "Unless I scrambled my brains more than I thought, that is *not* Zanzibar."

"Oh, yes. Kathy Shane, Ivor Jorgenson."

Ivor extended a hand and gave Shane a beaming smile, "Pleased."

Shane managed to find a full smile of her own and grasped his hand. "So, are you an innocent bystander, or are you one of Dominic's nutcases?"

Ivor shook his head. "Neither." His smile never wavered.

Tetsami stood. "Well, get dressed and we'll go down to the warehouse—"

"Uh, this is it. The doctors trashed my jumpsuit."

Tetsami looked Shane up and down. "Kind of drafty.

Sheesh—" she shook her head. "I didn't salvage any luggage—all I got was your case of armor and a few weapons. Damn."

Shane shrugged. "Don't worry about it."

"Here," Ivor shrugged out of the pseudoleather jacket he was wearing. He held it out. Shane wasn't much taller than Tetsami. Despite her being built like a weightlifter, Ivor's jacket draped her like a tent.

"Thanks—" Shane slipped her feet into a pair of hospital slippers by the bed. "Let's go."

Tetsami shrugged and led them out of the building.

Behind her she heard them talking.

"Tetsami told me what happened. I'm sorry."

"You don't need to—"

"I know how it feels when your own people turn on you."

"I turned on them."

"I know about that, too."

As they got to the exit, Tetsami asked, "Ivor, how'd you get here?"

He pointed out the window across the parking lot, "My rig's over there."

"Good, we have to empty out the truck I appropriated. I burned the transponder on it, but someone's going to trace it eventually."

"Appropriated?" Shane asked.

"Stole," Tetsami explained. "You were unconscious."

The three of them walked out to the parking lot.

CHAPTER TWENTY-THREE

Controlling Interest

"History is an accident."

—*The Cynic's Book of Wisdom*

"None climbs so high as he who knows not wither he is going."

—OLIVER CROMWELL
(1599–1658)

Dom walked through an ancient cavern, his thoughts as dark as the glassy black walls. He was more than two hundred meters beneath the commune. The only signs of humanity down here were the lights left behind by the construction crew and the omnidirectional hum of the overbuilt fusion generator.

Whatever the temperature was in the snowy valley that hid the commune, the temperature down here was a constant ten degrees C.

Dom's breath fogged, casting halos around the rectangular lights that lined his path.

It would be nice to walk down here forever. Nice to lose himself in the heart of Bakunin's only mountain range, the spine of Bakunin's only continent. It would be easy to do, too. If he took a few branches beyond the end of the lights, it would be unlikely that anyone would ever find him. The caverns down here allegedly ran the length of the continent, from glacier to glacier.

Dom was surprised that the option held any attraction for him. The impulse revealed a facet of himself he didn't like. Was he so damn used to running?

The walls peeled back as Dom walked into a huge chamber, losing themselves in darkness. The floor collapsed into blackness ten meters away. There was one lone light in here, fixed above the entrance behind him.

He'd been walking for nearly an hour, and he had reached the end of the construction crew's amateur spelunking. Dom was probably the first human being to stand on this ledge since the commune was finished, years ago. He was certainly the first one down here since the Diderot Commune had been abandoned, and that was at least a decade.

The commune complex had been his for less than a year, and it was barely operational. Dom was certain none of his people had been down this way yet; there was too much to do, too much to fix, and too few people. The commune was originally constructed to house ten thousand, and Dom only had around fourteen hundred people. Less than a thousand when he subtracted children, wounded, and elderly dependents.

Dom ran his hand over the wall. Someone had used a laser torch to carve a list of initials in the obsidian.

His fingers traced the carving. It was the most permanent thing that the construction crew had done. This carving, down here where the weather never changed, on a planet that was—for most practical purposes—tectonically dead, would probably outlast other signs of the human presence on Bakunin by a million years.

That made Dom think about the Dolbrians, who were supposedly responsible for this planet. Maybe that's what all their mysterious sculptures, mounds, and trenches were—cosmic graffiti.

Dom surprised himself by smiling.

His old boss, Dimitri, wouldn't appreciate that sentiment. Him with his almost spiritual worship of the Dolbrians.

But the idea struck a chord in Dom. After all, isn't that all anyone wanted? What *was* life but a frantic attempt to make some sort of impact on an indifferent universe? An effort to scrawl *"I was here!"* as big as possible?

The Dolbrians had left one hell of a mark. People were reading their graffiti a megacentury after they'd died out. Or vanished. Or whatever.

Dom turned and faced the dark cavern. He didn't adjust his photoreceptors to get a better picture. He stayed watching the darkness.

What kind of mark was he going to leave when he died?

His breath puffed out in a cloud as he said, "Brother, what are you doing to me?"

For the first time in a long while he was thinking in terms beyond the corporation he'd birthed.

"Mr. Magnus?" said a voice from behind, down the passage. Its owner was panting heavily.

"Mr. Magnus, sir?" the voice's owner ran up behind him, boots echoing across the rocky floor. Soon another plume of breath joined Dom's above the abyss.

"Yes?" Dom turned and looked at a short swarthy individual. Having an onboard computer meant he knew the names and history of everyone who worked for him. The gentleman next to him had run the third-shift carpool and dispatch back at GA&A. His name was Desmond.

"We've got the aircar you wanted out of stores. It's ready on the pad."

"The contragrav?"

"Yes."

Dom nodded. "Can we spare it?"

"We'll get by."

Silence stretched. Desmond remained standing next to him.

"Anything else?"

"Well, uh, sir—"

Dom turned around so he could face Desmond.

"We've installed the holos and the field generators. There are people who've seen that and feel we're much too vulnerable."

"The generators were supposed to compensate for that."

Desmond nodded.

Silence stretched and Dom finally said, "It isn't enough."

"The commune still feels too exposed. A lot of us are nervous, especially with the potential threat."

Dom nodded. He had purchased this bolt-hole less than a year ago, and there had been precious little time to prepare it.

With Klaus out there, this commune really wasn't safe. Klaus was behind a systematic targeting of GA&A personnel. If he became aware of the location of Dom's commune, he would eradicate it. Klaus would need only a fraction of the force he had used against GA&A.

Dom needed some way to make things more defensible.

He nodded to himself and started leading Desmond back to the fusion generators and the elevator to the commune. "Yes, Desmond. I think I have a solution, something I should have thought of earlier."

He spent a few hours drafting a plan, organizing an engineering detail and a construction squad, getting the ball rolling. That done, he delegated authority and satisfied himself that things would run fine without him again.

When he took the aircar—contragrav, *not* vectored thrust—Bakunin had settled deep into a moonless night.

Dom lifted off from a snow-dusted carpool on the fringe of the commune building. He let the computer handle the initial trajectory of his craft as he watched the commune recede.

The building was a massive, white, truncated pyramid with a skirt made by the hydroponics greenhouses. The structure filled the floor of this nameless valley. The craft rose, and there was a shimmer as he passed through the defensive screens of the commune. The force field dome here was not designed to block lasers or plasma, or to fry the delicate electronics of a missile—the building didn't have power systems that could cope with that. This field was designed with more passive thoughts in mind: reducing the stray infrared and EM signature of the commune down to that of the rest of the mountain around it.

There was another shimmer, and suddenly the commune vanished as Dom's craft passed through the floor of the holo screen. A dozen independent projectors ringed the valley, raising the image of the valley floor above the top of the commune. From this close it was obviously a projection, but from an overflight, another peak, or a satellite, the commune would be invisible.

Sadly, both the holo and the defense screens were jury-rigged measures that took two full Bakunin days to implement. Dom didn't want to leave until both were operational. They were last-minute compensations for the fact that he had never planned for the commune to be a target. The commune was housing for displaced refugees. Corporate wars almost never extended to targeting employees. Corporate battles were battles for assets.

Dom hadn't anticipated Klaus.

As the dead snow-capped peaks receded behind him, he hoped his late measures would be enough to hide his people.

He should have anticipated this. The *whole* commune should have been built underground, with adequate ground-air defensive weaponry.

Dom turned away from the mountains and decided it was too late for regrets.

Dom flew his contragrav in a wide circle around Godwin, above the hardwood forest that camped in the shoulder of the mountains. The forest seemed an afterthought, a result of the congruence of the equatorial "heat" and the chain of mountains blocking the moisture blowing off of Bakunin's world-ocean. It seemed almost providential.

The people who believed in Dolbrian intervention on Bakunin pointed to this as a sign of their intervention. They also pointed to the fact that, by all rights, Bakunin should be an iceball, but a combination of its proximity to its weak star, an infinitesimal axial tilt, and a thick moisture-laden atmosphere made the equator on the planet's one continent fairly comfortable. One side of the mountains was lush, one side desert, and the dead tectonics of the planet meant that it had been this way—except for the slow erosion of the mountains—almost since the Dolbrians existed.

Dom shook his head. He was still thinking of ancient civilizations.

It was Dimitri. Dolbrians were one of Dimitri's little obsessions. And, unless one of Dimitris' annual medical procedures—this year a kidney, the next his liver, nerve grafts, bone marrow—had gone wrong recently, Dimitri was in charge of the TEC mission that had cost Dom GA&A.

In fact, Dimitri would have to be personally overseeing something like this.

Dimitri.

Dom wanted to kill him almost as much as he did his brother.

The warehouse Dom had rented from Bleek was in the northwest corner of Godwin, sitting right on top of the gentle northward curve of the ill-fated Godwin-Proudhon commuter tube. That's where he was headed. A direct route straight for the warehouse from the commune would have saved him several hours and given him less of an opportunity for reflection, but it also would have carried him over the GA&A complex, as well as East Godwin. Those were two risks he wasn't ready to take. So his contragrav aircar had started north, away from everything, turned west over the white synthetic marble of Jefferson City, and turned around so he merged with eastbound air traffic from New Paris.

As he flew over the residential outskirts of Godwin—walked suburban enclaves patrolled by private security armies—the eastern sky beyond the mountains began to lighten. The slight ruddy glow that lit the mountains from behind made him think of what they must have looked like when they were sharp-edged and volcanically active.

A northern turn took him abruptly into a forest of warehouses.

He landed just as the mountains' shadow passed him,

slicing its way east, abandoning the dull black cubes of the warehouse district to the red dawn light.

The warehouse he was renting from Bleek Munitions was typical of its kind—blocky, windowless, over-engineered, and about as subtle as a slap in the face. Unlike GA&A, Bleek wasn't in a centralized location, so it needed way stations like this at various points in its logistical set up. This place was supposed to be a stop for munitions orders going off-planet via Proudhon, which was why it sat on top of the hypothetical commuter tube. Since the tube was never finished, this warehouse was fairly useless. It was badly placed and spent most of its time empty.

All reasons that Dom chose it to base his operation.

Our operation, he told himself, thinking of Tetsami.

The past two days had been the only point during the last dozen when he'd been without Tetsami's company. There was a numbing realization that in ten days he'd gotten used to Tetsami, perhaps even *needed* her. It gave Dom a vague feeling of unease. He didn't want to think of himself as using a colleague as an emotional crutch.

It was unprofessional.

And emotional involvement in his kind of work was dangerous, possibly crippling.

He had to shift mental gears.

Our operation.

This thing he and Tetsami had started, it was different from GA&A. There were different expectations. Tetsami had pointed out something. These people were *not* his employees. They were his partners. Whatever he did, Tetsami was part of it just as much as he was, and everyone involved would have a piece.

He pushed open one of the gull-wing doors and stepped out on to the roofside landing area.

An elevator mounted at the edge of the roof slid open, and two people stepped out. It was Sergeant Zanzibar and a giant white-haired gentleman who looked vaguely familiar.

Ivor Jorgenson, Dom remembered from his research. *Where have I seen you before?*

They were both armed with Macmillan-Schmitt wide-aperture plasma rifles. The things were close-combat jobs, scaled-down versions of a vehicle plasma-jet. Confed infantry liked them, even though they sucked power a few magnitudes beyond a similar-sized laser. Unlike a laser, one shot from a plasma rifle could probably clean this roof.

The marines nicknamed it "pocket sunshine."

When Zanzibar and her escort saw who he was, they lowered their weapons. Zanzibar walked up to him, and the white-haired man hung back by the elevator. "Welcome back to Godwin, Mr. Magnus. Did you run into any trouble on your way here?"

Dom shook his head. "No."

"Security here's been a nightmare. We've been ambushed twice by Confed marines. The last was an attempt on Mosasa and Random Walk when they came into Godwin."

"Mosasa was never a GA&A employee." Dom didn't like that.

Zanzibar nodded. "Some details of this op seemed to have leaked back to Colonel Dacham."

"Damnation and taxes!" Dom slammed his fist against the shell of his contragrav and only barely noticed Zanzibar's shocked expression.

"I've done what containment I can," Zanzibar said. "Everyone's locked down here in the warehouse. No communication is going out. I was worried about the commune—"

Dom shook his head. "Don't. The commune is all right."

"If Dacham IDs the commune and where it is—"

"Damn it, Zanzibar! What do you think I've been doing the last two days?"

"Sorry, sir."

Dom took a deep breath. "No. I'm sorry. It's been a rough few days." He surprised himself by putting his hand on Zanzibar's shoulder. "Don't worry about that. It's been taken care of. Your job's here."

"It's only a matter of time before somebody traces this warehouse."

"All we need is a few days. Is everyone here?"

Zanzibar nodded. "Mosasa and Random arrived yesterday."

"Is he all right?"

"Yes." Zanzibar sounded odd. "They tried to take us—me and Ivor were escort—by surprise. They got me and Ivor stunned, but apparently they missed Mosasa entirely." Zanzibar sounded suspicious.

"What happened?"

"Apparently Mosasa crisped three marines while we were out."

"He wasn't hurt?"

"Not a scratch."

"I don't like that."

"Neither do I."

"Any idea where the leak came from?"

Zanzibar shook her head and looked irritated. "No. I'd put my money on Shane. If there were any way she could have known who Mosasa was and how he was coming in."

"It could have been Mosasa."

"I know. A stunner miss seems too damn convenient. But the marines *were* crisped. Seems costly for a cover job."

Dom sighed. "Well, we keep a lid on for now. Take me down to meet the team. We don't have much time before we have to hit Klaus."

By mid-morning—after Dom was briefed by Tetsami—the team was all together in one place for the first time.

So all Klaus needs is one missile, Dom thought as he took his seat to the right of the display holo.

The warehouse could be subdivided by computer-controlled wall modules, and their meeting room was a large chamber constructed entirely of the programmed wall units. They sat in a cube twenty meters on a side and would have had one hell of an echo problem if Mosasa hadn't included sound dampers in with the more conventional countersurveillance devices.

Nine people sat in a ring around a circular table that had once been a pedestal for some piece of heavy machinery. Dom and Tetsami sat on either side of a holo generator aimed above the table.

Dom folded his hands before him and began.

"All of you've been given some idea of what we plan to do here. It's time for specifics. None of you is committed yet. Considering time and security problems, this is your *one* chance to back out."

Dom scanned the room. He had to make the offer. Levy looked a little nervous. The bird-thing's head was bobbing on a serpentine neck in a very inhuman manner. Mosasa's dragon tattoo showed more expression than Mosasa did.

No one backed out.

Dom nodded. "Good. Since this is the first time you've all been together, let's have some introductions—Tetsami?"

Tetsami stood. She was going to have to bear the brunt of the presentation since it was, for the most part, her plan.

She ran her hands through her hair. She looked as though she'd been missing some sleep. "Well, you all know me—in fact you're lucky if I haven't pumped you for information in the past sixty-four hours—but for formality's sake, I'm Kari Tetsami."

Funny, though it was in her file, it was the first time Dom had ever considered her first name.

"I'm coordinating this expedition. If you have a problem with the plan, you talk to me."

Tetsami waved at Ivor. He was putting away his third sandwich and washing it down with a mammoth container of coffee. "This is Ivor Jorgenson, the best pilot I know of on this rock. He'll be the one extracting the surface team from the complex."

She continued, counterclockwise around the table. Next

to Jorgenson was Shane, who was nursing a large bruise on the side of her face. "Kathy Shane, she's our marine. She was kind enough to defect with a full load of body armor. She'll be the one to get the ground team into the ship."

Mosasa was next. "Tjaele Mosasa is our expert on communications, electronics, security systems, and so on. He's already done worthwhile work on the transponder in Shane's armor, and he is going to make sure that the folks holding GA&A don't see us coming." Mosasa nodded politely, the glow from the holo projector reflecting off his scalp.

Floating next to Mosasa was a squashed metal sphere carrying what looked like an oversized briefcase in one of its manipulators. "The robot is actually being run by Random Walk, an artificial intelligence." Dom felt he heard Tetsami's voice lower a few degrees. "Random will be responsible for taking charge of the computers aboard the Paralian ship in the landing quad."

Johann Levy was next, short, balding, and perpetually nervous. Dom also noted that he was sitting between the two nonhumans. "Johann Levy is our demolition expert. He has the most important job, cracking the safe."

Next was the bird, a creature who had been getting his—her? its?—share of stares. "Flower is a Voleran," *just in case they hadn't guessed;* "it—please don't call Flower 'he,' that would be an insult—is our informant on the design and weaponry of the drop-ship that we have to deal with. Flower will not go in on the ground, but our success relies on it as much as on any member of the group."

Then there was Zanzibar. "Mariah Zanzibar knows the hardwired security setup in the complex. She's also combat-trained and will back up the team going into the safe.

"And, finally, Mr. Dominic Magnus, the man whose money we're stealing."

Dom nodded at the rest of the assembled team.

"What's at stake here," said Tetsami, "for each of us,

is a flat twenty megagrams. *Or* an equal share of a corporate takeover." She smiled. "Now that we know each other and why we're involved, shall we get down to what we're going to do?"

CHAPTER TWENTY-FOUR

Press Conference

"Mercenaries may not win as many wars as fanatics do, but they live longer."
                                    —*The Cynic's Book of Wisdom*

"Gold is everything; without gold there's nothing."
                                    —DENIS DIDEROT
                                    (1713–1784)

Sometime during the introductions it hit Tetsami. *It was actually going to happen.* This heist she had been planning—at least half out of desperation—was actually going down.

Until now, standing in front of the eight other team members, she'd been deep-down convinced that this whole idea was hypothetical. Something to mark time while she or Dom thought of some way to get out from under the Confed guns.

They weren't marking time, it wasn't hypothetical, and it was probably the only way to get a defensible position. Dom—damn the diabolical logic of all this—*needed* a corporate base to defend himself and "his people." It was that or everyone whom Dom even breathed on would have to dig a hole and hide until the TEC decided to leave the planet.

A vain hope when she had no idea why they were here in the first place.

She manipulated the holo and started reviewing the whole plan for the first time, all the while expecting the inevitable, "You're kidding," or, "That'll never work." It took an extreme effort on her part—especially with Ivor there—to avoid showing the nerves that tied her gut in a knot.

She consciously imitated Dom's control.

"First," she told the eight others as she called up a holo image of the current layout of the GA&A complex, "Here's the nut we're going to crack."

She zoomed in on each detail as she described it. "The complex is surrounded by a two-hundred-fifty-meter diameter circle of twenty perimeter towers. Each is—was—fifty meters of diamondwire-reinforced concrete, sensors, antiaircraft, and Emerson field generators."

She moved the pointer to the west side of the complex. "Here's the good news—half got scragged by TEC missile fire. The entire ass-end of the residence tower—the tall building west of the quad—is hanging out over Godwin. Ditto what's left of the old security HQ, *and* the extreme north end of the office building.

"The TEC is trying to fill the gap with their own equipment. The scragged perimeter towers, most have been chopped off at twenty meters for them to mount their own weapons and sensors. They're more twitchy about a ground assault than an air attack. There's enough computer-aimed hardware on the *Blood-Tide* to take out a decent airborne assault without waking their command. Their problem's that the *Blood-Tide* is useless versus ground-pounders. So the nests on top of those ten scragged towers carry plasma cannons. MacMillan-Schmitt HD350, I think—"

Shane nodded and some of Tetsami's audience whistled in appreciation.

"Again," Tetsami continued, "we got good news. They only have the ship's computers, and those are overloaded. They have warm bodies manning the plasma cannons, and they don't have enough marines to man the perimeter *and* patrol the interior."

Tetsami nodded at Shane. Shane elaborated for her, "There's a one-hundred-twenty-marine complement in there, and the HD350 requires a gunner and a tech to run. That's half the active-duty personnel at any one time."

Tetsami nodded. "Add to that the minimum of five people stationed aboard the *Blood-Tide,* and another ten marines lost to injury or misadventure since this began, there'll be ten marines on generic security as long as GA&A isn't on some sort of alert—"

"At which point an extra seventy marines land on us," muttered Zanzibar.

"—so with the exception of the perimeter and ship itself, we're dealing with civilian security."

"Until the alarm sounds," Zanzibar said.

"I hope to avoid that." Tetsami adjusted the focus of the holo so that everyone was looking at the central portion of the complex. She moved the pointer about, highlighting the buildings in turn, describing GA&A's layout, until she focused on the central landing quad, where the hundred-meter-long *Blood-Tide* barely fit. "Now, I want to get back to the TEC ship. Flower?" Tetsami prompted.

The birdlike alien scratched its long neck with one foot as it gestured at the holo with its three-fingered hands. The three joints made its arms move with a liquid grace. "The *Blood-Tide* is a class of ship that was first designed as a fast troop-carrier. He is as large as a cargo ship. He deceives with that. The original model was extremely overengineered. His design incorporates a tach-drive, conventional maneuvering drives, and a contragrav generator. A quantum extraction contragrav, not the slower, safer, catalytic injection drive. Because of the multiple systems his original model could never move more than five hundred troops—"

Flower went on at length on the ship that had landed on the GA&A complex. It was the third time Tetsami had heard it all. The important points of Flower's speech weren't the reassessing of the Barracuda Class-Five's military role—a reassessment that added dozens of weapons and heavier armor and reduced its carrying capacity. The important point was the multiple redundancies of the craft. Redundancies such as total separation of the defensive field generators from the drives, allowing the *Blood-Tide* to power a defensive screen over the whole GA&A complex without running the drives. Redundancies such as a spare computer system that could be hijacked to run the security system for GA&A from the ship—barely.

Flower took the holo's remote and called up various schematics. Some were public domain, some had been bought or hijacked from various nets in the last few days, and a few Flower had drawn up itself. The people paying the most attention to Flower's assessment of the *Blood-Tide* were Mosasa and, predictably, Ivor.

"Here, and here—" Flower used the pointer to indicate places around the landing gear, "are access points to the secondary Emerson field generator. Like most Confederacy battlecraft, the Barracuda has a multiple-layer system that can generate concentric fields of differing frequencies to deal with multiple laser hits. From the information I have been given, the *Blood-Tide* has only a single screen up, covering the diameter of the entire complex. Even one layer at that diameter would be a major drain on his power systems, even if he taps the GA&A power grid. With the landing gear down, it is possible to access the Emerson field generator directly through these circuits." Two spots lit up red. "This bypasses the control computer."

Random Walk's robot rose and tilted at the holo. "And what about accessing the computer itself?"

"Theoretically, he could be accessed from the GA&A security grid, since they are using the ship's computer to run the complex. This is not a good option since we know nothing of the interface they are using, only that it was designed by TEC programmers on-site. The better option is direct access to the core system of the *Blood-Tide* himself."

The image rotated, pulled back, and dropped electronic schematics in favor of structural detail. "Here is the secondary core. He is placed as central to the ship as possible—"

Ivor spoke up. "What's that big sphere crowding the starboard bulkhead?"

Flower shrunk the image even further to allow more of the internal structure to be seen. "That is the contragrav generator, which *is* at the center of the ship. The secondary core is central to avoid battle damage, the generator is there for maneuvering—"

"I was afraid of that," Ivor said.

"Isn't it dangerous to get that close to a quantum extraction system?" asked Zanzibar.

Flower bobbed its head. "There is only a radiation hazard when the drive is running, and he is shielded."

Ivor sighed. "Those things are hideously cranky."

Flower made a circular gesture with his foot. "We do not intend to fly him—"

"Right, we don't," said Tetsami. "Which brings us to the ground team, and how we're getting Random to that computer core."

The floating robot tilted in a bow.

"The surface team is Shane, Mosasa, and Random—or specifically, that briefcase Random's simulacrum is holding."

The robot placed an aluminum briefcase on the table. "I don't show this to just anyone, but in that case is a fifth part of my brain, a crystal matrix with RF and a few I/O ports, what makes me *me*."

"I was wondering how that thing was being piloted when we're supposed to be RF shielded in here," Zanzibar muttered.

The robot used a manipulator to open the case and revealed a keyboard, a number of cables, a small holo display, and a lot of access ports. One of them was a bio-interface jack. Tetsami didn't want to think about that.

"Mr. Mosasa built this for me," Random said. "So I could go out, see the world—etcetera."

"Anyway," Tetsami said, "Random is going to be the major cog in getting TEC security off everyone's backs. I'll be backing him up from the security grid end, but we need someone at the core of the *Blood-Tide* to make sure we pull this off. Stage one of the op is getting Random's briefcase to the secondary core of the *Blood-Tide*."

Tetsami took the remote back from Flower and changed the display. Now, floating above the table was the globe of Bakunin. The globe looked like a map someone had left unfinished, even though it was an accurate picture from orbit. Most of the globe seemed white, all except a strip around the equator where Bakunin's one continent shot from north to south at an angle, ice cap to ice cap. A little red dot glowed on the equator of that continent, on the western side of its mountainous spine. A large blue dot glowed to its immediate west. "The red dot is GA&A and the blue dot is Godwin."

Tetsami started to circle the table, pacing the slowly rotating globe. "Our first problem with the ground team is getting them in without flagging security. It calls for a distraction to misdirect everyone so we can get Shame up to a perimeter guard. The first problem we have is the Emerson field. A military screen can detect any EM active source crossing the perimeter—that includes Shane's armor and Random. Second problem is the RF traffic and the transponder codes—obviously altered since Shane defected. We need to knock out all that to give Shane a window. And do it without letting them realize something's up."

As she passed Zanzibar, Tetsami heard her mutter, "Good luck."

"Gladiatorial combat to the rescue."

Not a few people said, "Huh?"

Tetsami hit the remote and a small yellow speck appeared over the planet's equator, pacing the planet's rotation. "The problem of getting Shane in baffled me for a while—I mean, what kind of massive ECM could I pull on the whole GA&A complex that wouldn't *look* like someone deliberately fucking with them? The solution is bonehead simple—if you ever watch the public airwaves on this rock. That yellow speck there is a Troy Broadcasting Corp satellite." Tetsami realized that her smile had grown hard. This part of her plan was petty revenge. However, it did have an elegance about it.

"The sat's a new one, right over Godwin, and it's been blasting anything that gets close to it."

Tetsami punched the remote and on came footage from the wattage war between the gladiators and the demolition derby. "Troy Broadcasting has been beaming targeted high-power broadcasts straight into Godwin. They overpower any ground-based transmission, and when they really get happy, they bleed their broadcast over every holo channel available. Folks have been picking this stuff up on computers, aircar autopilots, power cables—you get the picture. Someone eventually is going to nuke that terrorist sat, but while it's there . . ."

"Oh . . ." Ivor always understood her sense of humor, even if he sometimes didn't appreciate it.

"I can hack that sat, and tightbeam their whole broadcast, full power, right on top of GA&A. They won't know what the fuck's going on, but for a while, this is what they'll be getting on their tac database. It'll take them at least fifteen minutes to get unscrambled. That's the minimum it'll take someone to directly program the main screen to block out the RF overload."

Tetsami returned the holo to the overview of the GA&A complex. Overlaying it was a timer and moving blue dots representing what they knew of the guard patrols—mostly Shane's info, supplemented by some clandestine observation from several tall buildings in West Godwin. The timer sped by as Tetsami reviewed the movements of the blue dots. After going over what they knew, Tetsami froze the image. The timer read 06:50:00.

"We're setting up the tunnel for the strike. In three days we'll have both access points excavated." Two red lights activated. One underneath the far southeast corner of the complex, almost directly underneath perimeter tower number seven. One at the fringes of the image in the woods four hundred meters away from the back of the office complex.

"The subsurface team is here." Tetsami highlighted the

red dot under the complex. "The ground team is here." The red dot in the woods glowed brighter.

"How in hell are you getting all that subsurface digging past them?" Zanzibar asked.

Tetsami shrugged and smiled. "They don't know what's normal, ain't got anyone to say a subsurface tremor is wrong. Especially when we time the digging to match Proudhon's departure schedule. Every launch at the spaceport brings us a centimeter closer. By now they've explained the vibrations to themselves and are busy ignoring them. A simple computer is down there now, maintaining the illusion. The intermittent digging is why it'll take three days."

"Isn't someone going to check that out?" Zanzibar went on.

For the first time since the presentation began, Dom said something. "What they'll find, if they bother to check, is that the mountain range they're at the foot of is riddled with holes, and rings like a bell if you hit it. Every contractor I know bitches about never getting accurate soundings; any audio picture of the rock around there is so filled with ghosts and echoes, that resonance from the spaceport would seem a logical explanation—if they even notice the digging."

Tetsami went on. "We are in position at 06:30:00, five days from now. I hack the sat. They're washed at 06:50:00. That's when we strike. The ground team breaks the surface. Ivor's getaway vehicle is waiting down the hole. Shane, Random, Ivor, and Mosasa have three minutes to make it to the edge of the woods. Where they should see this blue dot." Tetsami pointed to a frozen glowing point isolated all by itself behind the office complex. "This guard's isolated, all the towers back here are automated, and the other marines are in the quad, the buildings, or on the other side of the complex. Shane hits him with a long-distance stunner—one shot, but it should drop him. That leaves ten minutes for Mosasa to transfer the transponder coding and the data recorder to the modified systems in Shane's suit. Ivor gets to kill the systems on the marine's suit and drag him into the woods."

Tetsami accelerated the image of roving guards until the counter read 07:05:00. "By now—if they have any sense at all—they'll have locked out my RF interference. Shane and Mosasa are inside the screen perimeter. Mosasa has to turn on his cloak—that will hide him from cameras and eyeball search for ten minutes as he follows Shane's radar shadow. Shane keeps the guard's rounds. We're going to rely on Mosasa's modifications to Shane's transponder and comm unit here. The guard's path takes them here."

The holo accelerated to 07:10:00. "Right through the quad. For three minutes, Shane is the only guard patrolling here. Once she stops at the ship, she has that long before someone realizes she's no longer keeping the other guard's rounds. She has to be aboard the ship before then. Mosasa has to access the ship's defense screen through the gap in the landing gear and set up a neural stun field within the ship to take out the five marines on board—"

"Wait a minute," Zanzibar interrupted. "How the hell do you reprogram a whole system on the fly like that, in three minutes?"

"Not reprogramming," said Mosasa softly.

"No," Flower said, "a stun field is part of the command set in the Emerson field software installed in the *Blood-Tide*. It is part of Confed policy, especially in the Centauri Alliance, to—"

"Thank you, Flower," Tetsami said. "Once the marines are out in the ship, Shane has to get Random to the secondary core in a minute and a half and hook him up. This is the most critical part of the timing. Random has to take charge of the security setup in the space between 07:13:10 and 07:14:40, when there's no RF traffic between the guards and the ship. The transition has to be seamless, or the perimeter guards might be aware something's up. Next job Random has is to clear the shipboard security to let Mosasa onboard without a coded transponder, before his cloaking quits."

"Isn't that cutting it close for Mosasa if he's only got ten minutes?" asked Zanzibar.

"Random will make it," said Mosasa.

"So much for the hard part," said Tetsami. Levy snorted. "Since the Emerson screen on GA&A is blocking RF signals at this point, we'll have no comm between the two teams—which is okay. Less radiation for them to detect. However, team two has to assume that the ground team gets in. At exactly 07:25:00, team two is going to punch through into the warehouse sublevel. The subsurface team—Mr. Magnus, Zanzibar, and Levy—has to make their way up a floor and north until they reach the third sublevel of the office complex. This should not be difficult with our guardian angel running security—"

Did she actually say that about an AI? She shuddered. "The box we're cracking is hidden in the midst of plumbing, wiring, and suchlike. Odds are that our TEC friends don't even know what they've got there—so there probably won't be a guard. Levy is in charge of popping the safe, and inside . . ."

Tetsami had circumnavigated the table twice, and she was back to her own seat. She turned toward Dom and handed him her remote. She sat and Dom stood up. Dom suddenly seemed to reach a level of *presence* that he hadn't had up until then. Suddenly he looked like a CEO, a leader. He sucked in a breath and smiled. It was a small smile, and Tetsami suspected that the only other person to notice it would be Zanzibar.

"In that safe," Dom said, "is four hundred and thirty-five megagrams worth of the future."

CHAPTER TWENTY-FIVE

Conflict of Interest

"You can never know enough about a man's self-interest to be able to trust him fully."
                              —*The Cynic's Book of Wisdom*

"It is a sin peculiar to man to hate his victim."
                              —CORNELIUS TACITUS
                              (*ca* 56–*ca* 120)

"Six days ago, in the city of Godwin, three marines from this command were suddenly and deliberately attacked. Corporal Sterling and Corporal Higgins were both killed instantly. Two hours ago the third victim, Sergeant Robert Clay, died from extensive burns over ninety percent of his body."

Colonel Klaus Magnus paused to let this sink in. He had done this speech once before for the duty shift. From the look of the faces filling the cafeteria-cum-auditorium, he had their attention. The speech he was making was being broadcast throughout the complex to all the civilians, but Klaus made a point of gathering all the marines here in person. These were the ones who needed to see him face-to-face, to understand the stakes here.

Klaus let the anger creep into his voice. "These three marines were in Godwin to apprehend a deserter. They died in the line of duty. They died because of the treachery of this planet."

Klaus slapped his hand down on the podium in front of him. "Without reason or provocation, a gang of Godwin hoodlums attacked and killed three Occisis marines in the midst of their duty. Two marines crushed beyond all recognition, one burned past repair by a plasma explosion."

He slammed his hand again. "Why?"

He scanned the audience. Everyone alert. All eyes on him. Good. The "gang of Godwin hoodlums" might be an exaggeration, but he needed a little hyperbole to get his point across. Klaus could feel the anger in the air, even from the five marines he'd been forced to discipline a week ago.

"*Why?* Why this unprovoked assault? Why, when any civilized planet in the Confederacy would refuse to aid or comfort a deserter? When any civilized planet would aid in the capture and extradite such a deserter? *Why?*"

Each "why" was like a club he used to bludgeon his audience.

"By Bakunin's own rules, our only conflict is with the war profiteers we've neutralized. Our battle is with Godwin Arms and Armaments. We have made extreme, and perhaps even dangerous, concessions to avoid hostilities with any other organization on this planet."

Klaus watched his audience and felt a little internal smile when he saw a few marines nodding. One of them was Captain Murphy, Shane's replacement and an officer much more to Klaus' liking.

However, Klaus did not let his pleasure show; his face was a mask of anger and hard determination that he did his best to impart to his audience.

"Despite this, we've been under constant assault from without. Barely a week passes without the necessity of repelling an armed force from our perimeter—

"*Why?*

"We've played by this world's rules. At considerable risk to ourselves we have battled *only* with the forces of GA&A—and still, we are subject to undeclared and unprovoked attacks—

"Why?"

Klaus waited a beat for his last "why" to sink in.

"Because this is Bakunin and there are no rules here!"

"Wipe from your mind any notion that this is a normal world. This is a planet that, *by its very nature,* is at constant war with the Confederacy and all it stands for.

"No rules! Do you understand that? The evil out there? No rule of law, no rule of morality, no rule of engagement. The only rule out there is brute force and the passion of criminals rejected from every corner of the Confederacy.

"If you had any doubt in your mind, wipe it away. We are at war!"

Klaus could feel a flush inside him as he surveyed the crowd. He was winning them, had already won them.

"We've been at war ever since Bakunin accepted the seeds of anarchism into itself and opposed everything the Confederacy stands for—

"Unity,

"Diversity,

"and The Rule of Law!"

The entire room stood up and applauded him. He let the ovation wash over him in waves. Now that his marines had a concrete example of what they were fighting, they were his.

Klaus was glad he had decided to visit their burn tank. Unplugging Sergeant Clay had been a good move.

"Damn it, where have you been?" Klaus demanded. He managed to generate a spark of irritation, even after the heady experience of talking to the troops. He was locked in his office looking at a glowing blue sphere and talking to an electronically altered voice.

"I've been incommunicado—and you don't sound too happy to hear from me."

"You disappear for five days and I should be happy?" Klaus leaned back and turned the chair around to face the holo sunset over Godwin. He wondered where in that city Webster had set up shop. He wondered who Webster was.

As it was, he had no hold on Webster other than money, and that was no hold at all.

"Don't be ungrateful, Klaus. Remember who's doing who favors."

"Expensive favors."

"You accepted the terms I gave you. You're the tactical genius who screwed the grab for Shane."

Klaus spun the chair around and avoided—barely— sweeping the secure holo to the ground in fury. "How dare you—"

"I don't *have* to give you anything more, Klaus. I gave you Shane, I gave you Mosasa."

Klaus shook his head and regained his calm. Webster was lucky that he was anonymous. No one should be allowed to talk like this without repercussions. Klaus' patience had finally reached the breaking point. "I am afraid this relationship has reached the end of its usefulness."

"Don't do something stupid, Klaus. Not when I'm about to hand it *all* over to you."

Klaus' hand stopped halfway to the disconnect button. "What do you mean?"

"What do you think I mean? Why did you hire me?"

"*All* of them?"

"One thousand three hundred and eighty-seven as of last count. Plus Dominic, plus Shane, plus a handful of others."

"Where?"

"No."

Klaus was silent for a long time.

Finally, he spoke, his voice barely in control. "What do you mean, 'no?' "

Webster chuckled. "I wish you had your holo's video pickup switched on, just to see your face."

Klaus grabbed both sides of the holo, stood up, and shook it as if he could throttle Webster by remote control. "What do you mean, 'no'?"

"I mean that I have to be compensated for the risk I'm taking."

"What risk?"

"Believe me, you don't want to know. But you're go-

ing to have to quadruple the balance on my account before I hand you anything."

"You don't know what you're asking."

"I know exactly what I'm asking. I've got a monitor on
the account active right now, and I'll talk once I see numbers change."

"Right now?"

"Unless you want a nasty surprise or two in the morning."

"What do you mean?"

"Pay."

Klaus debated a moment, only a moment, before he
went to the main terminal on his desk and began to transfer funds. It only took a few minutes to do. With his account at TEC, his finances for discretionary spending
were effectively unlimited. If he hesitated at all, it was
because it galled him to be dictated to.

If he ever found out who Webster was, he was a dead
man—

Or woman.

"There, you have your money."

"Very good, Klaus. For a minute there, I thought you
were going to let your pride screw you up again."

"Talk, damn you."

"There are two pieces to this, and you better take notes
because I'm not going over this again. First, there's the
coordinates of a particular mountain valley you'll find
interesting—"

Klaus stored the location of Dom's little commune on
the computer in his desk.

"Next, if you want Dominic himself, you're going to
have to make a few modifications to your ship before oh-
six-hundred tomorrow morning. . . ."

PART THREE

Covert Action

"Whatever is not nailed down is mine. Whatever I can pry loose is not nailed down."

—COLLIS P. HUNTINGTON
(1821–1900)

CHAPTER TWENTY-SIX

Media Exposure

"Most of life is sitting around waiting for the shitstorm to start."

— *The Cynic's Book of Wisdom*

"Property is theft."

—PIERRE-JOSEPH PROUDHON
(1809–1865)

06:30:00 Godwin Local

"Twenty minutes, people. Get your shit together." Tetsami's voice echoed through the tunnel even though she was whispering into a tight-beam LOS communicator. Down the tunnel, Ivor's contragrav was invisible but for the red warning lights glowing through the digging equipment's scaffolding.

Mosasa, Shane, and Random were up there waiting for the signal to make the punch through to the surface.

Tetsami was under more scaffolding at her end. Above her, a trio of mining robots hugged the walls of a triangular hole. The hole went up at a steep angle to end facing a scarred concrete ceiling thirty meters away. From Tetsami's position she could barely see the concrete underside of the GA&A complex, lit by the targeting lasers from the robots.

In an hour that concrete ceiling wouldn't exist.

"Shane's made it into position," came Ivor's voice over the communicator.

The ground team would be up the hole. Shane and company were another thirty meters closer to the surface than GA&A's subbasement. They had to weave through a lot more scaffolding. The hole under the woods traveled through fifteen meters of clay, soil, and mulch after it left the rock that housed the maglev tube. Keeping the hole from caving in required a lot of scaffolding—and the last five meters would have no support.

Eventually, Ivor would have to get his contragrav van up that hole—he was the only person Tetsami would trust with *that* job.

"Tell the team to prep for the signal."

"Will do," Ivor replied. Shane and company were out of direct RF contact because of rock and soil. At the moment, Ivor was Tetsami's only link to them. Once the job started, the only comm they'd have would be the clock.

A clock that read 6:35. It was time to grab the sat.

Tetsami opened the back of the maglev van parked next to her hole. Inside, Zanzibar was checking the charge on their weapons. Beyond the front of the van, Dom and Levy were making final checks on their equipment. Flower's feathery form sat in the passenger seat in the van. It had insisted on coming, even though it had done its job during the planning stages. It wanted to see the operation personally, and right now it was watching everything with its serpentine, eyeless face.

Tetsami pulled a case containing the portable groundstation and attached it to a loose cable that was lying on the floor of the tunnel. The cable led off to the west, where it led to a surface sat antenna.

On the floor of the van she opened the case and powered it up. A holo globe began to rotate above the groundstation, and lights carved out the tracks of the orbital flotsam that surrounded Bakunin. Tetsami tapped in a few code sequences, and tracks began falling out of the picture. By the end of her key sequence, only one glowing yellow track remained, pacing Bakunin's equator as the planet turned.

Tetsami looked up at Zanzibar, who had finished with the weapons. "Zanzibar, I'm going to fugue out for a few minutes while I talk to the sat. Keep tabs on Ivor in case something ugly happens."

Zanzibar nodded wordlessly. Tetsami didn't like the expression Dom's sergeant wore. Zanzibar had never been enthusiastic about this mission, despite her loyalty to Dom. In fact, with the exception of Dom, she didn't seem to fully trust anyone else on the team.

Despite Dom's assurances, Tetsami understood the feeling. Attacks by Confed marines on two separate occasions made everyone a little nervous. However, Dom had assured everyone—Tetsami and Zanzibar included—that he was in control of the situation.

Besides which, they had a very narrow window in which to pull this off, leak or no leak.

Tetsami looked off, past Zanzibar and Flower, and at Dom.

You're hiding something. You're always *hiding something.*

Tetsami jacked into the groundstation and felt the shell software take over her senses. It was a high-class shell she'd written herself. It grabbed the whole sensorium in order to get the biggest shitload of info across in the shortest possible time. Every sense—vision, hearing, smell, kinesthetic—meant something.

She felt herself shoot through black space, a virtual universe that had every distraction edited out. There were only two things here. Her, and the commsat.

A glowing yellow dot appeared and, as she focused, shot toward her. In Tetsami's time-dilated world its approach was majestic, even though its appearance and orientation took only a fraction of a second.

It resembled a golden spider. Its body was a spherical golden shell made of geodesic hexagons, its legs beams of yellow light flying off to infinity. Tetsami skimmed the surface of the geodesic, a tiny fly darting through its web, looking for the hole.

Millions of command structures shot by her, glowing, golden, venomous. The defenses on this sat were active and waiting for her to take a single misstep so they could entangle her and suck her dry.

However, Troy Broadcasting wasn't quite as worried about the integrity of their transmission command set as they were about the integrity of the sat itself, or the content of their broadcast. It wasn't a major weakness, but it was enough for her. Her fly landed on a control node right next to one of the golden lasers, and she leeched on to the control driver for the sat's broadcast antenna.

The sat's whole instruction set shuddered as her commands rippled through it. It tried to poison the data, but she had venom of her own—and since the sat's first priority was to survive and its second to keep broadcasting no matter what, Tetsami's little fly finally melded into the structure of the spider.

Tetsami unhooked herself from her subprogram and slipped away from the sat's command structure. The golden sphere had changed. There was a black dot, a speck really, glued to its surface. Tetsami's program.

And now the legs were moving. They were brightening and slowly converging on a new leg that had sprouted below the sphere. One of those glowing legs of light passed by her like a searchlight, and she had a brief full-sensory image of a melee going on in TBC's gladiatorial stadium. An ax was swinging right at her as the contact was broken.

Mission accomplished.

She allowed herself a silent mental chuckle at the expense of Troy Broadcasting. It might not be a suitable payback for the death of her parents, but her little program might permanently lock up the sat's command structure and cost TBC a few megagrams in lost revenue and hardware.

Of course, all that was secondary.

Tetsami jacked out. The time was now 6:47.

"No problems?" she asked Zanzibar.

Zanzibar shook her head.

Tetsami got on the comm to Ivor. "We got the sat."
Tetsami waited until the minute rolled over. *"Two minutes
to zero."*

CHAPTER TWENTY-SEVEN

Crossing the Rubicon

"Anyone who doesn't fight for his own self-interest has volunteered to fight for someone else's."
—*The Cynic's Book of Wisdom*

"Every war, at its root, is a war of trade."
—ROBERT CELINE
(1923–1996)

06:50:00 Godwin Local

"... Two ... One ... *Now!*"

Ivor's voice, coming from the midst of the scaffolding below, was muffled by the helmet on Shane's modified armor. At his command, she activated the computers on the three mining robots that surrounded her.

Her visor polarized as the mining lasers fired, circling her, slicing through the few meters of soil that separated them from the surface. The scaffolding rang with showering debris. Fist-sized chunks of dirt rained down and shattered on the struts in a controlled avalanche. Shane tightened her grip as dirt and gravel pelted her.

Inside her helmet it sounded like ripping canvas.

Within a minute it was over, and the sound of raining debris was replaced by the sound of wind whistling past an opening above her. Shane looked up and saw a starry early-morning sky.

She was scrambling up the lip even before Ivor said, "Move."

Lights blinked on her helmet's display as she cleared the edge of the hole. The telltales said that her RF field was already soaking up a few thousand kilowatts of Tetsami's commsat broadcast. She turned around and helped move equipment out of the hole—Mosasa's long-range stunner, the huge powerpack for it, Mosasa's tool kit, and the briefcase that held Random Walk.

Ivor pushed Mosasa over the lip as he scrambled over himself. Then he scooped up the stunner and the fifty kilo power source. Mosasa grabbed his tool kit, and Shane grabbed Random.

No words were passed as they jogged to the western edge of the woods. They ducked around trees, over logs, and scrambled down the gentle slope toward GA&A. Shane almost blundered out into the open when they reached the edge of the woods. There was no thinning before the clearing. The forest simply stopped about a hundred meters from the perimeter.

The four of them, Random mute inside his box, faced the curving end of GA&A's office complex. It filled their entire view out of the woods. A curving concrete wall, seven stories tall, hid behind the spikes of the perimeter towers. It was overlaid by a distorting heat shimmer caused by the defensive screens of the *Blood-Tide*.

Not for the first time, Shane wondered what she was doing here.

She turned around, and Ivor and Mosasa had already set up the stunner. The device was an ugly-looking hybrid, cobbled together by Mosasa to fit the requirements of the mission: dropping a marine in full combat armor at one hundred meters without alerting the complex or damaging his suit.

I agreed to this, Shame thought. *Am I really saving lives?*

Or am I simply seeking revenge for my own people shooting at me?

"It's ready," said Mosasa.

"Good," said Ivor. "Because there's the target."

Ivor was right. The marine roaming the perimeter had just rounded the curve of the office complex and come into view. Right now, he was the only marine in line of sight. He would remain so for close to ten minutes. Shane got behind the ugly-looking gun and sighted through it.

The monster she was about to fire had begun as her own personal stunner. Then Mosasa got hold of it. Among a number of additions to it was the stabilized tripod, the targeting computer and integral sight, and the heavily insulated stock that kept the stunner itself from touching the computer, the tripod, or the gunner. The insulation was necessary because a pair of superconducting cables led from the stunner to a fifty kilo power sink that once was the emergency backup for a Hegira Starliner's tach-drive.

The principle was still the same as for her personal stunner. The small baton generated an Emerson field in a thin paraboloid—the generator at the tip being the focus—and it was programmed so that interference with a normal laser-damping field would create a neural stun field.

The difference was before Mosasa got hold of it, the effective range of the stunner was five meters before the field's parabola became too diffuse. Even at that range, the energy it sucked was on the order of a plasma rifle's. Mosasa had powered it up. It now carried about four hundred times the wattage and would probably melt when she fired it. The power spike would be so intense that GA&A security couldn't miss it—*if* they weren't having other problems with all their detection gear at the moment.

Shane looked through the sight and tracked her target.

She wondered if she knew the soldier out there. It wasn't Conner. The form was wary, not panicky. Shane watched the soldier sweep the plasma rifle to cover the woods. Very methodical. Shane wasn't worried about being seen. All the sensors on that suit—gray urban camouflage just like her own—would be washed out by RF interference right now.

The stunner's targeting computer, specially RF shielded by Mosasa, locked on the marine.

Shane wished there'd been time to test Mosasa's gadget. Her stunner had relied on a few gigs of sensitive programming to do what it did right. Mosasa had replaced that with his own programming, necessary to keep the stun field from dispersing against the defensive screens of the *Blood-Tide* instead of the intended target.

The plasma rifle swung back toward their position as the marine continued the patrol. The computer sight was still flashing "target acquired" at her.

Damn it, why was she stalling?

Did she know this person?

She'd never frozen in combat before, never.

An overwatted stunner could kill a person.

The marine stopped and turned. The plasma rifle tracked back to Shane's position. The image froze for a second in Shane's sights. Then the marine took a step forward.

Shane fired.

For the first time in her life, Shane felt a recoil from an energy weapon. The jerk she felt was the field generator exploding. Blue arcs from the discharging field shot out of the woods for ten meters. The cables to the stunner melted, smoldering in the mulch. The insulation cracked and blackened and the small targeting screen burned its last image permanently on its surface.

The image was of the marine dropping.

"Got 'em," Shane said. She looked across to the crumpled form and decided that she had finally chosen sides.

For better or worse. I can't go back now.

"Gods be with us today," Mosasa whispered. He started running to the perimeter. Ivor followed, and Shane took up the rear. The dead stunner was left where it was. It had served its purpose.

Shane wondered at Mosasa. At times the technical expert was prone to strange archaisms. But, then, stress could bring out odd things in a person. Especially combat stress.

As for instance, right now she was panting and grinning like a maniac. Whoever it was, she'd just dropped him. Poor guy didn't even know what happened. It got her adrenaline pumping double-time and brought a feral smile even if there was a possibility she'd just killed someone who'd been a friend.

When all this was over, she was going to have to have a long talk with her neuroses.

When she got to the heap of marine, Mosasa had already stripped the helmet and had cables leading into the body of the suit. "I got patches into the transponder and the data recorder. Open up."

Shane ripped off a patch that covered a few ports that Mosasa had installed in her armor. Mosasa had done extensive mods to the operating system of her armor, chief of which was modifying her transponder and data recorder to leech security codes from another suit's system.

Mosasa plugged her into the fallen marine, and she saw that it was Corporal Hougland. Ivor noticed her stare and said, "Don't worry, she's still alive."

That generated two thoughts. She thought, *You're not supposed to worry about the enemy's casualties.*

The other thought was that Corporal Hougland would have killed her without any hesitation.

Mosasa nodded a few times, looking at a readout mounted on Shane's midsection next to the ports he was using. "Good, the transponder codes took. You're her now." Mosasa gestured toward Hougland and disconnected the cables at the same time.

Mosasa was right. Shane could call up Hougland's tac database, the info on her data recorder, even the radio was modified to synthesize Hougland's voice with patterns lifted from the recorder.

"Okay," Shane said. "Ivor, take her. Mosasa, let's get moving. It's already past seven."

Shane and Mosasa ran to catch up with Hougland's patrol route while, behind them, Shane caught a glimpse of

Ivor grabbing Hougland in a fireman's carry and heading toward the woods.

I'm her now, Shane thought to herself.

It was an uncomfortable feeling.

CHAPTER TWENTY-EIGHT

Loopholes

"Never turn your back on the villain, especially when he's unconscious."

—*The Cynic's Book of Wisdom*

"God Almighty hates a quitter."

—Samuel Fessenden
(1847–1908)

07:01:00 Godwin Local

Ivor Jorgenson ran full tilt into the woods, toward the bolt-hole. Halfway there his shoulders ached and his lungs were on fire. The marine was too damn heavy. He had to put her down for a while.

Once he was out of eyeball range of the complex, he had time to set her down. The marine would be out for hours; they wouldn't need him to pilot things until everything was over, forty-five minutes from now. It was good that he had the time, because the minute he leaned his burden against a convenient tree, he felt every joint in his body protest the exertion of the last ten minutes.

He was too old for this.

In his prime he could have carried this woman across a few klicks of tundra. He knew that because, when he *was* in his prime and Fleet Commander of the Styx Presidential Guard, he had done just that for a soldier wounded in an aircar crash.

But that was two decades ago.

Or, another way of thinking, it was only nine years ago.

Or, yet another way of thinking, it had never happened at all.

Hands on his knees, catching his breath, he realized that this was the first time he had thought about Styx in years. What should have been angry thoughts were predominantly nostalgic now. The nostalgia was embarrassing.

You can be nostalgic for anything if you're far enough removed from it.

And Ivor's memories of Styx were as far removed from present reality as they could get. Because of his brush with the wrong end of a wormhole, a decade-long chunk of his memory just didn't happen as far as the rest of the universe was concerned.

Even if the universe didn't accept it, that decade was still credited to his body's account. He was twenty years older than he'd been on Styx, and he wasn't up to lugging heavy marines in full armor uphill through dense woods.

Slowly, he stopped hyperventilating and felt his muscles unkink.

Once he could move without pain, he decided to lighten his burden. Nothing in the plan called for him to take the armor, too. He was just supposed to restrain the comatose marine. He walked over to her.

The name-tag read Hougland.

"Pleased to meet you, miss." He told her as he felt for the emergency release on the suit. Triggering it would scrag the armor, but it needed to be there for medical access in field conditions. He groped around until he found the trigger.

"Forgive the imposition, but I just can't carry all this."

He hit the release and multiple hisses announced the separation of the seams on the armor. He picked up Hougland's chest piece and looked for a suitable place to ditch her armor. A few meters away he saw a deadfall that seemed to fit the bill. He picked up a few more pieces and walked over to the pile of old wood and began to dig a suitable hole for the armor.

He was in the midst of digging when he noticed a red light flashing on the inside of one of the leg pieces he had brought over.

He picked it up and examined it more closely.

The flashing light was the last of a series on the side of a small rectangular box that would fit snugly on the inner thigh. A sick feeling washed over Ivor when he saw it.

This box, and things like it, went by a number of names—hardwire lightning, express, black speed—all of which meant the same thing; military biological augmentation via drugs and electronic hardware that hyped metabolism, recovery times, and reflexes to screaming high levels. The cost to the body using such things—skyrocketing blood pressure, burned out neurons, not to mention addiction—was so high that it was insane to use the things outside of combat.

If the marines out there were wired with this, then they were expecting to be attacked.

Ivor was about to run for the bolt-hole to warn Tetsami and the rest of the team about the set up when the second thought hit him.

Maxed recovery time.

Ivor turned and ducked just in time to avoid decapitation by the branch Hougland was swinging. He hadn't heard her approach, and he was very glad that Mosasa had taken her weapons.

Hougland swung again and Ivor scrambled back, over the uncertain footing of the deadfall. He felt a breeze as a meter-long chunk of wood the diameter of his thigh swept by his face.

We took her weapons, but why am I unarmed?

Ivor backed over the precarious footing as the marine, clad only in briefs and a sweat-stained T-shirt, advanced on him.

Because we thought the driver didn't need any, idiot.

"Do you think," he said, nearly slipping on a loose branch, "that we could talk this out?"

Another swing. Not lethal, she was just testing the range. Ivor was beginning to feel that all this was a bit much. He glanced behind him and saw that he was backing toward the lip of a ravine.

The ground shifted beneath him, and he felt his right foot sliding downward. He still had Hougland's thigh armor in his right hand. "Corporal Hougland, I'm sure we can come to some accommodation before permanent violence is done."

A look of extreme distaste crossed her face. "I'm a marine, old man!" she shouted at him. She stepped forward and swung a skull-cracking arc at his head.

Apparently negotiation was not an option.

Ivor swung up his arm to block the blow with the thigh-piece from Hougland's armor. The two met with a crack and Hougland looked surprised.

"All my age means, girl, is I've got a dozen years combat experience on you."

Ivor kicked out with his right foot, spraying deadwood shrapnel at Hougland. She fell back, still holding on to her club, and Ivor had to make a complicated hopping dance to keep his footing as he stumbled down the front of the deadfall.

By the time Ivor was on solid ground again, Hougland had gotten up and was brandishing her log at him.

"You realize—"

She interrupted him with a sweep that he had to parry.

"—that this is pointless. This whole operation is in other hands now."

Sweep, block.

"Whatever happens, it'll be over before either of us can do anything."

A lie, but who was counting?

She pulled an obvious feint—however well someone's trained, a log is still an unsubtle weapon—and lunged to slam him in the groin. Ivor danced aside.

Enough was enough. Old man or not, he *needed* those.

Her next swing he made to block again with the thigh armor, but instead of blocking it, he let it glance off the armor and slip inside his guard. The log slammed into his side at a rib-bruising velocity. Before she could recover the log, Ivor wrapped his arm around it and held.

He grabbed it so hard that he thought he could feel the muscles in his arm tear. Hougland wasn't expecting that, and she froze for a second.

"Playtime's over." Ivor shot a vicious kick at Hougland's midsection, doubling her over. "Time for bed." Ivor backhanded her with his left fist as hard as he could. Her head snapped back and she fell, nose and mouth bloody.

As she fell back, Ivor tossed the log aside. The right side of his body felt like a gigantic bruise.

While Hougland was still dazed, Ivor grabbed her wrists and bound them together with his belt. Then he tossed her over his left shoulder and started back toward the bolt-hole. Ivor thought of the sixty-meter climb down the scaffolding and thought, *This isn't going to be easy.*

CHAPTER TWENTY-NINE

Securities Exchange

"Seeing is believing, but belief doesn't amount to much."

—*The Cynic's Book of Wisdom*

"Don't assume you know anyone."

—Sylvia Harper
(2008–2081)

07:11:00 Godwin Local

It was amazing how little everything seemed to have changed. The patrols, the guard towers, the *Blood-Tide*, all were just as Shane had left them. It was an eerie sensation. . . .

Hell, if it feels odd to me, I wonder how Dominic feels.

That thought brought the predictable internal debate about just who here was on the side of the angels. Shane was slowly coming to the decision that if God had any brains at all, he had washed his divine hands of all of this long ago. Her drill sergeant had once yelled at her, after a particularly nasty battle simulation, that there were no good guys or bad guys, only fuckups and survivors—

What are you, Shane?

God, she could still remember his breath.

Why did she agree to this?

She tried to lock her mind back in the present. She

checked the timer; it was twenty seconds after the last time she looked. Seemed longer.

The entire quad between the residence tower and the offices was bare of people. That would last another one and a half minutes. She glanced toward the nose gear and looked for Mosasa. She could find him, if she stared.

Mosasa had cooked up another toy for this job, in addition to her stunner and her transponder. He had built a personal cloaking field. Shane was sure that somewhere in the toy stores of the Confed Intel community there were much more advanced versions of what Mosasa had cobbled together. The principle was simple enough. Key an Emerson field for wide spectrum interference and cover the hole with a holo projection. Simple it was, but there were some major problems with it.

First was power consumption. The wider the range of wavelengths an Emerson field screened, the greater the power consumption—exponentially. A normal personal field relied on software and feedback from the screen itself to shift to whatever wavelength seemed threatening. The cells for a standard personal field could last for sixteen hours of continuous operation. With Mosasa adjusting his field to suck up the visible spectrum and into the UV and IR, he had ten minutes.

The other problem was the holo cameras and projectors which, obviously, had to project beyond the field to do any good. The little pea-sized cameras and projectors bounced outside the perimeter of the field on hair-thin wires. They not only provided the data for the cloaking holo projection, they also allowed Mosasa to see.

It took Mosasa one day to pull it all together, and the damn thing worked. Right now she was staring right at him—but what she saw seemed more like some floating pocket of denser air. The apparent refraction and heat shimmer, sometimes at right angles to the holo projection, sometimes looking reflective rather than transparent, made Mosasa look like a mirage or a trick of the light.

Shane stared and could barely see the cameras hovering over nothing.

The sight gave her a headache.

Mosasa was halfway up the landing gear, doing things to the *Blood-Tide*'s field control system. After a few seconds Mosasa said, "Step out from under the ship. I have the diameter programmed, but there might be some bleed-through."

"What about you?"

"Don't worry about me, just clear the ship. Ten seconds."

Shane moved out from under the *Blood-Tide* and around to the boarding ramp in the nose. She kept her eye on the timer in the corner of her headsup as she turned to face the ship.

07:13:08 . . .

07:13:09 . . .

07:13:10 . . .

Right on time, a warning light came on in her display. A too-weak neural stun field had washed by her, diminished by its expanding radius. Damn it, Mosasa was right next to it. Shane started for the landing gear and a voice near her wrist said, "What are you doing?"

It was Random's briefcase.

"I thought you were off," she whispered, making sure the suit's comm was still off.

"You turn off *your* brain just because you have nothing to do at the moment?"

"I was going—"

"I know where you were going. Don't worry about Mosasa; it was part of the calculations. A ship field control has a wide tolerance for the field diameter. He had to push the programming five meters past the skin of the ship. He's fine."

"But—"

"Get up the ramp!"

It was a choice between taking Random's word and possibly blowing the most closely timed part of the operation.

Fuckup, or survivor?

"You better be right, Random."

"Believe me. I know *exactly* what Mosasa's capable of."

Shane darted up the ramp and went through the security pass procedure with the computer, the same way she'd done a dozen times before. This was the first time she thought she'd get fried for her trouble.

After an incredibly long two-second pause, the computer accepted her as Hougland.

She stepped through the open air lock. At this point she was supposed to hear radio confirmation from the skeleton crew manning the *Blood-Tide,* who would ask why the hell Hougland was on board rather than scouting the perimeter like she was supposed to.

The fact that they didn't showed that Mosasa's stunfield jimmy had worked. The *Blood-Tide* crew was out of it for the next three or four hours, and if Random was patched into the security comm in time, no one in the complex would know the difference.

Shane went down a deck and ran half the length of the ship to get to the secondary computer core. It was deep, beyond the weapons stores. The corridor was yellow, black, and red, the colors of restricted access. Most of the doors she passed had blinking red lights—closed and locked.

The computer room was all the way back, at the end of the corridor. The last room before the start of the massive engine systems. The brushed-steel door was more heavily armored than the weapons lockers. Its light was blinking red.

Hougland's codes didn't work.

"Shit."

"No problem," said Random. A motor whirred, a panel on the side of the briefcase slid aside, and a small flexible cable snaked out. At the end of the cable was a needle-thin probe.

"There's a hole next to the keypad. Insert the end of this."

Shane picked up the silver probe and slid it in the hole.

Almost instantly, the light flashed green.

Shane tried the door and it slid to the side. The probe withdrew, and Shane walked into a chamber lined with screens, readouts, access panels, ports, and keypads. She set Random's case on a small ledge, waist-high, on the opposite side of the room.

"Turn me over."

"Oh, sorry."

Shane flipped the case over. The lid popped open and a cable slithered out.

"We have half a minute," Random said. "Do exactly as I say."

Suddenly, Shane was frantically following Random's orders, plugging cables that snaked from the box, punching instructions on keypads, popping access ports, and at one time killing the power for half a wall of protesting electronics.

When she was done, her headsup chronometer read 07:15:15.

"Oh, Christ, it's over."

"What?" came a voice from a speaker grille on the wall.

"We're nearly thirty seconds over. The routine radio checks to the bridge—"

"Oh no worry—the comm circuits were the first thing I patched."

Shane smiled weakly. "Of course."

"That's why they don't call it artificial stupidity. Come to think, that's as good a term as any for this security system. If I had some hands at the moment I'd slap the braindead hackhead who wrote up these interfaces. I'm losing sixty percent of my efficiency just talking to the rest of the complex."

Shane kept looking up the hall. "Where's Mosasa?"

"I keep telling you, don't worry about Mosasa."

"What do you mean, is he on board?"

"Look, he's not doing anything to jeopardize this mission."

"Then where is he?" Shane had a very bad picture of Mosasa crumpled in a heap by the landing gear, his cloak drained of power.

"We decided that it was just too close a thing for him to come through the dock before his cloak failed. He climbed up into the landing gear housing."

Shane tried to stare but had no idea what to stare at. She ended up rotating in a small circle, looking up at the walls of the computer core. "Didn't we go through that in planning? There's no space for anyone to crawl through the structure down there."

"Mosasa can."

"He's two-and-a-half meters tall!"

"Well, he has to partially dismantle himself to do it."

"Huh?"

One of the grates in the floor started to move, and Shane swung her laser to cover it.

"Don't worry, that's Mosasa. I guess we'll have to let you in on a little secret."

The grate slid aside and Shane saw a dark hand appear.

"How the hell?"

A leg appeared, sticking up at an unnatural angle, the hand gripping the upper thigh. The hand tossed it, and the leg—just the leg, by itself—fell over with a thump, landing by Shane's feet.

Shane took a step back and another leg was tossed out of the hole.

Then a left arm.

As Mosasa's dragon-tattooed torso chinned itself into view, Random said, "You see, Mosasa's as much a construct as I am."

CHAPTER THIRTY

Capital Expenditures

"It is a fundamental inequity of the universe that, while you have only one life to give, you can take as many as you damn well please."
— *The Cynic's Book of Wisdom*

"The torments of martyrdom are probably most keenly felt by the bystanders."
— RALPH WALDO EMERSON
(1803–1882)

07:24:30 Godwin Local
"Thirty seconds," Tetsami said over the comm.

Dom looked down the steep hole and could barely see the commuter tunnel. In less than half a minute he would be back in GA&A. A familiar calm frosted his nerves. The same icy stillness that had gripped him when GA&A had been taken over. Not numbing this time—

Exhilarating.

"Twenty seconds."

The three of them were in position behind the trio of mining robots. Levy was in the center; Dom and Zanzibar were leaning inward against either wall.

Each of them carried a Dittrich 1.5 mm Hyper-Velocity Electromag, a low profile weapon. An HVE wasn't the most powerful handheld projectile weapon, and it didn't

have the greatest range, but firing 300 monocrys steel flechettes per second it could probably handle anything
they'd run into—without causing a hideous energy spike.
The only problem with the Dittrich HVE was that the
ammo disappeared in a distressingly short period of time.

"Ten seconds."

They also all had backpacks filled with Levy's equipment. And trailing behind them was a buzzing contragrav
sled. It was custom-made, and the most expensive piece
of equipment going into the complex—if you didn't count
Random Walk, who was priceless. The sled was five meters long and two wide, a simple platform anchored on
top of a toroid contragrav generator that was rated for
nearly two tons. It was led by a taut cable whose handle
doubled as a control panel. The sled was made of an
aluminum-diamondwire composite and had only ten kilos
of inertia.

"Now."

His companions turned away, but Dom kept staring at
the concrete underside of what had once been his building. The photoreceptors scaled down the dazzling input as
he watched the mining robots cut into the concrete at the
top of the shaft. Three beams of intense light darted
across the concrete, too fast to distinguish as single
beams. They cut a repetitive grid pattern in the triangular
concrete face.

Gravel sheeted off the wall, showering over them and
down the floor of their tunnel. Dust billowed up, making
Dom want to sneeze.

In less than three seconds the lasers hit the reinforcing
rods.

If Random wasn't in charge of security now, the whole
team was in trouble. There were intrusion sensors to detect any breach in an external wall. They weren't as efficient as an Emerson field, but you couldn't trust feedback
from part of a field that passed through matter—too many
spurious readings—so intrusion detection under the complex was a matter of wires, computers, and cameras.

The reinforcing rods that the robots diced apart were

also a circuit in the security grid. Now they were so much
polyceram dust.

The lasers hit a point where the floor above them was
no longer sound enough to support its own weight. A
grinding snap filled the small space, and the wall erupted
into a cloud of dust. Gravel rained down on the three of
them and caused an odd resonant hum as it bounced
across the contragrav sled.

The range finders on the mining robots detected the
sudden absence of their target, and they ceased firing.

As the dust cleared, Dom queried his onboard computer. The time was 07:25:12. It had taken the lasers ten
seconds to slice through the wall. Dom decided to remember that fact if he ever put up another building.

"Let's go," said Zanzibar. She lowered her weapon and
darted to the edge of the hole, scanning the room beyond.
After a second, she waved Levy ahead. Levy had the sled,
and as he passed Dom, Dom had to flatten against the
wall to let the sled by. It was odd, watching the sled follow Levy. It wanted to stay horizontal, and in the steep
tunnel that meant that the front end had the same clearance to the floor as the rear did the ceiling. It could
barely get past the robots.

When Dom followed Levy through the hole, he heard
the robots begin their withdrawal. There was no sign of
alarm, nor even any sign of habitation. So far, so good.

The three of them moved through the silent warehouse
level. The warehouse was dark, filled with crates of un-
sold weapons Dom had ordered fabricated for the ficti-
tious ship *Prometheus*.

There were a few thousand crates of everything GA&A
made, and it gave Dom a moment's pause.

*Why did they use such a big order to cover themselves?
Couldn't they have punched in for a much smaller pretense?*

Did they want *five hundred tons of weapons?*

Dom had yet to allow himself to wonder deeply about
what the TEC was doing here. If he had managed to think
of it at all, lately, it simply seemed part of his brother's
age-old, possibly justified, vendetta.

But this was larger than his brother.

Even if Klaus had managed authorization for his own games, there had to be some larger pretense for the TEC to support him. Something the old man, Dimitri, would approve of. A TEC operation outside the bounds of the Confederacy was politically dangerous, and there had to be something here to justify the risk.

But what?

For the briefest instant, Dom flashed on the idea of conquest. Maybe the TEC wanted to take over—

That was ludicrous. The operation here had barely a thousand people by now, and only one hundred fifty—at most—had any military training. Something the size of GA&A was about the only thing they *could* take over. One hundred fifty marines wouldn't be able to take a moderate-sized commune. Much less a city. Or the *planet*. And if the TEC imported *that* kind of force anywhere, especially into non-Confed space where jurisdiction was open to any lawyer's interpretation, it would count as political suicide.

Planetary self-determination was one of the cornerstones of the oft-bent but rarely broken Confederacy Charter. It was probably the only reason that the planet Bakunin was allowed to exist in its current form.

However, after logically limiting the TEC activity to things less grandiose, he was left with one disturbing fact to consider: There was enough hardware down here to equip nearly a half-million infantrymen. And once they had the new computer on-line, they could make *more.*

Dom let those thoughts pass and concentrated on covering Levy's rear. They remained lucky. They wove through ten-meter cubes of boxes stacked for shipping, and saw no one. A few loaders were parked at odd angles, abandoned in the midst of their jobs. It looked as if nobody had been down here since the attack.

As they reached the point where the subterranean warehouse passed under the office complex, Zanzibar held up her hand and waved Dom up to her.

Dom stepped up and saw why Zanzibar had stopped.

"Sir, I just wanted a second opinion on how old this is."

Dom looked down at the wreckage.

One of the crate-cubes had partially collapsed, completely filling a five-meter gap between it and its neighbor. Both cubes had charred streaks that were signs of laser fire. A corpse was half-buried by the wreckage. In the dry, climate-controlled environment of GA&A's warehouse, the body was mummifying.

"They just left him here?" Dom asked no one in particular.

"If it's the Executive Command, I believe it," Levy said.

Zanzibar nodded.

Dom looked around and saw more scars of laser fire, on the packing crates, on the floor, on the walls. "It looks like he got lost in the general chaos of the invasion. They'd have no idea who they'd captured and who escaped. No reason to go hunting for corpses." Dom kneeled by the body.

"Did you know him?" Levy asked.

"Harrison Bradley." Dom's computer coughed up the data without comment. "Hired him five years ago. He was the foreman down here. Looks like he popped a crate and fired on the marines—idiot."

"Let's go, sir." Dom felt Zanzibar's hand on his shoulder.

"We have a minute. Go to the lift. If Random's on the ball, it's waiting for us."

"But, sir—"

"Wait for me. I need a few seconds alone."

"Sir—"

Dom heard Levy say, "Give him his minute," and he heard the two of them withdraw.

What the hell is this?

Dom knelt by the body of his second-shift warehouse foreman and wondered what the hell he was doing. It wasn't like he knew this guy. Damn, he'd never even met Harrison Bradley.

However, for some reason, instead of running for it as

he was supposed to, Bradley had found a crate of GA&A anti-armor focused plasma jets. Bradley—Bradley and others—if there was only one sniper they wouldn't have missed the body—had died trying to defend GA&A.

Dom thought that might be why he was crying.

CHAPTER THIRTY-ONE

Contingency Plans

"Screwups, like entropy, always increase over time."
—*The Cynic's Book of Wisdom*

"We have seen the bottom of the Abyss, and we fear the end is upon us."

—WILLIAM IV
(2126–*2224)

07:31:20 Godwin Local

Tetsami had watched the plan go forward flawlessly. The first try and no bugs.

Tetsami had flown all her life on her instincts. Right now her instincts were screaming at her. Nothing ever goes one hundred percent, and the better things look initially—

She would have almost preferred to have seen one big up-front unanticipated screwup. The longer she waited for it, the more nervous she got. When her LOS comm called for her, it was almost a relief.

But only a short-lived one.

She knew something had fucked the plan when she grabbed the headset off the door. Ivor's voice was chattering before she could even acknowledge the pickup.

"—ser me girl, we have a problem. A *big* problem. Tets—"

"I got you. Ice it and tell me what happened. Did the ground team get in?"

"That isn't the problem."

"What *is* the problem?"

"The guard Shane picked off had an augmentation biopack strapped to her thigh."

One of those? You don't put something like that on someone just doing guard duty. *Unless . . .*

"Sweet mother Mary and her bastard son Christ—"

"Get the picture? They're expecting us. We got to abort—"

"Damn it, Ivor, check your time! Dom and his team went in seven minutes ago. They could be at the safe already."

"Shit."

"Whafuck took your ass so long to tell me this?"

"I had to subdue a very pissed marine."

Oh. "Sorry."

"Forget it. We've got to warn our people in—"

"Shut up, let me think."

Jesus, this was bad. The TEC was expecting them to show up today. Someone in their party *was* passing info to the—

Don't think about that now, think about how you can warn everyone before all hell breaks lose.

How?

Of course!

"Ivor, leave it to me."

"Okay, what do I do with my prisoner?"

"Sit on 'em. If this goes bad, we can always try an exchange."

Tetsami stripped the headset and pulled out the groundstation that she'd used to hack the TBC sat. She looked around and saw Flower regarding her.

Why does Random give me the willies and I don't think twice about the damn alien? Never mind.

"Flower, can you handle a human gun?"

"I understand small arms operation. However, human sighting mechanisms forbid Voleran perceptions, and few arms have triggering mechanisms that are comfortable with—"

"Just tell me, can you shoot that thing?" Tetsami pointed at one of the spare Macmillan-Schmitt plasma rifles racked on the inside wall of the van.

Flower ducked its head and turned it side to side. Flower's head was hard, conical, and featureless except for the Rorschach yellow and black markings that covered its "face." Tetsami saw no eyes, but Flower's head bobbed as if it was scanning the weapon.

"Yes, after a fashion he will let me wield him. The area he covers should compensate for the aiming—"

"Good, grab him—it—and follow me."

Tetsami was getting sick of Flower's nasal wheeze. *Can you call it nasal when it doesn't even have a nose?*

Tetsami shook her head as if she could shake out all the irrelevant thoughts that were shooting around in it.

She led Flower in a race up the hole to the warehouse level. She nearly slammed face first into the ground a few times, tripping over the transverse support ribs that formed a half-stair, half-ladder up the steep-angled tunnel.

She glanced behind her to see how Flower was doing. She needn't have worried. Flower was using both legs and one arm in a fluid three-legged jog that made the alien seem to float up the tunnel behind her. Its head hovered in the geometric center of the tunnel, bobbing a meter ahead of the rest of the body. Its wings billowed behind it like a drag chute.

Tetsami was out the hole first with only a superficial scan of the room beyond. If there'd been marines down here, they'd've been down on her and the van already. No alarm had been raised yet. That meant that they had something of a chance. That also meant that Random *had* made it down to the computer core.

Assuming all that—too many assumptions but they were what she had—Tetsami might be able to keep the whole mission from imploding. If she got into the system before the marines on that damn ship woke up from Mosasa's stun field.

She opened the groundstation and pulled the connecting jacks. In a pinch the groundstation could be used as a regular terminal. She looked at Flower.

"Guess what. You get to play soldier after all."

"Something unanticipated?"

"Damn straight. The marines are prepped for combat. They're expecting us. You've got to find the safe team and warn them. You know the layout?"

"I studied every facet of the plan for my research."

"Then you know where they are—don't discharge that thing unless you're forced to. So far it looks like they don't know we're here."

"I appreciate that you believe me capable."

"Hell, you're all I got—*go!*"

Flower bobbed its head and glided down the length of the warehouse, toward the lifts to the office complex.

Tetsami took the leads from the terminal and walked over to a wall panel. The damn thing was restricted access, had a keypad, a red light, and was electromagnetically sealed. How the hell was she going to break into—

The light turned green.

"Random?"

She opened the door and found a jack for the leads to her terminal. Then she ran back and powered up the groundstation. In less than a second she was looking at a fish-eye holo of what had to be the core of the *Blood-Tide*. She saw Mosasa and Shane, but the voice the terminal relayed was Random's.

"I had a security flag on the hole—saw you come in, but there's no audio pickups down there and I'm not great at reading lips when your back's to the camera."

"Problem, Random."

"I figured."

"We've been expected. The marine you took out had a packet of black speed on her. If the guys on the ship are equipped that way—"

"Damn it," said Random, "I'm sealing the ship. All the bulkheads are coming down."

Shane said something on the holo screen, Tetsami couldn't hear it.

"Okay, I think we've got a handle on it here. Our babies are locked in, incommunicado. Worse happens and I can pulse the stun field. It'll lay out Shane, but I'll still be in control."

"Try to avoid that." *Shane? What about Mosasa?*

"I will—" Random paused for a moment. On the holo both Shane and Mosasa turned toward the now-closed door to the computer core. "You know," he continued, "your timing is impeccable. Our first marine just woke up, and he seems quite upset."

CHAPTER THIRTY-TWO

Liquid Assets

"Never say the problem is over, never mention what else could go wrong, and never say how lucky you are—there is no surer way of inviting disaster."
—*The Cynic's Book of Wisdom*

"Like liberty, gold never stays where it is undervalued."

—J. S. MORRILL
(1810–1898)

07:26:45 Godwin Local

"The easy way won't work," Dom said as he backed away from the first door. The three of them stood in one of a few dozen branching chambers sandwiched between the basement of the GA&A office complex and the subterranean warehouse levels.

Dom had tried his personal comm-code on the safe's keypad. Predictably, it didn't work. However, the attempt had shown him that the keypad was dead. It didn't flash "invalid command." It didn't flash at all. The invaders had burned the controls rather than reprogram it.

Levy looked at the keypad. "They did a low-level EMP on this. It would wipe anything volatile. They froze the doors in place."

Everyone unshouldered their burdens. Dom set up one

of the high-power cutting beams on a tripod. Then Levy
pulled out a small device and delicately placed it on top
of the nose of the laser.

"Stand back," Levy said.

Dom backed up. Levy tapped a few keys on his master
holo and there was a lightning-flash pulse from the laser.
Dom's photoreceptors compensated immediately.

"The test burst worked. This thing is calibrated."

Zanzibar was behind them, guarding their back. She
said, "You're going to cut through *that* with *that*?"

Dom saw Zanzibar's point. The outer door was only a
delaying measure. Even so, it was a square, featureless,
brushed chrome wall that reached five meters to the concrete ceiling, and five meters to the side. It was recessed
a meter back from the wall itself. The edges of the opening were faced with black metal. If there had been almost
anything else in this safe, the outer door would be
enough. Even with the lasers at their disposal it would
take hours to cut through.

However, the fact was that they had no intention of
cutting *through* the door.

Levy, grim and wordless, tapped at the holo display.
The display showed a computer model of the wall's internal structure. Levy ran his hands over the controls, and the
motorized tripod swung the laser into a new position. The
graphics on the holo changed as well, to show the area
now covered by the scanner on the laser's nose. The laser moved up and right a few millimeters. Once the laser
stopped moving, Levy began flipping through layers of his
display. Dom saw hoses and pumping equipment.

Eventually the holo showed a single two-dimensional
section of the interior under the safe. The laser and the
scanner were pointed down at a forty-five-degree angle.
Central to the picture was an s-shaped tube. Dom was
looking at a slice from it, and inside the black skin on either side of the pipe, Dom could see a grayish solid.

"What are you doing?" Dom asked.

"Time's important. The size of the hole depends on
density, pressure, viscosity and so on . . ."

He trailed off and Dom didn't interrupt him again.

A pair of green crosshairs focused on the center of the tube on the holo, and Levy tapped keys until he had a circle superimposed on the crosshairs about two millimeters wide. Levy pulled out a pair of smoked goggles and put them on.

"Now," he said.

Dom powered his photoreceptors down to minimum intensity and was briefly blind.

Then a lance of pure energy sliced open the darkness, stabbing from the tripod-mounted laser and into the ground a few centimeters short of the massive outer door. Dom began to feel heat—from the laser and its target. The smell of molten metal seared Dom's nose to the point where he turned off that sense.

It didn't keep his nose from itching.

One second, two seconds, three seconds.

By now the metal floor of the recess had sprouted a bubbling black flower around the beam of light. Beyond the black, the metal was glowing red in a circle about ten centimeters in diameter.

Levy began counting down. "Five ... Four ... Three ... Two ... *Got it!*"

Dom heard a long whistling hiss, and the hole in the floor vomited a cloud of noxious-looking steam. The hissing decreased in volume, and the door started sinking. The descent was inexorable. It had moved three centimeters, and the hissing changed in character as the steam stopped and a millimeter wide stream of hydraulic fluid shot up and hit the ceiling.

"Damn it," Zanzibar said as she stepped out of the way. "It's pissing on me."

Dom watched the door descend. Slow, too slow.

It seemed to take hours for the door to settle, but it was only 7:33 when the hydraulic fluid stopped leaking and the top edge of the outer door settled a half-meter from being flush with the floor.

Levy had three or four emergency sealant canisters— designed for spacecraft—that he had modified for this job. Instead of the bell- or fan-shaped nozzle that came with them, he had installed a hair-fine probe. Levy inserted the probe into the laser hole. He hit the button on the canister, and the can responded with an insistent hissing noise. Soon the hole overflowed with white polyceram sealant.

Levy left the can in place. The hissing continued for a few seconds, then stopped.

"So far, so good," Dom said.

Zanzibar grunted and kept looking down the corridor.

Levy loaded all the equipment onto the contragrav sled and manhandled it over the frozen door and into the room beyond. Dom followed.

The room was small, and became smaller as Levy unpacked equipment from the sled. The walls and the ceiling sloped inward toward the safe door itself. The next door was a black, featureless square about three meters on a side. Green, amber, and red lights were mounted above it. The red light was flashing; there was an interlock in the hydraulic system that was supposed to prevent both doors from opening at the same time.

Levy unloaded three lasers and tripods. One laser was much larger than the others. The extra size was its cooling system. He also unloaded probes, hoses, and more sealant canisters.

"Now," Levy said, "we come to the tricky part. Get number three pointed at the northwest corner of the door."

Levy went through much the same procedure he had gone through on the outer door. Only this time he was aiming two lasers simultaneously. The number one laser, the big one, was pointed at the door itself.

After a few minutes of aiming, Levy gave warning, donned the goggles again, and the two lasers fired. It began as before, brilliant beams slicing into the floor at a steep angle, but after a few seconds the beams dimmed, became intermittent. One would fire briefly, Levy would take off his goggles, look at his holo, don the goggles, and fire again.

It took nearly five minutes for Levy to be satisfied with the holes he had made. There was no hiss of hydraulic fluid, only a pair of millimeter-diameter holes set in blackened concrete craters.

"Half a millimeter to go, I think it's clean to the hoses themselves."

Levy handed Dom a very fine hose. The tip was metal and Dom could see an optical fiber peeking out the end.

Levy went to one hole, and Dom went to the other. The probe went smoothly down the hole. Dom fed it until it met resistance about three meters down. On the black tube there was a yellow mark that was now flush with the crater in the ground. That meant it was the end of the hole, not hung up on anything.

Levy tossed him one of the sealant canisters. "Don't overdo it. We just want to keep a vacuum. If the pump gets clogged, we're in trouble."

Dom knew. They had enough spare equipment to try one more pilot hole. But that probably wouldn't work if the hydraulic system was partially and unevenly drained. The holes were at very particular points.

Dom inserted the needle-probe into the hole next to the tube and slowly withdrew it as he discharged the sealant. The expanding polyceram goo shoved the needle-probe out, filling the crater. In seconds there was a small rock-hard white dome holding the hose in place against the concrete.

Levy examined his own handiwork and then went to examine Dom's. "Good."

Levy went to the pump. "Okay, Mr. Magnus. This is it."

That strange nervous exhilaration was back. He walked around so he could watch Levy at the pump. All the many readouts meant nothing to Dom—except maybe temperature and pressure.

Levy flipped a cover off of a red button and pressed it.

Instantly the pressure shot up as the hydraulic fluid began backfilling. Levy didn't look at the readouts. He stared at the sealant holding the hoses in place. It would be very bad if one began to leak. Neither did.

When the numbers stabilized, Dom realized he'd been holding his breath.

"Good," said Levy. He flipped a few more switches on the small pump, and it began sucking hydraulic fluid into its tank. The pressure dropped faster than it had risen. The pump whined, made a slight slurp, and the numbers dropped near zero. The readout slowed its descent until it hit some absurdly small decimal. The pump still worked, but the number stayed the same.

"That's as perfect a vacuum as we're going to get?" Dom asked.

"Yes," Levy said. "But it's enough. That was the last major technical hump." Levy smiled and Dom thought he could catch a hint of irony in Levy's voice. "We're going to have no more big proble—"

Zanzibar said, *"Shit!"*

There was a clatter outside and Dom hurdled the outer door to stand next to Zanzibar. Zanzibar was tensed to the breaking point and had her electromag pointed down the corridor, back they way they'd come.

The clatter had been the alien, Flower, dropping a plasma rifle.

"Damn it!" Zanzibar said. "I could have shot you."

"I understand, but the risk made me necessary. I come to warn you of a potential difficulty. It seems that we are expected."

Levy had been wrong. They were going to have a few more big problems.

CHAPTER THIRTY-THREE

Counterinsurgency

"It is never as bad as it seems—but sometimes it *is* worse."

—*The Cynic's Book of Wisdom*

"Distrust all men in whom the impulse to punish is powerful."

—FRIEDRICH NIETZSCHE
(1844–1900)

07:32:15 Godwin Local

Shane leaned against the massive door closing off the secondary computer core. She could barely hear the commotion beyond it. It sounded as though all five marines that manned the *Blood-Tide* had recovered from Mosasa's stun field.

The three insurgents seemed to have the momentary advantage. Random had sealed every door on the ship. He was still in charge of communication. If Random had to, he could still pulse the stun field.

In other words, all Shane had to do now was sit on her hands and brood on the irony.

Her own people were going to kill her.

Shane knew it was self-defeating to think along those lines, but she couldn't help it. After Random had been hooked into the ship's computers, her job on this mission was over. She had nothing left to do but worry.

Nothing to do unless shooting started.

And if shooting started, they were all dead.

"The safe team's opened the outer door." Random's voice came from one of the speaker grilles next to her. "Flower is making its way through the warehouse level. I see no resistance."

Shane nodded. The mission looked as though it would succeed, even if the three people in the *Blood-Tide* never made it back to Ivor's getaway vehicle. Random was checking all the sublevels constantly, and he wasn't picking up a single marine down there.

Not a single marine.

Why did that bother her?

The same reason the fact that a sentry was equipped with a bio-augmentation pack bothers me.

Those things improved combat effectiveness, but they did so much damage to the user that it was against Occisis regs to use them outside a hot combat situation. That meant the colonel was—*is*—expecting an attack.

But we're in.

"And we're trapped," Shane whispered.

"Are we?" asked Mosasa.

Shane snapped her head to look at Mosasa. Somehow she had managed to avoid thinking of him. Easier than admitting to herself that she'd once thought of him as human.

What was he?

"*I* am. You can squeeze through the vents you came through—"

Mosasa shook his head. "The emergency containment that Random used is to handle sudden depressurization. The vents are sealed. We are living off one of the redundant life-support systems now."

Shane looked at Mosasa a little differently. His dragon tattoo glistened a metallic green in the dim lighting. "I think that might be the longest speech you ever gave me."

"Perhaps."

"It's up to Random what happens now, right?"

"I trust him."

"Do you have a choice?"

"Right now neither of us does."

The grille spoke. "They've set up the equipment to take the big door. Flower's caught up with them. Flower's explaining the situation up here."

"Thanks," Shane said. Then, to Mosasa, "Who are you?"

"Tjaele Mosasa."

Shane shook her head and Mosasa gave her a surprisingly human smile showing a few decorative gold teeth.

"Your question really is, '*What* are you?' I'm what's left of a smuggler named Tjaele Mosasa who found the remnants of five old Race AIs. By the time Mosasa died, Random was his own person, but with the Confed feelings about AIs, he needed a human front. The only human he could trust was Mosasa."

"Random *built* you?"

"Custom-designed, with the addition of a chunk of Random's own memory core and what software could be lifted from Mosasa's corpse."

Shane shook her head. "Why—"

"Why anything? Survival."

The grille spoke. "Shane, Mosasa, we have a problem."

"What?" Shane and Mosasa said simultaneously.

"I just lost the interface between the ship and the rest of the complex."

Shane could feel her pulse throb in her neck, and she tasted copper in her mouth. "Can you get it back?"

"No, it was hardware. No warning, someone pulled the plug."

"Could you—" Shane began.

"We are in very deep trouble, children," Random continued, and a few holo displays began to flash scenes of the quad from various ship cameras. The *Blood-Tide* was surrounded by marines. "I've got a dozen invasive software probes attacking right now. I fused the doors and the life-support controls, I've lost communications, weapons, flight control— *Oh, shit!*"

After a pause, Random said, "They've got me locked back into the secondary core."

Shane kept staring at the holo display from the quad. They'd scrambled all the marines. It was over. The colonel had suckered them in, and now he had everybody. Shane could feel the adrenaline throbbing and desperately wanted a target to shoot at.

"They're piping in a message. I'm putting it on screen. I'm going to see if I can hack my way out of this box they put me in."

One of the holo views of the quad flickered and was replaced by the colonel's face. *He's changed,* Shane thought. *His eyes—there's a shine that wasn't there before.*

Klaus looked into the camera and talked as though he were addressing a crowd of thousands. He was perfectly choreographed—pressed, tailored and packaged for mass consumption. He looked like a man who'd been studying vids of every charismatic leader of the last three centuries.

"Dominic," he said. Shane could hear a sarcastic lilt to the name. "It has been too long since we've talked."

Huh?

"I'm afraid this is a one-way transmission. I suppose it is a shame that I cannot hear you justify yourself. Justice will have to be enough—"

"Do you know what he's talking about?" Shane whispered, even though no one could possibly overhear them.

"No. He seems to think Mr. Magnus is in here with us."

"—like my ship? You aren't going to leave it alive. We can poison the life support. We could pulse a lethal stun field tuned just for your artificial neurons. We could simply let you starve in there. This is the end, brother Jonah. You've been dead for ten years—"

"They're related?" Shane said. She had noticed the resemblance before, but—

"However, I have something to do before I finally dispose of you for good. I know you might have taken comfort in thinking your allies might have escaped."

The holo transmission shifted and Shane gasped.

On the holo was an up-angled shot of Dom's secret commune, where she had taken all the civilian prisoners. A truncated white pyramid girded by greenhouses. *How the hell?*

"We dropped a recon module from orbit just to get footage of this. We have another ship in orbit, Dominic, the *Shaftsbury*. And we have the location of that valley, down to the meter."

Klaus chuckled. The recon's cameras were looking up at the commune and past it, toward the sky. At first the sky was obscured by a holo projection; then the recon module shifted to something other than optical imaging, and the sky outside the rim of the valley turned slate-gray, the stars tiny black points. One of the stars seemed to vibrate.

"Remember 'pacifying' the coup on Styx? Or did you forget about it when you washed your hands of the TEC and the rest of your responsibilities?"

"My God," Shane said, very quietly. The star had swelled to a black blob, and it was growing. *Don't let it be what I think it is.*

"TEC called it 'shredding' when you wiped Perdition off the map. They've changed the terminology since. It's now called 'orbital reduction of the target.' "

It is.

Shane knew what she was about to see, but she couldn't pull her gaze from the screen.

Dropping large objects from orbit had always been a cheap means of mass destruction. Enough mass and enough velocity can wipe anything off the map. One problem it shared with nukes was the godawful mess it left behind. A big enough rock could make a tectonic wreck of the planet, cause ice ages, evaporate oceans, and do all kinds of other nonproductive destruction.

Needless to say, in three centuries of spaceborne warfare, someone had found a solution to that particular problem. Someone in the last century decided to try dropping a ton of polyceram filaments from orbit. That person discovered two things. First, that this particular brand of monomolecular filament stayed stable during the stress of reentry. The second discovery was that it reduced the surface to gravel to a depth of a hundred meters.

The vibrating black star now looked like a circular cloud.

Klaus kept talking.

"I want you to know that if you had come to me, surrendered, I might not have done this. Just as, had you acted differently, our mother might still be alive."

The black cloud grew, the growth accelerating. In an impossibly short time it eclipsed the entire sky. Then the camera died.

A few seconds later, as if to confirm the atrocity that had just been committed, a dull rumble vibrated the floor. When Shane felt that rumble, she could feel her stomach fall out. "God save us," Shane whispered.

Klaus' face returned to the holo, unfazed. "There went your army, Dominic. You aren't a special man any more, just some criminal Bakunin flotsam I have to flush from my ship. My only regret is that you'll be unable to attend your trial."

The holo died.

"Thirteen hundred people."

"Shane," Random said.

Shane leaned her forehead against a bulkhead. Was it her? Had she led that psychopath to all those people? Did she save eight hundred people just so the colonel could mop up the rest of the survivors?

She had just lost any justification she had for being here, fighting her people.

"Shane!"

Mosasa spun her around.

"What?"

"Random just lost life support. You have to turn your suit to full containment."

Shane flipped a few internal switches and winced at the power-level on her suit. "I only have fifteen minutes."

"That's okay," said Random. "It's only going to take them twelve to burn through the hatches to us."

CHAPTER THIRTY-FOUR

Loose Cannon

"The more complicated the situation, the sooner and more catastrophic the eventual screwup."
—*The Cynic's Book of Wisdom*

"Treason is loved of many, but the traitor hated of all."
—ROBERT GREENE
(1558–1592)

07:35:00 Godwin Local

Despite Flower's warning, there wasn't a choice. They had to finish the job.

Finish this, then think of the ground team.

So, after spending a minute burning the security cameras in their section of hallway, the job went on as planned. Levy pointed the huge number one variable-gamma laser at the main safe door. After triple-checking the team's personal radiation shields, a nervous-looking Levy began firing the laser.

The gamma-ray laser was powerful enough to cut through the door on its own, given unlimited time and power. However, that wasn't the point. The point was the fact that with the hydraulics drained the only thing holding up the door was the electromagnetic lock buried inside it. The lock's power supply also ran the field generator that was trying to soak up the energy from the gamma laser.

Levy was watching power readings and occasionally altering the frequency of the laser.

The whole process was invisible, even though Dom could swear he saw some infrared hot spots on the door.

"Now," Levy whispered as he pulled on his goggles.

Suddenly, the gamma-laser beam dropped into the visible spectrum. Despite the automatic compensations of his artificial eyes, Dom was still blinded for a second.

The floor shook with a sound like a massive bass gong. A breeze swept by Dom as his vision came back on-line. When his sight was back, the door was gone.

"We did it," Dom said.

The immediate shift from gamma radiation down to visible light had managed a microsecond-long overload in the door's power circuits. That microsecond failure was enough for the weight of the door and the vacuum hydraulics to pull it open far enough to prevent the electromagnets from closing it again.

Levy rose from behind his holo, and Zanzibar stepped up between him and Dom.

"Gods," she said.

Behind the open safe door was a long rectangular room. The visible walls, ceiling and floor were all the same black metal. The walls on either side were lined with dull-gray lockers with uniformly square doors.

Stacked on the floor ahead of them were three or four dozen white shipping containers—each the size of a footlocker, the same containers GA&A sold rifles in. One of the containers stood near the safe door. It was open.

It was half-full of Imperial Waldgrave ten-thousand mark notes.

"Zanzibar," Dom said, "help Levy load the sled. Flower can guard our rear."

"Yes, sir." Zanzibar's voice sounded distant as she stepped forward and closed the open container.

Dom felt his pulse pounding through his temple and his neck. It was a measure of how tense he was that biological imperatives were overriding his body's finely tuned mechanisms. He forced his thoughts into colder, smoother channels. *Don't get excited,* he thought, *no mistakes.*

He stepped into the safe and looked at the lockers. He tried one of the locks, and it winked green at him. These locks hadn't been wiped by the EMP that had scragged the outer door's lock. He ran his onboard computer for inventory and began popping doors.

It had taken them nearly fifteen minutes to open the safe.

It took them three to empty it.

During the loading Dom felt a sight tremor through the building. It felt minor, and no one else commented on it. Inside, however, Dom felt an irrational dread. He had no evidence, but he suspected he knew what that tremor was.

He hoped that the preparations he had started at the commune had gone according to schedule.

Again, Levy maneuvered the contragrav sled. It was burdened with a two-meter-high pile of currency from across the entire Confederacy. The boxes were filled with everything from holographic scrip from Khamsin to the exotic-matter coinage from Shiva.

Dom and Zanzibar guarded the rear of the sled, while Flower took point with the plasma weapon. Flower made a good forward observer, since it didn't seem to rely on light to see.

Their progress back to their hole was slower; the sled was now encumbered with a lot more inertia than when it started, and it moved sluggishly. Dom expected to run across marine resistance any moment. He expected Klaus to land on him every time they turned a corner. However, the lower levels were as empty as the first time they'd passed through.

After Flower's warning about Klaus' preparations, it seemed too good to be true.

It was.

Tetsami was standing by the hole when they arrived. At her feet was her portable groundstation wired to a panel in the wall behind her.

Dom knew something was wrong the minute he saw

her. She was staring at the holo; what little color she had was gone from her face.

Dom ran up to her. "What happened?"

Tetsami looked up with an expression that mixed anger, horror, and utter helplessness. "It's gone," she whispered. "Everyone's dead."

Dom looked back. No one else seemed to have heard her. "Flower, Zanzibar—get the money down to the van."

Flower nodded its serpentine neck, and Zanzibar gave him an abbreviated salute. When Levy started to go with them, Dom said, "No, Levy, stay up here. I might need you."

Levy looked a little confused, but he stayed.

Dom waited until Flower and Zanzibar disappeared down the hole before he turned back to Tetsami. "What happened?"

Tetsami looked up at Dom and opened her mouth. It took a few seconds before she said, "He wiped it off the map!"

Dom felt a familiar icy chill grip his stomach. *What have you done, Klaus?* He made sure to keep Levy in his peripheral vision. Dom noted that he backed away slightly.

The bastard targeted the Commune, didn't he?

"Tell me," Dom said softly. "The ground team, are they all right?"

"I don't know. I had contact, but—" She seemed to lose some of the disengagement and emotion began leaking into her voice, mostly anger. "He knew, Dom. He knew about the team going into the ship. It was a trap."

Dom nodded.

Tetsami shook her head and knelt at the holo. "He cut all contact to the ship, then he piped this in."

Dom watched the holo broadcast. Watched his brother for the first time in fifteen years. As he watched, the cold gripped him, freezing every nerve in his body. His racing pulse slowed, and he could feel things sharpen and draw into too clear a focus.

When he saw the holo of the polyceram net slicing

through the Diderot Commune, it seemed the world had achieved the perfect stillness of absolute zero.

"Tetsami," Dom said.

"Yes?"

"Go down with Zanzibar, Flower, and the money. Bug out now."

"But . . ."

"*Now!* Take the van and evac to Godwin. Blow the hole when you leave. Tell Ivor to give us and the ground team fifteen minutes. At eight hundred he bugs out, *no matter what!*"

Tetsami looked like she wanted to argue, but she simply looked at him with an expression of mute pain.

"We rendezvous at the commune site."

"But—" Tetsami looked at the holo that had so recently shown the destruction of the commune.

"The warehouse is compromised. Klaus won't be looking at Diderot. It just got 'reduced' from orbit. *Now go!*"

Tetsami left without further words.

Again Levy started toward the hole, and again Dom stopped him. Dom put his hand on Levy's arm and said, "No, I need you."

"But why?"

"Come on," Dom said, pulling the short old man after him. Dom went deeper into the warehouse levels, toward the elevators that would take them up into the office complex.

"What are we doing?" Levy sounded nervous.

Dom stopped by a stack of packing crates that had been upended in the chaos of the invasion. He ran the crate's ID through his onboard computer. It was what he was looking for. He pulled a crate roughly from the pile of debris and ripped the top off of it with his left hand, the artificial one.

"What?" Levy said.

"Long-range, high-frequency sniping laser." Dom pulled an arm-long rifle from the dozen that packed the crate. "Let me have your HVE."

Levy handed Dom the electromag, and Dom continued leading them toward the elevators.

"What are you doing?" Levy asked, a pleading note crept into his voice.

They made it to the elevator and Dom pushed Levy in. Dom hit the buttons for the second level of the complex and the codes for the air traffic tower on the roof.

"You're going to kill him, aren't you?" Levy was sweating.

"That's the whole point, isn't it?" Dom looked down at Levy. "*Or* each other. It doesn't matter much to you, does it?"

Levy paled.

"Someone's been feeding Klaus our plans. Someone's been a TEC plant. But not a good one, Levy. If the plant fed Klaus all he knew, we'd all have been dead long before now. It makes no sense, unless the plant had his own agenda." The elevator dinged as they rose above the warehouse levels and began passing the sublevels of the office complex.

Levy began shaking his head. "You have to kill him now. This is your only chance. He thinks you're in the ship—"

"Your first mistake was when I initially talked to you. I didn't notice at the time, but I'm cursed with a very good memory. You mentioned the TEC's involvement before anyone else knew about it. I let it slip by me because I was checking people for prior employment by the Executive. I forgot that there were other sorts of relationships." Dom looked down at Levy. "It's about Paschal, isn't it?"

Levy looked frozen.

"Klaus contacted you, and you saw it as a way to get close enough—"

"Stop it."

"You engineered all this to distract him. To give me a shot at his back. To make me want to."

Levy jumped up and grabbed Dom's collar. "You have to stop him. What he did on Paschal. You have a chance to do it—"

"I should kill *you*."

The doors opened and Levy let go of him.

Dom checked the corridor, saw it was empty, and held the door open. "I'm not going to kill anybody."

"But—"

"I don't want to know what's going through your head, Johann. But if you want Klaus, this elevator is going straight to the tower." Dom tossed the laser rifle into the elevator. "That weapon has a good range."

Levy looked down at the rifle.

The doors closed on him.

CHAPTER THIRTY-FIVE

Zero-Sum Game

"Never play chicken with someone who has nothing to lose."

—*The Cynic's Book of Wisdom*

"All men think all men mortal, but themselves."

—EDWARD YOUNG
(1683–1765)

07:45:00 Godwin Local

"The whole idea is insane," Shane yelled at Mosasa. Her suit was working overtime, and her breath tried to fog the inside of her helmet. The readouts were showing that the atmosphere outside the suit had reached a near-zero oxygen level and the pressure was dropping.

Mosasa showed no effect from an environment that would have KO'd any normal human in less than two minutes. "It's our only chance."

"You'll flood the compartment."

"You can set your personal field to block the radiation."

"What about Random? What about you?"

"Shane," came Random's voice from the walls, "we have seven minutes before the resident marines cut through that door."

"Damn it!" Shane didn't like what she was feeling. It

was all falling apart around her. "Can't *you* get to flight control from the computer?"

"They were expecting this," Random said. "I can't get out of the secondary core."

Shane looked up at the ceiling panels. Beyond them was the center of the ship, where the contragrav was.

"Can you do it?" she asked Mosasa.

"Once I crack the control box, I can make it do anything I want."

"What about the radiation?" Shane couldn't help but think of the legendary quirks of quantum extraction contragravs. The things were nasty when you ran them *within* the operation specs.

"I'm not human, Shane."

"Does that mean you can sit next to that thing while it's running?"

"Time, people," Random said. "Move it!"

Mosasa stepped on a ledge and pushed aside one of the heavily shielded panels. A warning light came on, filling the room with a flashing yellow glow. He looked at Shane and gave an all-too-human shrug. "I guess we're about to find out."

Mosasa disappeared up the hole.

"I do not like this," Shane said.

"Mosasa can do it."

Shane quietly adjusted her personal Emerson field to screen her from harmful radiation. The adjustment cost her three minutes on her environmental containment. She pointed her plasma rifle at the door and waited.

"I'm sorry, Shane."

"Why? This isn't your fault."

There was a pause. "I can't explain fully. My surface is a mimetic reproduction of human psychology, but my thoughts are—different. Most intellectual beings don't have the equipment to foresee the consequences of their actions."

"You saw this coming?" Shane asked.

"I could have."

"I'm the idiot who put myself in this position, Random. Don't blame yourself for my mistakes."

"A moral question."

"Hm?"

"Does prior knowledge of someone's decision—and the consequences of that decision—require you to share responsibility for that decision?"

Shane didn't have an answer for that.

Time seemed to stretch into infinity as she waited for something to happen. She watched the chrono in the corner of her headsup and watched the numbers change too slowly.

"Why weren't you horrified?" Random asked.

"Huh?"

"Two AIs, working independent of any supervision. Most Bakuninites would find that too disturbing. You're Confed material, you should be screaming in horror."

The chrono changed to read 07:48.

"Maybe I will, when I've got a chance to think." Sweat was rolling down her face, despite the cooling system, and she desperately wanted to wipe off her forehead. She blinked her eyes and wished for a sweatband.

"I just appreciated your concern for Mosasa."

Shane nodded inside her helmet and kept watching the door. She thought she saw something and began to run her visor through its enhancement modes.

Random kept talking. "He's the closest thing I have to a son."

Please God, Shane thought, *don't tell me the AI's losing it.*

"Look, Random, I chose my team, okay? That's you, Mosasa, everyone. Do you have any surveillance on the corridor out there?"

"No, they've locked me in. The only pictures I have are the ones they pipe in."

Shane kept staring at the door. Her visor's setting had locked into the IR, and the door was beginning to glow around the edges. Heat trails were piping in from the sides.

"Random, they're cutting in from the other side now."

"They're early," Random said matter-of-factly.

"Some of the onboard marines must've been in position when we boarded."

"It'll take them two to five minutes to cut open the door."

"How long for Mosasa—?"

"Seven to ten."

"Been nice knowing you, Random."

"You can hold them off. There can only be five at most."

"Only one of me."

Her chrono flipped over to 07:49.

Parts of the door were now glowing in the visible spectrum. The marines out there must have a cutting torch.

She dialed her MacMillan-Schmitt for maximum discharge. Not a setting recommended for firing inside enclosed spaces, especially with a fully charged wide-aperture plasma rifle. But a second shot probably wasn't going to happen.

"What're you doing?" asked Random.

"Setting this on full."

"Isn't that dangerous?"

Shane laughed. More like suicidal. There was a good chance of her filling this room with plasma backwash. That'd fry her just as bad as the troops outside the door. "The jet might vent out."

"There's only ten meters down that corridor before there's another emergency door."

"They might have cut through it." There was a long silence after she said that. And after a while she said, "Then again, they might not have. You don't have any idea, do you?"

"No, but if I were laying an ambush, I'd put them in one of the empty lockers down that hall."

Shane nodded. "So I'm taking a chance." After a moment, she added, "Maybe you should lock yourself up in that case of yours."

As she heard the sounds of cables withdrawing and Random's case closing, she considered the fact that she probably knew the marines on the other side of the door.

She could surrender and escape with her life. For some reason the thought shamed her.

I chose my team.

"I made my bed," Shane whispered. "Now it's time to die in it."

Smoke was wisping from the bottom of the door. The edges were glowing red and occasionally the light from the cutting torch flashed along the edge. Parts of the door were warping inward.

It was 07:50.

"Think the others made it, Random?"

"Yes," came the voice from the case's speaker, behind her. "All the force is surrounding the ship."

"Good. I'm glad."

"No regrets?"

"Only one."

"What?"

"I think I chose the wrong line of work."

At 07:50:30, the door to the secondary computer core of the Barracuda-class troop-carrier *Blood-Tide* fell open and ex-Captain Kathy Shane fired her weapon.

CHAPTER THIRTY-SIX

Extreme Prejudice

"Nothing is so fierce as a coward who is backed into a corner."

—*The Cynic's Book of Wisdom*

"A desperate disease requires a dangerous remedy."

—GUY FAWKES
(1570–1606)

07:48:00 Godwin Local

The elevator rose.

Johann Levy stared at the rifle on the floor in front of him and thought of Paschal.

Twelve years ago he had been a young lawyer rising in the Paschal hierarchy. There might have been a chance of rising in the secular arm of the Paschal government, if it weren't for the revolution. If he hadn't panicked. If he had stayed.

It was the colonel's fault. Klaus Dacham had been a captain then, and he'd ordered the TEC reinforcements to roll over all the demonstrations. Five hundred dead, ten times that injured, ten times *that* imprisoned. Even the Paschal Elders who had called for help were shocked.

Levy had been one of the liberal voices in the establishment, but when he had seen most of his friends from the university disappear at the hands of the TEC, he had run. Left Paschal, left the Confederacy, left everything he had known, to come to this nihilistic little dirtball called Bakunin.

Levy had never forgiven himself for that.

Worse, he had left *himself*. He hadn't even dared to apply for his own exit visa. He had stolen a friend's and had left the planet wearing that identity. The real Johann Levy was most likely in some unmarked student's grave on Paschal.

Somehow, the twisted process of his own mind had made him, a gentile lawyer on Paschal, metamorphose into an expatriate Jewish revolutionary on Bakunin. He had spent the last dozen years capitalizing on Levy's reputation as a revolutionary.

He was a revolutionary who had done nothing when the guns had begun to fire. A revolutionary who might have had a platform to condemn what was going on, who instead packed his bags and left before he attracted attention.

He had built a string of contacts, learned the arcane lore of security and armor, bombs and surveillance—all without ever putting himself in any physical danger.

He had long ago admitted to himself that he was a coward.

If he weren't a coward, he wouldn't be in the position he was in now.

What had he been thinking when he allowed the colonel to contact him and contract for his expertise in the Bakunin underground? Did he really think that he could use "Webster" against Dacham? Was that it? Or was he just too terrified to say no?

He had dealt with the devil, and his own hands were as bloody as Colonel Dacham's.

Levy wanted the colonel to pay for Paschal, but his own fear kept him from ever going through with it. He had built up "Webster's" credibility to the point where he knew he could've gotten a personal meeting. With Colonel Dacham's brother as bait, he could have had the colonel where he could have finished him off—

Why hadn't he done that?

The elevator continued to rise as Levy slowly knelt to pick up the weapon.

He hadn't wanted to do the dirty work. That was it. He was afraid to. He had been drowning in deception and manipulation for so long that it seemed easier to arrange for the colonel's own brother to do it. It would have been a perfect setup, if Jonah Dacham had cooperated.

Ironic, Levy thought, *how many deaths I am responsible for when I've never fired a shot.*

Levy stood straight and checked the laser. It had a full charge.

It's over, he thought, *all the duplicity, the lies, the running.* After dealing with the colonel, after this last betrayal, there was nothing left for him. Bakunin was the last place anyone could run. Bakunin was the end, and if you kept running from here, all that was left was an abyss.

Levy knew he was never going to leave this building alive.

He thought of the students cut down on Paschal. He thought of nearly fourteen hundred people cut down from orbit only minutes ago. He thought of the people on the *Blood-Tide* whom he'd betrayed. He thought of Klaus Dacham.

A dozen years of fear and anger gripped him like a tourniquet.

Then the elevator doors opened and he no longer had time to be afraid.

The elevator had stopped at the top of the air-traffic control tower for the GA&A complex. It was a massive room housed inside a ten-meter-high transparent dome. Control panels were everywhere, showing holo tracks of local aircraft. The view commanded the entire complex and the wooded hillside all the way down to Godwin.

There were five people in there.

Levy surprised himself by shooting first.

The guard Levy shot was standing next to the elevator. The man had a personal field, but it was a civilian model and it failed under the strength of the laser rifle Levy wielded. The guard was still turning to see what was happening when the power sink on his field exploded and the beam sliced through his abdomen.

As the guard collapsed, Levy felt something burn his right shoulder and he dove for the cover provided by one of the consoles.

The elevator was inside a pillar that rose into the center of the control room. There'd been another guard on the other side of it, and he was rounding it, aiming a hand-held laser pistol at Levy.

Levy screamed as he swept his laser across that half of the room. Consoles exploded, a chair erupted into flames and burning smoke, and the attacking guard's field proved as useless as his comrade's. The guard got one more shot at Levy before his field collapsed and his face turned into a hollow blackened groove.

Levy scrambled behind another console and realized that he couldn't feel his left leg any more.

There was moaning somewhere, and Levy looked for the four techs he'd seen when the elevator doors had opened. He kept close to the floor, pulling himself around the base of a console. Once he cleared the rank of consoles in front of the elevator, he saw two of the techs.

One was facedown on the floor with a hole burned in his back. The other looked as though his head had been too close to one of the exploding consoles. He was moaning and clutching his face with bloody hands.

The elevator doors dinged and Levy swung the rifle to bear on it. The doors closed on the third tech.

He was sitting up and felt a paralyzing pain through his body as something slammed into his back. He swung the carbine around, firing. He spun fast enough to see the woman swinging the chair at him before the rifle's beam sliced her in half. The chair still managed to slam into his right arm as the woman's corpse folded over in front of him. Levy heard a crack and didn't know if it was his arm or the chair.

For a few seconds the only sound was moaning from behind him.

Levy looked down and saw the reason he couldn't feel his left leg was that most of it was gone below the knee.

Strangely, that didn't upset him.

In fact, he laughed a little and told the woman folded over in front of him, "That wasn't as bad as I thought it would be."

Well, he was here. In a few minutes they were going to come for him. He fired into the elevator to keep that from being too easy.

That accomplished, he only had one thing left to do.

Slowly, Johann Levy began to drag himself toward the edge of the dome, all the time praying that Colonel Dacham was out in the open somewhere down there.

CHAPTER THIRTY-SEVEN

Market Crash

"It ain't over until the fat lady's *dead*."
—*The Cynic's Book of Wisdom*

"The popular method of pacifying a tiger is to allow
one's own consumption."
—LI ZHOU
(2238–2348)

07:48:00 Godwin Local

From what Dom saw of the office building, it was deserted. GA&A obviously had yet to restart commercial operations. Floor two was empty of anybody, including security patrols—

But then security had another problem at the moment.

Every time Dom passed by a window overlooking the landing quad—for security reasons, every GA&A building only had windows facing *in* toward the complex—he could see the backlit behemoth of the *Blood-Tide* surrounded by ground troops.

Dom quickly came to an office that fit his requirements. One of the benefits of having the floor plan of the GA&A complex in a computer inside his skull.

This second-floor office used to belong to Cy Helmsman, Dom's late veep in charge of operations. This particular office had been both RF-secured and given priority access to the GA&A network.

The office building was a U, cupping half the landing quad. Cy's old office was right in the center of that U, and normally it had a commanding low-angle view of the entire GA&A operation through its double-height picture windows.

That view, however, was dominated by two of the *Blood-Tide*'s main drives. The view out the window was like looking down the throat of a double-barreled volcano.

Dom looked out and thought of the caverns honeycombing the mountains between Godwin and Proudhon. He smiled briefly.

"While there's life, Klaus . . ."

Dom slipped behind the desk and powered Cy's terminal. This office was hardwired into whatever data lines survived in the complex. It took Dom less than thirty seconds to realize that the invaders had barely touched the original equipment.

"Why, Klaus," he whispered to himself, "you're being paranoid."

Even though there was still 20% of the processing capacity left aboveground, Klaus' people had done their best to avoid any of GA&A's old computers. Everything they used on the site they must have hauled in and coded themselves. It seemed a waste of resources to Dom.

However, it did mean that the system he was plugged into now was just about how he'd left it. His personal codes still worked, and while GA&A's original computer system had been disconnected from every sensitive area—such as the security system and what was left of the perimeter air defenses—it was still linked to the base communications network. Dom supposed that the marines had their own communications and weren't worried about the old system being compromised.

Dom set the commands up and paused—

He didn't have to do this. He could still slip out of here.

Dom queried his onboard computer. He had eleven minutes before Ivor bugged out.

No, Dom thought, *I can't let this go on. I can't keep running—*

Can I?

Dom flipped open the audio circuit on the holo in front of him, and his voice went out over every comm channel wired into the GA&A complex.

"Klaus."

Dom waited. He thought he could hear a commotion from outside, on the quad.

He walked over to the window. It was somewhat dangerous, but the quad was floodlit, and the office was dark. He knew even enhanced vision couldn't see through the mirror-tinted glass, especially in the veep suites.

"Klaus," he repeated, keeping his voice level. His broadcast was going out over the PA system, the intercoms, the closed-circuit holos—everywhere. It was disorienting hearing his voice vibrate the window in front of him.

When he was next to the window, the *Blood-Tide* occupied almost all of his field of view. The troop-carrier's massive drive-laden ass filled the cup of the office building's U. He could barely see the edges of the residence tower beyond the hump of the ship's drives, and most of the quad was covered by the stubby wings.

The *Blood-Tide* was fifty percent larger than the largest ship the landing quad was designed to handle. It was amazing that the ship had fit in the space at all. It was a hundred meters long, and Dom knew from his computer-remembered plans that the clearance between the residence tower and the office building was a hundred ten meters.

Dom felt admiration for the pilot who'd landed the thing. The engines were barely three meters from the window.

Dom had to get right up to the window and look down to see the marines on the ground. There must have been a hundred of them, in full armor, urban camouflage, and bearing enough hardware to lay waste to all of East Godwin. They were mustering, half of them coming toward the office complex.

"Klaus," Dom repeated. "If you want me, talk to me."

Marines began to surround the base of the office complex.

"Jonah."

Dom turned and saw Klaus' face on the holo. The view behind Klaus was mostly sky. The view seemed familiar. As Dom talked, he quickly ran possible locations through his mind.

"Hold off your marines. I want to make a deal."

"A deal for your surrender?" Klaus shook his head. "You are in no position to bargain. We have you pinpointed in the office complex. The exits are sealed. We can take you any time we wish. No deals."

"You had me trapped aboard the *Blood-Tide*."

Klaus hardly looked fazed by Dom's suggestion. "Obviously you were never aboard that ship. Surrender, Dominic, and I guarantee you will survive to see your trial."

Dom shook his head. "There are some conditions."

Klaus laughed. Dom stared at the holo image. *Where was he?* "Your arrogance is amusing. In less than a minute you are going to be in custody, conditions or not. You've always had an inflated view of yourself."

"And you were always dangerously rash. Do you think I'd be talking if I didn't have a card to play?"

"What can you possibly do?"

"Trigger a few thousand kilos of high explosives planted throughout the GA&A complex."

There was a long pause. "You're bluffing."

"I could be. Or I could have set the timer before I called you. It could be that if I don't say the right word in the next three minutes, the whole complex disappears."

"I don't believe you."

"Cy Helmsman might argue with you."

Yes, Klaus, you know I'm bluffing. But you also know where I'm calling from. Can you be sure? Can you afford to be sure? You've made it quite a point to remove everything you think I live for.

Klaus leaned out of the display and said something offscreen. Once Dom had an unobstructed view of the background, he knew where Klaus was. Behind Klaus was the same view of Godwin that Dom had seen every day for seven years. Klaus was on top of the residence tower. He was right outside Dom's old office.

Dom looked out the window and tried to see beyond the drives of the *Blood-Tide*. He thought he could see a mass of people on top of the tower, next to the matte-black office dome.

"Okay," came Klaus' voice. "You have three minutes. What are your conditions?"

"First, once you have me, you cease persecuting GA&A's former employees. Up to and including anyone who might have been involved in this operation."

Klaus smiled. "Agreed, with you in custody I will cease to have any interest in the survivors."

You evil bastard. You think you've won, don't you?

"Second, my people aboard the *Blood-Tide* are given passage off the complex and released."

Klaus smiled even more broadly. "Of course."

The ice gripped Dom's stomach. *They're already dead. He's killed them.*

He had wanted to give Shane, Mosasa, and Random a chance. It looked as though he was too late. Well, he would have to face it, he had run out of cards to play. He almost wished that he *had* peppered the complex with explosives, so he could set them off and take Klaus with him. Instead, Dom turned toward the window.

"You have two minutes left."

Dom noticed marines turning toward the *Blood-Tide*. The whole ship seemed to shift its weight slightly, as if in a gigantic shrug.

"I want this 'trial' to be public."

"I intend to air your crimes for everyone to see, have no fear. I am sending in marines now. I expect you to turn yourself over quietl—" Something offscreen was stealing Klaus' attention. Someone hit the mute, and Dom noticed a lot of the marines downstairs running toward the *Blood-Tide*.

What?

"Jonah," came Klaus' voice from behind him. Dom turned and saw Klaus riding the edge of fury. "While you talk of surrender and capitulation, your 'people—' your Bakuninite traitors—are setting off plasma explosions aboard the *Blood-Tide*. You get no deals."

"Damn it, Klaus!"

"I'm going to make you pay for *everything!*"

That was the point at which the world decided to explode.

Dom's brain, computer-assisted as it was, had to suddenly contend with processing a tremendous amount of information in a very short time. From Dom's point of view, this had the ironic result of slowing his thought processes down to a crawl.

Klaus was finishing his sentence, the word "everything" still on his lips, when a flower of smoke erupted from his arm. Dom watched his brother fall across the holo, knocking the image askew. In the cockeyed slice of the top of the residence tower, Dom saw telltale heat ripples cutting through the air, marking the passage of the otherwise invisible beam of a high-frequency sniping laser. The invisible laser cut through air, concrete roof, and defending guards with equal impunity. The angle of the shots marked them as originating from above the office complex, in the air-traffic tower.

It had to be Levy.

Dom had barely a fraction of a second to grasp that when the doors to the office blew apart.

Five well-armed marines fanned out into the room, even as the doors were still in the air. Part of the door landed on the desk, smashing the holo Dom was watching. Four narrow-aperture plasma rifles turned to lock on him. Dom started raising his arms as the leader shouted, *"Freeze!"* through the loudspeaker on his shoulder.

One marine didn't level his weapon at Dom. He was the last one into the room, and he never looked at Dom at all. He ran into the room to take his position between the front two marines and froze, weapon at his side, staring, through his faceplate, out the window behind Dom.

Dom stood there, arms raised, facing the marines across the desk. There was a second of silence. The floodlights in the quad cut abstract shadows in the wall beyond the marines.

The shadows were moving.

The one marine looking past Dom said, "My God." Dom never would have heard the hoarse whisper without his enhanced ears.

The light disappeared entirely and, despite the warnings, Dom turned.

The view out Cy Helmsman's picture windows was now entirely dominated by a pair of the *Blood-Tide's* eighteen-meter diameter main engines. As Dom watched, the engines moved slowly upward. Looking at the silent, majestic progression, Dom could swear that the engines were getting closer—nearly touching the window.

Then they touched.

The entire office complex tried to shake itself apart. Glass flew into the room. The floor tilted down toward the window, scattering marines and throwing Dom across the desk.

Two marines tumbled past him, stopping short at the window as Dom grabbed for purchase on the desk. The entire room shook. Dom looked behind him, right down the throat of the *Blood-Tide's* number three main engine.

"Shit."

The floor was still tilting, and the engine looked as though it was backing toward him. The desk was starting to slide. A marine fell into the gap between the edge of the floor and the engine, there was a grinding noise, a scream, and the marine disappeared.

The *Blood-Tide* continued to rise.

The building was shaking itself apart around him, and behind him the number three engine was sliding up, past him. Dom lost track of the marines. As the engine rose, the floor tilted back. Soon it would be shifting in the opposite direction as the bottom of the engine passed by this floor.

The engine was huge. It could swallow most of the room Dom was in. It looked more like a cavern than ever.

If the maniac who was piloting the *Blood-Tide* fired the mains, the blast would vaporize the whole building.

Dom felt a massive shudder through the surface of the desk, and part of the roof above him buckled. Dom jumped as pieces of the ceiling began collapsing. He landed on the still moving floor between the desk and the engine. Dom fell on his side and rolled as the floor itself began to crack and buckle. As he tumbled, he caught glimpses of the space beyond the floor. He saw one ugly scene of a marine being ground between multiton slabs of concrete on the floor below him.

Dom's mad scramble, avoiding collapsing ceiling and suddenly hungry floor, took him straight toward the window. He had hoped to get by the *Blood-Tide,* but by now that entire side of the room was slowly moving engine. Even with the edges of the containment nozzle shredded and torn by the impact with the building, it was the only stable refuge left.

He threw himself into a manic dive into the number three engine as the room behind him evaporated into a billowing cloud of pulverized concrete. He slammed inside the bell of the containment nozzle with a force that dimmed his vision; part of the room followed him, slamming across his back and making part of his world fade out.

As Dom sank his left hand into the electromagnetic mesh of the engine, he hoped the pilot wouldn't fire the thing any time soon. Then he let the world float away.

Dom was somewhat surprised that he didn't wake up dead.

His first conscious thought was that his back and his left arm were screaming pain messages at him. His self-diagnostics were telling him that nothing irreparable had been done to him. It didn't help much with the pain. Something huge had fallen across his back, pinning him to the inside of the engine.

All he could see was the mesh in front of him. He couldn't even get a view of what was pinning him down. Wreckage held him in place from the shoulders down.

At least the ship seemed to have stopped moving.

Dom pulled his left hand free of the mesh. It seemed redundant to clutch at the engine when he was pinned in place. As he let go, he tried to turn his neck—

"Shit!" he yelled in pain.

He was suddenly aware of what kind of trouble he was in. Wherever the *Blood-Tide* had landed, there would be marines surrounding the site in short order. He had just volunteered his location—and he was pretty damn helpless at the moment.

Dom held himself still, letting the pain fade for a moment, and hoped no one had been within earshot of his curse. It was a vain hope. In moments he could hear someone at work behind him, at the throat of the engine.

Dom steeled himself against the pain—even if he severed his spinal column, it was only a sheaf of easily replaced superconducting monofilament—and turned his neck to see the rear of the engine.

He finally saw that what held him in place was a ten-by-two-meter chunk of polyceram-reinforced concrete. Also, to his surprise, the engine was now clogged with wood. Chunks of trees had been broken off and wedged in the engine.

As Dom watched, a large log dotted with purple-orange foliage shifted and started to slide out. It was followed by another. And suddenly, there in a two-meter gap, was Mosasa.

"What the hell happened?" Dom asked.

Mosasa managed to answer that question as he did his utmost to quickly extricate Dom and get him to Ivor's waiting getaway vehicle before Klaus' marines showed up.

Mosasa told Dom what had happened aboard the *Blood-Tide*. Trapped inside the ship, with no way out, Mosasa had climbed into the support system for the contragrav and had wired control directly into the hardware. He had flown blindly north, eventually slamming into the wooded foothills high up on the Diderot Mountains.

Ivor had caught up with the *Blood-Tide* within a few

seconds. His vehicle had been up and ready to bug out on
Dom's orders, and the spinning-out-of-control troopship
was hard to miss.

As Mosasa—possessing a strength that Dom didn't
expect—helped move the concrete slab off him, Dom
asked about the other team members.

The news wasn't good. While Random *had* managed to
fuse the access to the hatch controls on the ship, five marines had been aboard the *Blood-Tide* to ambush the team.
Shane had managed to take out the marines when they'd
cut through the hatch of the secondary core, but only at
the expense of critically injuring herself in a plasma
backwash. The life support on her suit was barely keeping her alive. Ivor was waiting to evac her to Godwin.

As Mosasa helped to half carry Dom out of the engine,
he said, "We need to get you to a doctor, too."

Dom shook his head. "We can't risk travel to the city.
They'll see that. If we're north of GA&A, we might man-
age the commune unseen. There're medical facilities
there."

Mosasa clasped Dom's arm. "You don't know. Klaus—"

"I know what Klaus did." Dom looked up at Mosasa.
"We have to get to the commune rendezvous."

Mosasa looked at Dom and nodded.

Despite the plan going badly wrong, it *had* worked.
Dom knew it had all come together. Badly, and costing
more than it should've. But it had all worked.

Best of all, the way everything had gone, Klaus was
going to assume everyone was dead.

EPILOGUE

Economic Indicators

"You are free and that is why you are lost."
—Franz Kafka
(1883–1924)

CHAPTER THIRTY-EIGHT

Closing Costs

"No one can be quite as annoying as a potential lover."
—*The Cynic's Book of Wisdom*

"It is much more secure to be feared than to be loved."
—NICCOLO MACHIAVELLI
(1469–1527)

Kropotkin had dropped below the western horizon. The sky was fading from blood-red to the purple of a deep bruise. Below the ledge where Tetsami stood, the sprawl of Godwin glistened with blacks and browns like some divine compost heap saturated with human insects. From here she could see the speck of the GA&A complex, a small scar in the woods where the *Blood-Tide* had gone down, and the circular crater where Klaus' orbital attack had reduced a mountain valley to so much gravel.

Over, Tetsami thought.

That one word covered a hell of a lot of territory. She wished she knew if she'd blown it or not. It all worked, didn't it?

Didn't it?

She hugged herself and shivered in the breath-fogging cold.

Somehow they all had managed to pull themselves out of a potential disaster. All except Levy, of course. . . .

"Poor fucking Johann," she whispered.

It had taken her two or three days to sort out those last fifteen minutes or so. She still didn't understand it, exactly, and she probably didn't want to. The only really clear thing about the whole situation was the fact that Colonel Klaus Dacham had lost the final confrontation, and might even be dead.

Somehow, Dom had outmaneuvered his brother. Outmaneuvered him as cynically and heartlessly as he'd outmaneuvered everyone else.

Especially Tetsami.

Why didn't he tell any of us Klaus was his brother? She slammed her fist into her thigh in frustration. *Why didn't he tell us about the preparations at the commune? Why didn't he tell us that Levy might have been the one—*

Everything had knotted up into a burning little ball in her gut. Most of her anger was directed at her "partner," Dom.

Dom had seen the attack on the commune coming. He had *prepared* for it. By the time of the attack, almost all of Dom's people had moved into the tunnels in the mountains around the commune. Klaus' recon drone had given Dom's people enough warning to evac all the aboveground personnel into the retrofitted caverns. The buildings had been reduced to rubble, but only one person had been killed and a few dozen injured when an unstable cavern collapsed in the attack.

Part of Tetsami hated Dom for not telling anybody—hell, for not telling *her*—about that. Seeing the holo of the commune disintegrating and not knowing. . . .

Just the memory of how she'd felt made her want to throw up, or cry, or kill someone.

She had expected to rendezvous on a mass grave, and instead found Dom's people intensively involved in rendering the endless caverns habitable. There were medical facilities, hydroponics gardens, and all manner of things stripped from the main building before the balloon went up.

Dom could have told her, could have *trusted* her.

Worse was Johann Levy. She wanted to believe that Dom only knew of Levy's betrayals after the fact. But she couldn't shake the suspicion that Dom had used Levy as an exercise in cold-blooded manipulation. It was intimately tied up in the wretched feeling that had enveloped her ever since the completion of the mission.

It's not as if the project weren't risky. Sure, the ideal would have had no casualties on either side. But it's foolish to think everyone could come out unscathed.

Right?

Tetsami stared out at the wretched sprawl of Godwin and forced herself to admit her real problem.

It had been her idea, her plan, her command—and she hadn't been ready for it. She hadn't been ready for people getting hurt and killed. She wasn't ready for Shane.

Dom had had extensive medical facilities moved into the caverns, but they'd been barely enough to stabilize her. Shane had lost a considerable portion of her lower body, couldn't breathe without assistance, and—mercifully—had yet to regain consciousness.

Shane was somewhere down in Godwin now, Ivor having smuggled her back to the Stemmer Facility for major reconstructive work. Any prognosis beyond simple survival was anyone's guess.

Mosasa and Random were both intact after the episode, and for some reason that only made Tetsami feel more uncomfortable around the AI and its keeper.

On top of Shane, there were the five marines who'd been aboard the *Blood-Tide*. The marines who'd been in *front* of the weapon, while Shane had just been brushed with the plasma backwash.

Add to them the marines who'd died when the *Blood-Tide* backed into the GA&A office complex, the people who'd been shot by Levy in his manic attempt to assassinate Klaus, and Johann Levy himself who was almost certainly dead.

The more Tetsami brooded, the more corpses floated up to the surface.

Do we start counting the three marine snipers I had to kill at the construction site?

It was all so damn ugly, so damn brutal. It was nothing like the clean digital world of the computer net she had worked in until now. Sure there'd always been risk—but somehow it was a cleaner risk. No one's blood on her hands but her own. No one between her and the guns. No one out there taking shots for her.

Tetsami ran her hand across her eyes and wondered what she was going to do with her life.

No question, she could bail out now. She could cash in her share of the spoils—twenty megagrams, more money than she'd ever think to see in a lifetime—say good-bye to Bakunin, and find some civilized place to retire. She could even pay her way to Earth.

She tried to find some joy in the prospect, but the idea only filled her with a hollow dread.

"This is a wretched planet." Tetsami spat over the ledge.

"Perhaps," came a familiar voice behind her. "But it has its points."

"Hello, Dominic," she said without turning around.

"I've been looking for you. People get lost in these caverns."

"I wanted to get lost."

She heard him step up next to her. "Nice view."

"The view's shit." She turned and looked at Dom. He was staring down at Godwin. "What do you want?"

"To thank you—"

"You're welcome." Her mouth felt dry when she said it. The irony in her voice sounded extremely unsubtle in her ears.

"—and give you this." He held out to her a small plastic envelope.

Tetsami took it and tore the seal. Inside was a sheaf of plastic currency, all kilogram notes from the IBASC. Fifty of them. Tetsami looked at the cash, briefly unable to speak.

"That's what I owe you. In addition to your share, of course."

Tetsami suppressed an urge to toss the whole package off the edge of the cliff. She wanted to scream and cry, run around in circles, tear her hair out—

Hell, anything to get his attention.

"Dominic, you unfeeling bastard."

Dom turned to regard her, and the nonexpression on his face made her even angrier.

"Do you even see *people* when you look out of those eyes of yours? Was all this just some sort of weird economic transaction to you?"

Dom, for once, looked puzzled.

Tetsami took the sheaf of bills and jammed them inside Dom's shirt. "*Keep it!* I never delivered the damn data on Bleek anyway. And another thing—"

Dom was glancing down at his shirt and looking marvelously lost. "What?"

Tetsami grabbed both sides of Dom's head, cocked it to the side, and kissed him savagely, until she thought she tasted blood. Hers, his, it didn't matter. When she let go of him she said, "Think about that, you asshole."

She left him standing on the ledge as, behind him, the stars began to come out.

CHAPTER THIRTY-NINE

Propaganda Victory

"Once you have mastered the art of deceiving yourself, deceiving others is that much easier."
—*The Cynic's Book of Wisdom*

"No man spreads a lie with so good a grace as he that believes it."
—JOHN ARBUTHNOT
(1667–1735)

"There's been some loose talk about how bad off we are."

Klaus looked over the impromptu parade ground. It had been the landing quad, but now that they had the new mainframe and power systems on-line they didn't need the *Blood-Tide* in the center of the complex running the defensive screens. Now that they had the perimeter towers back, the *Blood-Tide* sat next to its cousin, the *Shaftsbury,* on a new staging area directly east of the complex.

Without a ship in the way, he could comfortably address all his personnel at once. With the last load from the *Shaftsbury* there were nearly two thousand civilian techs, plus the remaining one hundred ten marines.

It had been three days since the "incident."

Klaus stood there, at the focus of their uncomfortable silence. He had placed the podium inside the curve of the

office building's U. Someone else might have debated the
wisdom of having his audience face not only him but also
the shredded front of GA&A's offices where the *Blood-
Tide* had backed into them. It was an all-too vivid reminder of six presumed dead and five injured marines,
and a pair of dead and injured civilians.

The silence stretched.

Someone else might have seen the anger in the ranks,
the sinking morale, and feared it.

Klaus didn't fear it. Anger was good. Anger could be
used. Anger wasn't something to shrink away from. On
the contrary—

Anger was a gift from God.

Klaus scanned the front rank and made a sweeping gesture with his left arm. His right was still mostly immobile
due to a laser shot from the observation tower. "*Look.* We
fell under attack from Bakuninite terrorists, anarchists
whose sole aim is our destruction. But look around you—
are we destroyed?"

Hit them with the blatantly obvious, first. Klaus looked
around, getting a feeling for the mass of the crowd.

"Do you know what those terrorists planned to do?" Of
course not. Klaus had been good about putting a lid on
the security breach in the warehouse level. No more than
a half-dozen trusted people knew about the commuter
tube down there—a tube that had since been secretly
blasted shut.

"Imagine igniting all the drives in the *Blood-Tide* while
simultaneously decoupling the containment on the
contragrav's quantum extraction furnace."

Klaus smiled. He had most of them now. A good proportion of the civilians were technical, and *could* imagine
that. For the benefit of the rest, Klaus continued. "If that
had happened, you wouldn't be looking at the damaged
building behind me. You would be looking at a glass-
bottomed trench nearly a kilometer long from the bottom
of a crater fifty to a hundred meters deep."

He could feel the mood shifting like the tide. Slow, but
inevitable. And, properly used, just as hard to deny. It
was becoming hard to keep his gestures in check, and he

decided to hell with the laser wound. The medic could deal with it. He thrust out his right hand and the pain gave him a shot of adrenaline.

"Preventing this was a defeat? The five marines who died, died to prevent that. The terrorists were tampering with the contragrav by the time the marines managed to stop them—at the cost of their own lives. The flight of the *Blood-Tide* was the contragrav malfunctioning. *They were that close!*"

A bit overdramatic perhaps, but the sound of his own amplified voice from the PA systems buoyed him like a drug.

"If it had not been for my own intelligence sources and those five marines, we would not now be ready for the second phase of this operation. Every single one of us would be dead."

Klaus smiled.

It was time to dispose of the rest of his problems.

"Isn't it interesting that there are those here who call this defeat?"

A long silence followed. He let it hang as the implication of that sank in. There was another purpose—other than drama—for the pause in his speech. It was a cue for his loyalists to get ready.

"Isn't it interesting that among the missing is a marine officer whose duty was to guard the perimeter? Isn't it interesting that the transponder logs show this officer as the last person to board the *Blood-Tide*? Isn't it interesting that this officer was on a detail with the Bakuninite traitor Kathy Shane when eight hundred prisoners were *allowed* to escape?

"Isn't it interesting that I was nearly a victim of a sniper from our own air-traffic control tower?"

All his people were in position within the hushed crowd.

"It should be obvious to anyone, even without the intelligence sources I have access to, that there are traitors—Bakuninite anarchist sympathizers—within our own ranks. Traitors that have been there since the beginning. The trap I laid with the *Blood-Tide* had another

goal, in addition to taking out the terrorists who were im-
molated within it—

*"The trap was there to implicate the traitors within our
own ranks!"*

That was the signal for his people to grab nearly two
dozen liabilities from within the audience. Most of the
people sat in shocked silence as Klaus' security team
dragged twenty-four men and women out of the crowd.

Twenty-four problems, all counted as solved.

"Look at them! Two dozen secret assassins, every one
waiting for the right moment to destroy any one of you.
Each one would gladly give life itself to see this complex
blown off the face of the planet. But they overreached,
and exposed themselves—and now they're revealed for
the cowards they are."

All of them were making quite a hue and cry as they
were being dragged to the residence tower behind the
crowd. One of them, the marine Conner, was actually crying.

Every single one of them was denying everything.

Klaus would make a bet that not one in ten of the audience believed them. And that one would do nothing
about it—because anyone who did would be dragged
away with the others.

Klaus waited for the commotion to die down before he
went on.

"We are not weaker now. We are stronger.

"We have not been defeated. We have triumphed.

"We are not at the end. We are only beginning.

"Look around you. The future is ours. Bakunin is ours.
They will not stop us!"

The speech lasted another forty minutes. When he left
the podium, he got a standing ovation.

CHAPTER FORTY

Plausible Denial

"Those who are most sure of themselves are those possessing the fewest facts."

—*The Cynic's Book of Wisdom*

"I have been ever of the opinion that revolutions are not to be evaded."

—BENJAMIN DISRAELI
(1804–1881)

Sim Vashniya liked Earth. He liked the blue skies, the ash-free air, and the light gravity that made him feel as though he could do anything. Not only was he enjoying the environment, but his own plans were going very well. Everything was perfect.

Which made it all the more troubling to feel the edges of his mouth twitching toward a frown.

He stroked his beard to conceal the effort he made to maintain his smile. "What are you asking me?" he said.

There was no real reason for him to dislike Dimitri. The old Russian was only another professional trying to do his own job. But for some reason Vashniya was finding it difficult to maintain his good humor, something that usually never took a second thought.

For the first time in quite a long while, Vashniya was annoyed.

The two of them, Vashniya and Dimitri, were sitting in Dimitri's office. Surrounding them was bedrock, and the monolithic foundation of the Confederacy tower. They were deep in the bowels of the Confed bureaucracy, both literally and figuratively.

"I would like a straight answer, Vashniya."

Dimitri looked weary. Vashniya understood, but he didn't sympathize. Every decade, right before the Congress, things got hectic in the intelligence community. That was a given. Water was wet, deep space was a vacuum, and every ten years Confed politics reached critical mass.

It was no excuse for Dimitri to be so unsubtle.

"Am I now to abase myself and admit to all the imagined crimes of the Indi Protectorate?"

Dimitri rubbed his forehead. "I'm not accusing you of anything."

"I am relieved."

"You can't deny what happened on Mars."

"Nothing denied, nothing admitted."

Dimitri slammed his hand on the desk. "*Damn it!* I've been playing this game for twice as long as you've been alive. I am supposed to run the Security apparatus for the entire Confederacy."

Vashniya stood up. He felt his smile leave. "Thank you for inviting me, but I think I'll go now."

Dimitri sank back in his chair. "I'm sorry. Forgive the outburst."

"I don't think we have anything more to say."

"Don't you understand this at all? My job is to hold the Confederacy together. It's delicately balanced, and any change in the power structure *is* my business."

Vashniya did not sit down and he did not repair his smile. "What could possibly change?" He made no effort to withhold the irony in his voice.

"We both know the potential of planetary promotions in the next Congress. Especially now that you have the Seven Worlds here backing you—"

"I understand. Perhaps from where you sit any shift in power may seem too destabilizing. A threat."

Dimitri was nodding.

Vashniya sighed. "So much for the TEC's much-lauded independence. You've admitted that you are nothing more than an agent for the interests of Sirius and Alpha Centauri."

"Have you ever thought that any substantial shift in the Confederacy might erupt into something less desirable?"

"Everyone in power must fear change."

"I don't say that the current system is perfect, but there's a process in place—"

Vashniya stepped toward the door. "I deeply resent the implication that the People's Protectorate intends to violate the Charter. If you do so again, I will lodge a formal protest."

"I told you, I'm not accusing you of anything. Would you please sit down and listen to me for a minute?"

Vashniya sat down, thinking clean thoughts to calm himself. He felt his frown weaken a little. "Perhaps I overreact. But please, let us expedite this. We are both busy men. Ask me something I can answer, and I will."

"Okay. No specifics—but, Sim, I am going to have to deal with whatever happens afterward. Should I be worried?"

Vashniya sat back, stroked his beard, and felt the smile return.

"Perhaps, Dimitri. Perhaps you *should* worry."

Sim Vashniya's mood had returned to normal by the time he arrived back at the Indi Consulate. There was time left in the day for the more normal burdens of his duty, even this far from Shiva. Not the least of which was an appraisal of the Protectorate's intelligence operation on Earth. He was doing well on that, even if the local people took offense at being outranked by a non-Chinese—

Racism was an unhappy thought; he banished it.

The Consulate was part of the diplomatic sprawl that surrounded the spire of the Confederacy tower. Each building dotting the parkland at the tower's base represented another planet, or group of planets. Each building claimed a portion of land in the name of its own government—which was the reason why none of them was housed in the tower itself. Even though the kilometer-tall building could easily house all of them just as well as it housed most of the governmental bureaucracy that ran the Confederacy.

The only planet that housed its diplomatic function with the building itself was Earth.

The main Indi Consulate was central to a dozen lesser buildings that housed diplomatic staffs of various member planets. It was hard to tell just how many buildings there were because of the extensive landscaping. If Vashniya stuck to the path, he could pass buildings twenty meters on either side of him and never see anything but trees, gardens, and the occasional pond.

That's why he didn't notice the man until he was upon him.

Vashniya was crossing the ornamental stone bridge that led to the front courtyard of the Indi Consulate when a voice addressed him.

"Mr. Vashniya?"

Vashniya turned and saw a furtive figure step out from behind a tree. The man addressing him had appeared from out of nowhere, and Vashniya's first thought was he was about to be ambushed. The feeling faded. The trees around him concealed more security than anywhere else on the planet. The man could not be a threat and be within a kilometer of here.

"Yes?" Vashniya asked.

"I was told you may be able to help me." Now that Vashniya had a good look at the man, he began to wonder. The man had the unsure fumbling gait of a new arrival, unfamiliar with the gravity. *Heavier than he's used to,* Vashniya thought. The man's hair was bleached from heavy UV, but the stranger's skin showed no sign of burning. The clothes he wore were new—*very* new.

An enigma from off-planet.

"What can I do for you?"

The man raised his hand to brush through his hair, and Vashniya noticed that it was a rather crude biomechanic, scarred and pitted in contrast to the polished image the rest of the man was trying to portray. The man noticed Vashniya looking and put the hand in his pocket.

"There're no offices for the Seven Worlds here."

Vashniya nodded. "I believe they only maintain one embassy out of their own sphere, on Mazimba." The man had gone considerably out of his way to chase a shadow.

"But there's a Tau Ceti delegate here for the Congress."

"Actually, she's from Grimalkin."

"I need to talk to her."

Vashniya chuckled. "I am not a secretary. I don't make appointments for other diplomats. You have to talk to her."

The man looked exasperated. "If I knew *where* to find her, I would."

"Ah, I see the problem."

"Can you tell me how to get in touch with her?"

"Why?"

The man only hesitated for a fraction of a second, but Vashniya noticed it. "I'm tracking down relatives on Dakota."

It was a lie.

Vashniya decided to let it rest. He could question Hernandez about it if this man's meeting with her ever took place. "Francesca Hernandez, she's staying at the Victoria. They can ring her from the desk, and if she'll talk to you, she'll talk to you."

"Thank you."

The man turned to go, and Vashniya said, "Be prepared. She isn't human."

He turned, raising the metal hand to his cheek. "In that sense, neither am I, Mr. Vashniya."

"Can I have your name?"

There was another brief hesitation before he said, "Jonah. My name's Jonah."

Jonah disappeared into the woods as suddenly as he had appeared. Vashniya stood watching where he'd been for a long time.

A trivial incident, really, Vashniya thought.

Vashniya returned to his duties. However, try as he might, he was unable to put the "trivial" incident out of his mind. That and the phrase he had spoken to Dimitri: "Everyone in power must fear change."

Of course, his worries weren't warranted. Vashniya was in control of the powers he was unleashing. But for some illogical reason, his meeting with Jonah made him doubt himself, and he didn't understand why.

APPENDIX A

Alphabetical listing of sources

Note: Dates are Terrestrial standard. Where the year is debatable due to interstellar travel, the Earth equivalent is used with an asterisk. Incomplete or uncertain biographical information is indicated by a question mark.

Adyebo, Yoweri
    (2303–), Mazimban political leader, president.
Arbuthnot, John
    (1667–1735), Scottish physician, writer.
Astell, Mary
    (1666–1731), English feminist, writer.
Bacon, Francis
    (1561–1626), English philosopher.
Bakunin, Mikhail A.
    (1814–1876), Russian anarchist.
Blake, William
    (1757–1827), English poet.
Bradshaw, John
    (1602–1659), English lawyer, regicide.
Castle, Damion
    (1996–2065), American general, chairman JCS.
Celine, Robert
    (1923–1996), American lawyer, anarchist.
Cheviot, Jean Honoré
    (2065–2128), United Nations secretary general.
Cicero, Marcus Tullinus
    (106–43 BC), Roman statesman.

Cromwell, Oliver
> (1599–1658), Lord protector of England.

Diderot, Denis
> (1713–1784), French encyclopedist.

Disraeli, Benjamin
> (1804–1881), English prime minister, writer.

Emerson, Ralph Waldo
> (1803–1882), American philosopher, writer.

Fawkes, Guy
> (1570–1606), English Catholic conspirator.

Fessenden, Samuel
> (1847–1908), American lawyer, politician.

Galiani, August Benito
> (2019–*2105), European spaceship commander.

Goldsmith, Oliver
> (1730–1774), English writer.

Greene, Robert
> (1558–1592), English dramatist.

Guicciardini, Francesco
> (1483–1540), Italian historian, statesman.

Harper, Sylvia
> (2008–2081), American civil-rights activist, president.

Hobbes, Thomas
> (1588–1679), English philosopher.

Huntington, Collis P.
> (1821–1900), American railroad magnate.

Kafka, Franz
> (1883–1924), German writer.

Kalecsky, Boris
> (2103–2200), Terran Council president.

Lenin, Vladimir Ilyich
> (1870–1924), Russian political leader.

Li Zhou
> (2238–2348), Protectorate representative.

Machiavelli, Niccolo
> (1469–1527), Italian political philosopher.

Marx, Karl
> (1818–1883), German economist.

Montaigne, Michel de
      (1533–1592), French essayist.
Morrill, J. S.
      (1810–1898), American senator.
Muhammad
      (570–632), Founder of Islam.
Nietzche, Friedrich
      (1844–1900), German philosopher.
Proudhon, Pierre-Joseph
      (1809–1865), French journalist.
Rajastahn, Datia
      (?–2042), American civil-rights activist, political
      leader.
Shakespeare, William
      (1564–1616), English dramatist.
Shane, Marbury
      (2044–*2074), Occisisan colonist, soldier.
Tacitus, Cornelius
      (*ca* 56–*ca* 120), Roman historian.
William IV
      (2126–*2224), Monarch of United Kingdom in Ex-
      ile.
Young, Edward
      (1683–1765), English poet.

The Cynic's Book of Wisdom is an anonymous manuscript that first appeared on Bakunin in 2251. Since, it has seen innumerable editions, many with substantial additions or modifications. The generally accepted text is credited to "R. W."

Worlds of the Confederacy

The Alpha Centauri Alliance:

Number of member worlds: 14	Number voting: 13	Number prime: 10
Capital:		
Occisis—Alpha Centauri	founded: 2074	a
Other important worlds:		
Archeron—70 Ophiuchi	founded: 2173	c
Styx—Sigma Draconis	founded: 2175	b

The People's Protectorate of Epsilon Indi:

Number of member worlds: 31	Number voting: 17	Number prime: 15
Capital:		
Ch'uan—Epsilon Indi	founded: 2102	a
Other important worlds:		
Kanaka—Zeta^1 Reticuli	founded: 2216	a
Shiva—Delta Pavonis	founded: 2177	a

The Seven Worlds:

Number of member worlds: 7	Number voting: 7	Number prime: 5
Capital:		
Haven—Tau Ceti	founded: 2073	a

Other important worlds:

Dakota—Tau Ceti	founded: 2073	a
Grimalkin—Fomalhaut	founded: 2165	x

The Sirius-Eridani Economic Community:

Number of member worlds: 21	Number voting: 14	Number prime: 12

Capitals:

Cynos—Sirius	founded: 2085	x
Khamsin—Epsilon Eridani	founded: 2088	b

Other important worlds:

Banlieue—Xi Ursae Majoris	founded: 2146	c
Dolbri—C1	founded: 2238	d
Paschal—82 Eridani	founded: 2164	a
Thubohu—Pi³ Orion	founded: 2179	a
Waldgrave—Pollux	founded: 2242	d

The Union of Independent Worlds:

Number of member worlds: 10	Number voting: 2	Number prime: 1

Capital:

Mazimba—Beta Trianguli Australis	founded: 2250	b

Non-Confederacy Worlds:

Bakunin—BD+50°1725	founded: 2246	c
Helminth—Zosma	discovered: 2277	c
Paralia—Vega	discovered: 2230	d
Volera—Tau Puppis	discovered: 2288	e
Windsor—Altair	founded: 2146	x

Notes:
a = habitable Earthlike planet
b = marginally habitable planet

c = possible site of Dolbrian terraforming
d = definite site of Dolbrian terraforming
e = site of Voleran terraforming
x = planet uninhabitable without technological support

You are invited to preview

PARTISAN

the second novel in
S. ANDREW SWANN's
hard-hitting, action-packed
science fiction trilogy:
Hostile Takeover,
available at your local bookstore
in a DAW Books paperback edition
in December 1995

CHAPTER ONE

Friendly Fire

"One can watch everything and see nothing."
—*The Cynic's Book of Wisdom*

"Life happens to us while we are planning other things."
—ROBERT CELINE
(1923-1996)

"You bastard!"

The shout from behind caught Dominic Magnus completely off-guard. He turned away from the four board members he'd been addressing to face a fifth, Kari Tetsami.

"Excuse me?" Dom said to her.

Tetsami stood, blocking the doorway. Her normally pale skin was flushed a bright pink, her nostrils were dilated, and her hands were balled into fists. Dom could almost see her small body vibrating.

"Who the hell do you think you are?" she said.

Dom turned to the others in the meeting room. Mariah Zanzibar, his chief of security, was standing, arms folded, avoiding eye contact with him. Mosasa, their resident electronics expert, was seated, working at one of the terminals set into the conference table. He stared at the terminal while, from the side of his bald head, the eye of his dragon tattoo stared at Dom. Dom had no way to tell where the nonhumans were looking. Random Walk, Mosasa's contraband AI, was in the wiring and could be watching out of any of the cameras in the room, or not. And Flower, their alien military strategist, had no eyes in its bullet-shaped head, only black Rorschach patterns over leathery yellow skin.

"Perhaps you should excuse us for a moment—" Dom said to them.

"Let them stay. Why shouldn't they hear this? They're in on everything, aren't they?" Tetsami stepped into the meeting room and jabbed Dom with her finger. "Unlike some of us!"

I've done it again, Dom thought. He only wished he knew exactly what it was he'd done.

"Me and Mosasa have to check the security perimeter," Zanzibar said, snagging Mosasa's elbow. Mosasa glanced up, as if suddenly realizing that there was a situation in here. He let Zanzibar lead him out of the room.

Flower stood on its multijointed legs, draping its wings about it like a cape. Its long serpentine neck appeared as if it grew from some strange avian bush. "Observation of the defensive perimeter. He will give some opportunity to see static weaponry. He should be studied most closely, not?"

Even the alien can see it, Dom thought.

Flower glided out of the room, leaving Dom and Tetsami alone with the possible exception of Random Walk, silent in the wiring.

Tetsami paid no attention to the sudden exodus. "What the hell am I, Mr. Magnus? Some little twitch for hire whose usefulness has expired?"

Hearing her say "Mr. Magnus" chilled Dom's gut. For a confused second he couldn't figure out why. *Everyone* called him "Mr. Magnus."

But not Tetsami. Never Tetsami. They had been to hell and back together, through more life-threatening BS in the past five local weeks than any five lifetimes—even lifetimes spent on the anarchic planet of Bakunin.

Tetsami had never called him "Mr. Magnus." His *employees* called him "Mr. Magnus."

"No—" Dom began a belated response.

She wasn't waiting for an explanation. "After all this

shit! After I planned the whole op for you—great! Now that you have your money, you don't give a shit about your pet hacker anymore?"

"What—"

Tetsami jabbed him again. "How many times have you held out on me, Dom? Where the hell are you going?"

Tetsami's anger shot into focus for Dom. "I was going to tell you when I got the whole board together."

She just stared at him, as if his skin had suddenly gone transparent. Dom had to raise his hand slightly to make sure that it hadn't. His hand was fine, olive-colored and natural looking. Dom felt a vibration begin in his cheek, and he lifted his hand to cover it.

"That's it, isn't it?" she asked quietly.

Her sudden calmness was as disturbing as the anger of a few seconds ago. Dom hated seeing her like this, and he wanted desperately to fix whatever was wrong. "Just tell me what you want me to do," he said.

She shook her head. "I don't think you'd understand, Dom. You certainly don't act as if you would." She turned toward the door.

Dom felt a sinking in his chest. "Please. What's wrong?"

She stopped on the way to the door, her back toward him. He watched her head nod and her back shake. It could have been laughter. Or sobs. Maybe both.

"What's wrong? *Wrong?*" Tetsami sighed. "What's wrong is, after all we've been through with each other, that I'm just another fucking stockholder."

He walked up and tried to put a hand on her shoulder. She shrugged out of it and left him there, hand in midair. As he stood there, staring at his hand, he heard her say from down the hall, "Don't wait up for me."

Dom paced the loading dock, waiting for the techs to finish tuning the contragrav he was going to fly into Godwin. As he waited, he tried to will away the cold dread that clutched at his gut.

Dom's current enterprise, the Diderot Holding Company, was more successful than it had a right to be. In three weeks local, it had managed to convert the tunnel warrens under the mountains into living space for the thousand-plus refugees from the Godwin Arms & Armaments takeover. With Tetsami's planing, they had even managed to liberate 435 megagrams worth of liquid assets from Godwin Arms. . . .

Tetsami.

She was why Dom was depressed, even though, by all the standards that should have mattered to him, he should have been pleased with the operation. Her increasingly unpredictable reactions to him clouded any optimism Dom might have had. She should have been pleased with the way things were going.

It was becoming a mantra, counting the reasons why he shouldn't feel as if the world was crumbling around him.

The main reason was the fact that he, and most of the employees from GA&A, had survived to form a base of operations in the mountains. They had managed this despite the fact that Colonel Klaus Dacham, Dom's brother, had led the takeover of GA&A in what appeared to be a personal vendetta against Dom. A vendetta that might be over, now that Klaus must believe Dom and his people were all dead. There certainly had been no more militaristic activity out of Godwin Arms since Dom's raid back in there, to steal back his own money. Tetsami had planned that raid. . . .

"Cold in here," Dom said, watching his breath fog. They were high up the side of the Diderot Mountain range. The loading dock was a cavernous hollow in the rock. The entrance, at the moment, was open to the air. It gave Dom a view of purple sky, wispy cirrus clouds, and the fat orb of Kropotkin that did little to warm the biting wind.

There were other reasons he should have been pleased. Kathy Shane, who had suffered extensive injuries in that raid, was going to live. She was still bedridden, but the doctors had managed to replace the damaged limbs with cybernetics. . . .

That brought shadowy memories, too. Dom felt his cheek twitch.

Maybe he shouldn't leave.

He'd had the same thought dozens of times, ever since Tetsami had confronted him. Things were going well. He didn't need to go to Godwin. He could stay here and—

"And what?" Dom asked.

He walked to the edge of the cavern opening. The sky unfolded and suddenly he wasn't *in* the mountain. He was standing on the edge of a precipice, a fall of two hundred meters or so. Below and away, the weathered mountains gave way to rolling hills, and eventually disappeared under the chaotic sprawl of Godwin. The city of Godwin hogged a good part of the horizon.

"And what?" Dom repeated in a breath of fog. Icy wind tore the words away.

He could see no purpose a delay might serve. He shouldn't rearrange his business decisions to suit his personal problems.

He didn't even like to admit that his difficulty with Tetsami *was* a personal problem. He didn't like admitting that, despite his efforts to be fair to all his partners equally, he might be treating her differently. Treating her differently because of what he felt about her.

What do I feel about her?

"Too much," he answered himself. "I have over a thousand people I need to worry about right now. I can't delay things just because I think she—"

"Sir," came a voice shouting over the wind. "Your car's ready."

"Thank you," Dom said as he walked back to the waiting contragrav.

Business first, Dom thought. *I have to lay the groundwork to acquire another arms company. Take care of my people. Then I'll take care of myself.*

The setup was only going to take a week, two weeks at most. He'd figure some way to patch things up when he got back.

S. Andrew Swann

☐ **FORESTS OF THE NIGHT**   UE2565—$3.99

When Nohar Rajasthan, a private eye descended from genetically manipulated tiger stock, is hired to look into a human's murder, he finds himself caught up in a conspiracy that includes federal agents, drug runners, and a deadly canine assassin. And he hasn't even met the real enemy yet!

☐ **EMPERORS OF THE TWILIGHT**   UE2589—$4.50

She was the ultimate agent. Her name: Evi Isham, her species: frankenstein, her physiology bioengineered to make her the best in the business. Evi has suddenly found herself on the run from an unidentified enemy, and even the Agency might not be able to save her from those who sought her life!

☐ **SPECTERS OF THE DAWN**   UE2589—$4.50

This is the story of Angelica Lopez, a moreau descended from rabbit stock. When Byron the fox comes into her life, Angel finds herself dragged into the deadly underground of information peddling, and exposed to a series of confrontations that could blow the whole country wide open!
